The
Paperboy

THE PAPERBOY

PETE DEXTER

RANDOM HOUSE
NEW YORK

A signed first edition of this book has been privately
printed by The Franklin Library.

Library of Congress Cataloging-in-Publication Data
Dexter, Pete.
The paperboy / Pete Dexter.
p.   cm.
ISBN 0-679-42175-0
I. Title.
PS3554.E95P36   1995
813'.54—dc20   94-21523

Manufactured in the United States of America
on acid-free paper
23456789
First Trade Edition

Book design by Oksana Kushnir

For Irwin Potts and Gil Spencer,
a couple of pretty good paperboys
who never let it go to their heads

The
Paperboy

❏

My brother ward was once a famous man.

No one mentions that now, and I suppose no one is inclined to bring it up, particularly not my father, who in other matters loves those things most that he can no longer touch or see, things washed clean of flaws and ambiguity by the years he has held them in his memory, reshaping them as he brings them out, again and again, telling his stories until finally the stories, and the things in them, are as perfect and sharp as the edge of the knife he keeps in his pocket.

In his stories, the bass are all bigger than you have ever seen them, and always catch the glint of the sun in their scales as they jump.

And he always lets them go.

He has no stories about my brother, though. At the mention of his name, a change occurs—a small change, you would have to know him to see it—and my father, without moving a muscle in his face, slips away; retreats, I think, to that sheltered place where his stories are kept.

Perhaps we all have our places.

An hour later, you may notice he hasn't spoken a word.

❏

In august of the year 1965, a man named Thurmond Call, who had, even by Moat County standards, killed an inappropriate number of Negroes in the line of duty, was killed himself between the towns of Lately and Thorn, along a county road which runs parallel to and a quarter mile west of the St. Johns River in northern Florida.

Thurmond Call was the sheriff of Moat County, and had

held that position since before I was born. He was murdered on the eve of his sixty-seventh birthday, but had kicked a man to death on a public street in Lately only the previous spring. And so, while it is true there was some sentiment at the time—not only in Lately, the county seat, but in the larger town of Thorn, where we lived, and the little encampments along the forty miles of river in between—that it was time to wean Sheriff Call from the public coffers, it had nothing to do with his not being up to the job.

The sheriff's malady was viewed as having been imposed on him from the outside, and was therefore forgivable, even if it could not be cured. Like tuberculosis. Hippies, federal judges, Negroes—he couldn't keep track of what he was allowed to do to them and what he wasn't, and that had spawned a confusion in his mind which, the body of Moat County thought went, led him to more immoderate positions than he otherwise would have taken. And that, in turn, has spawned a certain unease in the general population.

Which is all to say that the man he had handcuffed and then stomped to death in the spring had been white.

❑

THURMOND CALL WAS FOUND lying on the highway early in the morning, in a rainstorm, a quarter of a mile from his cruiser. The engine had died but the wipers were still moving, in spasms, and his headlights were a dim orange. The wide-mouthed jar that he carried between his legs as he drove to receive his tobacco juice was sitting on the roof. He had been opened up, stomach to groin, and left for dead.

The question of how he traveled, disemboweled, to the spot on the highway where he was found, while probably unconnected to the murder itself, presented a haunting piece of unsettled business which lingers to this moment over Moat County, in the realm of those profound questions which have no answer. And perhaps lingers in other places, as at the end of his life the sheriff had become a symbol of one kind or another everywhere in the state.

My first opinion on the matter—and it was this sort of matter that at fifteen years of age I had opinions about—was that he was dragged by bears. I did not believe, as his friends did, that he crawled after his killer's car, an account which was presented as fact at his funeral.

It did not come to me until I was older that he might have just crawled—not knowing where, only wanting to be some other place.

Regardless of the manner in which Sheriff Call made his last four hundred yards, it is fair to say that with the exception of the war itself, no event in the county's history ever carried a more pivotal message to its citizens than his death, and not knowing how else to express the loss this message carried—not the loss of Thurmond Call, but of something more fundamental that people had felt themselves losing all along—a statue of the sheriff was commissioned to stand in the Lately town square. It is there today, celebrating the fracture in history that the passing of the sheriff represents.

On Halloween, a scar sometimes appears on the likeness, running from the stomach to the groin. This reminder of Sheriff Call's reward is routinely laid to juvenile delinquents, but there is a lack of embellishment in the gesture that suggests a colder purpose than vandalism.

❑

THE MAN SHERIFF CALL stomped to death in Lately was a former Chrysler/Plymouth salesman at Duncan Brothers Motors named Jerome Van Wetter, who was discharged finally not for being a drunk—which he was, but drunks, in fact, are not always bad salesmen; someone has to sell cars to other drunks—but because, even after he had been at the dealership many years and was as familiar a showroom fixture to loyal Plymouth buyers as the new models themselves, something in his deportment frightened customers off. He could not overcome it with clothes or talk of the state champion Little League team or his smile. The smile, in fact, only made things worse. I know this, having once been left alone with that smile and the new line of Plymouths while my father and Mr. Duncan went into the office to close a deal on a Chrysler.

The indistinct malevolence which Jerome Van Wetter carried hung off him at unexpected angles in much the way his suits hung on his bones, but gathered to its purpose in his eyes.

There was a predatory aspect to the way they fell on you, expecting something, waiting, a tiny interest finally stirring, like a slow smile, as he found the little places inside you where he did not belong.

He seemed to understand the effect he had on customers, and wore sunglasses indoors.

❑

I REFER TO JEROME VAN WETTER as a former car salesman not to underscore his eventual failure in the car business but because to my knowledge his employment at Duncan Motors was the only job he ever held, at least the only one that did not involve poaching. Even so, this venture into the mainstream of the Moat County business life eclipsed all the known social and professional accomplishments of all the other Van Wetters combined, past and present.

It was a family which kept itself apart, living on the edge of civilization, compared frequently in the Lately area, where most of them were, to the bears, which had finally lost all fear of humans and had to be killed because of it. But even the tamest of the Van Wetters was not tame in a way that would make you comfortable sitting beneath his pale blue eyes in a new Plymouth Fury, one foot resting on the paper protecting the car's carpet, the other still on the showroom floor, smelling both the new upholstery and the sweet, metastasized alcohol coming through his skin.

And because of that, in the end, Mr. Duncan let Jerome Van Wetter go, and in the resulting bout of drunkenness he was arrested and then stomped to death by Sheriff Call.

And it surprised no one when, a week after Sheriff Call was himself killed, Jerome's cousin once or twice removed, Hillary Van Wetter, was arrested for the crime. It was a known fact that the Van Wetters took care of their own.

By general agreement, Hillary Van Wetter was the most unpredictable and ferocious member of the whole Van Wetter family, a ranking that had come to him several years before when he had, in fact, attacked another policeman with a knife, cutting off the man's thumb in a dispute over a dragging muffler. That case, however, had never gone to trial. Half thumbless, the policeman yearned for his home in Texas, and once there, refused to return to Florida to testify.

And so seven days after Sheriff Call was found on the highway, county deputies raided Hillary Van Wetter's cabin in the dense wetlands just north of Lately, killing several of his dogs, and found a bloodstained knife in the kitchen sink. A bloody shirt was discovered in the washing tub, and Hillary Van Wetter—who was drunk and happy in the bathtub at the time the deputies arrived—was arrested for the murder, and within five months was tried and convicted in county court and sentenced to die in "Old Sparky" at the Florida State Prison in Starke. This in spite of being defended by the most expensive attorney in Moat County.

No one ever knew where the money came from for the lawyer.

My father's paper covered the trial and the appeals, of course—there were reporters in Moat County that fall from every paper of any size in the state, along with reporters from places like Atlanta, Mobile, New York, and New Orleans—but while the *Tribune* had, for as long as my father owned it, always employed a local death sentence to rail editorially against capital punishment, the paper was strangely quiet after Hillary Van Wetter's trial.

"People know where I stand," was as much as my father would ever say. And that was true. He had defied public opinion for as long as he had been in northern Florida—in 1965, the *Tribune* was the only liberal newspaper in any rural area in the state—but he had gone about it with a wink. The paper was liberal, but in a hopeless and harmless way that was designed not to offend, a posture which would not accommodate asking for mercy for the murderer of Thurmond Call.

❑

ON A COLD WINTER MORNING four years later, early in 1969—in the same year my brother would blossom as a journalist—I lost my swimming scholarship at the University of Florida. A few weeks afterward, I was expelled for an act of vandalism.

Specifically, I drank a small bottle of vodka and drained the swimming pool, which, while childish, is more complicated work than it may seem from the outside. I don't want to get into the mechanics of it now, but let me assure you that you don't just pull the plug.

I returned home, ashamed, and went to work at my father's newspaper, the *Moat County Tribune,* driving a delivery truck.

My father never asked what had happened to me in Gainesville, or if I intended to go back, but it was clear that he meant for me to drive the truck until I saw it was this life's one alternative to a college education.

He was not formally educated himself, and often spoke of the fact as if it were something lost. "Lord, I would have loved to study literature," he would say, as if he needed permission from a college to read books.

All that winter and spring I drove the north route for the *Tribune,* traveling 325 miles over the narrow, mostly shoulderless two-lane roads of northern Moat County. I loaded the truck in the dark, passing the sign marking Thorn's city limits by three-thirty in the morning.

Each morning at nine o'clock, if the truck didn't break down and the press runs were on time, I came to the clearing where Sheriff Call's car had been found. The spot was partially hidden from the road—a baked, treeless circle cut into a stand of pines, a picnic table and two outdoor toilets no more than twenty feet apart, the men's to the east, the ladies' to the west. A marker indicated the spot where the first school in the state had once stood, and a hand-painted sign attached to one of the privies showed a Confederate flag and a hand unconnected to any arm, and across these images the legend MOAT COUNTY EXTENDS A WELCOME HAND TO YANKEES!

Fifteen miles down the road was my last stop of the day—ten papers that I was required to place facedown on a makeshift wooden table just behind the gum ball machines inside a sun-faded country store run by an indeterminate number of members of the Van Wetter family, who did not want their patrons met with bad news as they came in the door.

What specific blood connection these Van Wetters had to the man Sheriff Call stomped to death, I do not know. The Van Wetters occupied half a column of the Moat County telephone book and their children rarely married outside the family. Calculating the collateral relations was beyond me, even if the Van Wetters had been inclined to discuss their family tree, which they were not.

I can only tell you that some mornings an old man was there, blind and freshly angry, as if the blindness had come over him in the night. He would make his way to the papers I had brought and count them, moving the folded edges up into the palm of his hand with his fingers, as if he were tickling them, his face scowling up into the window like a sour plant growing to light. And some mornings it was his wife.

Other times there was a young, pregnant woman with the most beautiful skin I had ever seen, whose children would run through a curtain and into the back when I came into the store.

This woman never looked up, but a moment after the children had disappeared, a man whose face had been burned—whose skin creased at his eye like a badly ironed shirt—would emerge from the curtain and stand a foot inside the room, his hands at his sides, watching until I had stacked the papers and left.

Once, when I had forgotten to collect for the week, I went back into the store and found him still standing where I'd left him, staring at her as she straightened boxes of candy bars in the case under the counter.

She looked at me then, for an instant, and it was as if I'd brought some bad news beyond what was in my newspapers. It was possible, I think, that anytime the door opened it was bad news for her.

I never heard her speak to the man with the burned face, and I never heard him speak to her. I assumed they were man and wife.

❑

I WOULD FINISH THE ROUTE before ten, park the truck, walk the six blocks home, and fall into bed with a beer and a copy of the newspaper I had been delivering all morning. Early in the afternoon, I would slip away from the stories in the paper into a jumpy sleep, full of dreams, waking up a few hours later in this, the same room where I had slept all the nights of my childhood, not knowing where I was.

Something like that had been happening at Gainesville too, and sometimes in those moments between dreams and consciousness, when I was lost, I glimpsed myself as untied to either place.

I would get out of bed then and walk to the city pool and swim laps. Or, when I could borrow my father's truck—he kept his new Chrysler in the driveway and left the garage for a beloved twelve-year-old Ford pickup which he used only to go fishing—I drove north to St. Augustine and would swim out into the ocean a mile or more, until my arms and legs were dead weight, and then slowly, allowing the water to hold me up, I would turn and make my way back.

I threw myself away and was returned intact to the beach, and in this way I was somehow saved from those moments it had taken, fresh from sleep, to recognize the room where my most private thoughts had been thought, and private courses set, for all my life. The walls of my childhood.

You could say I was afraid to sleep.

❑

My father came home from the paper every evening at fifteen minutes after six, slowly pushing open the door of his black Chrysler, moving his feet onto the ground, one at a time, then lifting himself out, then turning back into the car for his newspapers. He was a heavy man then, and at the end of his day, every movement was a task unto itself. He did not love his job the way he once had.

By 1969, he was leaving most of the newsroom business to his managing editor—a plain, square-jawed young woman with muscular legs and an embarrassing, unfocused ambition—and spent his time with the advertising department, his two-man editorial board, and preparing speeches to deliver to various journalism societies around the state.

I remember wondering if he was getting into his editor's knickers at lunch—if she was squeezing the energy out of him with those legs.

❑

MY FATHER HAD OWNED black Chryslers for as long as I could remember—a tradition that went back to simpler times when Chryslers were better cars than Pontiacs and Oldsmobiles, about as good as a Buick, and one step under the Cadillacs. A respectable car, but nothing too grand. He did not want his advertisers attaching themselves to the idea that he was making too much money.

Dinner was at six-thirty, served by the young Negro woman who had prepared it. She cooked and cleaned and kept the house, and rarely spoke to either of us without being spoken to first. In that way, she was unlike other housemaids of the time—who took pains to ingratiate themselves with their employers—but she was an intelligent woman, and the situation spoke for itself.

Her name was Anita Chester, and it seemed to me that she and the managing editor of my father's newspaper were better suited to each other's jobs.

After dinner, I would help clear the dishes and my father would thank the maid, whose name he could not remember, and drift through the big, empty house like an old ghost, visiting the bathroom a long time, then his bedroom—where he would remove his coat and tie and shoes, and slip a bathrobe over his shirt—and finally he would settle into his favorite chair in the study with a glass of wine, his head dropping back exactly into the spot where the Vitalis he wore had turned the material dark a long time before.

He would close his eyes a moment, and then, opening them, he would sip the drink and pick up the newspapers he had brought home and set them on his lap while he found his glasses and turned on the lamp.

The *Atlanta Constitution*, the *Orlando Sentinel*, the *St. Petersburg Times*, the *Daytona Beach News-Journal*, the *Miami Times*.

Half a dozen small papers from all over the state. He did not read them as much as inspect them; seeing what their front pages had that his own paper's did not. Or perhaps it was the other way around.

There was a rivalry at the core of the business, a race to deliver the worst news first, and when there wasn't bad news— there was always some, of course, but I am speaking now of calamity—the competition would move in another direction.

My father would stare at the *News-Journal* a long time and then look up, smiling, and hand me the paper. "They call that news judgment," he'd say.

As if I owned a newspaper, too, and had an opinion on what ought to be placed above the fold of the front page. As if I were the one who would take over his newspaper when it was safe for him to step aside.

He was more respectful of the *Atlanta Constitution,* as he had once worked with its legendary editor, Ralph McGill. He told his stories about Ralph McGill in a good-humored but reverent way, as if Mr. McGill were in the next room listening. The stories always centered around his bravery, which demonstrated itself entirely at the keyboard of a typewriter, and his single-minded pursuit of a better South.

It had occurred to me a long time before 1969, though, that there was something else behind my father's admiration of Ralph McGill.

He was famous.

I had been around reporters all my life—my father had been one once, and he often brought his favorites home for cocktails—and I saw early on that they were hungry in a way I was not.

His favorites were the most aggressive, but for all their scrambling to the scene, for all the research and investigations and prodding and cajoling and lying they did to get to their stories—they would brag about these things later—what they hated most was not to be wrong, but to be silent.

What moved them was not to know things, but to tell them. For a little while, it made them as important as the news itself.

And in a distant way, Ward was one of them. By that I mean only that there was something in the stories that he wanted for himself. Not that he craved celebrity.

At home, he had been like my mother. He would sit quietly, listening to my father's stories of floods and air show catastrophes and Ralph McGill, over and over, for as long as he cared to tell them.

And like my mother, he tired of the stories finally— knowing he could not compete against them—and left.

Their leavings were different, of course. He simply never came home from college, taking a series of jobs instead as a reporter, and finally arriving at the *Miami Times;* and she moved to California with a drama teacher from Moat County Junior College who had been a frequent contributor to the letters to the editor section of my father's paper and a supporter of his liberal views.

My father took his losses in stride, but while he regarded Ward's leaving as a stage of his development—a healthy experience, as he told it, and good preparation for his eventual editorship of the *Moat County Tribune*—he did not hold any such hopeful theories on my mother.

She had developed right out of his life.

And so after dinner my father would sit in the two-story white house he had built on Macon Street, empty now except for a maid who did not love him for his public tenderness toward Negroes, and a son who did not love his profession, and he would tell his stories and inspect his papers just as he always had, coming finally to the *Miami Times,* which he would check cover to cover for the byline Ward James.

On the days that he found it, he would quiet all the other, smaller things he was doing—sipping his wine, adjusting his glasses, rubbing his feet against each other—and read it carefully, sometimes twice, a smile slowly taking over his face.

When he had finished reading, he would move the paper farther away to judge the story's placement or size, I suppose estimating my brother's emergence into his world.

When he had finished, and the pile of newspapers had all moved from his lap, through his hands, to a pile at his feet, he would sometimes ask if I had been swimming that afternoon, and after I told him yes or no—it was a polite question; he had no interest in it now that it wasn't organized into competitions—he would look at his watch, stretch, and head off to bed.

"Six-thirty comes early," he'd say, always the same words, seeming to forget that by six-thirty I was four hours into my day. I watched him climb the stairs and then, when Ward was in the paper, I would pick up the *Times* and read the story he had written too.

In the beginning, until the airliner went down, it was usually a murder or a drug arrest. It was usually the Cubans. And I would think of the books Ward had studied, the formal and serious nature of his education, and try to imagine how it must have been, at the end of years of Latin and chemistry and physics and calculus, to see that it all led up three flights of stairs in a Miami ghetto.

Having spent some time in college myself, I imagined it was a relief.

❑

OF THE LAWLESS EPISODES that visited the James family in the year 1969, the most surprising to me was not my expulsion from the University of Florida but my brother's arrest for drunk driving.

In fact, until the Sunday he called, I was unaware that Ward drank at all. As children, he and I would sometimes sit in the kitchen before bedtime, eating cereal while my father entertained reporters in the next room—we were not allowed in there with them—listening as the pitch on the other side of the door gradually turned shrill, until all the words were shouted over other words, and the laughing was hard and vulgar, as if issued over the bodies of victims.

My father would come through the door for ice from time to time, swinging it farther open as the party went deeper into the night and he drank more glasses of wine, pushing it so hard finally that it would slam into the wall behind, his face by now flushed and sweating, the cigarette smoke trailing him into the kitchen. And after he had mussed our hair, gotten his ice, and gone back through the door into the wall of smoke outside, Ward would slowly smooth his hair and shake his head in a way that I took to be disapproving.

It never occurred to me that he wanted to be part of it.

He had been pulled to the side of the road on Alligator Alley at four-thirty in the morning, a Monday morning, driving a hundred and three miles an hour through the Everglades.

The trooper walked to the car from behind, carrying a flashlight. He leaned into the open window, the small circle of light moving here and there, stopping on the bottle between my brother's legs, then on the case of beer in back, then on my brother's face, then on his passenger.

"Sir, have you been drinking?" the trooper said.

Ward slowly turned and looked at the man sitting in the seat next to him. The other man laughed.

The trooper asked Ward to remove himself from the car, calling him "sir" again. The door opened and Ward poured out, still holding the bottle. He took a quick swallow before he handed it over. The trooper moved back into his headlights and placed it on the trunk.

"May I see your license, sir?" the trooper said, and my brother pulled his wallet out of his back pocket, upside down, trailing the pocket liner, and then, as he tried to open it, all his cards and money fell onto the pavement and into the wet grass at the side of the road.

He wandered into the grass and then the swamp behind it, looking for his license and his money, and fell in the mud. The trooper ignored the sounds of Ward in the swamp, and studied his driver's license, which he'd picked up off the ground, illuminating the particulars with his flashlight.

A minute passed, and my brother emerged into the lights of the trooper's car, glistening with mud.

"Mr. James," the trooper said, reading the name off the license, "you are under arrest."

And my brother, who, as far as I know, had never in his life asked another human being for a thing that was not his, stood on the road, swaying, and said, "Sir, I would be proud to wear your hat."

❑

THE MAN IN THE CAR with my brother that night was also a reporter at the *Miami Times*. His name was Yardley Acheman, and to the reporters and editors who worked in the newsroom with them, Yardley Acheman and my brother were exact opposites.

Exact opposites.

Some of the *Times* editors held the opinion that the differences between them accounted for their success, that it was keen management to know that opposites often generated a certain chemistry—they liked the idea of chemistry, these editors, the idea of magic—which the *Miami Times* had been wise enough to stir, and which had produced an investigative team of more potency than the individual ingredients would indicate was possible.

A perfect match, they said. *Exact opposites.*

And perhaps they were right, although it doesn't seem to me that people can be opposites, exact or otherwise—what, after all, is the opposite of six feet tall? Of being required in ninth grade to memorize the periodic table and never forgetting it? Of foot odor?

Still, people are different, and Ward and Yardley Acheman were more different than most.

It is my understanding that before the editors of the *Miami Times* first designed to throw him together with my brother to cover a plane crash in the Everglades—an arrangement more of chance and convenience than the chemists at the *Times* cared to admit later—Yardley Acheman was just another sulking and lazy reporter on the city desk whose name rarely appeared over stories in the newspaper because the editors who ran the desk weren't inclined to go through the long process of talking him into writing anything in which he had no personal interest.

On the other hand, when Yardley Acheman found a subject of interest, he was considered something of a literary genius. The editors agreed on that, and many of them held literary ambitions of their own. They all knew writing when they saw it; that was their job.

Between events of personal interest, however, Yardley Acheman would sit at his desk in the most distant corner of the city room, visiting an endless stream of girls and bookies on the telephone, trying to talk the new ones into giving him a chance, trying to talk the old ones into leaving him alone.

He was handsome in a spoiled way, a pretty boy, and it seemed to give him access to anything he wanted. It was often difficult for him to fit all his social engagements into his calendar.

The editors knew what Yardley Acheman was doing on the telephone, but all newspapers carry some sort of dead weight—reporters who do not want to be reporters, editors who care more for their titles than their jobs—and, as these things go, Yardley Acheman was less trouble than most. He considered other reporters, who did not possess his literary grace, beneath him, and was consequently never the sort of dead weight who became an agitator for the guild.

A guild agitator was a different kind of burden to bear, and the people who ran the paper were more inclined to relieve themselves of it.

Something happened to Yardley Acheman, however, on the evening that he and Ward were chosen—without forethought or ceremony, from the evidence, but because they were the only two unoccupied reporters in the room—to go to the wreckage of Flight 119, which had left its runway at Miami International Airport, stayed airborne two minutes and forty seconds, and then crashed into the Everglades, killing everyone aboard.

Yardley Acheman found his vocation in that night's carnage, in the enormity of the collision of 140 human beings and their sheet metal tube into the soft mud of the swamp, the enormity of the tearing—he became flush with the telling of it, with the cataloging of details; with the accumulative weight of their meaning.

It was like riding a bicycle, he got it all at once.

But Yardley Acheman, of course, had not amassed the details by himself. The most tearing of them had come from my brother, who had waded through the mud into the plane while Yardley kept outside, where, horrifying as the accident was, there were other places to look; room, as he would often say, to consider the larger perspective.

For his part, Ward walked the length of the tube, from the place in back where the tail section had broken off to the pilot's compartment, brushing mosquitoes off his face, counting the dead still in the plane, recording their positions, and through them the terrible velocity of impact.

By coincidence, the entire Dade County air rescue machinery had been sent to a smaller crash—a private plane—an hour earlier that night, and for more than thirty minutes Ward and Yardley Acheman had the disaster to themselves.

The plane yawned and settled as Ward made his way to the front; the only other sounds were those of the swamp itself. A

19

day later, subscribers to the *Miami Times* would hear those sounds too, and see, in the darkened cabin, parts of bodies still strapped to their seats.

And while careful readers might have noticed that the account of the sights and sounds carried a personal tone which alluded to matters beyond the accident itself, there was enough weight in the details to overcome it.

❑

LIKE YARDLEY ACHEMAN, my brother kept apart from the gossip and flow of the newsroom.

Even after the success of the airliner story, Ward would not be brought into the lives of the other reporters. He kept his desk spotless and neat, and checked facts compulsively; he worked hours beyond his scheduled quitting time and did not fill out requests for overtime pay.

All of this was misunderstood and resented by the reporters who witnessed it, who did not know that when he wasn't on a story, my brother was incapable of asking for anything.

It was assumed in the newsroom that Ward had gotten his job through his father's influence, and while I do not know if that was true—editors and publishers regularly hire each other's children, and I am not sure my father, for all his ethical posturing, was above that—I am sure that Ward was unaware of it. He would have never risked the embarrassment.

No one was more afraid of embarrassment.

Still, the story that rose from the wreckage of Flight 119 elevated Ward's standing with the other reporters, who were honest enough to see that he had done something that they themselves might not have done—a crashed airplane, still humming with current and warm from the friction of the collision and full of fuel, how many of them would have climbed into the hole where the tail section had broken off and walked the length of the cabin in the dark?—but he would not be complimented, could not think of words to say when they came to his desk that next morning with their congratulations.

He could not give and he could not receive, except in the course of collecting a story.

A story had an authority of its own to my brother, and under that authority he was able to approach subjects of intimacy that he would never approach on his own.

❑

A WEEK AFTER THE STORY of the crash appeared on the front page of the *Miami Times,* Ward and Yardley Acheman were called into an office where four editors in white shirts were seated around a long table, smoking Camel cigarettes and pinching pieces of tobacco off the ends of their tongues.

After a few minutes of desultory conversation—which Yardley Acheman was as good at as the editors, and which only made my brother uncomfortable—the lowest ranking editor in the room broke the news of the promotion: Yardley Acheman and my brother had been taken off their duties on the city desk and would work together as a team.

It is a fundamental principle of the operation of newspapers that all decisions, particularly personnel decisions, are delivered at the most local level. Under this principle, the managing editor, for instance, never appears to tell the city editor how to use his reporters.

If it were not for that, the reporters—who instinctively seek the highest authority—would come to the managing editor instead of the city editor to complain that their assignments were not suited to their talents or that their copy was being raped. And of the hundred reasons it's better to be a managing editor than a city editor, avoiding discussions of raped copy is near the top of the list.

❏

I was in only my second month on the north county route when Flight 119 went down in the Everglades, and it was seven weeks later that Ward and Yardley Acheman's next story appeared, a meticulous account of a fraternity hazing at the University of Miami which ended in a young man's drowning in a whirlpool bath.

As he had at the crash site, Ward went inside while Yardley Acheman kept the distance he required to preserve his larger perspective.

Over the weeks it took to gather the story, Ward was threatened by the fraternity members and one night was attacked and beaten by half a dozen of them outside their house. He could not see who they were. When they left, he drove to the hospital and took fifteen stitches in his eyelid and was back at their front door the same evening.

Later, his car tires were cut and his phone began to ring at all hours of the night, with no one on the other end when he answered.

And each morning he was back, hanging over the fraternity house like the death itself. Phone calls and beatings and having tires slashed—those were not the things that frightened my brother.

❏

THE FRATERNITY'S LAWYER had kept his clients out of court following the drowning, and now obtained a court order prohibiting Ward and all other employees of the *Miami Times* from coming within a hundred yards of the house.

Ward complied with the order, figuring the hundred yards trigonometrically and then waiting just outside the boundary two days a week, reminding them on their way to and from the fraternity house that he was still there.

On other days, he waited outside their classrooms. He called them at the fraternity, and wrote them letters, both at home and at school. The lawyer got another court order, prohibiting calls and letters.

But it was too late, my brother had gotten a letter back. The writer was a massive, long-haired football player named Kent de Ponce, who met Ward at his parents' home in Coral Gables and allowed him to set a tape recorder on the table between them while they talked. I have played that tape so many times now that I hear the voices sometimes in the hum of tires on the highway.

The football player sits so close to the machine that even his breathing is audible. He is drinking beer, and apologizing endlessly—for not speaking to Ward earlier, for his part in Ward's beating, for drinking too many beers, for not offering Ward a beer, for standing at the side of the whirlpool and watching while a boy only a year or two younger than himself was left upside-down and kicking underwater until all the kicking stopped, and his body was twice as heavy coming out as it had been a few minutes before, when it was lifted in.

He apologizes for these things as if it were in Ward's hands to forgive them.

He cries as he talks, and apologizes for that too.

The brothers, he says—that's what he calls the members of the fraternity, "the brothers"—were drunk and lost track of the time the pledge was underwater. They thought he was pretending to go limp. He wonders out loud if he will lose his scholarship. The football player's nose is running and he sniffs, making spasmodic wet noises, and once a line of spit drops from his lips onto the tape recorder itself. He laughs at that, and tries, at the same time to apologize. "Jesus, I'm sorry, man. . . ."

"You know, man," he says later, changing course just once toward the end, "I don't know if I should be doing this. . . ." There is a pause in the tape, as he realizes it is already done.

When he speaks again, it is as if he is trying out an idea on

---

23

Ward. "The only thing I could do now," he says, "I could break your neck and say I thought you were a burglar."

The tape is quiet a long time after that, and then he says, "I apologize, man. I don't know what I'm saying."

Waiting out the long pause—for as many times as I have heard the tape, I still strain for the words that end it—I think of my brother and wonder if, as he waits in the living room in Coral Gables with the football player and the prospect of violence, if he was drawn to those strange, kinetic moments before such things are decided.

If that is the heart of the attraction.

Ward met the football player again the next day at a restaurant near his house while Yardley Acheman, working from the perimeter, made notes on the football player's expensive shoes, his car, the houses that lined the street where his parents lived. His ten-dollar haircut.

In the story that appeared in the paper, these details and details of the appearance and belongings of other members of the fraternity—the piece begins with a description of a parking lot full of Jeeps and Mustang convertibles—occupy a place of importance that seems, on examination, to outweigh even the details of the drowning itself. It is written as if Yardley Acheman were arguing that his view was as meaningful as the one from inside.

There was no mention of the dead boy's car in this story, or the neighborhood where his parents lived, or the advantages he enjoyed. He was absolved of that, and presented with a purity that is familiar to readers of newspapers, who have always been willing to disregard what they know about human nature and believe that the people written about in stories are different from the ones they know in their own lives.

This does not include readers who have been victims themselves, of course. No one who is touched personally by such a story and then watches a newspaper report it ever trusts newspapers in the same way again.

On the other hand, I suppose that to those who loved him, the drowned boy was pure, and, if it were left to me, I would never take whatever comfort that might be away from them for the sake of accuracy. But even though it was never written, it is still true that if it were not for his drowning, the same boy a year later surely would have stood by drunk himself while blindfolded pledges were led in, shackled, and thrown into a whirlpool full of icy water.

Even if it wasn't written, part of the dead boy's story is that he wanted to be one of the bunch who drowned him.

❑

IT WAS EARLY in the morning of the day the fraternity story appeared in the newspaper that my brother and Yardley Acheman tripped a state trooper's radar gun at 103 miles an hour on Alligator Alley as they passed into territory belonging to the Miccosukee Indians.

They were headed, for reasons Yardley Acheman did not understand, back to the scene of the airplane crash. Ward, who was drunk, would only say it was something he wanted to check.

❑

BY THE TIME he walked out of jail the next morning on his own promise to appear in court and sat down in the sun on a bench in front of the courthouse to wait for Yardley Acheman—the dried mud breaking off his shoes and his face still stiff with jailhouse soap—my brother, while not famous yet, was on the way.

Yardley Acheman arrived with his girlfriend, who was a fashion model and was driving the car because he had lost his license to a drunk driving charge too. "The phone's been ringing off the hook all morning," he said, ignoring the fact that my brother had just spent the night in jail. "Everybody in the world loves us."

He was sitting in the front seat, with the girl; my brother was in the back. She looked quickly in the mirror, as if she were worried what someone who had just come out of jail might be doing back there.

Yardley Acheman turned in his seat, getting on his knees. His shoes left prints against the dashboard.

"Hey," she said.

"Right now," he said to Ward, ignoring her, "there's no place in the world we can't go. Keep that in mind. We can go anywhere we want." Then he turned back, slid closer to the girl, and dropped an arm around her shoulders as she drove. A moment or two later, he winked at Ward and moved his hand onto her breast. *Anywhere we want.*

"Hey," she said, pushing it away with her elbow, looking in the mirror again. But my brother could see that she liked Yardley Acheman, and didn't care where he touched her, or who was there when he did it.

Yardley, my brother told me once, had a way with the girls.

❑

UNROLLING THE *MIAMI TIMES* that Sunday afternoon, my father, still in his fishing hat, sat straight up on the chair after only a few paragraphs. Something big on the line. He leaned into it, gradually moving closer to the page, as if the print were disappearing, then turning the pages to get farther into the story. Occasionally, he stopped as he read, marking his place with his finger as he rocked back and looked at the ceiling, savoring some detail that struck him as particularly exquisite.

When he had finished, he returned to the top of the front page, moving from there to the middle of the paper, estimating the size of the story, considering its placement, and then he read it all again.

"This is what it's all about," he said finally, and set the paper down.

I had been two hours cutting the grass that day and was on the way outside to sharpen the lawn mower before it got dark. As I left the room I saw him go into his shirt pocket for one of his pills.

When I came back in later, the paper was lying on the footstool in front of his chair, still open to the inside pages where the story of the dead fraternity boy ended.

I found him on the porch, sitting in an old wooden swing attached to rafters, drinking a beer. The sun was going down; Anita Chester had made dinner and left.

"Do you drink?" he said.

A strange question, it seemed to me, considering what had happened at Gainesville. Perhaps he meant to ask if I still drank after what had happened. "A beer, sometimes," I said.

"Get yourself a beer," he said. And then, as I was heading back inside to get it, he said, "Your brother's a newspaperman."

And so we sat on the porch and drank to my brother, the smell of freshly cut grass on my shoes, my father moving slightly in the swing, smiling, but also shaking his head from time to time in a troubled way, as if Ward's sudden success in his world presented problems he hadn't considered.

"The plane crash," he said, "that could have been blind luck. . . ." I looked at him a moment, not understanding at first that he was talking about the newspaper account, not the accident itself. "But this thing with the boy in the fraternity . . . it's a Pulitzer. This could be the proudest moment of my life."

He stopped himself, as if to reconsider it all from another angle, and a few minutes later said, "I wonder who this Yardley Acheman is."

❏

THE FOLLOWING SUNDAY, I cut the grass again. If I didn't cut the grass on Sunday, my father would return from the river in the afternoon and go straight into the garage, without comment, and pull out the lawn mower—a hand-powered machine with rusted blades and bald tires—and begin to push it back and forth across the yard, a small supply of nitroglycerin in his shirt pocket against the onset of angina.

Before I came home, he hired one of the children from the neighborhood to do it, but with one of his own sons in the house, it embarrassed him to be seen spending the money.

I was in the backyard with this machine when Ward called. I left the grass, picking up a beer as I passed the refrigerator, and answered the phone. It took a moment to recognize his voice. I hadn't spoken to him since I left Gainesville, and there was something oddly reserved in the way he addressed me now, as if he were as worried as my father that I had gone crazy. That was at the center of things that spring, that I'd cracked.

But it was hard to know what Ward was thinking; he had always held himself behind the door to answer.

He had no talent for conversation, had never found a way to say the things he felt. It was as if even ordinary gestures—a smile, a turn of his head—didn't fit, perhaps were too imprecise for the exact, literal nature of his mind. He kept himself at a distance that no one could cross.

"How are things in the city?" I said.

And for ten seconds it was as if someone had cut the line.

"Good," he said, finally. And then, after another pause, "You're not swimming today?"

"No."

In the silence that followed, I caught a sudden reflection of what had happened in Gainesville, things changing one morning in the pool when the noise began to bounce off the walls and ceiling in a way that I could not follow back to the source. . . . How can I tell you this? I was terrifed that there was no source. That I was scattered, no longer intact.

28

The swimming coach, a Hungarian immigrant who had been wounded in the Russian invasion, pulled me out of practice ten minutes later and rapped on my forehead as if it were a screen door, and told me I had talent but would never amount to anything until I learned to commit myself to the swim. Commit everything to the swim.

"I'll get W.W.," I said, which is what my father—William Ward James—was called by everyone except Anita Chester, who called him Mr. James, and old friends who called him "World War."

But that was from a different time and a different place.

"Wait a minute," Ward said.

I waited, afraid he was going to ask about Gainesville. Moments passed.

"How are you doing?"

"It's going all right."

"W.W. said he's got you running the north county route."

"Six days a week."

The *Moat County Tribune* had no Sunday edition. My father had tried it for eight months a few years before, and nearly lost the paper.

"You want a job?" he said quietly.

"Is it driving a truck?"

"No," he said, "not a truck."

The line went quiet again.

"A car," he said finally.

"Whose car?"

"I don't know, a rental . . ." Something left hanging.

"You don't need me to drive a rental, Ward," I said.

"Yes," he said, "I do."

❑

I AM NOT SURE my father had a clock on it—he had worked each day for the next day most of his life, which is the fundamental rhythm of the news business, and he was happiest measuring his time in daily editions and unhappiest when he had to think further ahead, as the economics of the business required—but it was clear to me from early on that he meant for Ward to take over his newspaper.

His vision of this moment—a ceremony of some kind, surely—stayed constant, I think, even as all things around him changed.

He had always accommodated change, but kept this moment of his rewarding apart from that; perfect, unblemished, like the shapes of the things in his stories.

And it never seemed to me, until my brother called from Miami to ask if I would take a job as his driver, that I appeared in my father's grand reward ceremony at all. No more, at least, than in a place toward the front of the spectators, where I might stand with my mother and her new husband to witness the celebration.

But when I mentioned over supper later in the week that Ward had offered me a job which did not involve getting out of bed at two-thirty in the morning, my father, without realizing he had done it, set his fork down beside his plate and gazed past me and out the window. I remembered the look from the year my mother left.

He took out his pocketknife and opened the blade, testing its sharpness with the flat of his thumb. Then, just as absently, he went into his pocket for a heart pill. He had been doing more of that lately; sometimes it was hard to tell what made him happy.

Anita Chester came through the door a moment later, looked at the cooling food on my father's plate, then at the glaze over his eyes.

"Is something wrong with your meal, Mr. James?" she said.

"It's fine," he said, still looking out the window.

The heart pill had already made him more comfortable.

"Then eat it," she said, and went back into the kitchen.

He picked up his fork, reluctant to disobey her, and glanced down at the plate. Okra, black-eyed peas, pieces of ham, all lying together in a congealing pile. She took home what we didn't eat. He touched it, breaking the seal, and steam from inside came off the plate into his face and fogged his glasses.

He put the fork back down, a piece of ham speared at the end. "I thought you were going to stick around," he said finally. He looked quickly around the room, reminding me how empty the place would be.

"I'm not going to Miami," I said. "Ward's coming here." But he didn't seem to hear.

"Everybody's leaving," he said.

"I'm not leaving." I said it slowly. He looked at me as if he didn't know who I was. "Ward's looking into something here in Moat County," I said. "He needs somebody to drive him around."

He picked up his glass and finished all the water in it. When he put it down, he was back in the room. "Why can't he drive himself?" he said.

I shook my head, unwilling to tell him that.

"All I know, he and Yardley Acheman are going to be up here a few weeks."

"And after that?" he said.

Anita Chester came back through the door, studied my father's plate and his pocketknife, lying open near it, and put her hands on her hips. "You going to eat that or torture it?" she said. "I got things to do."

Without a word, my father picked up the full plate and handed it to her. She took it, then collected mine, then disappeared back into the kitchen. A moment later, we heard her scraping the dishes.

"What about afterwards?" my father said again.

I said I didn't know.

❑

LATER THAT NIGHT, after he had read the papers, my father got out of his chair, walked into the kitchen, and came back with a beer and a bottle of wine. One glass. He handed the beer to me and sat down, pouring wine into the glass.

"When I was young and first starting out in this business," he said, "there was a copy editor I knew at the *Times-Herald* in New York. His name was Henry McManus from Savannah, Georgia, and he is, to this moment, the cleanest human being I ever saw in a newsroom. He got a haircut once a week, kept the sleeves of his shirt buttoned right to the wrist all day, never raised his voice."

My father had a drink of the wine and then looked at me to see if he'd told me this story before. I couldn't remember if I'd heard it, but it wasn't an old favorite from his days with Ralph McGill. My father smiled and dropped his head backwards into the chair until it rested in the spot where the upholstery was stained.

"He labeled his glue pot so other editors wouldn't use it, and cleaned spills off the side before they'd hardened," he said, "that's how neat he was." He paused, thinking of Henry McManus's glue pot. "And he was so revered, other editors respected his glue, and never used it even when he wasn't there to protect it.

"Henry was an older man," he said, "he may have been thirty-five, which at the time seemed very old indeed, and he'd worked at a dozen newspapers. Still, he spoke to everyone, from the boss right down to the copyboys, with a respectful formality you rarely hear in a newsroom. He was fast and careful with copy, and some of us young Turks would sit in the bar across the street after we'd put the paper to bed and speculate on why he'd never become something more important.

"He had the demeanor of an assistant managing editor, and knew the city as well as any reporter, although he hadn't been there much more than a year. We decided, finally, that

Henry McManus didn't want to be important, and that was why he moved from paper to paper."

I nodded while my father drank his wine, wondering if that was the end of the story. Then he smiled again, watching as it rolled past.

"There was an annual party at Christmas," he said. "We went to Henry's apartment and collected him, against his wishes. We forced a drink on him and waited in his living room until he'd showered and dressed. And on the way to the party we gave him another drink, which he took with less coercion, and then another. . . ."

Anita Chester came through the living room, carrying her purse.

"I'll be leaving now," she said.

My father nodded at her, distracted, trying to keep his finger on the spot in the story. She lifted her chin half an inch and headed out of the house. The screen door slammed shut behind her. My father hated the sound of a screen door slamming.

He paused, as if he were waiting for some pain in his chest to pass, and then picked up the narrative exactly where he had left it.

"At the party," he said, "Henry stood in a corner, straight as a soldier, drinking punch that someone had spiked with vodka. He spoke only when spoken to, shook hands and smiled as the bosses told their wives kind things about his work. . . ."

My father paused again and finished the wine in his glass. He poured another. "And then something came over him," he said quietly, the wonder of it still in his voice. "One minute he was standing against the wall, the next minute he was in every detail a mad dog, right down to the foaming mouth.

"He lunged at one of the editors, and then another, getting the second by the throat. Several of us dragged him off, but he got loose—he was as strong as three of us, which was as

33

many as could get hold of him—and tossed aside one of the wives, trying to get at her husband. She went into the punch, and that seemed to set him off in another direction and that's when he began shouting. 'Jews,' 'kikes,' unimaginable language, howling it. . . ."

My father stopped again, then slowly shook his head. "He never even came in for his check," he said, "he just disappeared. Years later, I heard that he'd gone to Chicago, put six months on the copydesk, and then done the same damn thing. . . ."

My father looked at me then. "He was a newspaperman," he said, "but there's some people who should never leave Savannah."

I sat dead still, wondering what he'd heard about my expulsion from Gainesville, and if he thought I was also someone who should never leave Savannah.

❑

WITH HIS OWN ROOTS in suburban Miami, which is to say he had no roots at all, Yardley Acheman did not arrive in Moat County carrying a great esteem for local sensibilities. Nothing looks more foolish than tradition to those who have none.

He stepped off the bus in Thorn shirtless, his dark, curly hair falling almost to his shoulders, carrying an upright Underwood typewriter. It must have weighed twenty pounds. My brother was the next passenger out. The town was used to long hair, of course—it was 1969—but no one had ever seen a man climbing off the Trailways bus carrying a typewriter before, and even Hal Sharpley, Thorn's acknowledged hobo, moved away from him when he sat down on Hal's bench to tie his boots.

Yardley Acheman was shorter than my brother, and louder, and interrupted my father's stories at dinner with his own stories, which were not as good and had no polish. I was oddly offended by that—not that he'd cut my father short, but by the dismissive nature of the intrusion. It was as if the thousands of hours my brother and I had spent sitting at the dinner table politely listening to stories we'd heard hadn't been necessary.

He drank beer after beer, long after my father had excused himself and gone to bed, and smelled of it the next morning on the way to Lately. I had borrowed one of my father's delivery trucks, and it was a slow drive. A road crew was repaving a four-mile section of highway just outside Thorn, and from time to time, Yardley Acheman looked out the window and glimpsed something of the place—the wide, brown river or an old trailer park hidden in the pines or a small colony of shacks where citrus farmers kept Jamaicans during the harvesting season.

"Jesus Christ," he said. "Je-sus Christ."

He turned on the radio, punched in the stations, one after another, then turned the radio off. He put his feet on the dashboard.

"Je-sus Christ."

Ward sat between us, his feet straddling the gearshift, and he was staring at the countryside too. It would not have been impossible, judging his expression, for my brother to have been thinking *Jesus Christ* himself. He hadn't been home in a long time, and it was different to him now.

❑

MY BROTHER AND Yardley Acheman took two rooms at the Prescott Hotel in Lately and paid in advance for the month. Mrs. Prescott, who had run the place alone since her husband died unexpectedly the previous summer, stood still and smiled politely as Yardley signed in—without being offered the register—and then she studied the signature a long time, as if there was something in it that might have informed her whether or not to take a chance on the young men who had just come in the door.

"Is there a problem?" Yardley said, too loud for the room.

She was startled, and looked up from her register, smiled, and then shook her head. "Only the two of you are staying," she said, looking quickly at me.

"Only the two of us," my brother said.

She nodded, and stared again at the signature. "My husband always checked our guests in. . . ."

"Is there a problem?" Yardley said again. "If there's a problem, lady, we can go somewhere else."

"No," she said, taking the credit card that he'd dropped on the desk, "it's just that my husband always checked in the guests. I'm not used to where things are yet. . . ."

Yardley Acheman stared at the woman while she looked for the American Express machine and then ran his credit card through it twice—putting it in upside down the first time. Her fingers shook under his gaze.

She gave them two rooms on the second floor, sharing a bath. The rooms smelled damp, and the linoleum floor in the bath was warped near the tub and had began to curl where it met the wall. There was a window above the radiator which was sealed with paint and would not open even when Yardley Acheman climbed up on the radiator for leverage to force it.

"We'll get her to fix this," he said to no one in particular. Ward and I looked at each other a moment, and then Ward turned and walked into his room.

There was an ancient brass bed against the far wall in there, above it a copy of the Lord's Prayer hung in a frame. The paint all around the Lord's Prayer had blistered and peeled and broken, as if the battle for good and evil had been fought on that spot.

A floor fan sat in a corner opposite the door, and a smaller fan sat on the bureau.

Ward opened his suitcase, then the drawers in the bureau.

He studied them a moment, then went back into the bathroom and wet a towel. Yardley Acheman was still kneeling on the radiator, pounding on the window now, trying to get it to open. The noise carried everywhere in the house, something I realized a moment before Mrs. Prescott appeared, flushed and slightly out of breath, and knocked carefully on the open door behind us.

"Is everything all right?" she said.

Yardley Acheman stopped pounding and turned to her, still holding on to the window frame, and stared until she retreated a step and was back out in the hall.

"He was trying to open the window," my brother said.

"I'm afraid that window doesn't open," she said, so quietly we could hardly make out the words. "The windows in your rooms open."

Yardley Acheman slowly climbed down, the ridges of the radiator impressed into the knees of his pants.

"It's a window," he said, "it'll open."

She smiled, looking at nobody in the room, and shook her head. "It never has," she said, and then she was gone.

My brother went back into his room and cleaned the drawers with the towel, coming back into the bathroom twice to rinse out the dirt. Yardley Acheman left the window and followed him in, sitting on the bed, watching him work.

"She's supposed to do that," he said. "I don't care where the hotel is, you aren't supposed to clean up the room before you can use it. That's the whole idea of hotels. . . ."

Yardley Acheman hadn't opened the drawers in his own room. His things were still in two large, expensive, leather suitcases, dropped in the middle of the floor. He had set his typewriter on an unreliable-looking table near the window, which was covered by a sun-bleached shade. Filtered through the shade, the light outside turned the room yellow.

My brother finished cleaning the drawers, then placed his clothes in them carefully, organizing areas of socks and underwear and shirts in exactly the way we had been taught to at home by our mother. He closed the drawers slowly, not to disturb his things from the places he had left them, then put his suitcases in the closet.

Yardley Acheman watched all this from the bed. "You know, Jack," he said, more to Ward than to me, "there's a rumor going around that your brother's compulsive."

He was the sort of person who was comfortable offering a good-natured insult if there was someone else there to help absorb the reaction. He was also the sort of person who was comfortable with the fashionable psychological syndromes of the day, which he read about in the life-style sections of news magazines.

My brother looked at him, realizing the remark was intended as a joke, and slowly smiled. An unnatural smile, as if he had to stop a moment and remember the mechanics of how one was made.

On the way out, we passed the little apartment downstairs where Mrs. Prescott lived. The door was open, and she was sitting inside, wishing she'd never let us in.

❑

LATER THAT DAY, my brother and Yardley Acheman set up an office in a large second-story room over the Moat Cafe, at the east end of town. At some time in the recent past an effort had been made to change the appearance of the roof of the building to resemble a castle's, an attraction for tourists who came through on their way to and from the great beaches to the south. This remodeling was commissioned in spite of the fact that the café and the street and the county itself had nothing to do with castles but were all named for Luther Moat, a slave trader who had once owned the land which the town occupies.

The transformation of the Moat Cafe into a castle was abandoned perhaps halfway through, and the single finished area—a tower whose roofline resembled a dunce cap—had created a small room upstairs which the building's owner had rented to the *Miami Times* over the telephone for thirty dollars a month. The place smelled of cooked onions for as long as we were there.

My brother and Yardley Acheman brought in two heavy wooden desks purchased from the Moat County School Board and scarred with initials in a hundred places, two wooden chairs whose casters fell off whenever they were moved, a small refrigerator, and a leather davenport. All of it fit into perhaps one fourth of the truck, and had slid from the spot near the door where they'd left it (you cannot tell reporters how to load a truck; the way they look at it, if truck loaders are so damn smart, why aren't they reporters themselves?) all the way to the back, where the load had slammed into the wall, making a noise that was comparable to backing the truck into the loading station, something I had done on my first day of work at the *Tribune*.

They carried the stuff upstairs themselves, scuffing their knuckles as they negotiated the turn at the landing, taking paint off the walls as they went up. Knocking the top off an ornamental post which anchored the banister. Yardley swearing all the way.

I was a spectator for this show—the bottom half of it, anyway—as I stayed with the truck, which was parked in front of the café's door.

Neither Yardley Acheman nor my brother had done any physical work in his adult life, and they would arrive at the narrow door carrying the couch, for instance, before they saw they couldn't bring it in sideways. I would have helped, but the truck was parked in a loading zone—to my certain knowledge the only loading zone in Lately—and my brother wanted me to stay with it in case someone needed to get in and load.

Onions, I suppose.

———

He did not want to alienate the café owners or the police or the general population, as much of what he would do in Lately hinged on how he and Yardley Acheman were received.

Growing up in the county, my brother understood that anything foreign, even something harmless or barely noticeable—which he and Yardley Acheman were not—became an irritant on touch. Coming up from the south end of the county counted for nothing.

You were local or you weren't.

❑

CHARLOTTE BLESS ARRIVED in Lately as my brother and Yardley Acheman were negotiating the second desk up the staircase. I had been sitting in the loading zone watching for deliveries so long that a panting retriever of some kind had dropped into the shade of the truck to lie down.

She came in a rusted-out Volkswagen van with Louisiana license plates. The van had recently received a coat of house paint, and appeared from the east, catching my attention from a quarter mile away as the sun reflected off the flat glass windshield as she crossed the railroad tracks.

A block away, she slipped into the left side of the street and then slowed and finally parked, our faces no more than five feet apart when she stopped. Her side of the windshield was tinted blue. She stayed there a moment, staring at me until I looked away, and then climbed out. She wore jeans and a work shirt tucked into a tight belt, and as she left the truck she smoothed the shirt over her stomach and breasts and tossed her head in a way that evened the fall of her hair across her back.

She passed in front of my windshield without looking at me again, and then was out of view. A moment later she was back, her face just below my elbow, which was resting in the open window.

"Is that your dog?" she said.

The current shot through me six directions at once. I hadn't heard her return, and after one long, parting look at the rise of her bottom as it moved out of sight, I'd closed my eyes, trying to hold on to the picture of it as long as I could. The dog was standing next to her, looking up with his mouth open and his tail wagging, as if he expected something good was about to drop out of her pocket.

"No, ma'am," I said. I looked at him and then back at her. This close, she was perhaps twenty years older than she'd looked climbing out of her Volkswagen. Her skin was harder, and creased where it disappeared into her collar. I took heart from these imperfections, imagining that they made me more suitable. I had no idea who she was.

"He was lying right under your tire," she said, and I felt the accusation. She reached down and touched the animal's head, a ring on every finger of her hand. The dog came up slowly then, encircled her leg with his legs, and she pushed him down just as slowly, prying him off just as he started to pump.

Yes, she knew how to handle dogs.

I wondered if she might hold the same charity for me. I doubted it, as none of the girls at Gainesville who made a show of compassion for what went on in an animal's head had any sympathy at all for what went on in mine, and at that time in my life, when I was unsure of everything, sympathy was the only chance I had.

I looked back toward the place where the dog had been lying. He hadn't been right under the tire, or even in front of it, but I wasn't going to argue. In some way, her saying it made it so.

"I had an eye on him," I said.

She nodded slowly, as if we both knew that wasn't true, and then looked beyond me at the Moat Cafe, then up and down the street.

41

"I was looking for the office of Yardley Acheman of the *Miami Times*," she said.

❑

CHARLOTTE BLESS AND the retriever waited beside my window for Yardley Acheman and my brother to come down. I was dizzy with her perfume, and while I did not intentionally continue to compare myself sexually with this animal, it came to me then that somewhere in history, we, like dogs, were sexually aroused primarily by the sense of smell, and there are certain odors which all your life seem to call you to act on them. I was not thinking of roast turkey in the oven, which you sit down and eat, but something like gasoline, which stirred me from the first time I smelled it. But to do what? Drink? Bathe?

Is it possible the first thing I wanted to fuck was gasoline?

❑

MY BROTHER AND Yardley Acheman appeared in the open door which led upstairs to their offices. Yardley sat down on the bottom step, sucking alternately at a scraped knuckle and a long-necked bottle of beer he held in the same hand, while Ward walked back to the truck to shut the rear door. He did not see Charlotte Bless until she materialized next to him as he was reaching up for the handle.

She seemed to like appearing unannounced under your arm. He jumped at the sight of her, and then reddened as she stood still, her head slightly cocked, watching him recover. Suddenly he was doing everything too fast. Smiling, nodding, trying to close the truck.

"I'm Charlotte Bless," she said.

"How do you do," he said. She looked at him without saying another word. Whatever she had over men, she wanted to know it was there all the time.

Ward pulled the door of the truck shut and locked it, then dropped the keys on the street. She didn't move as he bent to retrieve them, not even a step. His face almost touched her pants. He stood up, flushed and stumbling under her gaze. Then she looked away, over to the doorway where Yardley Acheman was still sitting, drinking his beer. Handsome and remote.

"Mr. Acheman?" she said.

From the beginning, she liked him best.

He stood up slowly and walked out of the shade to the truck. She extended her hand—chest high, as if she were someone just learning to shake hands—and he took it, looking her quickly up and down, taking in the appearance of her skin. He had seen her only in photographs.

"Is this it?" she said, looking at the front of the building. Yardley Acheman looked at it too, and then back at her, as if he might be asking the same question.

He finished what was in the bottle and set it down on the curb. "You want a beer?" he said. "We've got a refrigerator upstairs."

"I don't drink before sundown," she said, but she sounded like she might make an exception. She walked to the back of the van, opened the door, and came out with a stack of flat boxes that rose halfway from her hands to her chin. She hesitated a moment, returning to my brother and Yardley Acheman, and then, deciding something, handed them to my brother, who accepted them without asking what they were and then stood still waiting for her to tell him.

"They're my files," she said, and headed back to the van. "Come on, there's boxes of this stuff. . . ."

I waited behind Yardley Acheman for my own armful of boxes to carry up the stairs to the office and saw the look on her face as she handed him his load; a quick look, something passing between them, and then she dropped the boxes into

43

his hands—he sagged under the sudden weight—and turned back into the van for mine.

❑

IT WAS CHARLOTTE BLESS's long-range ambition to become the wife of Hillary Van Wetter. That was what she pictured at the end. She acknowledged this matter-of-factly upstairs, sitting against a stack of gift boxes bearing the name of Maison Blanche Department Stores which went waist-high against the wall of my brother's side of the office. Each of these boxes was taped shut and filled perhaps halfway to the top with several pounds of "files," and the weight of those on top crushed the ones beneath, and the whole wall looked like a pile of forced smiles.

Yardley Acheman sat on the other side of the room, his chair tilted back until it rested against the wall behind him, his feet crossed on the desk, drinking another beer. He was considering her in a way that suggested he hadn't made up his mind. Or perhaps he was still getting used to her appearance. She had seemed much younger in the pictures she sent.

No one interested in how newspaper reporters find their stories should imagine that the compass needle is reset each time out. What they find attractive doesn't change, only where they find it.

My brother and I leaned against the sills of the two windows in the office. The windows were open and I could smell onions, and, beneath it, her perfume.

She sat as comfortably as if she were in her own living room. Her knees were bent almost to her head, and she was hugging her legs. "My personal feelings for Hillary aside," she said, looking at Yardley again, "what I have come here to do is correct an injustice and free an innocent man."

Yardley Acheman bounced the bottle gently against his lip, not committing himself. My brother sat still and waited.

"That is our intention, is it not?" she said.

"You're going to marry him," Yardley Acheman said.

"We're engaged," she said. I looked quickly at her hands, trying to decide which of the rings might have come from Hillary Van Wetter. The one on her index finger had a baby's tooth for a stone.

Yardley Acheman looked at my brother.

"It doesn't change anything," she said. The room was quiet. "What does it change?"

My brother stirred, and the movement drew her attention. He seemed ready to speak, but then something caught, and he stopped.

"Mr. Acheman?" she said. She leaned forward, showing more of her chest. He tapped the bottle against his lip, thinking it over.

"Nothing," he said.

❑

CHARLOTTE BLESS FIRST laid eyes on Hillary Van Wetter in a UPI picture which appeared on the front page of a four-day-old copy of the *New Orleans Times-Picayune* which had been left on a lunch table at work.

He was handcuffed in the picture and being led up the Moat County Courthouse steps in Lately, accused of the murder of Sheriff Thurmond Call.

She was sitting in the employees' cafeteria at the main branch of the New Orleans Post Office, on Loyola Street. The paper was lying on the table, gutted of its sports section and then discarded, stained with dried red beans and rice. She wiped off the food and studied the picture, which was out of register but still captured a certain intensity in the expression of the blond man standing between two moon-faced sheriff's deputies, and found herself pulled to his side.

Judging from her other killers, whose files she brought

along with Hillary Van Wetter's in the Volkswagen, she had a tender spot for blonds.

She read the story beneath the picture—it was only a few paragraphs, mostly recounting the career of Sheriff Call—and then, as her lunch break was ending, she tore the picture and the story out of the paper and put it in her pocket. You could do that in the cafeteria; on the floor it was a felony, and there were dark windows in the ceiling where supervisors sat, watching the letter sorters for just that kind of criminal behavior.

Charlotte Bless's previous ambition had been to end her career with the New Orleans Post Office as one of the supervisors behind the dark windows. It fit her, and she had decided early to turn down any promotions that were offered beyond it.

That night she wrote him her first letter, an airy, five-page note telling him exactly how she stumbled across his picture, and about her position at the post office and the food on the table that nobody ever cleaned up, and her "quandary," in the middle of other people's mess, that an orderly, clean-shaven man like Hillary Van Wetter had gotten himself into a situation like this in the first place.

She made a carbon copy of the letter, and put it into a box that she marked H.V.W.

While he wasn't the first murderer she had written to, he was the first one who had used a knife. "If it were myself," she wrote at the very end, striking an odd tone of familiarity, "I am sure that, having sufficient provocation to kill, I would also opt for the intimacy of the blade."

The letter brought no response.

In her next letter, she wrote that she understood he was early in his legal journey—those were the words she used—and still too distracted to observe normal social discourse. "Being the photogenic person you are," she added, "I am sure you are receiving more letters than you have time to sort out."

◻

FOR THE NEXT FIVE MONTHS, Charlotte visited the New Orleans Public Library every afternoon after work, and not only pored over the pages of the *Times-Picayune* and the *States-Item,* neither of which carried much news from beyond Louisiana, for some mention of Hillary Van Wetter, but the *Atlanta Constitution,* the *Miami Times,* and the *Tampa Times* too.

As the story cooled, she found Hillary Van Wetter and Sheriff Call mentioned less often, but later, during the trial itself, she was rewarded with daily reports, and she cut these out of the papers, along with each picture of Hillary Van Wetter that appeared, even when it was a file picture which she already had.

She also cut out pictures of Sheriff Call and the prosecutor and the defense attorney and the two jurors who were interviewed and photographed after the verdict. Sometimes she looked at these pictures in the morning, when she woke up worrying about Hillary; it comforted her to compare them to him. She had turned down men with those same soft faces all her life.

She removed the pictures from the newspapers at a small table hidden from the front counter, using a pair of rounded cuticle scissors that left the borders of the emptied frames frayed. She felt guilty stealing the pictures, and once dropped a note in the suggestion box that said the place could use a better security system, and referred the library to the dark windows in the ceiling at the post office.

At home, she pasted the stories and pictures against typing paper, and laid the paper flat on the bottom of the box marked H.V.W. When it was half full, she started another.

All the while, she was writing Hillary Van Wetter every week at the county jail—long, wandering letters full of descriptions of the post office and the people who worked there, of the

47

noises that came through the wall of her apartment in the Quarter at night, of the way he had appeared to her in a story or picture she'd seen. She asked questions but never asked him to write back with the answers.

It was too early in things to push.

The other killers she'd chosen had been anxious and faithful correspondents from the first letter, even before she'd sent them her picture, but in the end there was a sameness to their letters that deadened her interest. She still sent them all perfunctory cards at holidays, but neglected to even open some of the thicker envelopes that arrived with identification numbers for return addresses. They were all the same, full of legalese and stories of forgetful lawyers and prison routines and sexual longings; promises of sex that would last days and months.

Worse yet, the ones who read books were always quoting dead philosophers. Mostly Germans.

Nothing about the crimes themselves. Not a word about the victims or the rooms where the killings happened. No glimpse of that. It was as if the single exciting thing about them had never happened.

Still, she hadn't given up on them completely—she still liked to think of them at night, imprisoned in six different states, staring at her picture in the half light of their cells, the place completely quiet except for their hard breathing and their rattling cots.

With Hillary Van Wetter, however, she realized that she was looking for something more substantial than her ordinary killers could offer.

She wanted someone less compromised, and after Hillary was convicted—that was how she was addressing him then, "Dear Hillary"—and sent to death row at Starke, she sent him her picture, and autographed it: "For Hillary Van Wetter, an intact man. Warmest regards, Charlotte."

Coming across that same phrase—"an intact man"—in the

accompanying letter, I thought suddenly of my Hungarian coach at the University of Florida. Commit everything to the swim.

She knew the picture flattered her, but thought of it, in the whole, as honest. It fairly represented her features, and if it softened and smoothed her skin, it had also showed nothing of her body, which, even in critical moments, she could not fault.

And if she knew when she sent the picture that she would at some point appear in front of Hillary Van Wetter not precisely as advertised, it wasn't a deception on the order of, say, the cover of a TV dinner, which promised peas the color of green crayons that turned out to be gray.

She was not gray peas.

Eight days after she sent the picture, a letter arrived from Starke, Florida:

Dear Miss Charlotte Bless,

Thank you for writing your letter to me about my innocents. I am working on some things in that direction myself. Would you have a picture that showed more of yourself so I could see what I am talking about.

Truly,
Hillary Van Wetter, #39269
P.O. Box 747
Starke, Florida

She read the words and could hear his voice. No evasions, no lawyer jargon, no bragging. He was purer than her other killers, but she had sensed that from the start. Uncompromised by jail and attorneys, an intact man.

And even acknowledging a certain misunderstanding at the center of her developing romance with Hillary Van Wetter, no one who ever met Hillary in person could say that Charlotte Bless entirely missed the point.

❏

THERE WERE, by actual count, forty-one boxes of "evidence" that Charlotte Bless had accumulated over four years. Newspaper clippings, letters to and from Hillary Van Wetter as well as half a dozen other convicted killers, transcripts of the trial and the two appeals which followed, brief biographies of all eleven judges who had become involved in the case.

There were several newspaper reports on famous murder cases the same judges had been involved in before, along with a list of miscarriages of justice which had occurred at the hands of Sheriff Thurmond Call over the last fifteen years of his administration.

And through all the boxes, there was a kind of running diary, mingled with the other "evidence," which not only argued with rulings and pressed alternate theories of the killing, but contained Charlotte Bless's most intimate sexual thoughts over the entire period of the case.

In one paragraph she analyzed Judge Waylan Lord's death sentencing patterns, and in the next she noted that all the killers who had written her except Hillary Van Wetter wanted to press their mouths into her vagina and even the crack of her behind. Hillary had no such desire, which she considered "psychological proof" of his innocence.

He wanted to be sucked himself, like a judge.

❏

YARDLEY ACHEMAN AND my brother stayed in their office every day for a week, reading everything inside the boxes of evidence. Ward opened each box first, numbered it, and then examined what was inside, making notes as he went. When he had finished with a box, he turned it over to Yardley Acheman, who went through faster, and without notes, stopping occasionally to read something out loud.

"Listen to this," he said, "she's talking about blowing him through the bars of the cell with all the prisoners watching, and then, wait . . ." He stopped for a moment, finding the place. "Yes, right here . . . 'I would suck his shaft, if it comes to that, as they strap on the electrodes, to hold him in my mouth as he comes and goes. . . .' "

He looked at my brother, smiling, and then, getting no reaction, he looked at me. "I don't think she's thought that all the way through," he said.

Ward was back studying the pages spread out across his desk.

"If nothing else comes of all this," Yardley said, "we've got a strange story here about a girl who falls in love with killers. . . ."

My brother looked up again, about to open another of the boxes which, with all the others, held every private thought and craving that had come into Charlotte Bless's head since 1965, and which she had turned over to him and Yardley Acheman on blind faith and out of love for her fiancé, whom she had yet to meet.

"We didn't make any promises," Yardley said.

Ward struggled with it a moment, then, without a word, went back to the box. The betrayal was built in; it was in the boxes when she turned them over, in the grain of the story, and in the grain of the business.

❑

"So," SHE SHOUTED, "you're smart. Why aren't you in college?" Her window was open and the wind lifted her hair off the seat behind her, blowing it into the corners of her mouth.

"We could turn on the air conditioner," I said, but probably not loud enough to be heard over the wind. I moved my hand toward the dashboard, trying to remember how it worked.

She stopped me, touching my arm, shaking her head no,

and her hair was free in the air and turned red as it crossed the sun, which was hanging just over the horizon.

"I like real air," she said, and I nodded, and a moment later my own hair slapped into my eyes, making them fill with tears. "So why aren't you in college?" she said.

I rolled my window halfway up, and the beating wasn't as bad. "I was," I said.

She looked at me, waiting. As if because she gave up the details of her own life to strangers, strangers would give up theirs to her.

"Something happened," I said.

"What was it?" Not even giving that a chance to settle, but now at least she was watching the road. She'd wanted to drive, I didn't know why.

"I forgot where I was," I said. And hearing myself say that, it seemed like the truth. She leaned across the seat to hear me, and the wind beat the top of her blouse against her chest, and in the second I looked that way, speaking of forgetting where you are, I saw the pink of her nipple.

"You got lost?" she said.

"Not lost," I said. "I knew I was somewhere familiar, I just forgot where it was."

"It's the same thing," she said.

"No," I said, "it's not."

She went quiet a moment, thinking it over. We were on the way to Starke. She'd said she wanted to be close to the prison for a little while, to sit in the parking lot and see what it felt like to be near him.

She'd wanted Yardley to take her, but late in the afternoon he showed up at the office and told her he couldn't. "Jack'll have to do," he said. He'd met a girl at the laundromat that afternoon, and needed to explore the local milieu with her instead. He said he was way behind on the local milieu.

"How do you forget where you are at college?" she said.

I thought about it, trying to remember how it happened. "I was a swimmer," I said slowly.

"You can swim?"

"It's Florida, everybody can swim."

It was quiet between us again, and she pushed the lighter into the dashboard and when it was ready she stuck a cigarette in her lips and then, letting go of the wheel, cupped one of her hands over the top when she lit it.

"Where did you swim?" she said, no one driving the car.

"University of Florida. I was on the team."

"In a pool?"

She pulled on the cigarette and the wind caught the cigarette and blew sparks into her hair. "You weren't in the ocean or anything."

"Not at the University of Florida," I said.

"Good."

And it was quiet again, and a few minutes later we drove through Starke and turned north on Highway 16. She saw a mileage sign for the state prison and slowed before she went past, watching it until it was cut from view, as if it were something she wanted to remember, and then for a while seemed to immerse herself in the land—studying the flat, lifeless landscape as if each piece of it had a separate meaning, like a battlefield from the Civil War.

I was still thinking of Gainesville and what had happened there, how I had forgotten where I was. I wanted to tell her about that, I thought it might make me more interesting.

"The pool was indoors," I said, getting the feel of it back, "and the sound bounced from the ceiling to the water to the walls. You could never tell where it was coming from."

She turned away from the window, and the cigarette in her lips had blown out. "What sound?" she said.

"Yelling," I said, "a lot of yelling. Whistles. . . . The coach was a Hungarian, they love whistles. We were in the water four hours a day, sometimes more, every day but Sunday, six months of the year."

"We?"

"The swimmers. I was on the team."

"And you forgot where you were."

I nodded. That was what happened. There were two practices a day, early and late. I was in the water all the time, and at night, in my dreams, I was in it again.

And I would wake from the dreams at five-thirty in the morning to be at the pool by six, and somewhere in the missed sleep and exhaustion the dreams began to bleed into the day, just as the days had bled into them, and I would find myself swimming laps in the morning and suddenly not knowing which place I was.

I would stop when that happened, terrified, and then roll over onto my back and float, ignoring the yelling and whistling, looking only at the ceiling and the walls, at my legs and arms and chest, to watch them and know where they were.

Three times that last semester I rolled out of bed.

And then, of course, I lost my scholarship and was expelled, and went back to Moat County to my own room and my own bed, and discovered that the disease had followed me home.

She'd quit listening, and then I looked off into the distance and saw it too, the prison.

❏

SHE PULLED INTO a gravel driveway that led to a gate marked "Visitors." The prison was another two hundred yards in, surrounded by a chain link fence with rolls of razor wire at the top. Behind it was another, smaller fence, also topped with razor wire, and between the fences two dozen large dogs lay in the late afternoon dusk—would-be killers themselves, they were the most vicious cases, and had been saved by that from a carbon monoxide gas chamber at the county's animal control center.

"We want to sit in the parking lot," she said to the guard.

He looked into the car, front seat and back, and then shook his head. "You got to have a pass, miss," he said, "and it's too late now. Business hours is nine to four-thirty. Visiting hours available on request."

He stared at me then, I don't know why.

"It's all right," she said, "he's with the press."

❑

WE BACKED OUT OF the driveway and sat in the car for a while along the highway. She studied the prison, one end to the other, and then sighed and dropped back into her seat. She closed her eyes.

"You know where they keep them?" she said.

"Who?"

"Death row prisoners, you know where they are?"

I said, "It all looks like death row to me."

"Over on the far right side," she said, and I glanced that way, but it looked the same as the rest of the place. "They keep the lights on night and day."

She lit another cigarette. "They have the opposite problem of you," she said. "In there, you can't forget where you are."

It was quiet a while and she turned away from me to stare at the prison. "Hillary would know I'm here," she said.

I didn't think that was true, but it's hard to judge from the outside what goes on between a man and a woman who become engaged to marry without meeting each other.

She sat with her legs apart, smoking her cigarette as the sky got dark. Night insects flew into the car, and I slapped them off my neck and arms. There were lightning bugs in the prison yard. She sat still, immune to insects, her face glowing in the light of her cigarette as she pulled on it from time to time, then disappearing into the dark. Perhaps the mosquitoes didn't like the smoke.

I thought of undressing her, right there in the car with Hillary Van Wetter lying in his cell a quarter mile away, his intuition suddenly sitting him up in bed.

———

But it was only a thought; it lit and faded, like her face as she pulled on the cigarette. It seemed to me that even Hillary Van Wetter would have forgiven me for that.

❑

WELDON PINE WAS seventy-two years old and had practiced law in the northern end of Moat County for fifty-six years, grandfathered in from a time when a degree from an accredited law school was not requisite to becoming a lawyer. And while Mr. Pine did not have a degree—at least not in the academic sense, he did have an honorary doctorate of jurisprudence from the Christian University of North Florida—he was personally associated in one way or another with every human being who made a living in or around the Moat County Courthouse, and was the man who decided, in fact, if many of them made a living at all. It was an accepted fact in the northern end of Moat County that he was the best lawyer in the South.

Mr. Pine still occupied the office he had first rented when he began his career. It sat in a building across the street kitty-corner from the courthouse, and while he now owned not only the building that housed this office but the block of buildings behind it, he kept the corner room on the first floor as it had been when he moved in. An oak desk sat in the center of the room, allowing just enough clearance for the door to swing open. Shades were pulled over the windows, the metal file cabinets sat against the far wall.

Except for its location and roofline and the fact that it did not smell of fried onions, it was not appreciably better than the space my brother and Yardley Acheman had rented above the Moat Cafe half a mile to the north.

It seemed smaller, in fact, after all of us were inside. Mr. Pine sat behind his desk in a new suit and a new haircut, a large, heavyset man, his wavy white hair shaved half an inch above his ears.

There was one chair in front of the desk, which Yardley Acheman took.

"I wonder," Mr. Pine said, looking at those of us still standing, "if we might be more comfortable in the conference room."

"That would be fine," my brother said.

The old man held up a crooked index finger, and said, "But . . ." We waited out a long, dramatic pause. ". . . any and all photographs shall be taken here. Do we understand each other?"

Ward and Yardley Acheman looked at each other a moment, then Yardley Acheman stood up, his shirt soaked with sweat and sticking to his skin. There was a small air conditioner at work in the window, but it was not designed for five people in the room at once.

"It's a little early yet for pictures," Ward said, and that seemed to satisfy Mr. Pine.

We followed him through his secretary's office and down a carpeted hallway. The conference room lay behind the last two doors on the right, and there were enough chairs in there for us all.

Charlotte put her hands behind her back and examined the law books that lined the walls as if she were looking for something to read.

The old man took his seat at the head of the table and watched her. "She's the photographer, am I correct?" he said.

"This is Charlotte Bless, Mr. Pine," my brother said. "She wrote you she was coming."

The lawyer said, "Of course, of course," and smiled at her. She took a seat but did not smile back. Weldon Pine leaned his head back into his laced fingers and closed his eyes.

"It's been my experience in these expeditions," he said, "that the best place to start is the beginning. . . ." There was another long pause as he gathered himself to start.

"I was born in this county in 1897 of proud but poor parents. My mother was French, my father German. My early education was informal, but nevertheless at least equal, I would say, to what my compatriots received at the hands of the public schools. I was taught the importance of logical thinking, which has served me well over all the years since—"

Weldon Pine stopped suddenly, looked in front of himself at the empty table, and then got up and walked out of the room, closing the door behind him. Those of us left inside looked at each other, but no one spoke. A moment later he was back, out of breath, carrying his family album; it looked as heavy as a sandbag. The leather cover was ancient and dry and it creaked as it opened.

"Here," he said, pushing his finger into the book, "this was my mother. As you see, she was French. . . ." The finger was thick and brittle, like a farmer's. Charlotte Bless came a few inches off her seat to look, possibly coveting the photograph for her files; no one else moved. "I'm afraid it doesn't reproduce well," he said. "What kind of presses do you have? The *Palm Beach Post* managed to get a good likeness, but they have offset presses. . . ."

He turned another page. "This is my father and his brother. . . ." He smiled at them. "Germans," he said, as if that were a joke we all understood.

"Mr. Pine," Yardley Acheman said, "you think we could skip maybe sixty-five years here, save everybody some time?"

The old man looked up, his finger still resting beneath the picture of his father and uncle. He blinked.

"Nineteen sixty-five," Yardley Acheman said. "Hillary Van Wetter . . ."

The old man looked at the album again; he didn't seem to understand. "That isn't a significant case," he said finally. "It contributes nothing to the richness of the story. . . ."

"It is the story," Yardley Acheman said slowly.

And there was still another pause as that settled in. "We wrote you a letter and said we'd be coming up?" Yardley Acheman said. "You agreed to take us in to see him."

The old man began to shake his head. "I wouldn't have agreed to any such thing without my client's permission," he said. "He has his right to privacy, like anybody else."

"You have Mr. Van Wetter's permission," my brother said quietly, and the old man turned to face him; it was like he was fighting off a pack of dogs. "He wrote you, and a copy of that letter was enclosed in the envelope you received."

Weldon Pine's jaw went slack. "I'd have to check that," he said. He looked again at the picture of his father and uncle, the Germans, and then reluctantly closed the album.

"The letter would be in your files," my brother said.

The old man looked at him, closing the gates. "That's what you say, but I've got a client to protect." He looked around the table again, stopping for just a moment on Charlotte Bless, and then fixed a small, practiced smile on his face. "Will that be all?"

"Mr. Pine," my brother said, in the same quiet voice, "Mr. Van Wetter has asked us to review his case for the purposes of writing a newspaper story. To that end, he has instructed you to open all the pertinent files to us, and to facilitate interviews between ourselves and Mr. Van Wetter, as well as all other interested parties."

"Other interested parties," the old man said, finding something humorous in that.

"If you would just check your files—"

Yardley Acheman interrupted my brother. "Put it another way, Mr. Pine. If you don't check your files and arrange a meeting with Mr. Van Wetter, if we've got to bring a lawyer of our own up here to represent Mr. Van Wetter's interests in this—and I promise you that's what we're going to do if we walk out of here empty-handed—then as long as he's up here, we're going to have him look into every aspect of Mr. Van Wetter's case, including the competency of his defense, if you catch my meaning. . . ."

The old man sat still, his throat working. "There's nothing wrong with the defense Hillary Van Wetter got in court," he said.

"You've got nothing to worry about from us," Yardley Acheman said, his tone friendlier now. "We just want to talk to him."

"I took that case pro bono," the old man said. "I didn't make a cent off that man."

It was quiet again. "We are, of course, aware of your fine record of commitment to the public interest," Yardley Acheman said.

Charlotte opened her purse and found a cigarette. The old man watched her light it.

"You sent me your picture," he said.

She nodded and drew the smoke deep into her chest. "I'm his fiancée," she said.

"I think you're wasting your time," he said a moment later, but he was looking at the family album again and it wasn't clear which of us he was talking to.

"We have time," Yardley Acheman said.

The old man arranged for the meeting with Hillary Van Wetter, but would not be talked into coming along to straighten out any problems we might have getting into the prison.

"I have no desire to see Mr. Van Wetter again in this lifetime," he said formally.

"You're his attorney," Yardley Acheman said. We were back in the little office again, where Weldon Pine kept his files.

"Yessir, I am," he said, "and in that regard I will continue to defend Mr. Van Wetter's legal rights, but I have no interest in another personal encounter." He put a scalding look on us all and said, "That man has took as much of me as I intend to give him."

❑

ON THE MORNING she would first meet her fiancé in person, Charlotte came out of the apartment she had leased in a yel-

60

low dress. My brother and Yardley Acheman and I were sitting in the rented car outside, waiting. She was fifteen minutes late, and none of us had seen her in a dress before. She wore white shoes with modest heels, and she had spent some time that morning in front of a mirror.

From the distance of the curb, she could have been as young as she looked in her picture.

"Well, look at this," Yardley Acheman said. My brother looked, but said nothing. She walked from the door of her apartment to the curb in a natural way, as if she wore dresses and white shoes with heels every day of her life. She got into the car carefully, lifting her legs well over the bottom of the door, not wanting to run her stockings.

We'd driven five miles out of Lately when she suddenly reached across the seat and turned the rearview mirror so that she could check her face. One side, then the other, smoothing the makeup into her neck. She left the mirror where she could see herself when she finished and lit a cigarette. For a long time, no one spoke. The windows were closed, not to muss her hair, and the air was dense with the smell of her perfume and her shampoo.

I was afraid Yardley Acheman would try to say something humorous, but he didn't. He sat in the backseat with his hands folded in his lap, looking at her, then out the window, then glancing at her again, as if it were something he couldn't stop.

She didn't notice his attention; she barely noticed the prison. It seemed to startle her when I turned back into the gravel road where she and I had been before and rolled down my window to talk to the guard.

Yardley Acheman turned his attention to the sprawl of the prison, and the flat, empty ground surrounding it. Already working on his prose. Half a dozen prisoners were standing in ditches farther down the road, swinging sickles at the weeds. In his story, they would become thirty men.

It was the same guard at the gate, and he seemed to recognize us. He looked inside the car at Charlotte first, then into the backseat at Ward and Yardley Acheman, and then back to Charlotte.

"Straight ahead to Administration," he said, staring at her legs.

❑

HILLARY VAN WETTER WAS brought into the room in shackles by a guard, and the smell of the prison—disinfectant—came in with him. The guard held on to a chain that encircled his waist and attached to his handcuffs, and, after locking the door he had just come through, he pointed to an empty chair that sat by itself in the middle of the room.

Hillary Van Wetter moved easily to the chair, as if the shackles and handcuffs were no inconvenience, and then allowed himself to be pushed roughly down, as if he did not feel the guard's hands on his shoulders. As if the guard did not matter to him at all.

"Fifteen minutes," the guard said. "No physical contact of any type, no tape recording devices, no objects of any type may be passed to the prisoner." He paused for a moment, looking at us each in turn. "I am right outside the door."

Hillary Van Wetter sat in his chair and waited. He nodded once at Charlotte, but did not speak. She nodded back.

"Mr. Van Wetter," my brother said, "my name is Ward James. . . ."

"You look like your pitcher," he said to her.

She smoothed her dress, a familiar gesture now, and blushed, which was not familiar at all. "Thank you, I think," she said.

"This is Yardley Acheman," my brother said, but Hillary Van Wetter did not look at Yardley Acheman or my brother. He stayed on Charlotte like he was feeding.

"These the paperboys?" he said to her.

She nodded, and it was as if the rest of us weren't in the room. "And what good is they going to do us?" he said.

She looked at my brother quickly. "Save you," she said.

He considered us then, taking his time, his eyes resting on me for as long as they did on my brother and Yardley. Then he went back to her.

"They can't save themselves," he said.

"They can help," she said. Her voice was smaller than it had been.

A look of impatience passed over Yardley Acheman's face, and he turned his head away and looked at the tiny, round window in the door; there were wires inside the glass.

"Who they saved so far?" Hillary Van Wetter said.

"They're well known in Miami," she said.

Hillary Van Wetter turned to Yardley, examining what it took to be well known in Miami. Something that might have passed for a smile among the Van Wetters crossed his face, and then was gone.

"So who you paperboys saved?" he said.

Yardley Acheman looked quickly at the walls and the floor and ceiling. "Who else you got?" he said.

And now Hillary Van Wetter did smile; it creased his face and pulled his lips back off his teeth until you could see the gums. "I like that," he said.

"You been to college?" he said, looking at me now. Before I'd been expelled, there weren't three people in this world who ever asked if I went to college, and now it was happening every ten minutes. I nodded, half an inch, not wanting to go any further into it.

It came to me suddenly that if I had been alone in the room with Hillary Van Wetter, I might have been able to explain what happened. With his criminal mentality, he could have understood it.

"And you'd be well known in Miami also," he said.

"No," I said, "I just drive the car."

He nodded, as if that made sense. "The getaway driver," he said, and he laughed. And then, a long moment later: "You ever saved anybody?"

My brother turned and looked at me now.

"I saved somebody once," I said.

Hillary Van Wetter's eyes rested on me, waiting, and I remembered the other Van Wetter's eyes, who was dead now, as I sat behind the wheel of the Plymouth at Duncan Motors while my father signed the papers with Mr. Duncan.

"At Daytona Beach," I said. "I pulled a girl out of the water."

"He's a swimmer," Charlotte said, but Hillary didn't acknowledge that. You could see it annoyed him having her talk out of turn.

"Seemed to me," he said a little later, "if somebody is foolish enough to get themself into water they don't know, they deserve what they get."

And he did not expect an answer to that, and turned back to Charlotte, almost as if he had said it to her. She smiled at him, staring right into his eyes. The look caught, and then changed, and grew, until I was embarrassed to be there in the room.

My brother started to say something and then stopped; his stirring did not register in Hillary Van Wetter's face. Hillary did one thing at a time. Now he nodded at his lap, where an erection had pitched tent in his prison pants. He looked at it, and then she looked at it too. Ward began to study his nails.

"There's something you could do for me," Hillary said.

She nodded. "I wish I could," she said in a tiny voice, and then glanced at the door.

It was quiet a long time in the room, and then my brother stirred again, and this time he spoke. "Mr. Van Wetter," he said, and the man nodded, still looking at his fiancée. "There's some things we have to go over ... about your case ..."

"Shut up," Hillary said quietly. He stared at Charlotte and she stared at him. His nostrils seemed to swell as his breathing caught and changed. "Open your mouth," he said to her, asking her more than telling her, and her lips came apart half an inch and her tongue wet the bottom one and then lingered just a moment in the corner.

He nodded at her, slowly at first, and then the movement of his head was more pronounced, as if he were in a hurry, and then he closed his eyes and dropped his head over the back of his chair and shook.

He sat completely still a moment, his eyes closed, his face calm and pink and damp, like a sleeping baby, and then a dark stain appeared on his trousers and grew across his lap onto his leg.

I wondered if it would be like that when they electrocuted him.

❏

CHARLOTTE BLESS CRIED in the car on the way back. She sat in the front seat with me and rested her head against the open window, not caring now if the wind blew her hair. It was not a kind of crying you could hear, but the tears dripped off her nose and chin, and it shook her shoulders.

It made sense to me that she would be crying; there seemed to be things to cry about, although I couldn't have told you what any of them were.

❏

THE CASE AGAINST Hillary Van Wetter had taken three days to try in Moat County Court, and the transcript of that trial sat in boxes along the wall of my brother's side of the office, marked in red ink with the numbers 11-A, 11-B, 11-C, 11-D, 11-E. The pages inside the boxes had been typed with a machine that blotted out the enclosed areas of the keys e, o, r, d, and b. The s apparently had required a harder strike than the others, and stood out on the pages like splattered mud. Whole paragraphs had been whited out and retyped, and it was impossible to make out the things that had been changed.

Still, enough of it was unchanged.

There was a newspaper story in these transcripts about justice in the rural South.

And there was another newspaper story in the possibility that Sheriff Call, who had publicly killed sixteen Negroes and never been called to account for it, had met his own maker at the hands of someone who was never punished.

The champions of social change who set the editorial course at the *Miami Times,* the South's greatest newspaper, saw the beauty in that, in the irony, and it was the beauty of the story, not the injustice—there was enough of that to celebrate back in Miami—that in the end decided their commitment of money and time to Moat County.

Yardley Acheman understood that better than my brother, I suppose, but then it was his job to see the beauty in these things. That was why he kept himself outside while my brother went in and recorded the details of ruin.

Yardley Acheman sat at his desk now, scanning the portions of the transcript that my brother had underlined in green ink.

The legal injury done to Hillary Van Wetter was clearly delineated in these underlined sections. The ineptitude of his attorney, Weldon Pine, was at least equaled by the ineptitude of the sheriff's deputies who handled the evidence and the arrest. The knife and shirt which were found in Hillary Van Wetter's kitchen sink, for instance, stained with blood, had been lost on the way back to the sheriff's headquarters in Lately.

The story that Hillary Van Wetter told the deputies that night—that he had been working earlier with his uncle

Tyree—was never investigated or explained. Hillary Van Wetter simply said it once from the witness stand and was never asked to elaborate, even on cross-examination.

His uncle wasn't subpoenaed, and did not attend the trial. Which is not to say that he would have appeared if he had been subpoenaed.

To the Van Wetters, an arrest in the family was like a death. If you were gone, you were gone, and when news of that kind visited the family, they looked another way, not wanting to see it.

❑

YARDLEY ACHEMAN DROPPED a portion of the sheriff's department's arrest report on his desk and leaned back, perhaps having suddenly perceived that finding Tyree Van Wetter meant going into the wet regions of the county where the family lived, explaining newspapers to people who did not read them, who did not see how or why their lives belonged to anyone but themselves. People with knives and dogs, who hung animal skins from the trees in their yards.

Yardley Acheman pushed his feet against the edge of his desk until his head touched the wall behind his chair. He could have been posing for a photograph.

"I think we've got enough without the uncle," he said.

My brother looked up at him, waiting. Yardley Acheman began to nod, as if they were arguing. "We could write around the uncle," he said. "We could get away with that."

My brother shook his head. He was not inclined to ignore what was inconvenient. He was not that kind of reporter. He wanted things clean.

"All we've got to substantiate here is reasonable doubt," Yardley Acheman said, sounding whiny. "We get into too much detail, it ruins the narrative flow."

"Let's see where it goes," my brother said, and went back to his work.

❑

ACCORDING TO THE REGULATIONS of the Florida state prison system, prisoners waiting to be executed could receive visitors who were not of their immediate families only with the permission of their attorneys.

And so to visit Hillary Van Wetter again, we had to go back to Weldon Pine, who was less accommodating now that he understood the *Miami Times*'s only interest in his career was the trial and conviction of the most famous client he ever had.

He left us waiting outside his office for an hour, and then opened the door, looked at us, and turned back inside, expecting us to follow him in.

He sat down behind his desk and looked at his watch. His wrist was as thick as a leg. "I don't see good intentions in this," he said. "Building up a man's hopes . . ."

He turned to Charlotte suddenly and said, "Young lady, you are an attractive girl with your whole life ahead of you. . . ."

He stopped and my brother spoke. "We need to talk to him again," he said.

"For what?"

"He said he was working with his uncle."

Weldon Pine laughed out loud. "What was he out working on at night, Mr. Reporter?" he said. "You think I didn't ask him that? You know what he said?" The old attorney shook his head. "You come all the way up here to find out what Hillary and his uncle was working on, you wasted your time and everybody else's."

The air conditioner in the window shook and changed pitch.

"We need to talk to him again," my brother said.

Weldon Pine thought it over and then lit a cigarette and picked up the telephone on his desk and told his secretary to get him the state prison.

"I ought to charge you people by the damn hour," he said.

❑

"I'D LIKE TO FOCUS your attention to the night Sheriff Call was killed," my brother said.

Hillary Van Wetter was sitting in manacles, staring at Charlotte. She was wearing a pair of blue jeans and a shirt that she'd tied in a knot just under her breasts.

She had changed her hair twice on the ride from Lately, pulling it back into a ponytail once and then, a few miles later, disengaging the clasp holding it together and allowing it to fall more naturally across her shoulders. She checked herself that way in the rearview mirror and then took a can of hair spray out of her purse and went over it in small, circular motions, still looking in the mirror, until it glistened.

An hour later, I could still taste hair spray.

"Where's your dress?" he said.

She looked down at herself, surprised.

"Mr. Van Wetter," my brother said, "we only have fifteen minutes. . . ."

Hillary Van Wetter turned to him then. "Paperboy," he said, "I wisht you'd quit talking to me about time. It's depressing."

"You testified in court you'd been working with your uncle."

"I did, did I?" he said, and turned back to her. "Everybody in this place wears pants," he said. "I like a dress."

He fixed his attention for a moment on Yardley Acheman, who was sitting near the door and had been watching Charlotte, trying her on for size in some way until Hillary Van Wetter caught him at it. Something about the room or Hillary stirred Yardley's interest in her.

Charlotte nodded at Hillary and smiled, doing both those things slowly, drawing his attention away from Yardley Acheman.

"There ain't no point to come see me looking like that," he said.

"I'm sorry," she said, and he looked away.

In the silence that followed my brother said, "What kind of work were you doing?"

Hillary Van Wetter looked at him without answering.

"What were you out doing at night?" my brother said.

Hillary shook his head.

"Lawn work," he said finally.

Yardley Acheman sat up in his chair. "As in grass?" A smile played at the corners of his mouth. "Where?"

Hillary Van Wetter turned to Charlotte again before he answered him, staring at her until she crossed her arms, covering herself against him. "It ain't that hard to find," he said.

Then, without changing anything, he was speaking to her. "You wear a dress next time, hear?" he said.

"All right," she said quietly.

"I need to find your uncle," my brother said.

Hillary Van Wetter stood up, the chain connecting his leg irons dropping onto the bare floor. "Yessir, well, good luck on that," he said, and then he started toward the door, walking like a man whose trousers have dropped around his feet, without another look at Charlotte.

"Where is he?" my brother said.

Hillary walked to the door to be let out.

"Mr. Van Wetter? Can you tell me how to get to his place?"

He turned and looked at my brother again. "You got a boat, paperboy?"

My brother shook his head.

"Then I can't tell you how to get there."

And then the guard opened the door. "You entitled to another seven minutes," he said.

Hillary Van Wetter shuffled past him and out of the room. "I been visited as many minutes today as I can stand," he said.

❏

SHE SAT IN THE CORNER of the backseat on the way back, where I couldn't see her in the mirror. Yardley Acheman was back there too, and he lit two cigarettes and gave one to her.

She took it the same way it was offered, without a word, and when she drew the smoke into her lungs, I could hear the catching in her breath.

"Tell me something, will you?" Yardley Acheman said. "What do you want with them?"

She didn't answer.

"All these boys on death row, writing all those letters," he said. "What do you want?"

"I want to help them," she said, and he laughed out loud.

❏

EACH NIGHT AFTER WORK I drove back to Thorn and my father's house, always thinking of Charlotte Bless. You may have seen dogs rolling on something dead in the grass, wanting the scent in their coats. That was the way I wanted her.

I saw myself in competition with Hillary Van Wetter. I was taller and in better shape and had better teeth, and I wanted her as much even if I had yet to ejaculate in my pants just sitting with her in a room.

The Chrysler was always in the driveway when I got home. My father was preoccupied with things at his newspaper, and he often walked away from the car with the keys in the ignition and the door wide open. To someone approaching the house, it would resemble an emergency.

It was dark this particular night, and the small dome light inside had attracted insects. I felt them as I reached in to take the keys out of his ignition, like cold ashes, all over my arm. Dinner was over and my father was sitting in his chair, a glass of wine on the table next to him, going through his papers.

"I believe she left you a plate in the oven," he said, not remembering Anita Chester's name.

He followed me into the kitchen, bringing his wine, to watch me eat.

"How is Mr. Van Wetter?" he asked, making a small joke.

I said I didn't know, and that was the truth.

"Still innocent?"

I shook my head, and that was the truth too. And then my father sat still and waited, as he often did these days, and in the waiting I found myself talking. It was a reporter's trick, I'd seen Ward use it on the attorney Weldon Pine.

I told him what Ward and Yardley Acheman had done that day, what they had said in their office. Much of it was about Mr. Pine and his defense of Hillary Van Wetter. Weldon Pine and my father were casual friends, sharing a prominence in Moat County society.

"The man's reputed to be the best lawyer in the state," he said, and I shook my head, as if I didn't understand any of it either. But I had seen enough of what was inside the boxes holding the trial transcript now to know that he hadn't done much to help Hillary Van Wetter.

He made no issue of the knife and bloody clothes that the sheriff's department had taken from the kitchen and then lost on the way back to Lately. He hadn't found Hillary's uncle; there was no sign that he'd even tried.

"It might be," my father said, "that Weldon Pine knew what he was doing."

"It doesn't look like he did anything," I said.

And then, in the long moments that followed, I realized that my father hadn't done anything either. His paper had covered the trial without reference to Sheriff Call's record of violence against the Negroes of Moat County. While the sheriff had been alive, my father had fought him as hard as he could, but on his death even the *Tribune*'s routine plea for a convicted killer's life was never issued.

"Weldon Pine is a respected and beloved man," he said. "You do not earn that overnight."

I didn't argue with him, understanding that he was talking of himself as much as Mr. Pine. I ate my dinner, he sipped at his wine. An unopened copy of the *Daytona Beach News-Journal* lay on the table next to his arm, but he had forgotten it was there. He was joyless.

"Do you see much of this Yardley Acheman?" he said.

I nodded, my mouth was full of food.

"He's older, right?"

"He's older than Ward," I said.

"What, thirty-five, forty?"

"Maybe thirty-five, I don't know."

My father weighed that, and then finished what was in his glass. "What was he doing all that time before they put them together?" he said. "He's been at the *Times* a long while."

"I don't know what he does now," I said. "Ward's doing all the work. I think Yardley's supposed to be the writer."

My father nodded. It made sense to him that one of them would do the work and the other one would be the writer. He stood up and went to the refrigerator and poured another glass of wine. "You wonder who's supposed to be in charge," he said after he sat back down.

He said it as if one of them had gotten the other one lost.

❑

MR. PINE DECIDED he did not want us visiting his client again. "I believe it's time to leave the man have his privacy," he said, pained but kind.

"Mr. Pine," my brother began, "Mr. Acheman and I have a

considerable amount of work left to do, work that is in Mr. Van Wetter's interests."

The old man sighed. "I've done the work," he said. "The appeals been filed and rejected." He paused, as if the weight were too heavy. "With all due respect, gentlemen, there isn't a thing your newspaper can do for the man that I couldn't. His options been exhausted, and it don't do him any favors to raise his expectations."

"You haven't seen him one time since the trial," Charlotte Bless said. It was the first time she had spoken to Mr. Pine without being spoken to first, and the insult crossed his face as if he'd been slapped.

"The fiancée," he said.

She stood up, and moved to his desk. "What I am," she said, "is the only damn one in this room that cares what happens to Hillary Van Wetter."

He looked at her, taking in her clothes and demeanor, dismissing them and her all in one glance. "Vulgarities do not flatter a woman," he said.

"There are areas left to be explored," my brother said.

Weldon Pine turned the same look on him. "Is that your legal opinion, Mr. James?" he said.

"I've got a legal opinion for you," Yardley Acheman said quietly. "Hillary Van Wetter was entitled to a competent defense."

"You don't know one thing about this person," the old man said. "You been in this world five minutes."

And then he stood up and walked to the door and held it open. Slowly, my brother began to nod.

"All right," he said. "If we could just ask you a few questions . . ."

"What for?"

"For the newspaper."

The old man shook his head. "No comment. That's my answer, no comment." He pointed at the open door.

———

74

"You already commented," Yardley Acheman said. "Everything you've said to us since we met is a comment."

"Not for the newspaper," he said. "I am putting you on notice that anything I said was only informational, an effort to be helpful. Not for attribution of any sort. You are on notice. . . ."

He seemed to get weaker the longer he went on.

"In fairness," my brother said, ignoring what he'd said, "I'd like to give you the chance to answer the questions." He had them written down inside his notebook. The old man stood at the open door, torn between wanting us out and wanting to hear the questions. In the quiet, my brother began to read.

"Why was the prosecutor in Mr. Van Wetter's case never called to account for the missing weapon?" he said.

The old man stood still, waiting.

"Why was the prosecutor in Mr. Van Wetter's case never called to account for the missing bloodstained clothing?"

Weldon Pine stared across the room as if across a great distance. As if he were watching a dark sky rolling in.

"What efforts," my brother said, "did you make to locate Mr. Van Wetter's uncle, Tyree Van Wetter?"

The old man looked away from my brother then, taking in each of us around the room.

"What efforts did you make to ascertain Mr. Van Wetter's whereabouts on the night Sheriff Call was murdered?"

The old man watched the storm coming in, and then, helpless against it, he suddenly slipped through the door, as if stepping inside his house to wait it out. My brother continued to ask his last questions in Weldon Pine's absence.

"What efforts did you make," he said, "to secure a change of venue for Mr. Van Wetter's trial?"

Later in the afternoon, Mr. Pine reconsidered. His secretary called my brother and said that he was welcome to see Hillary Van Wetter again.

Ward went alone into the prison, and was back in the car in

75

ten minutes, carrying Hillary's signed request for a change of attorneys in his shirt pocket. Without Charlotte in the room, Ward said, Hillary was a more reasonable man.

❑

EARLY THE FOLLOWING WEEK, an Orlando attorney on retainer to the *Miami Times* filed a form with the court and became Hillary Van Wetter's attorney of record, replacing Weldon Pine.

Weldon Pine was informed of this action by mail, and appeared in the doorway of my brother's office on a Friday afternoon, his shirtsleeves buttoned at the wrist, pale and damp with sweat, holding the notification in his hand.

Yardley Acheman looked up from the magazine in his lap, stared at the old attorney a minute, then went back to his reading. Weldon Pine walked in, uninvited, and had a look around. He seemed huge. My brother replaced some papers he'd taken from two boxes behind him and stood up. We were raised to be respectful of our elders.

"Mr. Pine," he said.

The old man didn't answer at first; he was still taking in the room and the furniture and the three people in it. Charlotte was not there that afternoon; she had gone to Jacksonville to buy a dress.

"I have practiced the law more years than you been alive," Weldon Pine said slowly, speaking to us all. "I have been a good friend to the court."

He came in another step or two, the fan on the floor blew the papers he was holding back over his hand.

"I defended every type of criminal personality there is, and until yesterday afternoon . . ." He paused, taking a moment to reflect on the moment the papers had arrived. ". . . no client, no court, no judge has ever asked me to remove myself from a case." His voice had begun to shake.

"That is an amazing statistic," Yardley Acheman said, still looking at his magazine.

The old man considered him again, considered us all. The only noise in the room was the fan.

"And now," he said, "people that don't know who I am are saying I don't know how to do my job." My brother stood by the corner of his desk and waited for the rest, but the old man seemed out of things to say.

"Nobody has to know," Yardley Acheman said, closing the magazine and sitting back in his chair. "It's only as public as you make it."

The old man waited. The fan moved across the room, ruffling the papers in his hand again.

"In forty-six years, this never happened once. . . ."

Yardley Acheman shrugged. "People change attorneys all the time."

"They don't change Weldon Pine," the old man said.

Yardley said, "Who's going to know?" He looked quickly at my brother, and then said, "We don't need a lot of people poking around into Hillary Van Wetter's business right now, so unless you want to raise hell about it in court . . ."

"I want to keep hold of what's mine," the old man snapped. "I worked for it all my life."

"We don't want what's yours," Yardley Acheman said. "There is nothing you have that we want."

The old man looked at the papers in his hand, and then, without changing expressions, dropped them on the floor. He turned and walked out without another word.

His footsteps on the stairs were unsure; I pictured his death grip on the handrail. "Nothing to worry about," Yardley said.

My brother got up and went to the window to watch Weldon Pine walk to his car.

"We've still got it all to ourselves," Yardley said. My brother did not answer. "Take my word for it, the man is not going to contest this in court. He doesn't want to paste it in his scrapbook that he's incompetent."

"You never know," Ward said. "He seems hardheaded. . . ."

Yardley Acheman said, "He isn't that kind of hardheaded, not when it threatens him."

❑

YARDLEY ACHEMAN WAS RIGHT about Weldon Pine.

He was often right about people, as he always expected the worst. The request for new counsel went uncontested by Mr. Pine, and was routinely accepted by the court, and Hillary Van Wetter changed lawyers without public notice. Weldon Pine absorbed the insult privately and went back to work as the most beloved lawyer in Moat County, believing his unfortunate association with us and Hillary Van Wetter was a closed matter.

I sometimes wonder, looking back on his long and fruitful association with the black side of human nature, what he could have been thinking.

❑

DURING THESE INITIAL WEEKS in Lately, there was not much for me to do. I picked up my brother and Yardley Acheman at the Prescott Hotel in the morning and delivered them back to the Prescott at night. If records were needed from the courthouse—Ward had begun looking into both the sheriff's and the state's attorney's budgets—or books from the library, I would get them. I drove Ward to the scene of Sheriff Call's killing half a dozen times, and often we went from there to the dirt road which led back into the wetlands where the Van Wetters lived. We never saw their houses, although he had some intuitive sense of where they were. Perhaps they had been pointed out to him from the river, back in the days when my father was still trying to turn us into bass fishermen.

On the days we stayed in the office, it was my job to go for sandwiches and keep the refrigerator stocked with Busch beer, which Yardley Acheman began drinking before lunch.

He did not have much to do either.

The beer made Yardley moody, and some afternoons, when it had taken him the wrong way, he would call his fiancée in Miami and confess that he was incapable of fidelity. A discussion would follow, as if the failings of Yardley Acheman's character could be changed by debate, and about five minutes later he would begin asking the girl why she was crying, and then she would hang up on him, and he would look at the phone a moment before he dropped it back into the receiver, and then walk over to the refrigerator and get another beer.

"Women . . ." he would say.

Some afternoons I drank beer with him, some afternoons I didn't.

Later in the day, he would call her again and initiate a conversation pertaining to the details of their upcoming wedding. It was his way of making up. What the bridesmaids would wear, who would be invited to the reception, who would come to the ceremony itself. The girl came from a Palm Beach family and her wedding plans were conceived in the context of a grand social event.

Yardley had no objections to her family or her family's money, but arguments did develop over the vows they were writing together, and before long he was exasperated again, insisting on minutiae that no man I had ever met except Yardley Acheman would have an opinion on anyway, and then a few minutes later he would be asking her again why she was crying.

Yardley hated to be edited—newspaper stories or wedding vows, it was all the same insult.

On the days I was drinking beer too, I would sit in the window and openly watch, listen to his end of the conversations, wondering what sort of disfigurement the woman had that would make her still willing to marry him after his behavior on the telephone.

I had almost no experience with women then, and it had not occurred to me yet that some of them were as pathetic as any of us.

On days when I wasn't drinking, I found something to do in the office while Yardley Acheman and his fiancée were fighting it out. I would straighten the boxes against the wall or sweep the floor. My brother sat at his desk, making notes on the papers in front of him, and occasionally—when the argument got too poisonous—he would pick up his own telephone and make a call, removing himself from what was going on in the room.

But while Yardley Acheman's love entanglements embarrassed my brother, and embarrassed me when I was not drinking, they did not embarrass Yardley Acheman at all, and after she hung up on him, he would always offer some comment that seemed to invite us into the argument.

"What is the broad thinking?"

❑

It is a fair representation of the situation to say that at this time there were four people at work, one way or another, at something only one of them could do. My brother needed to have the story all in his head before he could see where it went, and the rest of us were only waiting until he was ready.

My own most pressing business was not driving the car or running errands, but keeping Charlotte Bless away from the office. Ward and Yardley Acheman needed her accessible for meetings with Hillary Van Wetter—Hillary had made it clear that he had no use whatsoever for us without her—but her visits to the office were tedious, circular, and, at times, close to evangelical in nature.

It was Charlotte's habit to drop in after lunch, blowing through the doorway smelling of perfume in some new dress or another, calling us to our purpose, the saving of an innocent life. She did not wear jeans again after Hillary Van Wetter walked out of the room during our second visit, not even to the office over the Moat Cafe.

It began with the same breathless question, every day. "Anything new?"

There was never anything new, at least not in the way that she meant it. The governor did not call to pronounce Hillary innocent, and my brother worked his way through the documents again more slowly, collecting bits and pieces as he came to them, and then moving it all ahead to whatever was next, as if he were sweeping a floor.

"We've got to hurry this up," she would say, going to the window. "Every night Hillary Van Wetter lies in that prison is a night off his life."

Once, after she'd said that, Yardley Acheman asked Charlotte if she had thought of writing a country western song about it, but more often he simply refused to acknowledge that she was in the room, although she was clearly addressing herself to him more than my brother or me. She seemed to think he was in charge.

When Charlotte started talking about the nights Hillary Van Wetter was losing in prison, it was time for me to take her away. If I didn't, she would begin walking around the room, looking into the boxes of files or the papers on my brother's desk, and every paper she touched was a starting point for a review of the case.

It could take half an hour to wait her out, and beyond the distraction itself, my brother did not like the papers touched after he laid them down. A kind of indexing was always going on in his head, and he needed things to lie still and undisturbed to accomplish it.

On the other hand, the papers—many of them, anyway—belonged to Charlotte, and he could not find a way to tell her to leave them alone. She was as childish in many ways as Yardley Acheman, and she had staked first claim to Hillary

Van Wetter, and would not subordinate herself in the matter of saving his life to lawyers, reporters, or anyone else. I suppose she was afraid of losing him entirely.

❑

IT WAS MY INTENTION to save Charlotte Bless from drowning in the ocean.

I had no plan to make it necessary, but I daydreamed of saving her, and of her gratitude at having been lifted, terrified, from the ocean and set down in the warm, safe sand of the beach. I thought of the texture of her skin when she was wet, and of the jumpy feel of her muscles when she was helpless and panicked.

But I could barely get her into the water.

Two or three afternoons a week, she would go with me to the beach at St. Augustine, but she went to tan her legs for Hillary, and got into the water only to cool off. And even then it was only knee deep, always keeping one hand on top of the straw hat she wore to protect her face and neck.

She seemed vaguely interested in my swimming, but had no interest in learning herself.

And so we would drive to St. Augustine and park the car and walk down to the beach, and I would take off my shirt and pants and swim straight out, conscious of my form, as if that mattered to her, and she would lay a towel across the hot sand, and then undress—we wore our suits underneath our clothes—and lie down, turn on her radio, and cover her face with the straw hat.

When I came back, I would drop into the sand next to her, out of breath, and study the lines of her body. Her skin was barely puffy against the elastic of her suit, there was no flesh hanging off her when she turned to lie on her stomach.

Her suit was one-piece, cut deeply in back to the exact spot where the line separating her buttocks began. It fit her cheeks as if it had melted over them, riding down into the crack. There was no angle of her bottom that did not strike me as beautiful, and lying in the sand next to her, feeling my breath against my arm, I would also feel the growing weight of my erection, and then I would roll onto my stomach too, so that she wouldn't see the effect she had on me.

I had a sense that she would feel betrayed.

No, I didn't know anything about women at all.

On our third or fourth visit to St. Augustine, she pulled the straps off her shoulders and handed me her lotion.

"I hate strap marks," she said.

It was the first time, I think, I'd ever touched her. Her skin was cool and my hand slid from her shoulders down her back, and finally stopped at the bottom of her suit, where her body divided and rose into perfect cheeks. My hand stayed in that place a moment, and then she lifted her head and looked at me, as if to ask what I thought I was doing.

"They look so ignorant," she said.

"What?" ·

"Strap marks. They look like white trash."

I put the top back on the lotion and stuck it into the sand. Without straightening up, I dropped back onto my towel. I had reached a condition, rubbing lotion over Charlotte Bless's back, that was a spasm short of Hillary Van Wetter's jailhouse ejaculation, which is to say you could have put a propeller on the thing and flown it.

"You're breathing through your mouth," she said a few minutes later, watching me.

"It was a long swim," I said.

And she smiled behind her dark glasses and turned her head away from the sun.

"You need a girlfriend," she said, still looking the other way. When I didn't answer, she picked her head up again and looked around, spotting half a dozen girls sitting around a cooler of beer. They were behind us perhaps forty feet, at the border of the beach where the tall grass began. Pink toenails and radios. They looked like sorority girls to me, the way they drank their beer.

"You ought to go over there and make friends," she said, teasing me in some way.

"I don't like girls like that," I said.

She lowered her sunglasses on her nose and looked over them at the girls again. "I'll bet you'd like that one in the red," she said. I couldn't think of a thing to say. She said, "Go over there and pick out one that bites her nails, and she'll blow you. I promise."

"I don't want anybody to blow me," I said, and she looked at me, vaguely disappointed. I remembered what she'd written then, about Hillary Van Wetter wanting himself sucked just like a judge. An intact man.

"It's not that I don't want it," I said, making the correction, "I just don't want any of them to do it."

She considered that a long time. "It's a good thing you're not in prison," she said finally, bringing it back to Hillary. "You wouldn't have any choice in there."

"I can take care of myself," I said.

She smiled and dropped her cheek back onto the towel and I got up, angry and coated in sand, and followed my cock— which for the first half of my life was always stiff and pointed in the wrong direction—back out into the water and began to swim. I was two hundred yards out, feeling strong and angry, feeling as if I were riding the very top of the water, like the flames in an oil fire, when I realized suddenly why the metaphor had suddenly come to mind.

I was on fire.

I stopped in the water and looked around, the burning feeling moving across me like air from a fan as it scans the room. A certain chill followed behind the movement, and it took my breath. Half a dozen translucent jellyfish floated just under the surface, several in front, that many more behind me in the water I had just come through.

I lifted one of my arms, dropping deeper into the water, and saw that tentacles had broken off the jellyfish and wrapped around it, crossing over themselves like whips. The burning passed over me again; I felt distinctly cold.

I turned and began to swim. The burning did not change as I went through the jellyfish again, but a few yards beyond them I noticed a heaviness in my arms, and then in my chest, and I thought it would sink me. I rolled over onto my back to rest and realized that something was wrong with my breathing.

I kicked slowly, listening to the sound of the air passing through my mouth, unable to pull it deeply enough inside. I closed my eyes and kicked, thinking that I might be dying, and a long time later the water turned warm, and I knew that it was shallow and that I was not going to drown.

When I felt the bottom, I sat down a moment, collecting myself, and then turned onto my hands and knees, crawling from the water to the beach, and then made it to my feet, dizzier than I had ever been, and walked toward Charlotte Bless, who was still lying facedown and strapless on her towel.

It was one of the girls drinking beer near the weeds who noticed me first. I heard her say, "My God." I looked down at myself then and understood the dimensions of the poisoning. The tentacles were embedded in my arms and legs, the skin around each of them was raised and pink. Necklaces, I thought.

I heard the girls coming, but when I looked up I couldn't see. I rubbed at my eyes and the lids were in the wrong place, swollen out beyond the bone of the brow. I tried to step again and fell.

The sun was warm and I began to shake. "He's having an allergic reaction," one of them said. She came over to me, blocking out the sun, so close I could smell the beer on her breath. "Can you hear me?" she said. "We'll get an ambulance. . . ."

I felt one of the girls scrubbing my leg with sand. And then someone else had my arm and was doing the same thing.

"I know it hurts," said the one over me. "I'm a nurse."

"What's wrong with him?" It was Charlotte's voice.

"He's having an allergic reaction," said the one who seemed to be in charge. "He must have got into some jellyfish out there."

One of them was still scrubbing sand into my thigh. I heard her, a long way off. "Jesus, look at this stuff. . . ."

And then the one over me was talking again, calmly. "Can you hear me?" Her voice faded. "What's his name?"

"Jack," Charlotte said, sounding timid.

"Jack," she said, closer again, "we're getting an ambulance. Can you hear me?"

The ground began to turn under me, slowly at first and then faster. "Listen, honey," said the one in charge, "we've got to do something a little embarrassing here."

I did not try to answer, and then I felt them pulling my bathing suit off, turning it inside out as it rolled down my legs. "Just hold on," she said, and then she stood up, the light of the sun turned everything red, and a moment later I felt a gentle trickle moving up my leg, as if one of them were washing me with a warm beer.

"What do you think you're doing?" Charlotte said, still scared. There was no answer—these were trained nurses—but the first trickle died and then another of them blocked the sun and I felt it again, this time on my chest, moving from my stomach almost to my neck. I distinctly smelled urine.

"Lie still," said the one in charge. "We've sent for an ambulance."

I sat up anyway, dizzy and sick. The sting—some of it, at least—had gone out of the places where they had urinated.

"Honey," said the one who was in charge, "it's on your face too. Would you rather we didn't urinate on your face?"

The real meaning of such a question, of course, is not in the question itself but in what it implies—that one moment you could be in perfect form, right on top of the water, riding the tops of the waves, and the next moment could be lying blind and helpless on a beach being asked if you would prefer not having strangers urinate in your face.

"No," I said, "don't do that." My lips were swollen now too, thick and stiff; the words sounded as if they were coming out of someone old.

"What did he say?" one of them asked.

"I think he's out of it," said the one in charge. Then, to someone else, "Go ahead." And then another one of them was urinating from my shoulder down my arm all the way to my hand. I lay back down, glistening in the sun.

"I never heard of anything like this," Charlotte was saying.

"He's poisoned," said the one in charge. "He's poisoned and he's having an allergic reaction."

"I can see he's poisoned," Charlotte said. "But you don't piss on somebody after they've been bit by a snake."

I remember thinking, *You suck on them.* Which, of course, was where I came in.

I heard the ambulance then, a long ways off. I heard voices in the siren.

❑

THE DOCTOR WAS OBESE, I saw that when he held open my eyelids to study the pupils. He examined my eyes with a small light, first one, then the other, then took the light away and considered my face, as if to estimate the problem for a moment in its entirety. He smelled of cigars.

And then he dropped my eyelid and the room was dark. "Give me some epi," he said.

"How much?"

"A vial, give me the damn vial, I'll do it myself. . . ." It was a quiet moment, and then he said, "Come on, come on. If we lose this one it's going to be embarrassing."

And then I felt a coolness on my chest as he washed a spot with alcohol, and then a slow, spreading sting as he pushed a needle down through it into my chest.

I slept.

❏

I AWOKE IN A dark room. A wedge of light from the door lay across the floor, and the sheet covering me from the chest down glowed a faint green from the heart monitor at the side of the bed. There was a needle in the back of my hand, connected to a bottle of liquid suspended overhead. The green, uneven line of the heart monitor reflected more distinctly in that.

I blinked and my eyes felt thick and unfamiliar, but were no longer swollen shut. They were dry, though, and they stung. I sat up a little in bed and knew I was all right.

"Jack?"

My brother was sitting in the darkest part of the room, in a chair beneath the heart monitor where little of the light from it or the door reached. He was wearing a white shirt and a tie; his bus ticket was stuck into his shirt pocket. I saw the word *Trailways*. In the darkness, his face was hollow. I was chilled and began to shake.

"Jesus, it's cold," I said.

He stood up and came to the side of the bed. In a moment, I felt the weight of a blanket, and, a moment behind that, the warmth. "The doctor said you might have another allergic reaction," he said. "They've got you hooked up to something here to keep you from going into shock."

I felt another chill. "I got pretty sick," I said.

Ward nodded, the monitor dancing in his eyes, and then he looked away. I was chilled again—the cold seemed to be coming from the bottle overhead—and when it passed, I was profoundly, unaccountably sad. It was as if I had fainted from some bad piece of news and was just coming back now, where it was waiting. The sadness lay over me like the blanket and gathered in my throat, and without warning I was suddenly blinking tears. Ward saw them, and for a moment he seemed about to touch me. I think he wanted to, but in the end he turned and sat back down on the chair.

"You had a bad time of it," he said in the dark. "That takes a lot out of you."

"Not too much," I said. And that was true, but it had done something else, and I didn't have a word for it. My brother didn't have the words either, and we sat listening to the sound of the machine monitoring my heart.

❑

THERE WAS A PICTURE of the emergency room doctor on the front page of the *St. Augustine Record* on the morning I got out of the hospital. It was above the fold, where you could see it as you passed the honor box. He was posed outside the emergency room entrance, his coat straining at the buttons, a cigar between his teeth. Smiling.

Charlotte had come over to pick me up, bringing clean clothes and a razor and a comb. She waited while I showered and dressed, and then took my arm as we walked through the door. She was still holding it when I saw the picture and stopped.

"What is it?" she said.

Above the doctor's picture, across the top of the page, was the headline FAST ACTION SAVES THORN MAN AT BEACH.

"What's wrong now?" she said.

I did not open the paper until we were in the van and moving.

> Five nursing students from Jacksonville and the emergency
> staff of St. Johns County Hospital combined Wednesday to
> save the life of a 19-year-old member of the University of Flor-
> ida's swimming team who suffered an allergic reaction to jelly-
> fish bites while swimming in the ocean.
>
> "Those girls deserve most of the credit," said Dr. William
> Polk. "Mr. [Jack] James [the victim] was a very lucky young
> man that they happened to be on the beach."

I closed the paper and closed my eyes. Charlotte stopped at
a traffic light. "What?" she said. And when I didn't answer, she
put her hand on my leg, just above the knee, and left it there.
"Are you sick?"

"How did they know I was on the swimming team?" I said.

"They came to the hospital," she said.

"You told them?"

She watched the traffic light, leaving her hand on my
leg. "It seemed germane," she said.

I shook my head, more aware now of the weight of the
newspaper on my leg than her hand next to it. She patted my
leg and moved her hand back to the wheel. "You shouldn't
read in the car," she said. "It makes you carsick."

A few miles farther west, I opened the paper and looked at
the picture of the doctor again. I could smell the cigar, and
the sweet, greasy odor that came off him in the intensive care
room when he dropped in to see how I was doing. He was
one of those doctors who also function as local characters—
and consider themselves, and all their odors, beloved.

> The students apparently saved Mr. James by urinating over
> the many areas of his body which were attacked. "The boy's
> arms and legs were covered with stings," Dr. Polk said, "as well
> as his back and chest, buttocks, genitals and face."

"Dear Jesus," I said, and closed the paper again.

"I told you not to read in the car," she said.

❏

THAT WASN'T ALL.

The story of my being saved at the beach by nursing students who urinated on me was noticed by an editor at the Associated Press office in Orlando who condensed it into six paragraphs and added it to the day's national wire stories. In this form, it went out over the Associated Press wire service to the offices of fifteen hundred newspapers across the United States and Canada, where other editors trimmed it for reasons of length and taste, put a humorous headline over the top, and ran it as a sort of antidote to the bad news of the day.

HOME REMEDY SAVES BEACHED SWIMMER.

That particular headline, while not the most embarrassing one I saw, was the most memorable, running, as it did, in my own father's newspaper. I do not know if my father saw the headline or the story before it ran. It was not the sort of story that would ordinarily be brought to his attention, although if his managing editor had noticed my name, she would have come to him for permission before running it.

It was brought to my attention by Yardley Acheman. I walked into the office the morning following my release from the hospital and he said, "Congratulations, Jack, you made the paper."

"I know."

I crossed the room to the window to sit down. I was tired of Yardley Acheman and tired of waiting around the office for my brother to finish what he was doing. I was thinking that if I had to be in the newspaper business, I'd rather go back to driving a truck.

"Not just St. Augustine," he said, smiling at me now, and then he picked up the *Moat County Tribune.*

"Home remedy," he said, and handed me the paper.

I walked over and took the paper out of his hand, and then

I turned to my brother, who had laid the entire trial transcript across his desk and on the floor that morning as if he were drying the pages, and stared at him until he looked up.

"What's he trying to do to me?" I said, meaning the old man.

"It's called the newspaper business," Yardley Acheman said, behind me. My brother blinked, still caught somewhere in the transcript of Hillary Van Wetter's trial, and the next thing Yardley Acheman said—I don't remember what it was, only his presumption that he could put himself into the middle of the private matters of my family—I turned and threw the newspaper in his face.

And then he stood up and came around the desk furious, a little speck of white spit coming off his lips, pointing his finger at my face, and I remember the look of bewilderment that replaced the other expression when I pushed his finger aside and grabbed his hair, and then his neck. He had no strength at all. And then I had him in a headlock on the floor, and I squeezed his head until all the noise coming out of it stopped, and then I noticed Ward bending over me, completely calm, a foot or two away, telling me to let him go.

"Jack," he said, "c'mon, you're going to mess everything up."

"Everything's already messed up," I said, and I was crying.

He said, "I'm talking about the papers," and turned around to remind me that he had arranged them across the floor. A moment passed, and I let go of Yardley Acheman's head, hearing a popping sound either in his head or my arm, and then leaned back against the wall and caught my breath.

Yardley Acheman got to his feet. His ears were bright red, and a patch of his skin over his eyebrows was scraped. He was shaking. "You *are* fucking crazy," he said. Then he looked at my brother. "I want him out of here."

Ward didn't answer.

"He's a time bomb," Yardley Acheman said. "The next thing, he'll be in here with a shotgun."

My brother looked at him, up and down. "He's all right now," he said quietly.

"He goes or I go."

My brother went back to his desk and found his place in the transcript of the trial. I thought about what Yardley had said, thinking he was probably wrong about the shotgun, and then I thought about my father, wondering if he had seen the story before it ran, and then realized it was something I would never ask him. I did not want to be lectured on the price we pay for freedom of the press.

"Did you understand what I said, Ward?" Yardley was back behind his desk now, calmer, rubbing at his ears. The scraped place on his forehead was more defined than it had been, it had raised and turned faintly blue at the edges. "I want him completely the fuck out of here, do you understand?"

My brother gave no sign that he understood any such thing.

I looked out the window and watched Charlotte park her van and cross the street to the office. She wore a yellow skirt, and her behind fit it like something dropped into the bottom of a soft sack. Yardley Acheman picked up the telephone and dialed a number. I sat still.

In the immediate aftermath of a wrestling match on the floor of my brother's office, while I was still trying to decide if it was possible that I would come into this place someday with a shotgun, I suddenly pictured her behind pressed into the bottom of a satin bag, a green bag with drawstrings at the top, about the size of a pants pocket, or a scrotum, and imagining that, and the solid weight of the thing loaded in this way, I felt a familiar stirring, and took that as a sign that I was myself again.

"I'm calling Miami," Yardley said.

❑

SHE CAME INTO THE office as Yardley was telling his editor what had happened.

"He fucking tried to kill me," he said.

She sat down on the chair near my brother's desk and inspected herself in a mirror from her purse. One side, then the other; touching her hair, running a finger along some line beneath her eye. We were going to see Hillary again that afternoon, and she was worried about her appearance. She closed the mirror, miserable, then looked at me for help.

"You look fine," I said, and she studied me a moment, still welty from the jellyfish, considering the source.

"Will somebody please get him laid?" she said.

"No, right here in the office," Yardley said into the phone. "I can't write in an atmosphere where I don't know when somebody's going to go off the deep end and strangle me. . . ."

Charlotte took that in, noticing the scrape on Yardley's forehead, and then took the compact back out of her purse, opened it, and looked at herself again. "Did you strangle him?" she said, checking her forehead for scrapes.

"No," I said, "we only wrestled."

"That's exactly right," Yardley said into the phone. "I don't have to put up with this shit. Not from him, not from anybody. . . ."

For a moment, the room was still while Yardley listened to the editor on the other end of the phone. I could hear the voice, but not the words. When it stopped, Yardley took the phone away from his ear and spoke to my brother.

"He wants to talk to you," he said.

"Who?" my brother said.

"Miami," he said. He seemed irritated my brother wasn't paying more attention. "I told you I was calling Miami. . . ."

Ward got up, reluctant to leave the transcript, and crossed the room to Yardley's desk and took the phone.

"This is Ward James," he said. He stood completely still as he listened; he could have been waiting for the correct time.

Charlotte put the mirror back again and inspected Yardley Acheman while my brother listened to the phone.

"All he needs is to get laid," she said finally.

"He needs a fucking straitjacket," Yardley said, feeling more removed all the time from that moment he was helpless on the floor.

"He's oversexed," she said.

Yardley Acheman seemed to consider that, and then turned on her. "Oversexed is a forty-year-old woman that dresses up like she's eighteen," he said, and the room was suddenly so still I could almost make out the words coming through the receiver into my brother's ear.

My brother broke the silence. "No," he said into the telephone, and then hung it up. Then he walked back across the room and stared at his desk, trying to remember where he was.

"So?" Yardley Acheman said.

My brother sat down, looking for something now.

"He goes or I go," Yardley said.

And my brother looked at him a long time and then said it again. "No."

And in some way I did not understand, he had closed the door on it.

"If he ever touches me again ..." Yardley said, but my brother wasn't listening. Charlotte turned to me and winked.

❑

WE WERE BACK IN the interview room with Hillary Van Wetter again that afternoon, and my brother was trying to get him to remember where he had been stealing lawns on the night Sheriff Call was killed.

"What town was it?" he said. "Can you remember the town?"

Hillary smiled at the question, and answered without taking

his eyes off Charlotte Bless. "It could be a thousand places," he said. And then, as if it had some secret meaning between himself and Charlotte, he said, "There's lawns to be mowed and ashes to be hauled everywhere in the world." He smiled at her and she smiled back.

Yardley Acheman, sitting against the wall, closed his eyes as if he were too tired to continue.

"Could it have been Orlando?" my brother asked. He had called police departments all over the north-central part of the state, asking about lawn thefts, and there were more of them than you would imagine, especially around Orlando.

Hillary Van Wetter thought it over. "That's a long ways to go for a lawn," he said finally. And then, to her, "On the other hand, sometimes the farther you reach, the sweeter the grass," and he laughed out loud after he said it.

She moved in her chair, and then crossed her legs. Hillary leaned forward a little to look as far up her skirt as he could. Charlotte did not seem to mind.

"These boys been taking care of you?" he said to her.

She nodded, about to tell him, I think, of what had happened on the beach, of who was taking care of what, but then changed her mind.

"Everything I need," she said.

He turned his head suddenly and stared at me, something in it clean and cold. If he hadn't killed Sheriff Call, I knew then that he could have. "Better not be everything," he said.

I stared back at him, feeling clean and cold myself. He either didn't see that, or didn't care. He turned slowly to my brother, and then to Yardley Acheman. "She's spoken for," he said.

"Do you have any idea at all?" my brother said. "You remember what direction you drove?"

"Going or coming?" he said, sounding interested.

"Either way," my brother said.

He thought a moment, and then shook his head. "No," he

said. It was quiet again as he stared at Charlotte and she stared back. "There was a night in there we took the greens off a golf course," he said.

"Where?" my brother said.

"That would have been down in Daytona, I believe," he said. "My uncle might remember. . . ." He smiled, remembering something funny. "He played it once himself . . . golf." The image welled up in Hillary Van Wetter and then spilled over. He held his nose and shook, laughing, from what I could tell, at the notion of his uncle on the golf course.

"You're sure it was Daytona?" my brother asked. The question stopped Hillary's laughing, and he stared at Ward as if he had just walked into the room uninvited.

"I was speaking of golf," he said finally.

My brother nodded.

"I was saying my uncle played it once." He was angry; it was hard to tell why. "I had this pitcher in my head of it," he said, "my uncle in green pants, and then you said what you did, and cut me off."

He looked around the room, as if he were seeing it all for the first time. "And where's that leave me now?" he said quietly.

My brother didn't answer.

"You paperboys so damn smart."

"Everything's the same as when we got here," Ward said.

"Exactly," Hillary Van Wetter said, slowly nodding his head. "Exactly." He closed his eyes, trying to get it back. "It ain't that easy to pitcher somebody you know playing golf," he said. He didn't seem as angry as he'd been a moment earlier.

"Sorry," my brother said.

"Sorry is the most useless thing in the world," he said. "A man tells me 'sorry,' and it just aggravates the situation."

I imagined Thurmond Call telling Hillary Van Wetter he was sorry for stomping his cousin. I wondered if the sheriff had done that, or if, in the end, he'd died without explaining anything to anybody.

I wondered how much he cared for his life; if he would have traded what was still left of it for a moment or two of humiliation on the highway in the rain. If he would have begged.

I didn't think so, but, then, I'd only seen the sheriff in parades.

"A comical thing like that," Hillary said a few moments later, "it don't sound like much to you, but there ain't nothing in here to laugh at but something that hurts."

He turned his attention back to Charlotte then, trying to enjoy the sight of her legs disappearing up into her skirt, but that was spoiled too.

"Are you sure it was Daytona?" my brother said. He was polite to Hillary Van Wetter but he was not afraid of him.

"It don't matter," Hillary said a moment later.

Ward said, "If it didn't matter, I wouldn't bother you with it." He paused a moment. "Are you sure it was Daytona?"

"Someplace over there. Daytona, Ormond Beach . . . one of them places. It was a golf course, and we took the lawn off all the greens."

"All of them?" Yardley Acheman said.

"All we could find, walking around in the dark," Hillary said.

"Where did you take it?" my brother said. Hillary looked at him; he didn't seem to understand.

"Sold it," he said finally.

"To whom?" Yardley Acheman said.

"Whom?" Hillary said. "Whom?" He reconsidered Yardley Acheman, and slowly a smile crossed his face. "Maybe I don't have to worry about leaving my fiancée alone with you boys after all," he said. He looked to her, to see if she thought that was humorous. Testing her somehow.

"Where did you take it?" Ward said.

"A developer," he said. "They pay till they bleed for golf course grass."

"What kind of developer?"

"Condos," he said. He looked again at Yardley Acheman, who hadn't spoken since Hillary insulted him. "You'd like condos," he said. "They're full of 'whom' boys. . . ."

"Not that it's any of your business," Yardley said, "but for the record, I've got a fiancée of my own."

A smile suddenly lit Hillary Van Wetter's face. "What record is that?" he said.

"Where were the condominiums?" my brother said.

Hillary rubbed his eyes. "You did it again," he said. "Everytime a thing is humorous, you want to know where something was."

"It isn't humorous," my brother said evenly. "We're running out of time." And as if on a signal, the door to the room opened and a guard walked in and put his hand on Hillary Van Wetter's shoulder.

"That's it, boys," he said.

Hillary stood up without looking at the guard who was holding his shoulder. It was exactly as if Hillary had decided to get up on his own. The guard's hand went to the crook of his elbow and pulled him toward the door. Hillary did not struggle, but for a moment he held himself where he was, and neither of them moved.

"Open your mouth a little bit," he said to Charlotte, but it was a joke this time, and he let the guard lead him out.

Yardley Acheman picked at a little piece of scab on his forehead, and in a moment it beaded blood. "This is fucked," he said to my brother.

Ward didn't answer.

"Hillary Van Wetter is an innocent man," Charlotte said.

Yardley Acheman turned on her then. "Who cares?"

"Me," she said. "That's what I'm doing here."

"What you're doing here is getting your pussy wet off the

idea that this guy's going to the electric chair," he said. And then, indicating me, he said, "You're crazier than he is."

Ward stood up, tired, and walked toward the door. I followed him out, and a moment later Charlotte caught up with me in the hallway.

"You all aren't going to quit on this ..." she said. Yardley Acheman was just coming out of the visitors' room; my brother was ahead of us, waiting at the iron gate to be passed through.

"Ward isn't going to quit," I said, "and he's the only one that matters."

❑

THERE WAS AN ACCIDENT that night on the highway, a couple of bikers from Orlando met a station wagon from Michigan, head-on, and the highway patrol was hours clearing the mess.

My father was still in his chair when I came in, the pile of newspapers sifted across the floor at his feet.

He was drinking a bottle of wine, which he'd set on the table next to him. Before my mother left, he'd leave the bottle in the kitchen and make the trip back and forth; he didn't like to sit still and drink, believing that was a signal of addiction, and that getting up and walking to the kitchen was a sign the other way. He always looked for signs of things, and not the things themselves.

"You're late," he said, looking at his watch.

"There was a big one out on the highway," I said.

"Local people?"

"No," I said, "bikers and tourists."

He dropped his arm and picked up the glass. He studied my face, and then my arms. "How are the bites?"

"Stings," I said. "They're all right."

"Stings," he said, and seemed to let that settle. He had

100

drunk most of the bottle, and it had begun to show. "They hurt much?"

I shook my head and walked into the kitchen and got a beer. Then I heard the door swing open behind me and he came in and sat down heavily at the table. He set his glass and the bottle in front of him. "That must have been a hairy situation," he said.

I sat down at the table too; there was no place else to go. I didn't know if it had been hairy or not; it was removed, like a story I'd read about someone else.

"This time of year," he said, "I understand jellyfish are common in this part of Florida." I took a drink of the beer, nodded. "You have to respect the ocean," he said a minute or two later.

To my knowledge, my father had never been in the ocean in his life. He liked the river. When I was six or seven, before my mother left for California, he would let me squirt him with the hose after he'd washed the truck, and that was the only time I remember seeing him wet. He stared at his glass, a speck of something black floating an inch below the surface. He picked it up and drank it anyway, and the speck was stuck to his lip when he finished. He looked at his watch.

"Working into the night," he said, "that's when you wear out, start to make mistakes."

It seemed to me that he wanted to know how my brother was doing. "Ward doesn't get worn out the way other people do," I said.

My father smiled, looking like an old man. "Everybody wears out," he said. "Sometimes it's because they don't know when to quit. Like racehorses, if there wasn't somebody there to stop them, they'd run themselves to death."

In some way it seemed possible, Ward running himself to death. My father filled his glass again and stared a moment at the bottle, as if he were confused at the amount he saw inside.

"They had a shark attack up in Jacksonville," he said.

———

❑

IN THE MORNING, Yardley Acheman loaded his suitcase and a cooler of iced beer into Charlotte's van, and then climbed in behind it, headed for Daytona Beach to find the golf course Hillary and Tyree Van Wetter had vandalized on the night Sheriff Call was killed.

Yardley Acheman had been complaining for weeks of heat and boredom and the lack of good restaurants in Moat County, but now, leaving the place, he wasn't appreciably happier.

He did not speak to Charlotte as he got in; did not, in fact, acknowledge her at all. He settled into the passenger seat, set his sunglasses on his nose, and folded his arms over his chest.

Charlotte smiled at me and forced the van into gear, and then rode off into the early sun, trailing black smoke from a tear in the exhaust system.

❑

WARD SPENT HALF AN HOUR that morning studying a navigational map of the river, and then we went looking for Uncle Tyree. We went to the store along the highway first where I had delivered ten papers each morning all through the winter and spring. There was a naked child playing in the driveway, squatted over something shiny in the dirt—perhaps a flattened can or a piece of glass—pounding on it with a hammer.

He looked up at the sound of the car, dropped the hammer, and ran inside when we stopped.

"This isn't going to do you any good," I said.

Ward nodded, and then opened his door anyway and got out. I sat still a moment before I followed him, not wanting to go in there again.

My brother picked up the hammer and carried it with him to the front door. I locked the car doors and watched him step inside.

Ward was standing in front of the counter when I came in, still holding the hammer. The place was dark and hot, a black spider sat in the jar of beef jerky sitting next to the cash register.

A voice came out of the back. "Where's your pants?" A man's voice, there was no answer. "I askt you a question, mister. Where's your pants?"

There was no answer. My brother looked around at the shelves. Cookies, candy, flour, tobacco, sugar, Hostess cupcakes—none of it in any order I could see, it was stacked in the shelves as it arrived, I suppose, put wherever there was an open spot.

There was another voice in back now, a woman's. "Jack," she said, almost softly, just that word, and for a moment I thought someone was speaking to me.

And then she came through the curtains, the woman with the beautiful skin, and saw us standing in her store, and at the same time I heard the sound of a strap hitting flesh.

"Where's your pants?" the man said again, sounding more angry now, and the question was followed by another smack, and then another, and another.

The woman moved to her place behind the counter, expressionless, waiting. There was nothing to indicate she remembered who I was. The beating in the back room continued, and I realized I was counting the strokes; the number twenty-two was in my head.

Ward put the hammer on the wooden counter in front of the woman and smiled.

Twenty-four, twenty-five.

The child had not cried.

"This was outside," my brother said. The woman stared at the hammer, but did not touch it. The beating went on, but the only sounds were the strap against the boy's body and a labored breathing that I took to be the man's.

It stopped for a moment and my brother said, "I was wondering if you might be able to tell us how to find Tyree Van Wetter's place."

It started again then, and a tiny tremor passed over her bottom lip; passed and was gone. My brother took out his wallet and began looking for his business card. "My name is Ward James," he said, putting the card on the counter next to the hammer. When she didn't look, he pushed it a little closer.

"I am trying to locate someone who can substantiate Hillary Van Wetter's whereabouts on the evening he is supposed to have killed Sheriff Call."

No answer.

"Mr. Van Wetter has told me," my brother said, "that he was with his uncle Tyree. . . ."

The strokes reached forty, then forty-one. They were coming slower now, as if the man was wearing out. "I suppose he would be another generation removed from you," my brother said. "Your grandfather, or great-uncle . . ."

The beating stopped completely for the second time, then began again.

"You want something?" she said. It wasn't rude, but she was asking us to leave. "You got to buy something, or you can't stay." She glanced back in the direction of the curtains.

My brother picked up a pack of Camel cigarettes and handed the woman a dollar. He didn't smoke.

She rang up sixty cents on the cash register, the drawer bell sounding exactly as the fiftieth crack filled the room and then receded, leaving the place quiet. She stood still, with the drawer still open, until the strap fell again. Lost in it.

She picked the change out of the drawer; the coins in there were not separated into bins but tossed randomly together wherever there was space.

"I saw Hillary yesterday," my brother said.

She did not seem to hear. Another stroke landed, and then a low, sustained howl started somewhere inside the building, you could not tell where, and grew as it changed pitch—a dog's sound—until it filled the place, and all of us in it. The tremor crossed the woman's lip again, and this time it did not stop there but shook her chin too, and then I saw the light from the window collected in her eyes, and then she was crying, without noise. The beating had stopped with the wail; fifty-four strokes; and the woman cried that it was finally over.

The man's voice came from behind the curtain. "Now you go find them pants and put them on," he said. The curtain moved and the man with the burned face came through it. He was flushed and bare-chested, the sweat glistening on his stomach. He looked at us, and then at her. I could tell that beating the boy had made him want to fuck her.

"My name is Ward James," my brother said. "I am with the *Miami Times. . . .*"

"Store's closed," the man said.

"I was looking for Tyree Van Wetter."

The man walked to the door and opened it, waiting for us to leave. "I'm not with the courts," my brother said. "This is about Hillary."

The man nodded and waited for us to get out. He looked quickly at the woman, blaming her for our being in the store. My brother waited, not moving, and finally the man shook his head.

"They ain't here," he said, "either one of them."

"I know they're not here," my brother said, staying where he was.

I remembered an afternoon then, outside the Paramount movie theater in Thorn. A kid named Roger Bowen with a ducktail haircut and a pack of cigarettes rolled into the sleeve of his T-shirt danced a foot in front of Ward, leaning into his face. He moved his arms like wings and made chicken noises while his friends laughed. I'd tugged at Ward's sleeve; he wouldn't move.

Roger Bowen died the following year crossing the railroad tracks in front of a train, and on the afternoon I remembered, the theater manager finally came out and chased him and his friends away for being white trash.

Or perhaps it was because we were the children of William Ward James, and were in some way protected.

"I'm trying to locate Tyree Van Wetter," my brother said again.

The man at the door reconsidered him and then smiled, the kind of smile that leads to something else, and shook his head. "I said the store's closed." His voice had turned polite, and I knew something bad was in the works.

"Who would know where to find him?" my brother said.

The man shook his head. "Tyree? He's got family all around here, up and down the river."

"You're his family," my brother said.

The man shook his head. "Ain't the same bunch," he said. And then, nodding to the woman behind the counter, he said, "She was one of them, but she married into my side of the family." It was a joke between them, one that wasn't funny to her.

"Jack, please . . ."

He looked at her a moment, suddenly angry, and then, just as suddenly, he seemed to give in.

"Honeymoon Lane," he said.

My brother walked past the man and out of the store. I hurried to get out with him, and the moment I was clear the door closed. I heard a bolt slide on the other side.

My brother got into the car and sat in the heat, thinking, without opening his window. I turned on the air conditioner and looked at him to see where we were going. He was still a moment, staring at his hands, then looked back at the store.

I drove the car out of the parking lot slowly, and turning

toward the road I saw the boy again, still naked, standing behind the store, something draped from his hand. He moved his arm in a long arc, and the movement gave shape to the thing in his hands, and I saw it was a pair of pants. He let go of the pants at the top of the arc, and they floated up into the air and landed on the roof, one leg dangling over, as if trying to crawl the rest of the way up.

He stared at the pants a moment, making sure they would stay, then turned, and squatted, and began pounding the bare dirt with his fist.

"They shouldn't beat him like that," my brother said.

❑

A MILE NORTH OF the store we turned east onto a baked dirt road identified as Honeymoon Lane by a sign that had been dented and perforated by shotgun pellets. There was marsh grass on either side of the road, and, a mile or two farther, where it turned wet, there was a long stand of trees. Insects crawled over the windshield of the car, trying to get in.

Honeymoon Lane itself lay ahead like rough water. It rose and fell a foot or more in a regulated pattern, and then, in some places, dropped more than that, banging the car's undercarriage onto the ground. I slowed, but it did nothing to improve the ride. I was beginning to feel nauseous.

Ward looked out the window.

"If people live back here, they don't take this road in and out," I said.

"If they come out," he said.

The road quit a dozen feet from standing water, and a path led off into the trees. The trees were thicker than they'd looked from the highway; the path resembled a tunnel.

"Last stop," I said, and turned off the engine.

He got out and started into the trees, and I followed him in. It was shaded there, and cool, and the trunks of the trees were covered with moss, some of them eight or ten feet around. They grew in eroding soil, their roots visible for yards.

Between the trees, the ground dropped away and was covered by water. River water, warm and brown. Reeds grew in some places, in other, deeper places, there were none.

Mosquitoes moved over the water in clouds and made a humming noise that was electric, a deeper sound than they make close to your ear. I slapped at one in my hair and the movement seemed to draw others, and a moment later they were everywhere, even in my nose and mouth.

I brushed them off my arms and head, and then, looking at Ward, I saw a dozen of them had set down on his face. He didn't seem to notice they were there.

We walked along the edge of the water for a hundred yards, and then took a narrow stretch of raised ground farther east, deeper into the trees. We turned north again, on a kind of peninsula, and the texture of the earth was softer, and our shoes made sucking noises as we walked. The car was long out of sight, and although I have a certain sense of direction, I was not sure, left alone, that I could have found my way out.

"There's a boat landing here somewhere," Ward said. His voice carried clearly, and seemed to come from the trees behind me, although he was a few yards ahead.

I looked for a boat landing. "Where?" The sound of my own voice startled me.

He stared into the trees without answering, trying, I think, to remember exactly how the shoreline looked from the river. It had been ten years at least since he'd been out there on a boat.

Farther ahead, a dead tree had fallen across the path, one end still hinged to the base of the trunk, the other resting in the water. A moccasin as thick as my wrist lay on it near the water, the same color as the wet, rotting trunk.

I stepped over the trunk, blind to what was lying on the

other side. My brother stopped again. There was water in front of him, perhaps fifty feet of it, and beyond that the ground rose into an island, a yard higher than it was here.

Standing still, he had sunk to his ankles in the mud.

"There's a house in there," he said.

I didn't see a house, but then I'd been watching for snakes.

"How do you know that?" I said. I wanted to turn around and go back to the car. I slapped my arm, killing two mosquitoes at once. One of them full of blood. The noise seemed to hang in the trees, unable to get out.

"What else would it be?" he said.

"What else would what be?"

He pointed into the trees, and I saw it then, a dark, familiar shape barely visible against the lines of the branches. A television antenna. A crow screamed, and when I looked, another inch or two of my brother had sunk into the mud.

"You're sinking," I said.

He studied the problem, buried to his ankles in mud, and then slowly pulled his feet out. His feet came out, his shoes stayed.

Water filled the holes his feet had left, and when he reached down to retrieve his shoes, he couldn't find them. Brown wing tips lost to the mud.

My thoughts turned to quicksand.

Ward's arm went into the mud halfway to the elbow. "It's some kind of suction," he said. He stood back up, his hand black, and looked at the soft earth and then the water. He said, "There must be an underground current."

I looked at the water too, but nothing in it moved.

"What I think," he said, still looking around, "the whole thing is eroded underneath." He looked at me a moment and smiled. "I think it's all floating."

I heard something behind me drop into the water, and turned to look at the fallen tree we'd crossed a few minutes before. The moccasin was gone. Ward lifted one foot and then the other, taking off his socks and sticking them in the front pockets of his trousers, and began wading across to the island. I studied the water a long time before I took off my own shoes and socks, rolled up my pants legs, and followed him in.

The bottom was cool and soft and came up between my toes. A few feet ahead Ward was in up to his waist. "Are you sinking or has it gotten deeper?" I said.

He stopped for a minute to consider that. "It's hard to say," he said finally, and then moved ahead. A moment later I dropped into the same hole and the mud was colder underfoot but more solid. Ward had reached the other side, and was using the low branch of a tree to pull himself up onto the bank. He struggled, half out of the water, his weight changing the equation as he emerged. His arms shook with the effort, and I arrived under him just before he fell back in, and put my hand on his behind and pushed him up.

And doing that, I sank deeper into the bottom, and when I pulled myself out I was caked in it to the knees. I stood where I was while Ward caught his breath. I was surprised that he wasn't stronger—he had always seemed stronger—and that the few moments he hung between ground and the water had used him up. The thought crossed my mind that he was sick.

The narrow spot of cleared ground that we were on was not much bigger than a closet, not really enough room for us both. The underbrush leading farther in was thick, and there was no trail here.

"There's got to be another way in and out," I said. "Maybe we can find it when we leave."

He nodded, his hands on his knees, still catching his breath. I noticed the mosquitoes had no interest in my feet, which were now covered with mud. My shirt stuck to my skin. Ward stood up, looking pale. "You want to go back?" I said.

A moment passed and he said, "What's the point of that?"

And then he turned and pushed away the undergrowth and branches with his hands, and slowly made his way through.

He was awkward in everything he did now, the branches came at him from unexpected angles. He stumbled once, then stopped to inspect a cut on his foot.

Still, he pushed into the trees toward the antenna. A broken branch caught his sleeve and tore his shirt, and, turning to loosen himself, a smaller branch slapped him in the eye. He stopped, holding it, and when he let go it had begun to swell. Tears ran from the corner as if he were crying.

I walked past him and took the lead, holding the branches until he was through them, making sure there was nothing unexpected waiting to hit him in the other eye. It did not seem impossible that I would have to lead him back to the car blind, and within a few minutes he was in fact tearing from both eyes. No one was ever more out of place than Ward was here, and yet he pressed through, starting to sneeze. It occurred to me that it didn't matter that he was no good at this; what mattered was that he was willing to do it.

The thing he was good at was born of a lack of talent. He did not need grace to push ahead.

He stopped for a moment and wiped at his eyes, using the bottom of his shirt. The mosquitoes moved off his face, then resettled even before he was finished. I whacked the back of my neck and the jolt carried straight through my head. "I'm beating the shit out of myself here," I said. I did not bother to speak softly now; there was no chance we had not been overheard already, if there was someone to hear us.

Ward blew his nose into his shirtsleeve and tried to clear his vision, closing his eyes and wiping the lids with his fingers. "It isn't much farther," he said, and a minute later I heard the chickens.

❑

THE HOUSE SAT ON cement blocks at the far end of the clearing. Dozens of chickens hunted under it and over the bare ground of the yard for bits of food; a rooster sat on a pile of shingles.

Beyond the shingles, a nylon line had been rigged, leading from the corner of the main house to the single tree still standing in the yard. Half a dozen alligator skins hung from the line, none of them more than four or five feet long. There was a tree stump not far away where they did the skinning. An ax and some knives had been left there, two of them stuck into the stump itself, the rest on the ground and on a four-legged metal stool nearby.

My brother walked slowly across the yard; one of the chickens crossed his path and dropped feathers hurrying out of the way. The house itself was prefabricated; I had seen hundreds like it in developments outside Jacksonville and Orlando. It had one story with a pitched roof and a large picture window in front, where the living room would be. Ranch style, the real estate people called it.

I wondered if it had been hard to steal.

Half of the front of the place had been covered with aluminum siding, the rest left in shingles like the ones in the pile. An outboard Evinrude lay in pieces on a blanket in the carport; the tools used to take it apart lay among them.

My brother walked to the front door and pushed the doorbell. He and I looked at each other a moment, waited, and he knocked. Nothing moved. He took a few steps back and looked at the roof, one end to the other. It was covered with tarpaper which was torn here and there, exposing the wood underneath. Chicken droppings were everywhere.

He went back to the door and knocked again. He called out Tyree Van Wetter's name.

I had moved to the side of the house, and from there I saw the inlet behind it. A small boat had been left upside down in the backyard. The yard itself was wet and grassless, a strip of dirt no more than ten feet wide that sloped from the house to the water.

My brother's voice carried out over the water and bounced back. "Mr. Van Wetter ... I am here to ask you about your nephew Hillary."

I walked back around to the front. "There's nobody home," I said. My brother looked at the house, undecided.

He knocked again, much louder this time. "Tyree Van Wetter?"

The chickens resumed their search of the yard, as if we were of no consequence. My brother sat down on the step leading to the front door and began unplugging the mud between his toes with a stick. I sat down next to him. The step was warm from the sun. I smelled tar, probably from the roof. I looked at my brother, waiting to see what he intended to do.

"Let's give it a little while," he said.

I watched him clean his feet. "You know," I said, "this might be somebody's fishing cabin."

He was studying one of his toes. "No," he said, "it's the right place, I think." And then he said, "Someone's in the house. I heard them."

We sat on the porch and waited. The sun moved, and the house took more of it for a shadow. The place began to feel cooler.

"I'm sorry about what happened with Yardley," I said, sometime later.

He was staring at one of his feet; it had been a long time since either of us had spoken. I had not heard anything from inside the house. He frowned, I couldn't tell why. "Nobody was hurt," he said.

"He acted hurt."

"Yardley thinks he's protected," he said. " 'You can't do this to me, I'm with the *Miami Times*. . . .' " Hearing the words, he began to smile. Ward knew that no such protection existed. He had no misunderstanding about that.

❑

THE SUN HAD JUST DROPPED behind the trees at the west end of the clearing when I heard the boat. Ward and I stood up and walked to the backyard and watched it come across the inlet—a small aluminum fishing boat with an ancient Johnson motor. There were two men inside, one about my father's age, the other one younger, perhaps his son. They were both blond, and they did not seem surprised to see us standing at the edge of their property.

The one in front—the younger one—stood up as the boat approached land, holding a Coleman cooler under his arm, and jumped to shore. The boat rocked violently behind him; the old man sat at the motor and waited while the younger one set the cooler down and pulled him onto the landing. The younger man's arms were long and clearly defined, the sort of arms you get from work or swimming.

The old man pulled the motor out of the water, the shape of his own arms changing, and then stepped out himself.

My brother stood still, waiting for one of them to speak. The younger man tied the boat to a stump and then reclaimed his cooler and walked between us and up to the house. When he was almost there, the back door opened and a pale-faced woman stood in the crack and began to speak to him in whispers. He nodded, without answering her, and then stepped past her and disappeared inside.

The old man put his hands in the back pockets of his pants and approached my brother. He was wider than the younger man, but not as hard or as tall. He stopped in front of Ward, studying us like a problem. "You lost your shoes," he said finally, a smile playing somewhere behind the words.

Ward nodded and looked over to the place we had come in. "Yessir," he said.

"There's snakes all through here, you was lucky that's all that happened," the old man said. He seemed good-natured, and looked at me a moment to see if I was afraid of snakes, and then turned back into the boat and pulled out a full bag of groceries. A sack of potato chips was perched at the top. His whiskers were coming in, a gray line that followed his jaw and in the failing light made him seem just out of focus.

"Mr. Van Wetter?" Ward said.

The old man nodded.

"My name is Ward James, I am with the *Miami Times.* . . ."

The old man started up the bank to the house. His legs looked heavy. My brother followed, a few feet behind. "I wanted to talk to you about your nephew . . ."

The old man stopped before he went in the door. "Which nephew would that be?" he said.

"Hillary," my brother said.

The old man shook his head. "You come walking through them snakes for nothing," he said. "Hillary ain't my nephew. That's the other branch of the family." A moment passed.

"Which branch is that?" Ward said.

The old man stopped and scratched his head, still holding the groceries. "You might to ask Eugene there, he's Hillary's first cousin." He nodded toward the house.

My brother looked at the house, trying to put it together. "Eugene's married twict," the old man said, "and bridged the two sides of the family. He'll be out in a bit, we got to eat some ice cream."

We walked back to the front and sat down again on the porch and waited. There was movement inside the house; a baby cried. The sun dropped farther into the trees, taking the house in the shade. There were specks of spit in the corner of my brother's mouth. We had been a long time without a drink.

He stared into the treetops, sensing the place, the people in it.

Half an hour had passed when the door opened and the old man came out carrying a half gallon carton of Winn-Dixie vanilla ice cream. The one named Eugene stepped out a moment later, carrying a spoon in his shirt pocket, and, after they had each settled in a spot on the ground with their backs resting against the blocks supporting the house, the old man slowly opened the top of the ice cream, looking up at

Eugene after he had pulled back all four covers to reveal what was underneath.

It was a kind of ceremony.

The old man went into his pants pockets and came out with a spoon. He considered it a moment, and then dropped it into the ice cream. He put the spoon in his mouth and left it there a long time. When he pulled it out, half the ice cream came out with it.

The door opened a few inches and the woman stepped out sideways, carrying a baby. She wore a man's T-shirt, her breasts loose underneath. She kept her eyes down, not wanting to look at either my brother or me, and took a seat on the ground beyond Eugene.

The old man put the spoon back in his mouth again, and when he brought it out this time it was clean.

"You're Hillary's cousin?" my brother said suddenly. Eugene had been watching the old man eat, and his head snapped in my brother's direction. He stared at Ward as the old man balanced a load of ice cream on the spoon and guided it into his mouth. The ice cream was soft and some of what had melted dripped out of the bottom of the carton onto his pants.

"Hillary Van Wetter," my brother said. "You're his cousin?"

The old man chuckled with the spoon still in his mouth, as if the ice cream had made him happy. "Don't mind Eugene," he said. "He gets irritable waiting his turn."

My brother nodded, and Eugene looked away, back in the direction of the ice cream. Farther down the line, the woman was stealing looks in that direction too.

The old man caught her at it and said, "Ice cream," before he put the spoon in his mouth again. Barely, the woman nodded.

We sat outside the house for twenty minutes while the old man ate vanilla ice cream. Swamp etiquette. He seemed to enjoy the feel of it in his mouth as much as the taste, and once, after he had slid the spoon out of his lips, he put it against his cheek, and smiled at the way that felt too. The ice cream melted in the carton and dripped into his pants, and the stain there spread until it covered his lap.

And suddenly he stopped and closed his eyes and dropped his head back until it touched the bricks he was leaning against. He seemed to be waiting for a pain to pass, and when it was gone, he had a last, long look into the carton—it was still half full at least—and passed it along to Eugene.

The carton dripped as it was moved, and Eugene lifted it over his face and sucked on a corner.

The woman watched more carefully now, brushing insects away from the container, ignoring the ones that lit on her arms and shoulders. Her nipples were clearly defined under her shirt, and I looked other places, not to be caught staring.

The old man folded his hands over his stomach and closed his eyes. "Getting dark," he said, I didn't know to whom.

My brother nodded, as if that had been on his mind too. He had a quick look around the clearing. "Is there another way out of here?" he said.

The old man opened his eyes to consider that. "Two ways," he said, "the way you come in and the boat."

It was quiet again; my brother would not ask for the ride. The old man smiled at him again. "You proud, ain't you?" he said.

Ward didn't answer. The old man turned to Eugene, who had closed himself around the carton of ice cream. "These paperboys is proud, Eugene. I like that. . . ."

Eugene nodded.

"I might just give you proud boys a ride home," the old man said. He started to get up—pretended to get up—then dropped back onto the ground. He shook his head. "Too much ice cream," he said. "I'd sink that old boat with all this in me."

He smiled at the woman, who had forgotten the baby in

her arms and was watching the ice cream. Eugene was in it to his wrist now, and it had puddled on the ground between his legs; I couldn't tell how much was left.

"Looks like you two got to leave the way you come," the old man said. I thought of the moccasin lying on a branch in the dark, imagined putting my hand there to climb over.

"I have to talk to Tyree Van Wetter," my brother said, and it seemed to ruin the old man's good humor, that my brother didn't care if we had to go back the way we'd come; that snakes didn't frighten him.

"Can't do you no good," the old man said.

Eugene picked up the carton and sucked from the corner again. He seemed ready to turn what was left over to the woman; he looked at it, he looked at her; then dipped his spoon into it again.

"He could help Hillary," my brother said.

"Hillary's gone," the old man said. "They got him, and they ain't going to let him loose."

"Hillary says he was with his uncle the night Thurmond Call was killed," my brother said.

The old man thought about that, but didn't answer. When I looked at the ice cream again, the woman suddenly turned in my direction, glaring, as if it had just come to her that I might be ahead of her in line.

"They're gone keep that boy," the old man said.

"They're going to strap him into a chair and electrocute him," my brother said.

The old man nodded. "That's good," he said. In the quiet that followed, Eugene put the container on the ground beside his leg. The woman looked at him, then the ice cream, and then, on some unspoken signal, she picked it up herself. The old man said, "Then it's settled."

"He says he was in Daytona Beach when it happened," my brother said.

The old man shrugged.

118

"Stealing sod . . ."

The old man rubbed his chin. "That's against the law, ain't it?"

"Yessir."

"So they'd put poor old Tyree in the pokey too."

My brother shook his head. "There's a statute of limitations on that. They can't arrest anybody for that now."

The old man smiled again. "I seen your statues," he said. And he caught Eugene's eye and held it, as if they were deciding something, and a little later the woman put down her spoon and ran her finger along the inside of the ice cream carton and stuck it into the baby's mouth.

❏

THE AIR TURNED COLD as we made our way back, and we stepped on bare feet into pinecones and rocks that we could not see. The sky was dark and, looking up, it was impossible to distinguish it from the trees. A breeze came up from the east, the direction of the water, and behind it was a soft roll of thunder.

I walked ahead and heard him behind me, breaking through the trees even though I held the branches after I had gone through. He was breathing hard, and sniffing. I could hear him clearly, but I couldn't see him, even when he was so close his hand touched mine on the same tree branch.

And then there was a flash of lightning, and in that flash I did catch a glimpse of him, walking with his hands out in front of himself, his head slightly turned away, like someone in a water fight at the swimming pool. I straightened my own posture, seeing his, and dropped my hands to my sides. A moment later I walked into a tree branch that felt as if it had taken off my ear.

There was a moment then, as I held the ear and waited for the pain to pass, when it suddenly seemed to me that the old man and his son were in the trees somewhere, watching, and I straightened up again, not wanting to look foolish.

Later, I slipped on some wet ground and caught myself with my hands. Ward walked into me from behind, but managed not to fall. "How far do you think we came in?" I said.

"Someplace in here," he said.

"I can't see a damn thing," I said. And a moment later I thought I heard a smothered laugh; someone else was there in the trees and mud, watching. I was furious. "You know what I think?" I said. "I think these fucking people are too stupid to know you're trying to help them."

"If we just keep headed straight a little longer," my brother said, "we'll find the path to the car."

It was quiet while I got back to my feet, and then we began to walk again. "They aren't stupid," Ward said later. "They were playing with us."

And then the earth gave way under my feet and I dropped off it, catching my arm on something solid on the way down, and then landed, it seemed like a long time later, sideways in the water.

"Jack?" His voice came from a distance, and from behind something. "Jack? Are you there?"

I got myself up and stood in the mud, which closed around my feet. The water itself seemed warm and came about to the top of my pants.

"There's a drop into the water here," I said. "I'd say five feet."

It was quiet then, while Ward reconsidered the terrain. "We must be too far east," he said finally. His voice was muted; I felt my feet sinking into the mud and moved to another spot.

"The edge gave way," I said. "You better watch where you're standing or you'll be down here on top of me."

"Can you move around?"

A pattern of lightning lit the sky, and was followed a few seconds later by more thunder. In the light, I saw the root system of a tree in the bank over my head. It resembled a nest. Farther down, to my left, I could see a fallen tree lying one end in the water, and beyond that the ground dropped level to the water. I was suddenly cold.

"I think we came in over here," I said.

The lightning moved in and the thunder behind it shook the sky. It began to rain. Underneath that noise, I could hear my brother above me on the bank, making his way through the trees.

And we walked that way back to the place where we crossed to the island earlier in the day; Ward contending with bad footing and branches he could not see, and me, waist deep in water, ankle deep in mud, thinking of snakes.

❑

MY SHOES WERE ON the bank where I had left them. The car was where we had left it too, but had been rolled upside down and left with its doors open, glowing inside from the small light in the ceiling. We stood in the rain looking at it.

"You know the worst part?" I said, "we can't even get in to wait out the storm." Ward didn't answer. He seemed tired and weak; his clothes clung to his skin and underneath them he was frail.

Without a word, he began walking toward the highway. I waited a moment longer, watching the car rock in the wind, hoping in some way that the wind would blow it right and we could drive home. And then I turned and couldn't see him, and felt a quiet panic that he might be lost. I jogged up the dirt road in the direction of the highway, calling his name, and found him standing still again, staring back into the darkness where we had been.

He looked at me and blinked. The rain washed across his face and dripped off his chin. He looked pale and desperate, but then, looking back at the swamp, he smiled, and I understood that he'd gotten what he came for. That we had spent the afternoon with Uncle Tyree.

❑

I SLEPT IN YARDLEY ACHEMAN's bed that night, too tired to make the trip back to my father's house in Thorn. The pillow smelled of his cologne, and I woke once in the night, full of the smell and nauseated.

❑

HE AND CHARLOTTE RETURNED from Daytona Beach at two o'clock the next afternoon. When they came in, I was sitting at Yardley's desk, on the phone, going over the particulars of the overturned car with a claims agent at the car rental company headquarters in Orlando. I had been over the same story three times, starting with the clerk at the desk in Palatka, where we'd rented the car, and ending up with the man in Orlando, and at each step the person receiving the information seemed to take what had happened more personally.

"You just *left* it there, in the swamp?" he said. He had a distinct, mouth-full-of-grits north Florida accent.

"We parked it at the end of the road," I said. "We didn't leave it in the swamp."

"And when you found it, it was upside down," he said. Something in this was hitting a false note with the claims agent, and he wasn't trying to hide it.

"It was upside down," I said. I was tired, and I was wearing Yardley Acheman's shirt and a pair of his pants, which did not fit in the crotch and smelled faintly of his cologne.

"And you didn't leave the keys in the ignition. . . ."

"You think it rolled over because I left the keys in the ignition?" I said.

"I don't know what to think," he said.

And that was when Charlotte and Yardley Acheman came through the door. Charlotte appeared first—it looked as if Yardley had held the door for her—and I could see in that moment that something was different.

"Mr. James?" said the man in Orlando.

"I've gone over this four times with you, and three or four times with two people before you, and nothing's changed," I said. "I didn't turn the damn car over."

Yardley recognized his shirt, I don't know how. It was a plain white shirt with long sleeves that I'd found in his drawer; I'd never seen him wear it.

"What's he doing in my shirt?" he said to Ward.

"We had trouble with the car last night," my brother said. "He had to stay over."

Yardley Acheman nodded as if he understood. "What's he doing in my shirt?" he said.

"He didn't go home last night," Ward said.

"Your shirts don't fit him?"

"We'll send it to the cleaners," my brother said. "We'll expense it." As much as Yardley liked to expense things to the *Times,* he shook his head no.

"I don't want the fucking thing now."

Ward and I looked at each other, then I glanced at Charlotte, hoping she was about to tell Yardley off, but she stood quietly, listening to him, as if this discussion of a single shirt made sense.

"I hate people wearing my clothes," he said. And then he turned back to Ward and said, "And I hate people sitting at my desk."

"He's getting us a new car," Ward said.

"He's sitting there in my shirt, on my telephone. . . ."

He was angry, but I'd seen that before. Then I found myself noticing the way Charlotte was looking at him.

I stood up and opened the shirt without unbuttoning it,

then balled it up and threw it at his head. It landed in his hands. He took a step back, remembering the headlock. Then I kicked off my shoes, still frosted in mud, and stepped out of his pants and threw them at him too. I stood in Jockey shorts and socks, daring him to say anything else.

Slowly, he began to nod, as if this were the sort of behavior he'd been expecting all along. I realized I'd spent myself, or at least had nothing else to tear off, when Charlotte interrupted.

"Yardley found the golf course," she said.

And in that second, ripping Yardley's shirt off without unbuttoning it was all for nothing.

Yardley turned to my brother and nodded, acknowledging it, then dropped the shirt and pants on the floor. As if to say, *"And this is the way you treat me."*

"Where is it?" Ward said.

I walked around the desk in my underpants, brushing past Charlotte, and sat in the window. A breeze I hadn't felt before blew over my skin. She watched me a moment, then turned away, disinterested.

"Ormond Beach," Yardley Acheman said. He took a notepad out of his back pocket and read from what was written down. "August twentieth, 1965, six thirty-five A.M., the grounds super-intendent phones the Ormond Beach Police Department to report that his greens have been vandalized; somebody's stripped the sod in the night."

"Where'd you find it?" my brother said.

Yardley Acheman shrugged, as if it were some intuitive talent he couldn't explain.

"He saw it in the newspaper," Charlotte said, and for a moment I embraced the thought that the change in her was only that he had found the way to save Hillary Van Wetter. But then she looked at him again, and I knew I was wrong.

"It was in some old clips at the *Ormond Beach Satellite*," he said.

"It was in all the papers," she said. Charlotte was bragging on Yardley, but she did not understand that the size of his accomplishment depended on its difficulty. I folded my arms and leaned back into the window frame.

"You talked to the man. . . ." Ward said.

Yardley Acheman nodded. "Not the superintendent, he got cancer from the weed killer out there, but another guy. He remembered it because the membership voted to ask the governor to declare it a disaster area, they could get funds to replace the green without going into their own pockets. It made all the papers."

"They were old," Charlotte said. "A bunch of old men, walking around in plaid pants, still mad that somebody took their grass four years ago." She smiled at that, and smiled at Yardley Acheman. He was handsome, all right, and something from Daytona Beach had intruded on her feelings for Hillary Van Wetter.

Yardley Acheman walked to his desk and sat down, stepping over the shirt and pants on the floor.

❑

WE HAD TO SEE Hillary again, and Charlotte did not want to come along. I saw it even before she told my brother that her period had just started and she had cramps and bled too much the first day to go anywhere.

Another woman would have just said she was coming down with a cold. "I bleed like they cut it off," she said.

A little later she said that the prison was beginning to depress her. "I don't know how much longer I can go out there and see Hillary waiting to be executed. . . ."

"We've got to ask him again," Ward said, "about where he sold the sod."

"He already said he didn't know," she said.

"He's had time to think."

A little later, Charlotte went over the details of her menstrual cycle with my brother again. Ward stared at his hands as she explained how much she bled, and did not try to talk her into coming along. "I got to take a bottle of Midol and go to bed," she said, and a minute later, throwing an uncertain look in the direction of Yardley Acheman, she disappeared through the door.

"Will he talk to us without her there?" I said.

"I don't know," Ward said.

"If he won't," Yardley Acheman said, "fuck him. We'll go find somebody else. . . ."

But my brother, at least, didn't want to find somebody else. He wanted Hillary Van Wetter, he wanted the story he'd begun. It didn't have anything to do in the end with whether Hillary had killed Sheriff Call, or if he'd been fairly represented at his trial.

At the bottom of it, my brother wanted to know what had happened and to get it down that way on paper. He wanted to have it exactly right.

❏

COTTON HAD BEEN PACKED into both sides of Hillary Van Wetter's nose, the last bit of fuzz hung beneath the nostrils. It was hard to say if the swelling across the bridge was due to the cotton or the injury. His eyes were both bruised underneath, the streak of black running at similar angles on both sides, as if they had grown from the same spot.

"Where's my intended?" he said. It sounded as if he had a cold.

"She didn't feel well," Ward said.

It was a quiet moment.

"What's wrong with her?"

My brother began to shake his head, looking for a way to explain it. Yardley Acheman moved in his chair. "She's on the rag," he said. Hillary turned and looked at him, the sound of his leg irons the only noise in the room.

"The monthlies?" he said finally. He was handcuffed, and there was a guard outside the door. Yardley Acheman checked these things before he spoke again.

"That's what she said."

"Just come in and discuss it, did she?"

Yardley nodded.

"Pussy bi'niss, in front of paperboys," Hillary said.

"We ought to talk about Ormond Beach," my brother said, but Hillary Van Wetter continued to stare at Yardley Acheman.

"Mr. Van Wetter?"

Finally Hillary turned away from Yardley and considered Ward. "She told you about it too?"

For a moment no one spoke. "I've got to know where the sod went," he said finally.

"For what?"

"I have to find the person who bought it."

He turned back to Yardley Acheman. "You got a smoke?" he said.

Yardley nodded in the direction of a sign on the wall warning visitors not to give anything to inmates. "Not allowed," he said.

Hillary nodded. "Follow the rules," he said, "follow the rules. . . ."

Ward asked what direction Hillary and his uncle had driven from the golf course.

Hillary closed his eyes, picturing it. "International House of Pancakes," he said finally. "We had pancakes and ice cream."

"In Daytona?"

"Must of been."

"And then what?"

"And then we got paid and went home."

It was quiet again. "I need to find the place," my brother said.

"We all need something," he said. And then he had another long look at Yardley Acheman. Yardley stared back briefly, then he turned away. He checked his watch, then the door, reminding Hillary of the guard outside.

Hillary Van Wetter watched him, his gaze as flat as still water. He watched until Yardley got up and crossed the room and stuck an open package of cigarettes in Hillary's shirt.

Hillary never took his eyes off Yardley until he was back in his place by the wall. Then he nodded, slowly. You couldn't tell if he meant to say thanks, or if everything he'd been thinking about us had been confirmed.

"How far from the pancake house was the condominium?" Ward said.

There was no answer.

"What direction? It was early morning by then, right? Were you driving into the sun or away from it?"

Hillary Van Wetter shook his head. "Overcast," he said.

❑

"FUCK HIM," Yardley said. The new rental was a Mercury with a noisy air conditioner that shook the car as it came on and off, but didn't do much in the way of cooling. Yardley was sitting in the backseat with the windows rolled down.

"He isn't worth it," he said. He was talking to my brother as if I weren't there. He did that more often than he needed to, reminding me that I didn't count.

"We have to go through the building permits," Ward said. "They were putting condos up in sixty days back then, before the building inspectors had a chance to see what they were doing, and this one would have been almost done if they were ready for a lawn. . . ."

"He isn't worth it," Yardley said again. He pulled himself up in the seat.

My brother said, "There can't be more than a dozen that started construction the same time, some of them might be the same builder . . ."

"And then what?" Yardley Acheman said. "The guy's going to admit he bought sod off a golf course?"

"He might say he didn't know it was stolen."

"He isn't going to give a shit," Yardley said. "The lawyer doesn't give a shit, Hillary Van Wetter doesn't give a shit. . . . We got too many people here, Ward, that don't give a shit." He thought about it, still sitting up in the seat. "The truth is, I don't give much of a shit anymore myself."

Yardley stopped and considered what he'd just said, perhaps how it would sound if it somehow got back to the editors in Miami.

"I mean, what am I supposed to write?" he said. "I picture myself at the typewriter, trying to interpret this person to the reader, and I don't have a damn feeling in my body about him except if he wasn't the one who opened up the sheriff, he was probably out that night fucking owls."

It had long been Yardley's premise that his obligation was to interpret for the reader.

The air conditioner kicked in again and the engine sagged under the weight. "If the contractors are local, it won't take more than a couple of days," Ward said.

Yardley Acheman dropped back into his seat. "I can't write what I don't feel."

My brother nodded, as if he agreed with that. "You want to go back down to Daytona," he said, "or you want me to do it this time?"

Yardley Acheman shook his head. "What I want, we fold the tent on this guy," he said, "go find something fresh to do back in Miami. . . ."

Ward smiled politely, as if that were a joke. I suppose he'd heard the same thing from him before. A newspaper story, like anything else, is more attractive from a distance, when it

first comes to you, then it is when you get in close and ago-
nize over the details.

Which I presume is how Yardley got in the habit of keeping
himself at a distance.

❑

AT HOME THAT NIGHT, I told my father that Yardley Acheman
wanted to quit. Anita Chester was still in the house, doing
some late cleaning, and we were sitting on the porch.

"Hit a dead end, did you?" he said, having a sip of his wine.
He set the glass on the uneven boards of the floor next to his
chair. It sat at an angle, the wine closer to the lip on one side
than the other.

"No, it isn't that. Ward's still working."

My father thought it over. "Your brother's a damn good
newspaperman," he said finally, "but he doesn't know everything yet." He stretched his arms over his head and yawned.
The sound of the vacuum cleaner came through the window
to his study. There was no light left in the sky; it must have
been ten o'clock. I wondered why he hadn't just told her to
go home. She had children to put to bed.

"Ward knows what he's doing," I said. I hadn't told my
father about the visit to the Van Wetters' home in the wetlands. It was the kind of story he would have liked—at least it
was the kind he liked to tell—but there was some residual
exhaustion from that day left inside me, and I was not up to
taking it on again yet.

In some way, telling a true story puts you back into it.

My father nodded his head. "He knows how to get stories,"
he said, "but what he doesn't appreciate fully is that the stories go into a newspaper, and the newspaper goes out into a
community."

The sound of the vacuum stopped, and he looked quickly
in that direction and at the same time reached for his glass.

"She's been late every day this week," he said, and then, softening, "I hope she isn't having some sort of trouble at home."

His hand touched the glass and it rocked a moment, then fell, three or four inches onto the floor, and shattered. He stared at it, and then slowly reached for the bottle, which was half empty on the other side of the chair.

"She have children of her own?" he said. "I can't remember? . . ."

"A couple of them," I said. "Six and nine."

He picked up the bottle and held it to the light, as if to read the label. "I hope they aren't sick," he said.

She came through the screen door a moment later, carrying her purse and her working shoes, wearing white tennis shoes that came up over her ankles. She always walked home. Tonight she was in more of a hurry than usual.

"Good evening, Mr. James," she said, heading for the steps.

"Good evening," he said, and then, before she reached the steps, he said, "I wonder would you mind taking an extra minute. I smashed a wineglass over here. . . ." She stopped in her tracks for a long moment, then turned without a word and went back into the house for a broom.

"I hope she isn't having trouble with those children," he said.

❑

WARD WAS WAITING ON the sidewalk alone outside the rooming house in the morning. He got into the car and slammed the door, a departure of sorts, as we were brought up not to slam the Chrysler's doors.

"No Yardley?" I said.

He took his time answering. "He's an adult," he said finally, but I knew he didn't want Yardley out sleeping with local girls. It made him furious. He was still dependent on the town for his story, and did not want to poison the source.

There was something else too. Ward had certain standards of virtue, which he kept to himself, but which were always at work. I didn't know anything then about how many girls he had slept with himself, but I had never seen him with a girl of his own and assumed he would not sleep with one casually. He didn't even like being in the room while anyone talked about sexual matters, particularly Charlotte Bless, who talked about sexual matters constantly.

"As long as it's with another adult," I said, preparing him for the inevitable day when I'd arrive for work late and sticky too. He turned to look at me. "Somebody over eighteen," I said, thinking he'd misunderstood what I'd said, and then realizing, even as I said it, that I'd missed the point. And half a second later, the point came home.

Yardley was with Charlotte.

We drove in silence, mutually outraged, to Moat Street and climbed the stairs to the office.

The van appeared beneath the window just after eleven o'clock. The passenger door opened first and Yardley came out, holding a beer, and then waited for Charlotte, who came around from the other side. I studied her carefully, looking for some sign of self-loathing. He put his hand in the middle of her back when she was close enough to touch, left it there a moment and then, as she moved past him toward the door leading inside, he patted her behind. They were a long time making it up the stairs.

I did not look at either of them when they came in, and Ward stared at the papers on his desk. They came inside the door and stopped.

"Uh-oh," Yardley said, "I think Mom and Dad have been waiting up." She laughed at that, a nervous laugh. Yardley drained the beer in his hand, went to the cooler and found a fresh one.

"You sure you won't have one?" he said to her. "Nothing tastes as good as a beer in the morning, before you're supposed to have it."

"I'm fine," she said, and I didn't care for the way she said it. She was not just speaking of being fine without a can of Busch beer.

Yardley Acheman walked to his side of the office and sat down. He leaned back, holding the beer on his stomach, and put his feet on the desk. He looked at my brother and burped. Ward did not look up. Charlotte crossed the room to the window, leaned into my line of vision and said, "Good morning."

I thought I could smell Yardley Acheman on her.

"Good morning," I said. I tried not to forgive her.

"What I was thinking," Yardley said to my brother, "I might take one more crack at finding this condominium guy they sold the lawn to after all." He looked at Charlotte, and I saw it was something they'd decided before they got to the office.

"We could go back down to Daytona, spend a couple of days knocking on doors."

Ward nodded but didn't answer. Yardley Acheman said, "It probably won't work, but we're not doing any good around here."

Another looked passed between them, she seemed about to laugh. My brother's face had flushed, as if he were embarrassed.

"I thought we might as well go today."

❏

YARDLEY'S FIANCÉE CALLED late in the afternoon, after they were gone. Ward had stepped outside to visit the bathroom on the main floor of the building, and I picked up the phone only after I realized it was going to ring until I did.

I told her Yardley was in Daytona Beach on business. She said he'd just been in Daytona on business. "I guess he didn't finish," I said, and gave her the number of the motel he'd written on the notepad on his desk when he'd called for reservations.

She took the number and then repeated it back to me twice, to be sure it was right. "I know he's a great reporter," she said, "but sometimes I wish he wasn't so devoted to his work."

❏

CHARLOTTE AND YARDLEY ACHEMAN stayed in Daytona Beach four days. They took separate rooms at a motel on the beach, but Yardley was never in his room when his fiancée called, not even at night. She would call me in the morning, to be reassured that he was not doing dangerous work.

I wondered at the things he told her.

❏

WARD AND I WENT to the sheriff's office, which occupied the second floor of the county courthouse. The cells were in the basement, some of them with barred windows which looked out over the town of Lately at grass level.

We had been there before to look at the report of Hillary's arrest, and knew what to expect. The deputies would not speak to anyone from the *Miami Times,* knowing the paper's liberal slant, and referred all inquiries to the departmental spokesman, a smiling, white-haired man named Sam Ellison who had once been a deputy himself.

Mr. Ellison was retired from active duty, and worked mornings at the department, Tuesday through Friday, even though the department did not need to be spoken for nearly that often. He did not seem happy to find visitors waiting for him outside his office door.

"The *Times,*" Mr. Ellison said. He had seen us in this same hallway the last time we were at the courthouse, but had not spoken to us because it was four minutes after twelve. The sheriff's public information office closed at noon, Tuesday through Friday.

134

Ward said, "Yessir," and Mr. Ellison unlocked the door and walked into the office. We followed him in, uninvited. He opened the shades, lighting the room, and the dome of his head shone under his thin hair.

"You're World War's boy? . . ."

"Yessir," my brother said, still standing.

He went to his desk and sat down. "Gone to work for the competition," he said, and shook his head. He opened his desk drawer and stared inside.

"How is your daddy?"

"He's fine," Ward said.

Mr. Ellison closed the drawer and leaned back in his chair, smiling. "The most contrary man in Moat County," he said in an admiring way. Ward did not reply to that, and Mr. Ellison sat up, ready to do business.

"What may I do for you gentlemen today?" he said.

And my brother told him we were in town looking into the murder of Thurmond Call and the conviction of Hillary Van Wetter for the crime. He said, "There was some physical evidence that was lost. . . ."

Mr. Ellison nodded, as if he knew everything Ward was going to say. As if we were all in agreement. "Yes, there was," he said.

"Significant evidence . . ."

"Yessir," Mr. Ellison said. The room went quiet.

"We were wondering," my brother said, "what sort of explanation . . ."

Mr. Ellison was shaking his head. "There is no explanation," he said, "unless you ever been in a situation where your life was endangered. Unless you ever felt an attachment to someone who was murdered. That's the only explanation, that our officers are human."

My brother sat still and waited. Mr. Ellison looked at him, then turned for a moment and stared at me. "I don't believe I caught your name," he said.

"Jack James," I said, and he smiled again.

"The swimmer," he said, and I didn't know if he was talking about the University of Florida or what happened on the beach up in St. Augustine. He looked at us both, a wax smile fastened to his face.

"You going into the family business too?" he said. "World War must be a very proud man."

He smiled, Ward kept himself still. "Mr. Ellison," my brother said, when enough time had passed, "what happened to that evidence?"

He shook his head. "I wisht I knew," he said.

"Mr. Van Wetter has told us the blood on his clothing was his own," Ward said. "That he'd cut himself on some equipment he was using that night."

Mr. Ellison nodded thoughtfully. "Mr. Van Wetter has been known to use his equipment at night before," he said, and then paused while that sank in. "Cut a deputy's thumb off, as I remember." There was another pause, a long one. "Over a traffic ticket," he said.

And then he looked at his own hand and dropped his thumb until it was pressed against the palm. "A man can't do much without his thumb," he said. "It's what separates us from the primates."

"Is there a deputy we could talk to?" Ward asked. "Somebody who was out there when they arrested him?"

Mr. Ellison was still looking at his hand, working the fingers. "A little thing like holding your wife's titty . . ." He stopped moving his fingers and looked up suddenly, directly at my brother. "You married yet, Mr. James?"

Ward shook his head no.

Mr. Ellison looked back at his hand. "A little thing like that, you can't do it." He put his hand on his own chest and tried to cup the breast through the shirt. "You can poke a titty," he said, looking up, "but they don't like that, you know. They like to have them held. You go poking around all the time, before long they won't allow you to touch them at all."

He looked up again and smiled.

"Can I talk to somebody who was there?" Ward said.

"You can talk to whoever you want as long as they'll talk to you," he said. "But when you talk about Mr. Van Wetter, keep in mind what it'd be like, not to be able to hold your own wife's titty in your hand."

A moment passed and he said, "Oh, that's right. You aren't married." He seemed to be teasing him.

We went from Mr. Ellison's office back to the dispatch room, passing two deputies in the hallway, and arrived finally in front of a belligerent, overweight woman sitting at a desk reading a copy of *Motor Trend* magazine and wearing a name tag on her blouse that said, "Patty." There was a swinging door next to the desk, no more than waist high, and a sign attached to it prohibiting entrance to anyone not employed by the sheriff's department.

My brother and I stood in front of her a long time, waiting to be acknowledged. When she did that finally, looking up, she did not speak or smile. She only waited. "My name is Ward James," my brother said. "I was talking with Mr. Ellison, and he suggested that I come down here."

She took us in a moment longer, then went back to her magazine. I saw a deputy then, thirty feet behind her, leaning across his desk to watch her work us over. The deputy was smiling.

"Excuse me," Ward said, and she looked up again. "I would like to speak with any of these deputies. . . ." He took a pen from his pocket and wrote down the names of five deputies who were at Hillary Van Wetter's house the night he was arrested. He slid the paper across the desk. She looked at it a moment, then looked at us, and then picked up the paper and dropped it into the wastebasket.

Someone behind her laughed. She went back to the magazine, aware that her performance was being watched and appreciated.

I turned away, wanting to get out of the room, but Ward stayed where he was. She looked at *Motor Trend,* he waited. Minutes passed, and she reached into her purse for a pack of cigarettes, looking up once at Ward, then lighting a match and going back to the magazine. She had been on the same page a long time. Half a dozen deputies were watching now, waiting to see how it would come out.

She shifted in her chair and stole another look, and then suddenly slammed the magazine down on the desk in front of her, stood up, and walked off into the back. There was some laughing back there, and then it was quiet. No one came to the front to take her place, and the deputies seemed to have gone back to wherever they had been before.

"Are we just going to stand here?" I said.

He didn't answer.

"They aren't going to talk to us," I said. And he nodded at that, but he didn't move.

The woman returned perhaps fifteen minutes later. She did not seem surprised to see us still standing in front of her desk. "Is there something else?" she said.

My brother reached across her desk to a pile of paper, took one of the sheets, and wrote down the names again. He pushed the paper toward her without saying a word. She looked at it and then at him.

"You're slow, aren't you?" she said, sounding concerned, and dropped that paper into the wastebasket too. She looked at me then, as if I might be a faster study. "I can do this all day," she said.

But she couldn't. In another minute or two she stood up again and walked into the back. There were no chairs, so we stood in front of the desk. Half an hour passed, and a deputy took her place. He nodded at my brother and sat down at the woman's desk.

"May I help you?" he said.

My brother leaned over the rail and reached into the woman's wastebasket for one of the pieces of paper. He put it on the desk in front of the deputy. "I would like to speak to these men," he said.

The deputy looked at the list a moment, then slowly shook his head. "These officers don't have time to speak to you, sir," he said. "They're busy with their duties."

"When would they have time?" Ward said.

The deputy shook his head. "You might come back tomorrow. . . ."

He waited.

"Are you one of these officers?" Ward said. The deputy looked at the list as if he couldn't remember. There was a place above his pocket where the color was brighter blue than the rest of the shirt, and there was a hole in the material there. He'd taken off his name tag.

"I don't see where that's got anything to do with it," he said. "I told you we don't have time for you now."

"Are you one of these officers?" my brother said, sounding patient, as if it were the first time he'd asked.

"What I am," he said, "is the one telling you to cease and desist and allow us to get back to work."

My brother looked at the list of deputies. "Which one are you?" he said. And a murderous looked passed over the deputy's face.

"You know, there's some people," he said finally, "they won't let you treat them well."

Ward nodded at that, as if it were a compliment.

The deputy left and we stood in the room until four-thirty, when the cleaning lady came in and said that the place was closed.

"Thank you," my brother said, and we walked past her out the door, and then, in the hallway, I could hear people cheering. I went back to the door and saw that the deputies had come out from the back to applaud the cleaning woman. She was still in the middle of the floor, holding a mop that was set into a bucket on wheels, looking embarrassed but not entirely surprised at the sudden attention. As if it was about time.

We drove through Lately at quitting time. Citizens were coming out of their stores and offices, locking the doors behind them. Schoolchildren were on the street too, some of them smoking cigarettes and eating candy bars at the same time. The older ones, from high school, hung out of the windows of their fathers' four-door sedans, the drivers tearing up the engines, revving them until the noise was like a scream.

Ward and I had watched the same ceremony in Thorn, but had never had any part in it.

"Imagine what it would be like," my father would say from time to time, "if your name appeared in a police story in your father's own newspaper."

He was telling us, in his way, that there would be no favoritism; but we already knew that. Ward and I grew up in a house where my father's principles were a regular topic of conversation, and we were often asked to imagine the embarrassment which would be visited on the family in the event either of our names had to be put in the newspaper.

Ward seemed better at imagining the embarrassment than I was; it threatened him in ways I didn't understand.

At some point, of course, my father realized that there was no need to warn my brother to stay out of trouble. And perhaps by then, he was already beginning to worry that Ward had never been in any trouble; that he hadn't any friends to get into trouble with.

I looked at him now, wondering if he thought of Yardley Acheman as a friend. "Another fine day in the newspaper business," I said.

He shrugged. "It wasn't bad."

I stopped the car and let a woman pushing a baby carriage cross in front of us. Behind me, a load of kids in a Plymouth honked, and the woman jumped at the noise, looked up into the front seat of the car I was driving, frightened, thinking that I'd honked, and then hurried across to the other side. I had never seen her before and never expected to see her again, but I thought of getting out of the car and telling her that it was the driver behind me who had blown the horn.

I was triggering a hundred misunderstandings a day, and I couldn't seem to straighten out the important ones without straightening out them all.

"I don't see what it accomplished," I said, speaking again of the afternoon at the sheriff's department.

"We were there," he said.

"That's all?"

"It's enough," he said.

And I saw it then, clearly, that he found something in the waiting—or the shunning—pleasurable.

"We're going back?" I said.

He was looking out the window when he answered. "Of course," he said.

❑

We stood in the sheriff's department all the next day, and the day after. The woman behind the desk did not speak to us except to tell us to move out of the way when other visitors came through the door.

"Please move to the side of the room and do not interfere with the orderly business of this office," she would say. Words a county lawyer had given her, probably, the groundwork for our arrest if we failed to get out of the way.

But my brother and I moved politely to the side of the little room and listened as stories of stray dogs and dead chickens or children who did not belong in neighbors' yards were laid out across her desk.

"Do you wish to fill out a complaint?" she would say, cutting off their stories. And those words seemed to make them afraid.

"We don't want to get nobody in trouble. . . ."

"There is nothing this office can do until a complaint has been filed. . . ."

And then, more often than not, the visitors would leave, nodding to my brother and me politely on their way out. Thinking that we were a different kind of people, that we were not afraid of the law.

Still, none of the deputies on my brother's list had come out of the office behind the desk to speak to us, not even to say they wouldn't speak to us. My brother was not discouraged. If we were constant enough, things would fall into their natural place.

❑

WE ARRIVED AT OUR OFFICE late in the afternoon and found Yardley Acheman sitting in the stuffed chair against the wall and Charlotte sitting in front of him on his desk. From there, he could see up her skirt.

They were both drinking beer, and when Yardley saw us, he lifted his in a toast.

She smiled at us, wiping her mouth with the back of her hand. Something had been going on in the room before they heard us on the stairs, and I felt a familiar, quick heat in my face. "The guy who bought the lawn," he said, "I found him."

He walked past her then without a glance, as if she were a panhandler on the street asking for his change, and she saw that she'd been discarded.

He picked up a reporter's notebook, opened it to the front page, and found his notes.

"He remembered them," he said. "They showed up at six in the morning in a truck. He said he looked at the two of them and what they had and thought they'd stolen it from a cemetery."

My brother nodded slowly. "You showed him pictures?"

"Of Hillary. That's when he remembered thinking they'd robbed a graveyard."

"And he bought it anyway. . . ."

Charlotte got off the desk and walked to the window. She crossed her arms under her breasts, as if she were cold, and stared outside.

"He doesn't want to be connected to this in any way," Yardley Acheman said. "He doesn't want to talk to anyone else about it." He glanced quickly at Charlotte, who was still facing the window, and then at my brother. "You can't blame him for that," he said.

"Who is he?" Ward said.

Yardley scratched his chest. "This is the hard part," he said. "The only way the guy would talk to me, I had to promise to keep him completely anonymous."

Ward nodded. "What's his name?" he said.

"It's *completely* anonymous," Yardley said. "I had to give him my word. He's in a position to get some work with the state. . . ."

"But who is he?"

Yardley Acheman shook his head. "You're not listening," he said. "I had to make a promise to get him to talk to me, and I can't break it. There's a principle here. . . ."

Ward looked at him a long time. I do not know if he believed him or not.

"It was the only way it could be done," Yardley said. "I can only tell you he exists, and he recognized the picture."

"How did you find him?" Ward said.

"The hard way," he said. "We went through the county records."

Ward thought it over.

Yardley Acheman shrugged. "It's a matter of trust," he said. "I can't violate that."

Charlotte turned suddenly away from the window and

walked, without a word, out of the office and down the stairs, as if she had just realized she didn't belong in the room.

❑

IT WAS NECESSARY to see Hillary Van Wetter again before a story could be written. Charlotte and Yardley Acheman, for reasons that were not clearly drawn, were no longer speaking to each other, and she sat next to me in the car on the drive to the prison, with Yardley and my brother in back. She wore a blue dress and did not seem as concerned with her appearance as she had on the earlier visits. She looked in the mirror only once, after we had stopped in the parking lot.

What had happened in Daytona Beach had taken the excitement out of things for her, I think, and she was left with a situation which, while of her own making, bore no resemblance to the one she had envisioned.

❑

HILLARY VAN WETTER WAS led into the interview room in leg irons and handcuffs and pushed down into his chair. The bruises under his eyes had faded since the last visit.

The instructions were familiar now, mindless and repetitive. The smell of the place, the way words sounded in this room—it was all the same. Charlotte crossed her legs, showing some thigh, and lit a cigarette. And in some way that was the same now too. Hillary studied her a moment and then looked directly at Yardley Acheman.

He knew.

She smiled at him, unsure of herself.

"Don't you look nice," he said, sounding too polite, as if he were talking to tourists.

"Thank you," she said, and crossed her legs the other way. She felt his eyes and tried to hide from them. Every move she made to hide herself seemed to please him more.

"We found the man in Ormond Beach," Yardley Acheman said, and Hillary turned to him, nodding as if he were interested.

"The one who bought the sod," he said.

"That's good news," Hillary said, smiles all around.

"He made a note of the day and the amount he paid," Yardley said. "He remembered you from your picture."

Hillary looked back at Charlotte, and from her to Yardley Acheman.

"That's good," he said again, without looking at Ward, and then he moved his gaze to Charlotte. "These newspaper boys done me a big favor, wouldn't you say?" She nodded back, trying to diagnose the nature of the change that had come over him.

"It isn't done yet," Ward said.

"They're going to let me loose now," he said.

Charlotte had begun to nod again when my brother said, "We don't decide that."

For a moment the smile disappeared from Hillary's face, but he was acting. "I know that," he said, and then the smile reappeared, narrower than it had been before. He looked right at Charlotte and spoke to my brother. "I know your limitations," he said, and she blushed.

"Open your mouth a little bit," he said to her.

She looked at the rest of us, then back at him. She shook her head no. "That's private," she said, almost whispering.

My brother said, "There's one thing we need."

"What thing is that?" Still looking at her.

Ward didn't answer at first, and Hillary said, "What is it?" sounding suddenly angry. Never taking his eyes off her.

"To speak with your uncle again," Ward said.

Hillary turned slowly back to my brother. "I expect that's up to him," he said.

"It could help if you give us a letter to take to him," my brother said.

"A letter," he said.

"A note, something to tell him to trust us."

On that word, Hillary turned and stared at Yardley Acheman. "What do you think about that?" he said. "You think I ought to tell my uncle to trust you?"

Yardley Acheman didn't move. The smile spread across Hillary Van Wetter's face again. His teeth were yellow, the whole place smelled of disinfectant. A long ways off a man yelled, and the sound was hollow as it echoed down the halls. A light shone through the small window in the door and particles of dust hung in the air.

I stood up, wanting to move, and walked from one side of the room to the other, passing within a foot or two of Hillary's chair. He smelled like disinfectant too. The door opened and the guard leaned in with his head.

"No contact with the prisoner," he said. "Do not pass on any materials, written or otherwise."

"Mr. Van Wetter is going to need a pen and paper," my brother said.

"You'll have to see the warden," the guard said and closed the door.

When he was gone Hillary said, "The truth is, Tyree ain't much of a reader anyway."

My brother looked at him, becoming impatient. "He'd recognize your handwriting."

Hillary thought it over. "Numbers," he said. "He can read numbers."

"Is there something we can tell him," Ward said, "he'd know it came from you?"

Hillary shook his head as if he didn't understand.

"A story, something that happened, so he'd know you want him to talk to us."

"A story that happened," Hillary thought, and he stroked his chin. The chain holding his wrists rattled once against the handcuffs and then was quiet. "There was a girl," he said, "something happened to her." He waited, but that seemed to be as much about it as he wanted to say.

"What girl?" my brother said.

"Lawrence's wife," he said. "A girl from out of the family, he'll remember her."

"Lawrence," my brother said, and Hillary nodded. "What happened to her?"

Another pause. "Went away," he said. He stared at his legs, studying the irons attached to his ankles.

Ward looked toward the door. "They can't hear what you tell us," he said.

"Sometimes you don't have to hear a certain thing to know it."

"Prisoners talk to their attorneys in here. . . ."

"Attorneys," Hillary said, and as I watched, his mood turned dark, or perhaps was only revealed. "It comes right down to it, they can't do nothing more than paperboys. Come right down to it, the only ones can do something in here is the man, and he can do whatever his whimsy is. They ain't nothing to stop him."

In the corner, Yardley Acheman closed his eyes and dropped his head into his hands, as if he'd had as much of this as he could stand. Charlotte lit another cigarette and leaned toward Hillary, her elbow resting on her knee. He could see some of her chest.

"Look at it this way," Yardley Acheman said, "what do you have to lose?"

Hillary turned slowly to the corner where Yardley was sitting.

"What are they going to do, electrocute you twice?"

"Shut up," Charlotte said, and that made Yardley smile. He shook his head, as if he would never understand women, and then he shut up.

"It doesn't have to be about the woman," my brother said. "Just something I can tell your uncle, he'll know we have your confidence. . . ."

"My confidence . . ." He played with that a little while.

"What happened to her?" my brother said. "Lawrence's wife . . ."

Charlotte dropped the cigarette she'd just lit onto the floor and ground it out with the tip of her shoe. She didn't want to hear what happened to Lawrence's wife, but she said, "Tell the damn story," and for that moment, she and Hillary already could have been married.

"There ain't a story, the way you tell it and somebody listens," Hillary said. "The girl's gone."

"Gone where?"

"She was from the outside; one day she was there, the next day she was gone."

"Did she go back to her family?" my brother said, and Hillary began smiling again.

"I wouldn't think so, no sir," he said. Hillary stared at my brother and then finally turned himself back to Charlotte, and looked at her as he spoke to Ward.

He said, "I would think she went back whence she came."

He knew she had been with Yardley Acheman. He was telling her he knew.

"Ashes to ashes," he said. And then he smiled at her in the way he was smiling earlier. "Tell Tyree," he said, "ashes to ashes. See what he thinks about that."

❏

MY BROTHER AND YARDLEY ACHEMAN got in the backseat again on the ride to Lately, Charlotte was in front with me. She'd said good-bye to Hillary when the guard came for him and hadn't spoken since. She hadn't even waited at the car door for someone to open it.

"Ashes to ashes," Yardley said, "what a subtle guy."

It was humid, and the air conditioner was dripping on Charlotte's shoes. She was staring straight ahead, as if she were fixed on something a long ways down the road.

"What is that supposed to mean?" she said, sounding tired.

"Worst case," Yardley said, "they ate her."

Charlotte put a cigarette in her lips and punched in the lighter on the dashboard. After it popped back out, Yardley Acheman said, "Not that it makes any difference."

Charlotte turned suddenly and stared at him over the seat back. Her shirt pressed against her side and took the shape of her breast. "Will you shut up?" she said.

"You don't mind, we're trying to figure something out back here," Yardley Acheman said, and he sounded hurt, the same tone he took when he argued with his fiancée on the telephone. "Trying to save your intended from the state of Florida's electric chair."

"Ashes to ashes doesn't mean they killed a girl," Charlotte said, and she was furious, "it's biblical."

Yardley laughed out loud.

She turned back around, disgusted with everyone in the car. "Hillary was right about you," she said, meaning that for all of us. "You've got no empathy."

"Hillary said that?" Yardley was playing with her now.

"In so many words." And then she closed her eyes, exhausted. "Everybody in the world isn't stupid, Yardley," she said. "And even if that was true, it wouldn't make them any smarter, working for the *Miami Times*."

Yardley laughed again, and she seemed discouraged.

"You see right there, that's what I'm talking about," she said. "I'd rather have one compassionate person on my side than all of you put together."

Yardley was laughing again; feeding off her.

"I'll tell you something else," she said, "I'd feel sorry for your fiancée, but I think you deserve each other."

❑

WE HAD TO GO BACK into the wetlands. Yardley did not want to come along, and pretended he'd hurt his ankle. "I can write it without going out there," he said, but my brother shook his head.

"You better come," he said.

"I sprained my ankle."

"You need to see it," Ward said, and in the end Yardley gave in, his limp becoming more exaggerated as we got to the marina where we rented the boat. Even Ward did not want to try walking back in.

We followed the west bank of the river, moving slowly, looking for the television antenna in the tree line. The boat was powered by a small outboard which coughed and stopped at low speeds, and I sat at the throttle nursing the choke to keep it going. There was something in the quiet when the engine quit that none of us liked.

Yardley Acheman was in front, holding on to the sides with both hands. My brother sat in the middle, studying the shoreline. World War had taken us fishing on this part of the river when we were young, pointing out the cabins in the trees and recalling the stories he knew of the people who lived in them, the Van Wetters, who in his stories were pioneers. And those stories, along with the color of the water and the smell of the air and the vegetation along the bank, were married in me to the sight of a river bass slapping the bottom of the boat, sometimes leaving its blood on our legs.

And to the sight of a dozen bass a foot or two under water, hanging from a single piece of nylon cord hung over the side, some of them still alive, their white bellies glowing through the brown water.

My father did not make fishermen of his sons, and by the time I was ten or eleven, he had stopped trying.

It seemed to me that we had come too far down the river. "We must have missed it," I said, and began a slow circle back into the current.

"A little farther," Ward said.

I said we were too far south.

"Keep on a little farther," he said, and looked at his watch. I did not like to be told where to steer the boat, but Ward had a good compass in his head, and mine always told me to circle.

Still, it seemed to me that matters of the water, and driving, were my area.

Yardley Acheman turned around without letting go of the sides. "We're lost, right?"

Ward didn't answer him.

I steered in closer to the shoreline and the boat moved in the shadows of the trees growing out of the water. Some of the branches were so low I could have touched them without standing up. The last time my father took me fishing, a moccasin dropped out of one of those branches onto the floor of the boat, and he grabbed it by the tail while I was still realizing what it was, and tossed it into the air. The snake straightened to its full length, wheeling through the sky, and my father stood in the rocking boat, watching it, gradually smiling as he realized what he had done.

"Don't tell your mother," he said, but it was the first thing out of his mouth when he saw her at home.

❑

WE SAW THE CHICKEN before we saw the antenna. It was tethered by one leg to a stake not far from the water's edge, left there as bait. The other chickens kept their distance. I took us in to the shore and lifted the engine out of the water a moment before we landed. I got out and pulled our boat next to the one already in the yard. Yardley waited until I'd stopped to get out, holding on to the sides until both his feet were down on solid ground.

My brother walked ahead, around to the front of the place, carrying a picnic cooler. He set the cooler on the porch and knocked on the door. "Mr. Van Wetter?"

The door opened before he could knock again, and the young man who had been there before stood in the doorway, looking at us. First my brother, then me, then Yardley Acheman. He spent longer on Yardley than either of us.

"Is your father in?" Ward said.

The man in the door moved to one side and the old man appeared, naked below the waist. "Y'all brought reenforcements," he said, looking at Yardley. Yardley would not meet his eyes. He looked around the yard instead and found himself staring at the alligator skins drying on the clothesline.

"This is my associate Yardley Acheman," my brother said. "He is also with the newspaper."

The old man stepped out onto the porch. His balls hung like an old dog's. My brother took off the top of the cooler.

"He's pretty, ain't he?" the old man said.

"Ice cream," Ward said, and the old man looked inside and then cocked his head as if to reconsider us, "strawberry and vanilla."

"You want what you want, don't you?" the old man said.

"Yessir," my brother said. He took out one of the cartons and handed it to the old man, then took out the other and offered it to the man still standing in the door. When he didn't take it, Ward set it back in the cooler. The old man opened the carton and looked at the ice cream.

"Go get us some spoons," he said.

The man leaned back into the house and shouted, "Hattie, get some clothes on and bring us spoons," and then resumed his posture in the door.

"My associate talked to a man down in Ormond Beach," my brother said.

The younger man reconsidered the strawberry when the woman came out with the spoons, ate most of it and then passed the dripping container on to her. She did not speak once.

The old man was eating the vanilla, sitting on the ground, still naked below the waist. "That so?" he said.

"Yessir," my brother said. "He recognized a picture of Hillary, had it written down in his books when he bought the sod from him."

The old man nodded and stuck his spoon into the ice cream. "That was convenient," he said.

The woman's chin was sticky with ice cream, and there were specks of dirt in it. She wiped at her mouth with the back of her wrist.

"He said there were two of you," my brother said.

"You didn't show him no picture of me, did you?"

"I don't have a picture of you."

"That's right," the old man said. "That's right."

"But it was you, wasn't it?" Ward said.

The old man smiled, not unkindly. "You want what you want, I'll say that." Then he looked up at Yardley, who was sitting on the step holding his ankle. "You hurt yourself on my property?" he said.

Yardley Acheman shook his head no. "It was before," he said.

"Good," the old man said. "You ain't going to get a lawyer and change your mind. . . ."

"It isn't that bad," Yardley said.

"I didn't think so," the old man said.

"You were with Hillary?" my brother asked.

"Hillary's in prison," the man said.

"Not for that," Ward said. "He's there for murder. If Thurmond Call was killed the night you two were in Ormond Beach stealing sod off the golf course . . ."

The woman brushed the hair back off her face and glanced quickly at her husband, then at the old man. I wondered if she belonged to them both.

"Let me ask you something," the old man said. "You in prison, how much difference does it make what you're in there for?"

153

"The statute of limitations . . ."

"You told me about your statues," the old man said. "What about this man that owns the golf course?"

My brother smiled at the question, as if he were relieved. "He was insured. You can't have a golf course without insurance. It's a long time ago, and he can't do anything about it anyway."

"He could come looking for me," the old man said. He glanced quickly at his son. "He could come looking for my family."

"It's a lot of years," Ward said. "He wouldn't do that."

"I would," the old man said.

The woman set the carton of strawberry on the ground. The old man took one last spoonful of the vanilla and handed her that carton too.

"It's your nephew's life," my brother said. "If we're going to do something, we have to do it."

"You push too hard," the old man said, not accusing him, just an observation.

"I don't know any other way to act." Ward said, and the apology in those words was not lost on the old man. He looked at Ward and smiled.

"We're all born a certain way, aren't we?"

The other man moved forward a little, blocking his wife from Yardley's view, and bore into him with his eyes. Yardley rolled down his sock to inspect his ankle. The old man leaned back and laced his fingers over his stomach.

"You don't talk," he said to me. "I can't decide out how you ended up with these two."

"We're brothers," I said, indicating Ward. Making sure he knew which one I meant.

The old man smiled at that and addressed Ward again. "They's always family hiding somewhere in the shadows, isn't there?"

Ward did not answer.

———

"I was with him," the old man said suddenly. "Dropped him off at home, the next time I went over there, he was in county jail for cutting open Sheriff Call."

It was quiet again, and then Ward said, "Thank you." He thought a moment and said, "What time would you—"

The old man interrupted him. "I've said as much about it as I'm going to," he said. "This is as far as I go."

He meant it, and there was nothing more to say. We stood up; the old man stood up with us. The other man sat where he was, glaring at Yardley Acheman.

"He didn't hurt himself that night, did he?" Ward said.

The old man closed his eyes, trying to remember. "Not that I remember," he said. "I sliced a toe half off, myself, trying to work in the dark."

"It bled?"

The old man looked at Ward as if he didn't understand the question. "Shit yes, it bled," he said. "We're mammals."

"You go to a hospital?"

The old man began to nod. "Just go in, the middle of the night, covered with dirt and tell them I cut myself in my sleep. . . ."

❑

WE PUT YARDLEY ACHEMAN back in the boat—he sat down facing the motor—and then pushed it into the water and got in ourselves. The woman came into my line of sight then, standing at the edge of the house for a second or two, the tip of her finger in her mouth, as if she did not want to let go of the taste of ice cream, and then there was a sound in the house, a squalling, and she looked that way and was gone. She had round shoulders and clear skin, and I wondered what she would have looked like in another place. I pulled the starter cord and the engine caught, sputtered, and then smoothed as I corrected the choke.

"Thank you," my brother said again.

The old man nodded and his son came to the edge of the water and stood next to him. Yardley sat backwards in the boat, clutching the sides, nervous even before we pushed it off into the water.

The old man smiled at him and said, "Hold on to that boat now."

❑

THE RIDE BACK TO the marina was faster than the ride down had been, partly because we weren't looking for the house in the trees along the bank, and partly because the river itself runs north, from the middle of the state to Jacksonville, where it empties into the ocean.

The engine was less erratic at the higher speed and the nose of the boat bounced against the plane of the river. There was a certain pleasure in holding the stick and in the smell of the engine and the feel of the water passing beneath my feet. Ward sat in front again, thinking about what the old man had said, in some way not satisfied with it, and Yardley held himself still, his eyes closed against nausea.

At the marina, he leaned over the side and vomited. My brother hardly seemed to notice. "The man in Ormond Beach," he said when Yardley had finished, "did he show you his records?"

Yardley nodded, as if he knew what Ward was asking, as if the question had been asked a hundred times before. "They were right there on his desk," he said.

"And he was sure about the date."

"He was sure about the date."

We left the boat and started back to the car; I could still feel the lift and fall of the water.

"He was absolutely sure," Yardley said again, as if saying it would make it so.

Neither of them spoke again until we were back in the car and pointed toward Lately. "Did you give him the date, or did he give it to you?" Ward said.

Yardley came up in his seat to get a closer look at my brother. "What's wrong with you?" he said.

Ward spoke more slowly. "Did you say to the man, 'Was it August fourteenth, nineteen sixty-five,' or did he look in his books and say the date to you?"

"What difference does it make?"

"It doesn't feel right," my brother said.

"Look," Yardley said, "I've been doing this a long time, and I know when something doesn't feel right as well as you do."

❑

"You know the trouble with you?" Yardley Acheman said.

We were back in the office and Ward was going over some of the notes he'd made in the car after one of the early visits to Starke. He was missing some scrap paper, a word or two on it that he couldn't remember.

Yardley was impatient to finish the story and get back to Miami. "You don't understand that you have to let go of it to get it done," he said.

My brother found the paper and set it carefully on his desk, uninterested in it now that it wasn't missing.

❑

That day or perhaps the next, Yardley Acheman called an editor in Miami and reported that he was ready to write the story, but Ward would not let it go.

I am not sure how Yardley Acheman presented the situation—he did not make the call from the office, at least not while my brother and I were there—but at the end of the week a man with a beard and eyeglasses half an inch thick appeared in our doorway, knocked once, and walked in.

My brother was sitting at his desk, going over the early court proceedings again, and Yardley was on the phone with his fiancée back in Miami. My brother stood up when he saw the man with the beard, and in doing that knocked over a bottle of Dr. Pepper, spilling some of it on the papers. He opened one of his drawers and found the shirt I'd borrowed from Yardley, which he'd subsequently refused to touch, and used it to blot the mess.

The editor—he was the Sunday editor, that was his title—was smiling, looking around, admiring the ambience. He went to the window and had a long stare at Lately while, on the other side of the room, Yardley Acheman was finishing up with his intended.

"Right," he said, "I got to go. Right. Not now . . . tonight, I'll call tonight. Yeah, me too, right . . ."

"What's that smell, onions?" the man from Miami said. He was older than Yardley Acheman, perhaps forty or fifty. He didn't look like he'd been out of his office in a long time.

"There's a grease shop downstairs," Yardley said. "The whole street smells like onions." He smelled his own arm. "It gets in your skin," he said.

The man from Miami opened his eyes wide at the news, as if he had never heard of such a thing, then looked over to my brother. "How are we coming?" he said.

"We're getting there," Ward said. He had finished blotting the papers and was sitting in his chair again, not trying to do any work.

The man from Miami sat down on the chair against the wall. He looked at me a moment, not knowing what I was doing there.

"How much longer do you think it might be?"

"Not too long," Ward said. "There's some things here I'm not satisfied with. . . ."

"You think a couple of days, a week?" he said.

"Until what?" Ward said.

"Till Yardley can start writing." He smiled, but there was an edge to it too.

My brother looked at Yardley Acheman, Yardley would not meet his eyes. "It's hard to put a time on it," Ward said.

"What's left to do?"

My brother shook his head.

"It sounds to me like you're ready now and just don't know it." The man from Miami paused and then he said, "I was the same way. I never wanted to let go of a story; I suppose that's how you end up in an office." He smiled at that, as if his own shortcomings amused him.

"I'm not comfortable yet," Ward said.

"I appreciate that," said the man from Miami. "It means you're a good reporter, it means you're cautious. But from what Yardley's told me, it looks like things have turned up as black-and-white as you ever find them."

"I don't know," Ward said.

"I know you don't," said the man from Miami. "But the thing is, you could stay here the rest of your life and still never be sure of every little detail. That isn't our job. Our job is to get as much of it right as we can, and get it in the newspaper."

Ward didn't say a thing.

"You're too valuable to be sitting out here in the middle of nowhere," he said. "There's other stories to write."

"I don't think this one's finished," Ward said.

"Yardley's satisfied," he said. Yardley Acheman nodded from behind his desk. "He's the one who's got to write it."

The air was suddenly heavy with the smell of onions. Things had been decided outside this room, away from my brother, and there was nothing he could do about it. He rubbed his eyes as if he had not slept in a long time and then looked at me. He seemed to be asking for help. I did not how to help him, I did not even know how to start.

"It isn't finished," he said again.

"It's going to take Yardley a while to write," the man said. His voice was reasonable and friendly. "You do what you need to do and he'll do what he needs to do, and one way or another, we'll get this thing in the paper."

And my brother didn't say anything more to the man from Miami, even when he told a story about the days when he was a reporter himself and how he had gotten so close to a story that he finally couldn't write it.

"That story," he said quietly, "won me the Pulitzer Prize."

The prize was the proof that he was right about my brother's story, and about anything else that came up, and he allowed a few seconds for the weight of his accomplishment to sink in. Then he said, "And if it wasn't for an editor kicking my ass to put it on paper, I'd probably still be sitting at my desk at the Broward County bureau of the *Miami Times*, trying to get it written."

The man patted Ward on the shoulder when he left, and then three of us were alone in the room.

"I just thought we needed a fresh perspective," Yardley Acheman said. "I didn't know he was going to come up here and start telling us what to do."

Ward nodded and stood up. He collected all the notes on his desk, all the transcripts and depositions, and walked across the room to Yardley Acheman and dropped them in front of him. He looked back at me a moment—I didn't know if he wanted me to come with him or leave him alone—and then walked out the door.

I stood up to follow him, and Yardley Acheman said something to me, thinking I would repeat it to Ward. "It had to be done," he said.

It occurred to me then that I had been in Lately too long. I had spent too much time staring at the people who lived here and too much time staring at Hillary Van Wetter in the visitors' room at Starke, and too much time staring at Charlotte Bless.

When I stared at something long enough, the lines blurred and I could no longer see it for what it was. One thing became another.

❏

My FATHER WAS RELIEVED at the news that Yardley Acheman was finally writing the story.

"So now it's time for Mr. Acheman to go to work," were the words he said, but my father didn't care if Yardley Acheman worked or not. He was satisfied that my brother had finished poking through Moat County.

"They'll be going back to Miami to write it," he said, asking me the question.

"I don't know," I said.

"There's no reason to stay up here," he said.

We were eating fried chicken and boiled potatoes, and he was into his second bottle of wine. My father watched me, his lips against the rim of the glass, waiting for me to agree with him, as if my agreement would make it so.

I found myself thinking of an afternoon not long after my mother left, my father walking into the kitchen while Anita Chester was boiling potatoes for dinner. He'd drunk three bottles of red wine, a glass at a time, and he put a fork into the boiling water, pulled out a whole, soft potato, and stuck it that way—whole—into his mouth.

He reeled backwards across the kitchen, reaching into his mouth, trying to take it out, falling across the table first and then through the screen door into the backyard.

Anita Chester followed him out, carrying a spatula, and stood over him in the yard. Unable to get the potato out, he finally chewed and swallowed it. "Mr. Ward," she said, "have you lost your mind?"

He looked up at her through tearing eyes, beginning to cough, and nodded that he had. She stared a moment longer and then turned and walked back into the house, as if rich white men confessed to her all the time.

I looked at him now and thought of him on his back in the yard. "Unless I miss my guess, Mr. Acheman isn't going to want to stay in Lately one hour longer than he has to," he said.

And that was true, but it was also true that he would stay in Lately if Ward did. He could not write a story without someone there to lead him through the parts that could be checked. He had no interest in facts. It was a shortcoming for a newspaperman, I suppose, but he never saw it himself.

To see certain things, you have to be lying on your back with tears in your eyes and a scalding potato in your mouth.

It's possible, I think, that you have to be hurt to see anything at all.

"Ward wants to satisfy himself about some things before he leaves," I said.

"I thought the story was ready to write."

My father refilled his glass. "It's ready to go or it isn't," he said.

I had not told him about the argument between Ward and Yardley Acheman, or about the visit from the Sunday editor from Miami. It seemed to me it was something Ward ought to tell him himself if he wanted him to know.

My father drank half of what was in the glass and relaxed. "So what do you think?"

"I don't know," I said.

"About the business," he said. "You've had a look, what do you think?"

"I don't think much one way or the other."

"It's better than driving a truck."

I said, "It's better than loading one."

And he looked at me and smiled. "We all have our own

speed," he said, meaning, I supposed, that Ward had never been expelled from the University of Florida. "One way or another, we do things when we're ready." He thought about something else for a moment, then looked at me and smiled again. A kind of peace had settled over him with the last bottle of wine. "Don't be so serious about everything, Jack," he said. "Your turn will come."

I said, "I do things when I have to," and that made him laugh, and I laughed with him. I'd had a few glasses of wine myself.

"Sometimes," he said, fondly, as if he were remembering a story, "the only way you find out you're ready is that when you have to be, you are."

I had another drink of the wine, and felt peaceful myself. "Can I tell you something?" I said.

"Anything."

"I don't know what you're talking about."

And that made him laugh too. "I'm talking about you," he said. "I'm talking about you."

But he wasn't.

He was still talking about handing his newspaper over to Ward.

❑

WE WENT TO DAYTONA BEACH, Ward and I and Charlotte. Yardley stayed in Lately with the Sunday editor to begin his writing. Ward told them he was going down for a look at the golf course, but his intention was to find Yardley's contractor for himself.

Yardley Acheman's interest, of course, was in the flow of his stories, in interpreting events, in exposing hypocrisy wherever he saw it, which is to say that it was not impossible that he had never found the builder at all. That he'd seen what he needed and made it up.

WE STAYED AT A HOTEL on the beach—my brother and I shared a room, Charlotte took another—and I lay awake and restless for an hour after Ward had fallen asleep, and finally got out of bed, being careful not to wake him because it was after midnight, and walked through the lobby and out onto the beach, passing the drunks and the lovers, almost stepping on a boy and a girl wrapped around each other, naked on a blanket.

She held on to his neck, holding him inside her, and followed me with her eyes as I passed.

An open bottle of liquor was stuck into the sand.

I swam out into the ocean. It was calm and the moon lay ahead of me on the water, and it was endless. I swam a long time and never felt the familiar weight of my arms and legs which signaled I was getting tired. I thought of the girl on the beach, holding on to the boy's neck in the dark, her cheek pressed into the side of his head as he worked himself in and out, watching me.

I would have liked someone to hold on to myself.

I had a thought then about my brother, and the way in which we were different. He would not have ached over a girl he had only glimpsed a moment, lying with someone else in the sand. There was nothing in Ward that attached itself easily. And then I was suddenly chilled, as if the thought had done it, and I stopped—there was nothing to prove that night, nothing to exhaust—and rolled over onto my back so that I could watch the moon as I swam back to Daytona Beach.

Why had he attached himself to Yardley Acheman?

❏

I CAME OUT OF the water shaking like a man with his finger in the light socket, and could not stop even when I got under the blankets back at the hotel. I got up finally and stood under hot water in the shower.

When I came out of the bathroom his eyes were open, and he could not go back to sleep. From my earliest memories, Ward was a light sleeper.

❏

WARD SPENT THE NEXT DAY trying to find the builder. I drove him from county offices to building sites, exhausting the contractors one by one who had been building condominiums in August of 1965.

At the end of the day he had not found the builder, and while it was possible that such a builder was no longer operating under the same name—several of the ones he found listed in the county's building permits could not be accounted for—or had left the business, such a possibility presented the question of how Yardley Acheman, who had no interest in facts and no talent for research, had found him when my brother couldn't.

Charlotte was no help, remembering only that she had other things on her mind at the time. "Handsome men are the worst," she said.

❏

WE STOPPED LOOKING late in the afternoon and went back to the hotel. At the desk, Ward paid for another room and gave me the key, without mentioning that I'd kept him up the night before.

A band was playing in the hotel bar that night, and the restaurant, which was adjacent to the bar, filled up with smoke and music and noise and people from the other room as we ate. I studied the girls carefully, looking for the one from the beach.

Charlotte was bored with Daytona Beach and the newspaper business, and wanted to go back to Lately. "How much is all this going to help him?" she said, speaking of Hillary.

My brother said, "It would help if we could find the man who bought the sod."

"Yardley already found him," she said, but it didn't sound as if she believed that either.

She put a cigarette into her lips and dropped her face into her hands to light the match, her hair falling over her hands, dangerously close to the flame. I have set my own hair on fire in restaurants, bending over a candle on the table, and it makes a horrible smell.

"We need to find him again," Ward said.

"Shit," she said. She was tired of stolen sod and contractors and of us, and she was tired of Yardley Acheman, but in a different way.

The cocktail waitress arrived after we'd eaten. She was dressed in a ruffled blouse and a black skirt that did not quite cover the bottom of her panties. I ordered a beer, Charlotte ordered a Cuba libre—pronouncing *Cuba* the way it is pronounced by the Cubans—and my brother, who did not ordinarily have a drink in bars, asked for a vodka and Coke.

I looked at him, wondering what he was doing, but his attention had strayed in the last few minutes and was now drawn to a table across the room where a couple of sailors, probably on leave from Jacksonville, were sitting with a middle-aged man who wore a bow tie. They were baby-faced boys, the sailors, one of them with a mustache.

The man in the bow tie was paying another waitress for their drinks, taking the money, one bill at a time, from his wallet.

❏

THE WAITRESS LEANED over me to set the glasses on the table, brushing my cheek with her skirt. Her perfume was bitter, mingling with Charlotte's. Ward finished his vodka before she could leave. He handed her the glass and asked for another. I had never seen my brother drink anything beyond a few beers.

"You must be thirsty," she said.

He did not answer, but continued to glance from time to time at the table and the two sailors. They were drinking rose-colored daiquiris. One of the sailors looked up and caught my brother staring.

Ward and the sailor looked at each other, and then the other sailor was looking at our table too. He picked up his glass, never taking his eyes off us, and finished everything that was in it. The hard knot in his throat moved as he swallowed.

Charlotte saw what was going on. "For Christ's sake," she said, "we're going to have a fight." I assumed she had been around fights before, and knew what she was talking about.

"There's no problem," my brother said. And he drank his next drink almost as quickly as he'd drunk the first, and ordered a third.

"I think maybe I remember where Yardley found that builder," Charlotte said, trying to pull him away from his drinking and staring. He nodded at her, as if he already knew they would find him. "I couldn't concentrate today," she said. "Emotionally, I'm wrung out."

Then she looked at me and shrugged. "Thinking too much about Hillary," she said. As if I were the one who would understand.

"What about him?" I said.

She said, "I don't know, he's just been on my mind." None of us spoke for a little while, and when I looked again the sailors were still fixed on our table. Staring at Charlotte now more than my brother or me, but it seemed they wanted us all, one way or another.

The man with them was talking, but they had all the drinks they wanted for now and had stopped listening.

"Maybe we ought to go somewhere else," I said.

Ward took his next drink off the waitress's tray and gave her a ten-dollar bill. Then he stood up, leaving her the change, and headed off toward the bathroom.

"He's sociable tonight," Charlotte said.

I said, "He isn't used to drinking like that."

She said, "Nobody's used to drinking like that," and we watched him pitch left and then right on his way over. The sailors had seen him staggering too, and then one of them stood up, not as tall as I'd thought, and came to the table. He stood over Charlotte, looking down her blouse.

"Your friend got a problem with us, momma?" he said.

The other sailor was smiling now, watching everything this one did. Somewhere along the line he had lost a front tooth.

The man in the bow tie stopped talking, stirred by the possibility of violence.

"Nobody's got a problem but you, asshole," Charlotte said.

"It looked to me like he's got a problem," the sailor said, and now he looked at me.

I shook my head. The sailor frightened me. He rested a hand on the table and leaned closer, and the table moved under his weight. He moved his face in front of mine, a foot away, then slowly turned and looked at Charlotte and smiled.

"What do you think?" he said to her. "Your friends got a problem with me? Maybe they got a problem with each other, because, you know, they look like a couple of dick suckers. We got one over at our table too, maybe we ought to work out a trade."

"They're brothers," she said, and then, looking him over, she said, "and I think you've all got problems." A moment passed and she said, "You're all assholes."

Meaning men.

It was a voice I'd heard before. She got down on one of us, she got down on us all. The sailor continued to stare at her, continued to smile. "My friend and I got a bet," he said, "are you over fifty."

And he laughed at what he'd said, and then turned his head violently away and was suddenly so close to my face I couldn't make out his features. I jumped at the motion.

"What about that?" he said. "You think we're assholes too?" His breath smelled of strawberries and rum.

I did not answer.

"You don't say much, do you?" the sailor said. He stood up, looking us over. "One of them runs, one of them won't talk." He looked back at Charlotte and said, "You're a very lucky old woman."

"And you're an asshole," she said, and finished her drink. And then, when the sailor had left the table and gone back to be with his friend and the dick sucker, she looked at me and said, "Where's Hillary when you need him?"

❑

I WENT LOOKING FOR my brother. It was more what Charlotte had said than what the sailor had said, but I was suddenly ashamed, knowing that something had been taken away from me, in public, in front of her.

I walked past their table, brushing the one who had spoken to us, but he was occupied with the third man and did not seem to notice. He was asking the man for money.

"Come on, Freddie," he said. "You told us we was going to have a good time."

In the bathroom men and women were standing at the mirror, and some of them were smoking marijuana. A woman was on her knees behind the door of a toilet stall, her shoeless feet and part of her lower legs sticking out into the room. Runs in her stockings.

The bathroom was more crowded than the bar, and

warmer. I found Ward at the far end, combing his hair in front of a mirror, a sight that struck me as humorous.

❑

CHARLOTTE WAS TIRED, and I walked her back to her room, neither of us speaking. She kissed me on the cheek in the hall, and I went to the room Ward had gotten for me. My brother had stayed at the bar, drinking Scotch and Cokes.

I slipped toward sleep, thinking of the sailor, imagining that I'd stood up and choked him with a headlock. I wondered what Charlotte would have thought of that, and then I could see it all clearly. She would have thought we were all assholes.

I could have choked him, though, I was stronger than he was, and I'd known that even as I'd felt myself shaking because I was afraid.

I thought of Ward and how quickly he'd found the sailors staring at us. I wondered what sort of thoughts went through his head when he drank.

I lay in bed, thinking of my brother driving Yardley Acheman's car across Alligator Alley at 103 miles an hour.

❑

CHARLOTTE WAS POUNDING the door, calling to me from the other side of my sleep, something in her voice I hadn't heard before. I got out of bed in my underwear and knocked over a beer on the table, looking for the light.

The pounding shook the room. "Jack," she said. "Jack, get up." A harsh whisper.

I walked to the door in the dark, stepping into the beer I'd spilled, caught again for a moment between places, not knowing which one was real.

I opened the door and the room flooded with light. She stood in the middle of it, wearing a terry cloth robe. Her hair was pulled away from her face and held there by a rubber band, I think, and what fell across her shoulders was tangled in a way I'd never seen it, not even driving home from Starke with the windows down. She smelled of sleep.

It came to me that she would not like it when she took the compact out of her purse and looked in the mirror.

"Something's going on in Ward's room," she said. And I understood then, and I was awake.

The first rooms we'd taken adjoined each other; the new one—mine—was at the far end of the hall. I went past her, and out the door.

"I think they're killing him," she said behind me, trying to keep up. I turned to look at her.

"Who?"

"The sailors," she said. "I think it's the sailors."

My foot hit a tray of dirty dishes set outside a door for room service to pick up, scattering glasses and French fries across the carpet. I slipped, started to fall, and then got myself upright again and ran in earnest.

I lost the sound of her steps behind me, lost them in the sound of my own steps, and then suddenly realized I didn't know one room from another. His was near the lobby, I remembered that from the night before, walking up the air-conditioned hallway in my bathing suit. I slowed, looking at doors, and thought I heard the sailors. I stopped, shaking with fear, listening.

It was nothing hurried or sharp, just the noise of a beating, evenly spaced. Blunt. A few words between them as they worked.

I threw myself into the door. It held, but the spot where I'd hit it splintered and took the shape of my shoulder.

The noise inside stopped, and then was replaced by a different sound. This one coming out of Ward. It was not a moan or a cry, it was almost as if he were trying to talk.

I backed up and hit the door again, as frightened as I have

ever been. And then I heard Charlotte behind me, the catch in her breathing, the urgency of it, and as I turned to see her the door in front of me came open and one of them stood in the threshold, a bottle in his hand, blood all over the front of his shirt.

Behind him, on the floor, was my brother. He was naked and his eye was swollen shut and he was hobbled in some way, and when he tried to push himself up off the floor a line of blood followed him up, as if it were elastic, and then pulled him back down.

I was looking at my brother when the sailor hit me in the forehead with the bottle, and for a little while things went black.

When the light came back, they were running toward the far end of the hall, back in the direction of the room I had left. An Exit sign glowed from the ceiling. Charlotte was chasing them up the corridor, screaming words that did not make sense to me. She stopped to pick up a plate and threw it just before they hit the exit, briefly setting off the alarm. Doors along the hallway opened a few inches and then shut.

I got to my feet, suddenly nauseated, and walked into my brother's room. He was still on the floor. I put my arm under his chest, feeling the blood on his skin. It was drying now and sticky, and I lifted him off the floor. I carried him like that, facedown, toward the bed. A drop of fresh blood splattered against my foot.

The covers were torn from the bed, and one of the sheets had been ripped into smaller pieces and lay on the floor near the far chair, still tied in knots. They had used the strips of sheet to tie him. He moved in my arms and then went limp.

I laid him carefully on the bed, first his head, which hung half a foot lower than his body, as if his neck were broken, and then the rest. He coughed and tried to speak, a wet noise that fell off his lips like the blood.

I rolled him onto his back and saw the sweep of the beating. His teeth in front were sheared at the gums, the cartilage of his nose had been flattened and moved sideways and lay under his left eye. The eyes were both closed, swollen shut, one of them strangely out of place.

In some unexplainable way, I knew he had lost the eye.

There were marks over his chest and stomach, and on his arms, where he had tried to fend them off, and all around the groin. Most of these marks were red, but some—the ones where he had been stomped—were raised and dark.

I did not know where to start.

She came into the room a moment later and covered her mouth.

I do not know if it was the sight of her or of my brother, or—more likely—if it was the bottle which had slammed into my forehead, but I was sick. I walked into the bathroom and drank cold water from the faucet and then threw up in the sink. When I came back into the room, she was sitting with him, holding his hand. She had not tried to clean up the blood on his face. She sat still, holding his hand, and that was as much as either of us could do.

"I called the front desk," she said. "The ambulance ought to be here soon."

I picked up what was left of the sheet off the floor and covered him. "What happened?" I said.

"I don't know," she said. "I heard it through the wall, one of them screaming, your brother begging them . . ."

"Begging them?"

"Begging," she said again, "just begging."

He stirred under the sheet, and turned his head on the pillow.

"It must have lasted a long time," I said, and a moment later my eyes teared, and then the room began to spin. I went back into the bathroom and drank more water from the tap. I looked at myself in the mirror, and the place where I'd taken the bottle was swelling up into my hairline.

Then I stepped back into the room itself, and the place was somehow museumlike. Scattered furniture and bedclothes, blood soaking into the carpet. Something had happened, but it was quiet now, completely still. My brother's head rolled toward the far wall, and I could no longer see his face.

"They'll be here any minute," she said. I didn't know which one of us she was talking to.

"How long did it last?" I said. I could not dislodge the picture of my brother begging.

"Not too long," she said.

I needed to know it hadn't been long.

The curtains were torn off the windows, and I noticed there were lights in the parking lot. Some of them belonged to the police. My brother stirred again—it was as if he could not stay still—and his head moved back until I could see his expression. I don't know how with all the damage. Something strained, then relaxed.

"Any minute," she said.

I thought of trying to dress him, to make what had happened here look like something that was not as bad.

❑

THE POLICE CAUGHT ONE of the sailors in the parking lot, hiding in the backseat of a car that belonged to the man who had been with them in the bar. The other sailor had run out to the beach, and the police had chased him a minute or two and then given up, knowing they could get his name from the one they had.

"Mr. James," one of the policemen said to my brother, "Mr. Olson here says you lured him and his friend up into your hotel room and tried to engage them in sexual activity."

Mr. Olson was the sailor who had come to the table. He was standing between the policemen in the doorway, his hands were cuffed behind him.

174

"Mr. James?" the policeman said. There were ambulance attendants in the room, but neither of them had touched Ward. He was still naked.

"This asshole and his friend followed him out of the bar," Charlotte said.

The sailor looked at her quickly and said, "That's a goddamn lie," and the policeman standing at the door, who'd had trouble with sailors who came down from Jacksonville before, hit the sailor with his nightstick, catching him just under the ear. The sailor dropped to his knees, holding his head.

Charlotte smiled.

"We didn't follow the faggot anywhere," the sailor said. "He invited us to his room."

The first policeman looked at my brother in a sad way. "Is that true, Mr. James?" he said. "Are you a faggot?"

"He's no faggot," I said, looking at the sailor.

"Who are you?" the policeman said.

"Another one," said the sailor. And then the sailor laughed, but he looked at me strangely, as if something were out of place. I turned to the policeman. "I'm his brother," I said.

The policeman nodded. "So what's he doing naked?"

"It's his room, maybe he was taking a shower. Maybe he was in bed."

The sailor laughed again, and got to his feet. There was dried blood in the hair on the back of his wrists.

"I hate this," one of the ambulance attendants said. We all looked at him and waited, but that was as much as he intended to say. The other attendant stood looking at Ward, frowning.

"So what are we going to do?" the first policeman said to me. I saw Ward's flesh had risen tiny bumps along his arms, and I took the blanket off the floor and covered him with it.

"If you don't need us," the ambulance attendant said to the policeman, "we got a head-on out on the highway."

175

He looked at Ward quickly, then at the policeman who did not like sailors. "He's all right," he said, "he just got beat up."

Charlotte wiped at the blood still leaking from my brother's nose, and then at the creases that were his eyes.

"Get everybody's name," she said.

The policeman who did not like sailors rolled his eyes.

"The guy's a faggot," said the sailor, and the policeman hit him again, flush on the chin, and he fell against the door, his hands still cuffed behind him, dropping his face in such a way that it seemed as if he were trying to pick up his jaw with his teeth.

"Uh-oh," said the cop who didn't like sailors. "This one fell down."

"We got to go," said the ambulance driver, but he was afraid to leave without permission. He was waiting for someone to say it was all right.

"You saw that," said the sailor, but there was something wrong with his speech. He sounded as if he were begging now too.

The ambulance driver shook his head. "I didn't see nothing, I didn't hear nothing." He turned again to the policeman. "What do you want us to do?" he said.

The policeman looked at me.

"He's hurt," I said.

The sailor moaned, and seemed to be suffering. The first policeman picked him up from behind, using the collar of his shirt, and set him against the wall to wait.

"Don't move," he said.

"I didn't do nothing," said the sailor, but he was afraid now and stayed where he was against the wall. He started to speak again and the policeman near him slapped his face so hard his nose began to bleed.

The first policeman motioned me over into a corner of the room.

"You know you've got a problem here," he said, quietly

enough so the others couldn't hear. "What I'd suggest, it's easier on everybody if your brother had a few drinks tonight and went for a walk down by the beach. Things like this happen down at the beach, even if you don't see anything about it in the papers."

I looked at Ward, trying to figure it out.

"It could have happened at the beach," the cop said again. "The only thing is, in that case we didn't catch the perpetrators."

The sailor was watching us carefully, as if he understood what was being decided. He was bleeding and his jaw was swollen beneath his ear. He had begun to cry.

Charlotte was standing against a wall now with her arms folded across her chest.

"They tried to kill him," she said finally.

The first policeman took a deep breath and let it out slowly. "These things happen," he said. "I'm not telling you what to do, but these things happen."

The sailor groaned, slumping against the wall. The policeman with him used his nightstick across his leg, and the sailor dropped to the floor again.

"Uh-oh," the policeman said, "slipped again."

"What happens to him?" I said.

"What do you want to happen?" the policeman said. "A lot of things can happen on the beach."

The sailor began to cry out loud. "We didn't mean to hurt him like that," he said.

The policeman talking to me looked at the ambulance attendants, suddenly angry. "The fuck are you waiting for?" he said. "The man's hurt."

❏

I DO NOT KNOW WHAT they did to the sailor after I left the hotel room. I know he was still slumped near the door, trying to look more injured than he was, or perhaps it was simply that he knew what was ahead for him when he and the policeman were alone in the room again, and the thought of it had made him ill.

I walked into the hallway, hearing the sounds of the stretcher's wheels as they rolled over the carpet, my brother's form beneath the sheet, the toes of his feet exposed at the bottom, bouncing gently. The first policeman walked with us as far as the elevator, staring from time to time at Charlotte.

"We'll be by the hospital," he said, and smiled at her as the doors closed and the elevator began its drop to the basement. There was a service door there leading to the parking lot, the exit which the hotel preferred ambulance drivers use for emergencies.

❑

I SAT IN THE WAITING room while the doctors worked on my brother's face. They called for a plastic surgeon, but were unable to find one willing to come in at that time of night.

Charlotte sat with me, wide awake as I slipped in and out of sleep. She woke me once touching the swelling on my head, and again when I heard her asking one of the doctors who had come out to report on Ward's progress if I shouldn't be in the hospital too.

He examined me from the doorway. "Do you need to be admitted?" he said. "We're short eleven beds as it is."

"No," I said, "I don't think so."

He nodded and disappeared back into the place where they were working on Ward. "He's going to need reconstructive surgery," she said. I looked at her, wondering how she would know something like that. "They're going to have to rebuild the bone structure of his face."

I looked away from her then; in the end she knew too many things I didn't want to know. I felt her hand on my leg. "It doesn't mean he won't look right," she said. "I've seen plenty of people had their faces restructured, and most of them looked just fine."

She squeezed my leg, trying to get me to look at her. "Jack," she said, "you probably don't know it, but you aren't acting like yourself ever since you got conked with that bottle."

But it wasn't the knock on the head that changed me, it was the sight of my brother streaked bloody and wet like a newborn baby.

I put my hands into my face and closed my eyes. The room moved. "Jack?" she said. I shook my head, meaning I did not want to talk. I was suddenly afraid I would start crying like the sailor.

"It isn't as bad for a man as a girl," she said quietly. "That's something to be thankful for, right there."

And then for a long time neither of us spoke. She left her hand on my leg and from time to time ran her other hand over the back of my neck. Then I was sick again and stood up, her hand still on my leg, and hurried to the bathroom at the far end of the waiting room.

I sat on my heels in front of the toilet, rocking slightly, waiting to see if the vomiting would pass. My face was cool from the spray of the flushing toilet and my arms and legs were weak and shaking. I remember thinking that I did not know how to get up.

She came in behind me, stood at the door of the stall. "Are you going to be all right?" she said.

Her voice echoed in the room. I flushed the toilet and got myself together. She bent closer and I smelled her perfume again, and then her hands were under my arms helping me up.

I went to the sink and ran water into my hands and dropped my face into them. She stood patiently behind me, waiting until I was ready to leave.

The door opened and an old man in a robe moved slowly to one of the urinals, using a walker. He saw her there, but he had been in the hospital a long time, and was used to urinating in front of women.

"When your brother's out of surgery we'll go back to the hotel and call Yardley," she said. "Then we can get some sleep."

I looked at her, trying to track what she'd said, but the words had too many meanings and went too many ways.

I shook my head and grabbed at the sink to keep my balance. "Don't call anybody," I said.

"He's got to know," she said. And then, a moment later, "Your father's got to know too. . . . He'll want to come down."

"Don't call anybody," I said again.

"You have to."

"Let me think," I said.

She found a Life Saver in her purse and put it into my mouth, and then took my arm and led me out of the bathroom to wait for the doctors to come out of the operating room and give us their assessment of the damage my brother had suffered.

❏

AT SIX IN THE MORNING, Ward was moved from surgery to the recovery room. He lay in the room alone, although it was built to accommodate half a dozen patients. The room was cool, and the nurse covered his chest and arms with an extra blanket, being careful not to tear loose the tubes that ran from the bottles overhead into his arm.

He was conscious, she said, but he was tired and he did not move when I stood beside him and touched his shoulder. I spoke his name.

There was no answer, and I looked at the nurse again. She came to his side, reaching beneath the blanket for his wrist, counted the beats of his heart, his breathing; she checked the lines leading from the bottles into his arm to make sure they were dripping at the proper speed.

She looked at her watch, then at my brother. "He was under anesthesia a long time," she said. "Sometimes they don't start back up all at once."

She picked up the chart at the foot of his bed, entered his statistics, and headed for her other patients.

❏

AT THE HOTEL, she took me by the hand and led me to her room. I lay on her bed, kicking off my shoes and my pants, and she lay down next to me. A little later, she pulled me into her neck, holding me there, faintly rocking.

"Tell me if you feel sick," she said.

I burrowed myself into her, smelling her familiar perfume right against her skin, a different odor this close.

I was surprised at the weight of her breasts against my chest.

I did not move again until the middle of the afternoon.

❏

I WOKE UP ALONE. The door that connected this room to Ward's was open, and she was in there, packing his things into his bag. She had showered and washed her hair and put on her makeup. I stood in the doorway, watching her from behind. I swayed on my feet, and she turned, as if drawn to the movement.

"I called Yardley," she said.

I walked in and sat down on the bed. The sheets had not been changed and they were stiff in places with dried blood. "He had to know," she said.

I sat looking at the sheets, trying to decide what that changed. I could not make any of it stay in one place long enough to see it.

"He had to know," she said again, as if we were arguing.

"What did you tell him?"

She studied me a moment, and gradually I realized she was looking at my forehead. "They shouldn't have let you out of the hospital," she said.

I touched it with the tips of my fingers, pushed slightly into it, and felt the push straight through to the back of my head. My forehead was softer than it had been before and it bulged, as if it were growing a head of its own.

"A crack like that, you could have died."

"What did you tell Yardley?"

The phone rang and she picked it up. "Don't tell him anything else," I said, but it was only the front desk, asking if we intended to stay an extra day. She threatened to sue the hotel if we were bothered again and hung up.

"I told him Ward took a walk out on the beach," she said. "I told him the policeman said it happens all the time."

A moment passed, I tried to make those words a sentence, to find a beginning and an end and the meaning.

"What did he say?"

"Yardley? He said he was working."

I looked at her, waiting. She liked to make you wait, even when she was feeling sorry for you. "He asked if Ward was going to make it, and when I said yes, he said he was in the middle of writing and couldn't leave."

I saw that he'd believed her, because if he'd thought that Ward had compromised himself in a hotel room, he would have been on the way to the hospital.

That was Yardley Acheman's nature, and it was better that he was sitting in Lately writing his story about Hillary Van Wetter and Moat County than in Daytona Beach, putting together what had happened to Ward. He was not the sort of person to leave hurtful things alone.

She crossed the room and kissed me quickly on the cheek, smelling of soap and shampoo. I wondered how I smelled to her.

"He'll be down after he finishes Hillary's story," she said. "Maybe next week."

"I don't think Ward's going to be able to work for a while," I said.

"That man from the newspaper is still there, and he's checking it as they go along, instead of Ward . . ."

I smiled at her and the things she didn't know about the newspaper business, and about my brother and Yardley Acheman. "Yardley doesn't know it well enough to write it alone," I said finally.

"That's not the way it sounded," she said, and I got up and went into the bathroom and stood for a long time in the shower, and decided again that nothing Yardley Acheman did with the story about Hillary Van Wetter mattered. My only interest was to keep him removed from what had happened in Daytona Beach. And as I was thinking that, I came back to something else that had been going through my head, something which was there even the night before as I was following the ambulance attendants down the corridor of the hotel.

I didn't know if Ward would lend himself to the story that he was walking along the beach. I was not sure he could lie.

❏

I SAT BESIDE HIM in the hospital all the next day. He had suffered a fracture of the skull, and for that reason could not be given pain relievers. Charlotte came and went, leaving flowers, medical opinions. If her estimation of my brother had changed because of the hotel beating, it didn't show. To her, it was exactly as if he had been attacked walking along the beach at night.

It was not that simple for me, although I understood that Ward hadn't changed, that the change was in the way I saw him.

He had made his way through a crashed airplane, after

all, while Yardley Acheman, who slept with women regularly, found his reasons to stay outside. He'd returned to the fraternity house at the University of Miami the same night they had beaten him, he had walked into the Van Wetters' camp in the heart of the wetlands near the river. And none of that was recast because one night in Daytona Beach he craved sailors.

"Listen," I said, and then could not think of the words. The room was quiet a long time, I wondered if he was still listening.

"Listen, I don't care what you were doing with those guys, it doesn't matter to me."

He moved his head slowly, rolling it across his pillow until he was looking at me through the slit in the tissue around the eye that was not bandaged.

"How bad is it?" he said. His voice was dry, and I could barely make out the words.

"Pretty bad," I said.

He waited, blinking.

"You're going to need more surgery, to reconstruct your face."

He nodded, as if he already knew that. "It's like the ocean." He lifted his hand from beneath the sheet and moved it over a series of small waves. He smiled then, showing a black crust inside his mouth. "We should go swimming," he said.

His hand dropped and a moment later his breathing was deep and dry and regular and I knew he had fallen asleep.

His eyes opened the moment I stood up, on the way out to find a drink of water. I settled back in my seat and said, "The police caught them. Did you know that?"

He shook his head no, uninterested.

"They beat one of them up, I don't know about the other one. I think they've had trouble with sailors before."

My brother had no investment in what happened to the men who nearly killed him. "They either had to let them go," I said, "or the whole thing would have ended up in the newspapers."

It was quiet in the room, and then someplace down the hall a woman screamed.

"When you were hurt in the ocean . . ." he said finally, and then he stopped, as if he couldn't find the frame for what was next. Or as if his throat was so dry he had lost his voice.

"You want me to get you a Coke?" I said.

He shook his head no.

"When you were hurt in the ocean," he said again, "was it like this?"

I said I didn't know. "It was bad, though. I think it's always bad when you come close to dying."

"It's a strain," he said, and smiled again. There were a few teeth left in back. His lips were swollen and he barely opened them to speak. "Did you feel like crying?" he said a little later.

I stared at him a moment, remembering it.

"Not when it was going on," he said, and the words were stripped bare, "but afterward, when it was over. Did it make you weep?"

"Yes, that's what it does to you," I said.

He nodded his head, and in a moment his unbandaged eye shone with tears, and when he blinked they ran over and down his cheek.

"There is something sad about almost dying," I said. "It comes to you later."

And tied together in this way, Ward and I, for a little while that afternoon, were as close as we would ever be.

❏

I DID NOT TELL WARD until the next morning that Yardley Acheman was continuing alone with the story. Ward had showered before I came in, but because of the stitches he could not wash the blood out of his hair.

He looked better, though, and even with his face half covered in bandages, he seemed more himself. The swelling was down, for one thing, and I could see more of his good eye.

He would not cry again at the sadness we'd spoken of, although I know from experience that the feeling itself does not disappear because you give in to it. He had cried once, though, and I suppose that was as much of it as he was allowed.

"Yardley Acheman is going ahead with it," I said.

Ward was drinking a Coke through a straw, taking little sips. He put the bottle on the table which bridged the bed and dropped his head back into the pillow.

"The editor's with him, and they're writing it," I said. My brother lay still, thinking, jumpy with apprehension.

"What difference does it make?" I said a little later. "It's a story in a newspaper."

He didn't seem to hear.

"They don't know what happened at the hotel," I said, thinking that might have been on his mind. "They know you're in the hospital, that's all. . . ." I stopped there, not wanting to enunciate the thing they didn't know, not wanting to say it out loud.

"The police said you were out walking along the beach," I said. "That's what they wrote in the report."

My brother blinked, he understood the reasons.

"Tell them to bring it down, so I can see it," he said, meaning the story.

"I'll tell them."

He nodded his head. "It would be good if I could see it," he said. And then he closed his eye and went to sleep.

❑

I CALLED THE NUMBER in Lately half a dozen times; it was never answered. I called my father in Thorn and told him that Ward had been hurt. "He was walking out along the beach," I said.

"How bad is it?" he said.

"Not too bad, but he's going to need some teeth and a little surgery to fix his cheeks."

It was quiet.

"Did they use weapons?"

"I don't think so," I said, "he was kicked. . . ." I paused, trying to hear the way it would sound to him. "He's going to be all right."

"Is he talking?"

"A little. It's not easy, though. He's got a mouth full of stitches."

The line went quiet again; I could see him going into his shirt pocket for one of the tiny pills he kept there, setting it carefully under his tongue. "He's going to be all right," I said again.

"I could be there tonight," he said.

I told him it would be better to wait a day or two, until Ward felt more like company.

I knew that my brother wouldn't want to see him now. I could not think of a way to say those words, though, and so I said only that it would be a good idea to wait until he could wash his hair to visit.

I have spent most of my life keeping the truth from my father, and I suppose he has spent most of his in the same pursuit.

❑

THE NEXT MORNING my brother worried out loud about the story Yardley Acheman was writing in Lately. I took that as a sign of recovery, and told him that Moat County would survive anything the *Miami Times* might do to it in print.

We did not talk about the other story—the one the policeman wrote in his report. I did not mention that I worried at the prospect of ever seeing Yardley and Charlotte in the same room again. She had lied for my brother once, but you could not count on her to maintain it, one day to the next.

She brought fresh-cut flowers that morning and the next, but as my brother's condition improved she lost interest, and by the time my father finally arrived in Daytona Beach, she was planning her trip back to Lately.

"I can do more good up there," she said.

"You'll be in the way," I said.

"If I am, they'll say so. I don't have any clean clothes here anyway."

In the end, I agreed to take her back.

She and my father crossed paths in the hospital waiting room, Charlotte heading one way, my father heading the other. He was dressed in a suit, she was wearing the same clothes she'd had on the night Ward was beaten. I began to introduce them, but my father was diverted by a patient coming through on a stretcher and looked past her, afraid now of what he would see when he went farther into the hospital.

❑

"Well, you don't look so bad," he said.

It was something he had prepared himself to say no matter what condition Ward was in. In fact, the swelling had receded in some of the places Ward was hurt, but his bottom lip had become infected, and left him almost unable to speak.

My brother nodded at him, then looked at me. I did not know if he wanted me to leave or to stay. Charlotte's flowers stood at both ends of the one chest of drawers in the room, beginning to fade, and my father pushed them aside and sat down. He did not go near the chair beside the bed.

"I tried to call your mother. . . ." His voice disappeared, and he looked at my brother more carefully. "Did they catch them?" he said to me.

I shook my head. "There's been a lot of it down by the beach," I said. For some reason, it seemed necessary to repeat the policeman's exact words, to say it the same way it had been said to me. My father nodded, imagining the carnage at the beach.

"How long before they'll let you out of here?" he said, speaking again to Ward. There was a heartiness to his voice that was planned and unnatural, part of the costume for the visit.

Ward shrugged, looking around the room for help. It was hard to watch them together; it was hard to leave them alone. "They'll do some more surgery the day after tomorrow," I said. "They'll have a better idea then of how much longer."

"I can tell you the *Times* is worried," my father said. "I talked to my friend Larson there, and they're wondering what they'll do for news while you're getting better."

He would have liked to have told Ward that the *Moat County Tribune* couldn't get along without him, I think. It would have seemed more personal than the *Miami Times*.

My brother nodded at that and tried a smile. His lips hurt him, though, and his face moved only a little and then stopped. It was characteristic of my father that on seeing his oldest son lying in the intensive care unit of the hospital, beaten half to death, coming face-to-face with that thing he feared most, he would talk about going back to work.

Having been in the business of shorthand all his life—of using certain words to evade other words that are easier or more politely left unsaid—he could not find any words at all when it mattered.

My brother understood that and forgave him, and hoped, I suppose, that he would be forgiven in return. And perhaps that was what happened.

"They miss you at work," he said.

❑

MY FATHER AND I had dinner that night at his hotel, and he spoke infrequently, once to ask which newspapers Ward would want in the morning. After he had gone to his room for the evening I drove Charlotte back to Lately, arriving at her apartment at one in the morning, having to shake her awake.

"Jesus," she said, "was I snoring?"

I was tired in ways that had nothing to do with sleep. It occurred to me, sitting in the car with her, that I had been trying to hold too many things together that were meant to fall apart.

She was looking at herself in a compact, touching her face here and there with lipstick or an eyebrow pencil. In all the time I knew her, she never went from one place to another without looking at herself in a mirror. She had turned on the light overhead, and it cast shadows across the dashboard of the car.

"What do you want with him?" I said.

She leaned over and looked at me a moment, the light falling across her hair and face. "What do you think, I've still got something going on with Yardley?" she said.

I didn't answer, and a moment later she patted me on the leg and then turned in her seat and opened the door.

"The things you don't know, for a smart kid," she said, and then she closed the door and was gone.

❏

I FOUND YARDLEY ACHEMAN and the editor from Miami the next morning, both sitting at Ward's desk in the little office over the Moat Cafe. Ward's notes and his files were open all around them, on the desk and on the floor. In the center of the desk was a typewriter with a piece of paper in the carriage.

The editor's sleeves were rolled almost to his elbows and he wore a tie loosed at the neck. Yardley also wore a tie. There were no beer bottles in sight.

I walked in without knocking, and judging Yardley's expression, I was not welcome. The man from Miami had no idea who I was. He was not good at faces.

Yardley looked at me, then his eyes went back to the type-writer. "How's he doing?" he said, and typed for a moment or two and then stopped, as if he were taking it all down, and waiting now for my answer.

"He tried to call," I said, and looked at the telephones. Both of them had been taken off the hook.

"Tell him everything's all right," Yardley Acheman said. "He doesn't have to worry."

"He'd like to see the story," I said.

Yardley went back to typing. "Tell you what. Let me write the fucking story, Jack, then we can all read it," he said.

"He doesn't want to read it in the newspaper," I said. "He wants to read it before it goes in."

The man from Miami seemed to have put it together, who I was. "We've got a real time problem right now," he said. "We're trying to get this thing ready for Sunday."

I stood still, and Yardley went on with his typing. "These are the most organized, thorough notes I've ever seen," the man said. "If it weren't for that, we wouldn't have a chance." Thinking I would take that back to my brother.

"Why does it have to be in the paper Sunday?" I said.

Yardley Acheman threw the editor a tired look but contin-ued to work. The editor smiled again. "There always comes a time," he said, sounding patient, "when you've got to push the thing out the door. It's hard to let go, but you've got to do it or else you'd never get anything done."

I thought of the weeks Yardley Acheman had spent in Lately, getting nothing done.

"Beyond that," the editor said, "there's a man on death row. Time's running out on him, and it doesn't do him or us any good if he's executed before this situation can be corrected."

I stood still a moment, wanting to argue issues I didn't know anything about. "Ward ought to look at it first," I said finally. "It's his story."

"John," Yardley Acheman said to the editor, "I've got to

have some quiet." He was the only newspaper reporter I ever met who could not write unless it was quiet. The editor moved then, putting his hand in the middle of my back, smiling, heading me toward the door.

"If anything comes up we need his help, we'll call him at the hospital," he said. "And as soon as this thing's finished, we'll send him a carbon copy. . . ."

We had reached the door, where he had stopped and was waiting now for me to leave.

"It's his story," I said again. "He wants to read it before it goes in the paper."

"He can read it," the editor said, and put his hand on my back again.

"First," I said. "He can read it first. . . ."

Yardley looked up again from his typewriter, impatient for me to leave. The editor only smiled. "At the first opportunity," he said. "We'll have it sent to the hospital directly."

I stepped through the doorway, unsure of what the editor had promised. "Before it runs," I said.

"As soon as humanly possible," he said, and he shut the door.

❑

I RETURNED TO DAYTONA at night. It was late and warm and the highway was empty except for an occasional tandem loaded with oranges blowing past on the way to the processing plants north, rocking the car.

It was palmetto season, and in the glare of the trucks' headlights, the spatter of dead insects across the windshield made it impossible to see, and I could only hold the steering wheel steady and trust that there was a road beyond the glare.

❑

IN THE MORNING, my brother went back into surgery and was there most of the day. I had lunch with my father at the hospital cafeteria and he remarked a number of times that the food was better there than it had been in the army.

"This isn't bad," he said, and inspected a piece of chicken on his fork. "That girl that cleans and cooks for me . . ." He shook his head. "Ward's probably eating better than I am." Ward, of course, was taking his meals through a straw.

My father looked at his watch every few minutes. The doctors had said they could not predict how long the reconstruction of Ward's sinuses would take until they got inside and saw the damage.

"You should go home," I said.

"Not yet."

We went from the cafeteria back to my brother's hospital room and waited. The air in the room seemed stale, even with the windows open, and about three in the afternoon I became conscious of a problem with my breathing. I did not seem to be getting the air deeply enough into my lungs.

My father was sitting in a corner, reading one of the papers he had brought for Ward, and we had not spoken more than a few sentences since lunch. I stood up and walked to the window, wanting air. He looked up from the paper.

"If you want to get out of here for a little while, go for a swim," he said, "I can hold down the fort."

I looked at the clock on the wall and promised to be back in two hours. He nodded, telling me there was no reason for us both to wait, vaguely disappointed at the same time that I would leave the place with my brother still in surgery.

"I'll be back by six," I said, giving myself a little more than the two hours.

"No hurry," he said, and I left the window and started out the door. "He probably won't feel much like company afterward anyway."

I went to the ocean and drove the rental car out onto the

beach and headed north until there were no sunbathers. I took off my clothes in the car and swam for perhaps half an hour, straight out and back, not far enough to feel tired, and not far enough to get away from the hospital.

I came out of the water and lay on the sand, letting it press into my chest and legs and arms and my cheek, lying there with my mouth so close to it that little grains stirred as I breathed, and for a little while I slept.

❏

THE DOCTORS HAD FINISHED with Ward. He was lying in a recovery room again, his face more elaborately bandaged than it had been before, and he was drained, completely spent. My father looked at me from the chair beside the bed. We did not speak. Every ten minutes a nurse came in to record Ward's vital signs, which were ordinary enough, or at least were nothing that she didn't expect.

She spoke to him slowly, as you would speak to a child. "Would you like a sip of water?"

He nodded, and she lifted the cup to his lips and then took it away. "Just a little," she said, and then left the room. I refilled the cup and put it in his hand and he drank what was in it.

"That might make him sick," my father said, but it didn't seem to me that he had a claim on my brother's care.

Ward's good eye wandered the recovery room, resting here or there on his bare toes or the bottle which hung overhead, then moving on, stunned. He did not look at either of us.

My father said he remembered having his appendix removed and the sickness afterwards. He did not seem to appreciate the difference between illness and violence, or that the recoveries were not the same process.

Ward did not speak to us that evening, and barely spoke the next day. But once, when my father left the room to call his newspaper, my brother's head finally rolled in my direction and he stared at me a moment and then said, "Jack, something went wrong."

"Nothing went wrong," I said. "I talked to the doctors." There was a long, empty moment.

He closed his unbandaged eye and breathed deeply, in and out, until he seemed to have fallen asleep, and then, without opening his eye, he told me the doctors hadn't given him enough anesthetic.

"I was awake too long," he said slowly. "I heard them talking, I felt them lifting the bones in my face, cutting them."

"You couldn't move?" He shook his head, keeping the eye closed.

"I tried to move a finger," he said, "make some signal that I was still there with them, but it was all dead." And then he did open his eye, and I saw that the doctors had done something to him that the sailors couldn't.

He did not speak of what had happened in the operating room again, at least to me, but the shadow of it was always there. He had been terrified, and once that has happened, you are never quite the same.

❑

FROM TIME TO TIME, my father asked about the men who had beaten Ward, how many there were, if they were black or white; he wondered out loud when the police would catch them.

My brother did not acknowledge the questions, even in some polite way that would have dismissed them. He simply stared, one-eyed, at the ceiling.

❑

AS THE EDITOR FROM Miami had put it, the story was pushed out the door, and ran in Sunday's newspaper. My brother did not see it until it appeared in print, under his and Yardley

Acheman's names. It was spread across the upper fold of the front page—A SHERIFF'S LEGACY LINGERS OVER MOAT COUNTY— and began:

Officially, Sheriff Thurmond Call killed 17 people in the line of duty during his 34 years in office in rural Moat County. Sixteen of them were black.

Officially, it was the 17th killing—a white man named Jerome Van Wetter, who died while being arrested in Lately in 1965, the county seat—which led to the sheriff's own demise. It was Van Wetter's cousin, Hillary Van Wetter, head of a large and violent local family, who was convicted of stabbing the sheriff in revenge and leaving him to die on the narrow highway connecting the isolated county to the rest of the world.

But while Hillary Van Wetter is now officially convicted of the murder and waiting on death row at Starke, there is evidence that Van Wetter was not the killer, and that is something that has been known, unofficially, in Moat County for four years.

My father had gone back to his home and his own newspaper the day before. He and Ward had been in the same room together for three days, and almost all of that time passed in silence. Ward did not tell him what had happened in the operating room, and did not complain of the aching in his face. The infection had settled in, and he was taking antibiotics every six hours.

By the time I got to the hospital on Sunday morning, the paper was lying sifted into its sheets on the floor, where it had fallen from the side of his bed. I'd gone swimming and then read the piece over a long breakfast.

Yardley Acheman had not so much written a story about Hillary Van Wetter as a story about Moat County. In it, the lawyer Pine became all its lawyers, Sheriff Call spoke for the charity of all its white citizens. The finances of the state's attorney's office and the sheriff's department were called into question, and there was a list of relatives of county officials who were employed in both places, many of them in jobs that did not require their attendance. There was a suggestion, laid to unnamed sources, that civil and criminal cases were not settled in court, but in "smoke-filled rooms, late at night."

In Yardley Acheman's hands, the county became an enclave of ignorance and smallness in a state which was growing in another direction, and Hillary Van Wetter and his naive defender Charlotte Bless were the casualties of an inevitable war of clashing cultures.

❑

MY FATHER, who had called every evening after dinner, did not call on Sunday, or on the three days that followed. Yardley Acheman called, however, from Miami. First on Monday with the news that the newspaper was deluged with phone calls from readers, and then on Wednesday to say that the governor had ordered an investigation into the procedures inside the Moat County court system.

Ward did not take either call. I picked up the phone each time, repeated the things that Yardley Acheman said to my brother, and then hung up.

"Put him on," he said the second time. "We're going to return the Van Wetter boy back home to the swamp."

But Ward simply looked at the phone when I offered it to him, and then at me, and I told Yardley Acheman that Ward did not want to talk to him.

"How's he doing, anyway?" he said.

"He's all right," I said.

"Did they catch the guys?"

I didn't answer.

"The ones that mugged him, did the cops get them?"

"No," I said, "the cops didn't get anybody."

There was a pause and then Yardley Acheman, who was still full of the news that the governor had been pushed into opening an investigation, said that perhaps he should come to Daytona Beach and ask them why not. "A little nudge might get things going," he said.

"I don't think that would be a good idea," I said. "I think they're doing all they can."

It was quiet again, and then he said, "So, did Ward see the story?"

I didn't answer.

"What did he think?"

"He wanted to read it first," I said, and looked quickly at Ward. He was staring at something out the window.

"It's the business," Yardley Acheman said. "He understands deadlines. . . ."

The connection went quiet.

"It was one of those things," he said finally. "He'll get over it."

I hung up and he called back.

"Put him on," he said. "He's right there in the room, isn't he? Tell him I've got some good news. . . ."

"It's Yardley Acheman," I said to Ward. "He says he's got good news." My brother closed his eye.

I hung up again.

Ward stared out the window and refused to take phone calls from the *Times* for five days, and then the infection cleared and he was discharged, and went back to his apartment in Miami to recover. He could have gone instead to my father's house, where Anita Chester would have fixed his meals and done his laundry, but he did not want to go home.

❑

I DID RETURN TO Thorn and resumed my career as a delivery driver for my father's newspaper, and it was immediately evident that the publication of the story of Hillary Van Wetter and Moat County under Ward James's byline in the *Miami Times* had changed my father's standing.

It wore on him, not to be beloved.

To the citizens of Moat County, his son was another in a series of sons who left the place and came back thinking they were better. Ward, however, had done this on the front page of the state's biggest newspaper. He had caused the retirement of the county's most famous lawyer, had brought on a state investigation of the local government—they were auditing the sheriff's budget now, and people would be losing their jobs—and he had defended the most lawless and violent member of the Van Wetter family at the expense of the memory of Thurmond Call.

My father was held responsible for these things—not for the story itself, but for imbuing his oldest son with his liberal inclinations and, in doing that, insulting the place where he lived.

As he came to understand the wide breadth of this sentiment, he withdrew, retreating into that realm of memory where he was safe, and intact. He became remote even in his own kitchen.

The Dodge dealership where Jerome Van Wetter had worked canceled its advertising, along with Woolworth's and the Pie Rite bakery and all three of the real estate offices that operated within the county. On one hand, these cancellations were gestures aimed at identifying with the customers' sensitivities, on the other hand, they were personal. People who had not liked my father's politics suddenly disliked him personally, and a kind of resentment set in all over the county that would last long after the advertisers came back and the story of Hillary Van Wetter itself was forgiven.

My father spent the weeks after the *Times*'s story driving his Chrysler at eighty miles an hour from Thorn to Lately and back to Thorn, trying to plug a dozen leaks at once, explaining the ethics of the newspaper business to people who had no interest in it at all. Mostly, they listened politely and promised to think it over.

He returned home exhausted and worried and remote. He

would sit in his chair after dinner, the pile of newspapers next to it untouched, too tired to read. He would drink his wine and nod off to sleep, and sometimes, half asleep, he would absently take a pill from his shirt pocket and place it under his tongue. He must have been taking half a dozen a day.

Still, he told his stories; he told them against the evidence that he was being ushered out of the business, against the feeling that things were coming apart.

When it was time to retire for the evening, he would head up the stairs, his feet moving as if each step were a different thought. Sometimes he would sigh, "This too will pass," as if a conversation had been going on in the room before he left.

Other times, I would hear him in the kitchen, on the phone with my brother. Obligatory calls, asking about his recovery. The conversations were tense, as much as I heard of them, as if something had been acknowleged between them which, once in the open, could not be ignored.

He laid off one of the three members of his advertising staff, a young man named Lauren Martin who had been his best salesman, but who had no family to support and could most easily find another a job in Orlando or Daytona Beach or one of the papers in the Tampa Bay area. My father agonized about the firing out loud to the editors and reporters he brought over to the house for drinks. He wanted them to know he was not ruthless.

These evenings with his reporters were as drunk as they had even been, but the optimism was gone. The party was over, and the people left behind had in fact been left behind.

I did not generally care much for these occasions or the people who attended them, but I was briefly attracted to a woman named Ellen Guthrie, whom my father had recently hired as a copy editor, and who came to the house alone. She was perhaps Charlotte's age and, like Charlotte, paid an extraordinary amount of attention to her appearance. From what I saw, she had been ostracized by the other women at the paper. I had noticed, even then, that there were certain women whom other women instinctively disliked, and that these women invariably had more bait in the water than the women who disliked them.

I found Ellen Guthrie sitting alone one night on the steps leading upstairs. It was ten o'clock at night, and she was holding a bottle of beer in both hands. The rest of the reporters and editors and my father were outside on the porch.

She looked at me with a certain curiosity that the others did not have.

"The party's outside," I said, and she smiled, set her drink on the step next to her leg, and lit a cigarette. She moved a little to the side and patted the step.

I sat down next to her, noticing the smell of her shampoo, the sheer material of her blouse. The outline of her breasts beneath it.

"You're the son that isn't the reporter," she said.

I was unable to think of the correct answer.

"I kind of admire that," she said. "You didn't just jump into the business because your father owned a newspaper."

An impulse to defend my brother came and passed. "I drive one of his trucks," I said.

"That's not the same," she said.

"No, it isn't," I said. "It's about five hours earlier in the morning."

She nodded and moved her cigarette to her lips, and in doing that brushed her arm against mine. Her skin was cool and soft. I guessed she was thirty-seven years old. I moved a little, and in doing that my cock broke loose from the folds of my pants and stood up in the pocket. It looked something like a tongue stuck into a cheek. She did not look at my lap, but smiled as if she knew what was there.

"Your brother's story caused a lot of trouble for the *Tribune*," she said.

"He didn't write it," I said, "he was in the hospital."

She nodded, as if she knew everything, and nothing left could surprise her. "It was a good story," she said. She said that as if it were in her province to decide. She looked quickly through the window to the porch, not caring for the people she saw out there. "He's a good writer," she said.

"He didn't write it," I said again. "The other guy, Yardley Acheman, used his notes . . ."

"It was still a good story."

When I didn't say anything else she leaned forward, looking into my face more from the front, and smiled. "Sibling rivalry?" she said.

I shook my head no, but she didn't seem to believe me. "Big brother's the most famous reporter in the state?" She was smiling at me, teasing. And now she did look into my lap.

"I don't care about being a reporter," I said. "That's not what I want to do."

"You like driving a truck," she said.

"It's honest," I said.

"Are you good at it?"

"I haven't backed into the loading dock in a while. That may be as good as it gets."

She leaned back to a more natural position and opened her legs. She considered driving trucks. "I think you ought to be the best at whatever you do," she said. "Even if it's collecting garbage, you ought to be the best at it."

"Did you ever collect garbage?" I said.

I had a hard dick, but I would not sit on the same steps with the President of the United States and listen to him tell me that whatever menial task I might be qualified to do, I ought to do it well. The people who say these things are never the garbage collectors themselves.

She shifted her weight, sipping at her beer, and her side pressed briefly into mine. It was firm and felt solid, the way Charlotte's did.

"If I did, I'd be good at it," she said, and set the beer down

---

202

on the step next to her. When she moved back, somehow our legs were touching. I kept my leg precisely where it was, not pressing into hers, not moving away. "I always try to be the best."

We were not talking about collecting garbage now.

There was some noise out on the porch, something—someone—falling, the sound of laughter. Nothing especially happy, and I couldn't hear my father's voice in it. She looked in that direction, uninterested.

"Your father's a good editor," she said, "but he needs better people."

"He had to fire somebody in advertising this week," I said.

"He ought to fire some more of them," she said.

We sat quietly for a minute or two then; it came to me I was expected to do something, but I didn't know what. I considered taking her by the hand and leading her up into my room, but the moment I thought of that, I also thought of the shelves up there still filled with models I'd put together when I was eight or nine years old, along with the trophies from swimming meets in high school which, in some way, seemed to come from even a younger time. I don't know why I never took those things down, except I suppose there was nothing else to put in their place, and they were still there, the artifacts of my childhood, and it did not seem possible, even in the abstract, to have sex with a woman in the same room.

"Don't tell him I said that," she said.

I stared at her, gone completely south. "About firing his people," she said. "It just makes things complicated."

As if she were someone who minded complications.

"I heard he was badly hurt," she said a little later, speaking of my brother.

"He's back in Miami now," I said.

"Was he working on the story?"

"I don't know," I said.

"I got hurt once, working on a story," she said. "It's no

fun." I did not ask her in what way she was hurt, not wanting it leading back to Ward. She took a long swallow of beer, and then put the empty bottle down next to her. "Is there a bathroom upstairs?"

"On the right," I said. She was to the top of the stairs when I realized that my room was also on that side of the hall. I heard her footsteps stop, a door opened and then closed, and then she moved farther down the hall. I wondered if she'd seen my models.

❑

SHE GOT ANOTHER BEER from the kitchen, and brought one for me. She sat down, and there was a certain familiarity between us that had not been there before.

"I was sodomized," she said. Just like that.

For a moment I saw the sheets in the room where I had found Ward, twisted and lying half on the floor, still wet with his blood.

"It's no fun," she said.

"No, I wouldn't think so."

"A couple of drunks." And that was as much as she said for a while. Someone was laughing on the porch, one of my father's reporters.

I heard myself ask if they'd been caught. It was the same thing my father asked at the hospital, when he didn't know what else to say.

She shook her head. "They let them go," she said. I leaned forward and tried not to say anything else that sounded like my father.

"You're nice," she said a little later. "Most guys want to hear every detail. They get off on it."

I sat still.

"The complicated thing is, the guys who did it are dead. I knew who they were. Most rape victims are acquainted with their attackers, did you know that?"

I shook my head. She said, "So it complicates things. I mean you hate somebody and then they're dead, and how do you feel then?"

I didn't know. "How did they die?" I said.

She shrugged. "Too quickly."

"It doesn't sound so complicated," I said.

"You'll never know until it happens to you."

I checked the clock in the kitchen again, finished my beer, and stood up. She looked at me from beneath, and from that angle could not miss the fact that my cock was hinged like a sprung car door. She smiled.

"If you wanted to know about it, you could have asked," she said. "I'm not ashamed."

"I don't want to know."

"It happened while I was working, that's the reason I brought it up. In a way it's like what happened to your brother." I looked upstairs and then back down at her, catching the outlines of her legs under the gathered wrinkles of her lap.

"They did it together," she said, and I sat back down. For a moment, though, she appeared to have lost her place. I saw that she was drunker than I'd thought; it seemed to me that she might be one of those people like my father's friend who, one night, after six months of impeccable behavior, had tried to kill all the Jews at the party.

It occurred to me that my father collected these people on purpose. "Fuck it," she said. She leaned back against the stairs, her blouse tightening over her chest. She stared at the ceiling and then closed her eyes. "How old are you?" she said.

"Twenty."

She frowned. "That's too bad," she said. Then, "I'm forty-one."

"That's not so old," I said, as if I knew anything about it. "You don't look old."

She opened her eyes and drank from the bottle, spilling beer down her chin. She wiped at it with the back of her hand. "Forty-one next week," she said, "and you know what I want for my birthday?"

"A swimming lesson," I said. All these years later, I still have no idea why.

She laughed out loud, and her head rolled in my direction. "I want a sixteen-year-old boy all night long," she said. "Four years ago, you'd have been just right."

I stared at her, blinked. Not knowing what she was talking about. "You're washed up," she said. "Men hit their sexual prime at sixteen, it's a fact."

I began not to like Ellen Guthrie.

"If you wait about six hours, the paperboy will be by," I said.

And that made her smile, and she drank more of her beer and mussed my hair. "You know," she said, "you could pass for sixteen." And then she kissed me lightly on the ear and headed out onto the porch.

I went upstairs, wondering what I was supposed to make of that. I was still thinking it over in the morning, on the highway south in a loaded truck, and it seemed to me then that she had not meant any of it; that she tortured as many of us as she could to get even for being sodomized.

I thought she'd probably told both of the copyboys in the *Tribune* newsroom that she wished they were sixteen too.

❑

THE PRESSES MY FATHER used were in the bottom of the same three-story building where the editorial and advertising and business departments had offices. My father's own office was on the top floor, at the far end of the editorial department. From there he could look out his window down at the loading dock and see his three trucks coming and going in the morning.

There was a stairway from the newsroom leading to the presses and beyond them, to the loading docks, and many of the reporters and editors who parked their cars out in back—my father liked to keep the spaces in front of the building available for the citizens of Thorn, not wanting them inconvenienced as they did their shopping—used this stairway to enter and leave the building.

It was not unusual then for me to meet a reporter or an editor on my way inside late in the morning, coming in from my route. They were usually on their way to lunch.

I rarely saw my father, as he was in the habit of using the building's front door. It was a good feeling, I suppose, walking out of his own newspaper onto the street of his community, but since the publication of the Van Wetter story in the *Miami Times,* the feeling had changed.

A week after I'd spoken with Ellen Guthrie on the steps, I returned from the route an hour late—I'd lost a radiator hose just as I left Thorn—and found her standing with my father near the docks. He was speaking, she was listening, a little closer to him than she needed to be, smoking a cigarette, smiling at the things he said. They looked up and watched as I backed the truck into its space in the dock. The other trucks were already in.

I climbed out and my father checked his watch.

For as long as I can remember, he worried when the papers were late, believing—correctly, I think—that the business was fragile. That newspapers were read largely out of habit, as part of a daily ritual, and that when they were not at the reader's door on time, as promised, the habit could be broken. There was television to take their place.

The Van Wetter story in the *Times* had effected a loss in advertising, but it had not as yet cost him subscribers, and he was afraid of that, and did not hide it well, even in front of Miss Guthrie.

I told him I'd lost a radiator hose just outside of town, and that it took me a couple of hours to get it replaced.

"They were all late," he said, forgetting she was there.

"All of them in my truck," I said, and my father turned, taking Ellen Guthrie by the elbow.

"It's Ellen's birthday," he said. "Come with us for lunch."

I walked along with them, sometimes falling a step behind, watching Miss Guthrie's behind swing as she walked. It seemed to me that she was more expensive-looking than Charlotte, although not as principled.

"It's Ellen's fortieth birthday," my father said as we walked. I had looked at her quickly, remembering she told me she was turning forty-one. "We're going to drink the sun right out of the sky."

My father always took his employees out for a drink on their birthdays, at least the ones he liked. As a rule, however, he did not start out with the intention of drinking the sun out of the sky.

We passed through the door of the Thorn Grill, into darkness and cool air. It was the only place in town you could drink liquor and eat anything except pickled meat before six o'clock at night. He put his hand on her elbow as he walked in, as if to guide her in the dark, and left it there, it seemed to me, a little longer than he needed to. We sat in a booth with plastic cushions and I looked across the table at my father, having never been out drinking with him before, having never thought of myself in the same bar.

We drank four margaritas before Ellen went to the bathroom. My father stared at her all the way there, then turned to his drink and killed what was left in the bottom.

❑

"I WAS TELLING Jack before that I thought the story on the man up in Lately was well done," she said to my father when she came back. "No matter how unpopular it was locally."

She had put fresh color on her lips and done something to her eyes. My father dropped his chin into the palm of his hand, as if he were thinking it over.

"The reporting, I mean," she said. "The reporting was very solid. . . ."

He nodded, and then picked up his margarita. The first drinks had come with paper umbrellas hinged on the ledge of the glass, but we had run them out of umbrellas now.

"Ward is a hell of a reporter," he said finally.

"It was awful, what happened to him in Daytona Beach," she said. My father stuck his finger into his drink and stirred it.

"Yes, it was," he said, "but Ward's tough."

"I was hurt once on the job," she said a little later, and she and I looked at each other again before she went on with it.

"It's the kind of thing that stays in the back of your mind," she said. "Maybe it's why I'm not a reporter anymore."

My father backed a few inches away, as if to see her more clearly. She returned the stare, steady and long, a little heat in it.

"What happened?" he said finally.

She shrugged. "I was attacked," she said, leaving the word there for him to chew on. She took another sip of her margarita and stared at him again.

"Sodomized," she said.

He blinked, and then looked away. She was still staring, waiting for him, when he looked at her again.

"While you were on a story?" my father said.

She shrugged and ran one of her fingers along the rim of the glass, and sucked on the salt.

"There were two of them, and they took turns."

My father caught the waitress's attention and held up three fingers to signal more drinks. He was sweating, even in the path of the air conditioner.

"One of them held me," she said, and then stopped. "Do you mind hearing about this?"

"Not at all," he said.

"One of them held me, and the other one raped me from behind. They changed places, and after they'd rested they raped me together."

For a moment the only noise at the table was the sound of the air conditioner. She leaned closer to my father, half drunk now, stopping a few inches from his ear. "That's why I know what it feels like, the thing that happened to Ward."

"Nobody raped Ward," I said.

She stopped and looked at me. "What I think is, one kind of attack is like another. It's the same thing when somebody can do whatever he wants to you."

If my father was bothered by what she'd said, it didn't show. He smiled at her, boozy and full of understanding.

"I didn't need surgery, at least," she said.

Neither of them looked as I got up and made my way to the bathroom, but a moment after I'd closed the door it opened again, and my father came in. He checked himself in the mirror, combing his hair back off his forehead, and then took one of the pills from his shirt pocket and stuck it under his tongue. He splashed his face with water, then carefully dried his hands.

"She seems like an intelligent woman," he said, looking at me in the mirror. I had no comment on her intelligence. "She seems to know what she wants," he said.

I looked at him, wondering what he thought that was. On his way back through the door he clapped me gently on the back, a gesture from my childhood, but somehow meaning something different now.

"You don't have to stay," he said.

She was sitting across the table from my father when I came out, ignoring a man staring at her from the bar. The man was drinking red beer and hadn't shaved in two or three days. He continued to stare at her for a good minute after I sat down, dancing in one spot to some music on the jukebox, his pants nearly sliding off his hips, and then my father, who was full of tequila and full of Miss Guthrie, stared at him murderously until he turned away.

The man was thin and dirty, and he had an Adam's apple the size of a walnut. There were mermaids tattooed on his forearms, and he reminded me of the trustees I'd seen on the way in and out of the prison at Starke. I watched him light a cigarette and finish his beer, and then span the bar with his gaze, taking in as much of Ellen Guthrie as he could.

My father caught him at it. "Is there something you want?" he said.

"Jesus," I said, and her hand touched my leg under the table, as if telling me to hush. The man smiled, looking at my father, and then at Miss Guthrie. It was as easy to count the teeth as the gaps. His head was strangely elongated, and it seemed very unlikely that he was not carrying a gun.

He looked quickly at me, and dismissed what he saw. He took his first step away from the bar and moved toward the table. "Listen," I said, "nobody wants any trouble."

He stared at me with as much malice as he could collect, but I had been in a room with Hillary Van Wetter, and knew the real thing when I saw it. This one was a born trustee.

"Was anybody talking to you?" he said.

And then he was at the table, leaning over us, smiling. "Now," he said, "what bi'niss was it you said we had?"

The bartender noticed what was happening and called the man back. "Cleveland, leave them people alone and get back on your stool," he said.

But the man stayed where he was. "You smell sweet," he said to my father, "you know that?"

"If I were you," I said to him, "I'd go back to my stool."

"I can handle this," my father said, but the man had already turned to look at me.

"What's that supposed to signify?" he said.

"Cleveland, goddamnit," the bartender said, but the man held out his hand, as if to hush him.

211

"It means you came to the wrong table," I said, and in that moment, with the memory of what had happened to Ward so fresh in my mind, I was prepared to take things as far as they would go.

The man seemed to sense that, and went back to his stool at the bar, complaining to the bartender. "Working people got rights too," he said.

My father glared at him, and then turned his attentions back to the matter at hand. "Don't let him bother you," he said to her.

She batted her eyes at him, making the moment last. "Thank you," she said finally. "Men like that terrify me."

The truth, of course, is that she could have sent a man like that home boneless.

The man at the bar left a few minutes later, and when he was gone I got up to leave too. The margarita glasses were all over the table, the ashtray was full of cigarette butts. It was her habit to smoke perhaps a third of each cigarette and then put it out, as she used this gesture to punctuate her sentences.

❏

I MET MY FATHER coming in just as I was going out in the morning. His Chrysler rolled up into the driveway, then off the driveway into the front yard, and he stumbled out. His shirt was hanging free of his pants and he had no socks. He was bleary and drunk and wet, and I had not seen him so happy since the days when my mother was still at home and things had not started yet to go against him.

It was close to four in the morning. "A very intelligent young woman," he said, and stumbled past me to the steps.

I watched him climb to the porch, almost in slow motion, rocking at the top before he continued inside. It made me smile, to think of him staring down bar rats and then taking her to bed. It seemed to me he'd had a good night.

❏

LATE THE NEXT MORNING, after I had backed the truck into the bay and climbed down, she appeared from the rear door of the building, looking around her as if she were afraid to be seen.

"Happy birthday," I said.

"I wanted to talk to you about that night at your house," she said.

"Don't do that," I said.

"I just don't want any misunderstandings."

"We don't have to understand each other," I said, trying to get away. She stayed where she was, refusing to move until she'd finished.

"Sometimes when I drink old problems come back to haunt me," she said.

"We were both drinking," I said. And then, because she was still standing in front of me, not moving, I said, "It wasn't a bad night."

"I just don't want you to get the wrong idea," she said.

"I didn't." No inkling of what the right idea was. She looked at me as if she couldn't make up her mind.

"I'm twice as old as you are," she said.

"There is no problem," I said, and started around her.

"I'm not a tease," she said. And we stood in the garage, looking at each other. It is an uncomfortable thing, to lie to someone about things when you both know what is true. It asks too much of your authority, even if you're talking with a child.

In the end, we all know what we know.

The tip of her tongue appeared at the corner of her mouth, and then she bit her lower lip. "I've got to go punch the clock," I said. "I never got off the clock yesterday."

It was one of my father's rules, all employees punched time

clocks except the editorial staff. I remembered about half the time. Generally speaking, the reporters and editors didn't make any more money than the truck drivers or the mailers, but my father drew a distinction between the classes of workers, believing that those in the city room were above lying.

I stepped around Ellen Guthrie and walked back into the plant.

❑

SHE CALLED ME at home that afternoon. I had been swimming and I'd drunk a beer, and when the phone rang I was half asleep and thinking of Charlotte.

"I don't know what to do about you," she said.

I said neither did I, most of the time.

"Why don't you come over?" she said.

"Where?"

"My apartment," she said. "Right now if you want."

I told her I would be there in half an hour, and then, after I hung up the phone, I thought of my father coming in drunk and happy the night before, and I decided not to visit her after all.

I was never one to take a bite off someone else's fork.

I showered slowly and then went into the kitchen, took another beer from the refrigerator, and lay down on the couch in the living room with the newspaper.

She called again an hour later. "You're mad at me, aren't you?" she said.

"No," I said.

"Why don't you come over?"

"I don't know," I said, and stopped talking.

And then she hung up. When she called again, fifteen minutes later, my father was home and picked up the phone. His voice changed when he realized who it was; he laughed out loud, then he whispered. He stayed on the phone half an hour, and when he'd finished he came into the living room, carrying a bottle of wine for himself and a fresh beer for me.

"That was Ellen Guthrie," he said, and he sounded happy and surprised. "A very smart young woman," he said.

Which, of course, was absolutely true.

❑

ONE MORNING A MONTH LATER I found my father sharpening knives in the kitchen—a signal that things had not improved at the newspaper. It was his idiosyncrasy to sharpen blades when he was worried. During the year after my mother left, you could not reach into a kitchen drawer without drawing blood.

I was walking through the kitchen on the way to the garage. He was keeping steady company with Miss Guthrie now, coming home late and smiling every night, smelling sweetly pickled. In the mornings, the problems settled back in.

It was a Sunday and I was going to St. Augustine. I'd bought a car that week, an eight-year-old Ford station wagon with a decaying exhaust system and an accelerator which stuck when it was pressed to the floor. It cost three hundred and fifty dollars, and knowing it embarrassed my father to have a three-hundred-and-fifty-dollar automobile parked in front of the house, I left it along the narrow dirt alley that separated our property from the neighbor behind us. Sometimes at night, when I was out late myself, I turned off the engine at the street and allowed it to coast up the alley until it stopped.

He'd laid the pumice stone on the counter next to the sink, and pressed near the blade's edge with his fingers, working it in small circles. He was a perfectionist with his knives, and seemed to possess some innate sense of the spot where the stone and the steel touched; a certain understanding of the nature of friction.

"I see the Van Wetter fellow has been given a new trial,"

he said. He had seen that, among other places, on the front page of his own newspaper. The story had been there, one way or another, every day that week, as it had been on the front pages of most of the other newspapers in the state. Unlike the other papers, the *Moat County Tribune* did not include the names of the *Miami Times* reporters who were responsible for generating the new trial.

Three of my father's lost advertisers had not come back.

He was staring at the point of the knife, his fingertips bright red. He moved them slower now, more cautiously, as if he could feel the moment to quit coming.

"Maybe they'll hold it somewhere else," I said, thinking it would be better for him if they took the trial out of Lately.

"I doubt that they'll hold it at all," he said, still pressing, the sound of it in his voice. "People have moved, evidence has been lost . . ."

His voice died away, and I heard the blade working into the stone. A small, unobtrusive, chewing sound, you would never notice it except in the kind of silence that is made between two people, which is a different sound than silence you come across, say, underwater.

"They'll let him go," he said, and then his hands stopped and he looked up at me, a note of accusation in it. I shrugged.

"Then he'll go back to the river," I said.

I had been locked in a small room with Hillary Van Wetter, and knew what he was. I'd felt the cast of his bad intentions, and then the relief when he moved on to my brother or Yardley Acheman, or to Charlotte, and even understanding what he was, I didn't see that it made much difference if he were electrocuted by the state or living in remote regions of the swamp.

"Well," my father said, "I suppose he will."

It settled and then he said, "Have you spoken with your brother?"

I'd called half a dozen times that week, but he had not been at his apartment, or if he had, he was not answering the phone. "I don't think he cares about Hillary Van Wetter anymore," I said.

My father smiled, a small, brittle smile, knowing that wasn't true. Ward was not the son who quit on things when they became difficult. "He cares," he said.

I waited a moment, then started for the door.

"Was there something else that happened in Daytona?" he said suddenly. I turned and looked at him.

"You were there," he said.

I nodded but I didn't answer his question. I did not think he wanted me to answer.

"There's a story . . ."

He didn't finish the sentence, but left it there between us, waiting for me to tell him the story wasn't true.

"There are always stories when things happen," I said. Slowly, his fingers began to move again, and when I looked at the stone, there were beads of his blood on it. As I watched, the blood flattened, absorbed into the stone, staining it.

"You cut yourself," I said, and he looked at his fingers, finding the one he'd cut, and examined it first from one side and then the other.

"I've heard there was something . . . untoward," he said. "That the police cleaned up a mess."

"Why would they do that? No one cares who we are down there."

"I don't know," he said. He put his finger under the faucet. "It's just a story I heard."

"I don't think you should pay attention to stories about your own family," I said.

And we looked at each other again, wordless, full of accusations, and the water ran over his finger, both of us knowing who'd told him that something *untoward* had happened in

Daytona Beach. He turned off the faucet and wrapped the finger in a dish towel.

"It was nothing malicious," he said.

"What did she say?"

He shrugged. "Nothing specific, just that there was a story that was different from the one the police gave . . ."

He seemed to hear how weak the words sounded.

"She isn't a malicious person," he said. And now it was uncomfortable in the kitchen in a way that was different from the ordinary discomfort we suffered in each other's presence, as if some agreement between us had been broken off.

"Then she shouldn't be out repeating easy rumors," I said.

"She isn't easy, Jack," he said.

"Rumors, I said rumors. . . ."

"They aren't her rumors," he said, raising his voice, and there I was, standing in the kitchen, arguing with my sixty-one-year-old father about his girlfriend.

I said, "I'm going to the beach," and turned again to leave.

"People misunderstand Ellen," he said, and I heard her voice in that, whispering in his ear. "They take her the wrong way."

"In the end, I think people take you the way you are," I said.

"May I speak to you frankly?" he said. I waited, wishing I'd made it out the door before any of this started. "Ellen thinks that perhaps . . ."

He looked for the words.

". . . that you may have misunderstood . . ."

I didn't move an inch, not wanting to make it any easier.

"That you may have thought she was interested in you in a way that she isn't."

"In what way?" I said.

He held up his hand as if to say none of this was as important as I was making it. "These things happen," he said. "She knows that . . ."

"What things?"

He thought for a moment, deciding on the word. "A crush," he said, "younger man, older, experienced woman . . . perhaps it would be more comfortable for everyone if you didn't call her."

"I haven't called her," I said.

He smiled. "Then none of us has a problem," he said. And he peeked underneath the towel at his finger to see if the bleeding had stopped. I turned and headed out the door, letting it slam.

❑

A MONTH LATER, Ellen Guthrie was promoted to assistant managing editor of the *Moat County Tribune,* and a month after that, on a Friday, she moved into my father's house.

The following morning I met her in the hallway outside the bathroom; her hair was wet and she was dressed only in a University of Miami T-shirt, which barely covered her behind. My father was downstairs making flapjacks and sausage for breakfast. They were going bass fishing together out on the river. Ellen Guthrie had become inordinately interested in bass.

We stopped for a moment and I moved closer to the wall, not wanting to touch her accidentally as we passed, and then a certain bemused look crossed her face, a look which stirred me, and I walked past her into the bathroom and shut the door.

The air in the bathroom was still heavy from her shower, and the place smelled of the makeup and toiletries she'd put on, getting ready to deal with hooked fish.

I shaved and brushed my teeth, thinking of the look she'd given me in the hallway, and later in the day, while she and my father were out on the St. Johns River, I threw my best clothes into the station wagon, wrote a short note of resignation from my truck-driving duties, and fled Moat County.

It was the first time I left home, if you were willing to overlook Gainesville, and I'd driven south for an hour before I realized that I was headed for Miami.

It is probably true that, one way or another, I was always going home, even when I was leaving.

❑

MY BROTHER LIVED in a small apartment building overlooking Biscayne Bay, not far from the newspaper where he worked. I found the place and sat outside it in my car for half an hour, occupying myself with an imaginary swim across to Miami Beach. It was not much of a swim, an hour or less in the water, but the boat traffic was heavy, some of the ski boats pounding through at thirty or forty miles an hour, and I picked a spot on the beach where I would go in, and then followed my progress across into the channel, making allowances for the current and tide and the weeks it had been since I had trained, and following this route I was cut to pieces about a hundred and fifty yards offshore by an ancient Chris-Craft being driven by two fellows in beards, one of them in a white sailor's hat.

I looked back at the apartment and followed myself, disemboweled or worse, up the steps that led to the hallway. Before I could imagine Ward's face when he opened the door, I turned on the car.

The engine swelled then dropped into a low rumble, and I drove up and down the streets near my brother's apartment building for hours, looking at the apartments with vacancy signs in the windows, and finally stopped at one, more because there was a place to park in front than anything about the apartment itself, and rented a furnished room for a month.

"It's just one of you," the woman said, "you sure."

"Just me."

"They sometimes come in here, one person, the next thing you know, there's twelve of them inside, sleeping on the floors. . . ."

"I don't know twelve people," I said.

She nodded, thinking it over. "You want clean linen service?" she said.

I did not answer at first, thinking the question might be some sort of test to see if I would be sleeping twelve.

"You got your own linens?" she said, impatient now.

"No," I said.

"I put you down for the clean linen service," she said, and then, in the same breath, she told me the house rule: "Don't bother with nobody and they don't bother with you."

❏

I TOOK THE THINGS from my car to the room, making two trips, walking past a thickset man with frog's eyes who stood outside his door, smoking a tiny butt of a cigarette, staring at me as if he might be interested in asking for a date. I understood right away that Miami was not like the other two places I'd lived.

I shut the door to the room and locked it, dropping a hook into an eyebolt, and sat on the bare mattress. I felt the bedsprings yawn and hold. There were dark stains in the carpet, almost a crust. I thought of my brother's apartment building, which had not looked so different from this one from the street, and wondered if the rules were the same there. *Don't bother with nobody and nobody will bother with you.* Perhaps that was why he liked the place, why he liked the city.

There was a knock at the door, and then a man's voice. "You home, buddy boy?"

I lay down on my mattress, trembling.

"Buddy boy?"

The man came back half a dozen times over the next few days, but I did not answer the door.

❑

I WENT OUT OF the room to swim and to eat, and at night I would walk in the neighborhood, looking at the girls.

I hoped to run into Ward on the street, to have him spot me alone in the city and take me back to his apartment, back into my family, but I saw there were too many streets for that, and too many people on them. And in the end I went to the newspaper to find him, thinking that was somehow less of an imposition than appearing on his doorstep.

❑

THE CITY ROOM WAS a maze of desks and telephones and type-writers, all of it submerged in smoke, and I wandered into it unnoticed and asked a woman sitting in front for directions to Ward's office. She did not look up from her typewriter, but cast her fingers in a short arc toward the back. There was a stub of a cigarette between the fingers she used to point, about the size of an engagement ring.

I crossed the city room, passing a hundred reporters and editors who never looked up, who understood intuitively that I was not important, and asked for my brother again.

❑

HE WAS SITTING ALONE in an office with two desks. The office was smaller than the room he had occupied over the Moat Cafe in Lately, and it had no windows except the one that faced the larger room outside. The place smelled of Yardley Acheman's toiletries.

My brother was wearing a white shirt and a tie, and studying a bound, familiar-looking document which was several inches thick. He did not leave his reading immediately to see who had walked through his door, but held up one finger, asking for a moment to finish. Then he looked up and saw me.

He had lost his left eye, and covered it with a patch, and there was something different in the shape of his face, a certain roundness which took a moment to find. There were small white scars at the sides of his nose, and a larger scar an inch below his lower lip, which followed the line of the lip for most of its run and then reeled down and then straight up, intersecting it just at the corner of his mouth. The flesh billowed on both sides of the cut.

He smiled and the lip flattened against the teeth underneath it, and he looked more like himself. He stood up, leaning across his desk.

"Where have you been?" he said, and I could hear that he was glad to see me. I felt my eyes begin to tear.

"Miami," I said, "looking around."

"World War said you might show up. . . ." It was quiet a moment while we looked at each other. It was not the eye patch that caught me again, but the roundness of his face. It did not seem like such an unnatural thing to have lost an eye.

"He's worried," Ward said.

"I left him a note."

"It didn't say where you were going."

I shrugged and my brother settled back into his chair, still smiling at me, happy that I was there. "Sit down," he said, but the only empty chair in the room was behind the other desk. I hesitated, remembering how Yardley Acheman behaved when he'd found me behind his desk before.

"He's gone for the week," Ward said.

I sat down, feeling the chair turn under me. A soft, well-oiled chair, better than the chairs that the reporters and editors in the main room had. And his desk was wood instead of metal, and the typewriter was a brand-new Underwood.

"He said you bought a hot rod and took off," Ward said.

I nodded at that, not wanting to go into the rest of it then;

it felt like I'd been on the road since I left home. I looked out the window, I rocked back and forth in Yardley's chair. "Yardley's taking a few days off?" I said.

"Celebrating," he said. "The prosecutor's decided not to take Van Wetter back to trial."

"He celebrates a lot."

Ward nodded and fingered the document in front of him, straightening it with the edges of the desk. I recognized it then, the first hundred pages or so of the transcript of Hillary Van Wetter's trial.

"Well, I guess it's what we wanted," I said.

He stared at the transcript again, then he reached under his eye patch with one finger and scratched. A moment later he put the trial into one of his filing cabinets and recovered his good mood. He asked about World War's new girlfriend.

I told him it wasn't going to feel comfortable calling her "Mom."

❏

THERE WAS A LETTER from Charlotte a few days later. It was addressed to my brother, but was written to us both. Yardley Acheman got a letter of his own, which lay unopened on his desk with the rest of the mail that came while he was gone.

The letter to Ward and me was strangely detached, thanking us for our help in saving Hillary. It said that she still intended to marry him, but had no details on the date. We were on the guest list. Common-law marriages were traditional among the Van Wetters, it said, but she was holding out for a ceremony with a Baptist minister. It was signed "Fondly, Charlotte."

My brother showed me the letter over lunch at a cafeteria a few blocks from the newspaper. There was another place where most of the younger reporters ate which was closer, but my brother preferred not being around them.

Too many of them were "journalists" now, enamored with the importance of the calling and anxious to tell their readers what stories meant, not so enamored with the stories themselves.

The letter had been folded in half and then turned and folded again twice the other way to make it fit into the envelope. It was written on lined paper in careful loops. Good margins, no misspelled words, a formal sort of letter, in its way.

"It's like the thank-you notes Mother used to make us write to Aunt Dorothy after Christmas," I said.

He nodded, but he was not thinking of it that way. "She's trying to close it off," he said finally.

"Close what off?"

"We're unfinished business," he said, and then he picked up the envelope the letter had been mailed in and studied the postmark: Lately.

"She has what she wants," he said, and the words stabbed me. A glass of milk had been sitting in front of Ward all during lunch—we were taught not to wash down our food—and now he picked it up and drank it. As he lifted the glass, I noticed the scar beneath his lip again.

"It's bothering her," he said.

"What?"

He did not speak again for a little while, and then he said, "You have any luck this morning?"

I had gone to the employment office at the *Times* and applied for work in the newsroom. Under references, I had put my brother and, at Ward's encouragement, Yardley Acheman. "I'm supposed to take a test," I said.

He nodded at that, still thinking about Charlotte.

"You wonder," he said finally, "why she sent a separate letter to Yardley."

"He was the one fucking her," I said.

He shook his head, not wanting to get near that.

I didn't push the subject. When I first began hearing stories about fucking, perhaps in second grade, hearing them from so many places I knew there was something to it, I had the distinct thought walking home from school one afternoon that the world would be a better, simpler place if none of it were true.

My brother, I believe, carried that same sentiment through his life.

"A lot of people sleep with each other," he said. "I don't think it matters much to her." We looked at each other over the empty dishes. "It's something else."

"Then open Yardley's letter," I said. He smiled at me; we both knew he would never do that. The waitress came, and Ward gave her a five-dollar bill.

"How are you for money?" he said.

"I've got some left."

"Whatever you need," he said.

"No," I said, "I've got as much as I need."

It was awkward; we were not used to taking care of each other. "So the girlfriend moved into the house," he said finally.

"The medicine cabinet's full of makeup," I said. "Little brushes all over the place . . ."

He nodded, picturing it.

"She spends a lot of time on her face," I said.

"Well," he said a little later, "as long as World War's happy."

"He seems happy," I said, "but he spends so much time pretending to be happy, you can't always tell."

For all our lives, every time the library or the highway got money from the federal government, every time a sixth grader went to the state finals of the spelling bee, or Weldon Pine was named lawyer of the year, or a barn fire was extinguished by the volunteer fire company in Thorn, my father was happy. He was expected to be happy. And when the federal government did not come through with money for the highway, or when the fire company did not get to the barn in time, he was hurt.

It is difficult, of course, to ride the pulse of community life in this way, as invariably you are required to be happy and sad at the same time. For the editor and publisher of the *Moat County Tribune,* however, it had become as natural as getting dressed for work. Perhaps it was part of getting dressed.

At the bottom of it, however, what made him happy had nothing to do with the content of the news itself, but the process of distributing it. There was a confusion and loss of direction in the process, and it was finding a way through that he liked.

I wondered if that somehow applied to his flirtation with Miss Guthrie, but it was not the sort of question he would entertain, not even in retrospect, if she'd left and he was lost. He did not second-guess himself, for fear of what would unravel.

❑

AT LUNCH A DAY LATER, Ward asked if the lost advertisers had returned to the *Tribune*; then he asked about World War's angina.

The nerve had been severed in his lip, and occasionally milk or soup would leak from the spot where it had been cut and run all the way to his chin before he felt it there and wiped it off.

We had been brought up with table manners, but the food falling from the dead part of his lip seemed to cause him no embarrassment now.

❑

ANOTHER DAY, he asked suddenly what had become of the lawyer Weldon Pine, if he had stayed in Lately after he retired or moved to a city. I sensed that he regretted the trouble the story had caused the old man.

Later, he was preoccupied with Uncle Tyree.

"What if it turned out that the old man and his whole family, right down to the mutes, are all smarter than we are?" he said.

"What if they are?"

He held up his finger, wanting me to wait while he finished the thought. "What if they know us better than we know them? What if they knew what we would do?"

I waited until I was sure he was finished. "It still doesn't matter," I said.

He looked at me and smiled, as if I'd missed the point. "Things got out of hand for a little while," I said. "You got hurt and Yardley wrote his story and now it's over. Hillary's gone back to the swamp. . . ."

He picked up a hamburger he'd ordered and took a bite. A trickle of grease ran from his lip. "What if they used us?" he said.

The grease reached the part of his chin where his sense of feeling was intact, and he wiped at it with his napkin.

"What if we used them?" I said. "That's the game, isn't it? You use them, they use you. . . ."

"It isn't always like that," he said. "It doesn't have to be . . ." He thought a moment, perhaps trying to remember a case when it wasn't.

"It's like fishing," I said. "You really aren't up to it if you start out worried about the worm."

He leaned across the table, lowering his voice. "You haven't seen it when you get it exactly right, Jack," he said. "When you get things down just the way they were . . ."

"What then?" I said.

He smiled at me, his chin shining with grease. "It makes it bearable," he said. And it seemed for a moment that his voice was coming to me from the recovery room.

"You can't ever know exactly who somebody is," I said, and that lay on the table between us a long time.

228

❏

ALTHOUGH YARDLEY ACHEMAN could not be reached for his recommendation, I was hired as a copyboy in the *Times* newsroom, and started at more money than any of the reporters at my father's newspaper were paid.

Yardley stayed in New York an extra week, interviewing for jobs at both the *Times* and the *Daily News,* and socializing with famous writers and journalists at a bar called Elaine's.

He liked being with famous writers, and would labor to work their names into conversation when he got back.

While Yardley was in New York, my brother stayed at his desk, eight hours a day, going back again and again over the boxes of papers that he had accumulated in Moat County. There was nothing new in any of the boxes—he could by now recite all the times and dates and names—but he was unable to shake the feeling that there was a hidden order in them which he hadn't seen.

He had begun to believe that the Van Wetter clan had somehow designed the story which eventually appeared under his name.

Ward had arranged for my hiring and now he arranged for my hours to coincide with his, an accommodation which infuriated the copyboys who had been in the newsroom longer. One or two had gone so far as to file grievances with the union.

But if my brother had interfered with the normal processes of seniority, he had not done it out of partisanship. He wanted me close by because I had been with him in Moat County; I had seen what I had seen.

He was entertaining the idea now that Tyree Van Wetter had paid a man to represent himself as the contractor who bought the sod, that being the only real option to Yardley's having made the whole thing up.

He spent whole afternoons in search of honorable explanations for Yardley Acheman.

"How did they find him, then?" I said one afternoon as we were leaving the *Times*. "If he was there when Yardley went down, he'd of been there when we went down. If Yardley could find him, you could find him. . . ."

He trusted me in a way that I could never define, or earn, but still he fought what was in front of him. I knew it wasn't finished.

I asked if we were going back to Daytona Beach.

"I think we'd be better off talking to some of the Van Wetters again," he said.

I thought of the black moccasin dropping from the dead tree into the water that first time we waded in.

"Not me."

"Sometimes," he said, "you've got to watch people a long time to see who they are."

I stopped on the sidewalk and looked at him. "You mean you're worried they were on their best behavior?"

And he smiled a little at that, flattening his lip across his teeth. And I knew he was going back, and that I was going with him. I could not stand to see him hurt again, unless I was hurt too. To borrow a word, that was the only thing that would make it *bearable*.

❑

YARDLEY RETURNED TO MIAMI the next week with the news of his engagement to a magazine writer from New York. He had not told the one in Palm Beach yet that they were quits, and wondered out loud how that was done.

A story about the Van Wetter case had appeared in *Time* magazine that week which referred to Yardley as an important new voice in newspapers, one of the emerging "new journalists." My brother was hardly mentioned in this piece, but then, he had not returned the phone call from the reporter from *Time.*

The story and the accompanying picture were clipped out of the magazine and pasted on the city room bulletin board, and a caption was written beneath it: "WHAT IS MISSING FROM THIS PICTURE?"

Yardley Acheman was despised in the newsroom now by all but a handful of young reporters—some of them with college degrees in journalism—who wrote stories imitating his style. Not having my brother to supply these stories with the weight of incident and facts, however, the pieces they wrote were masturbatory in nature, stuff that even I—a dropout of the University of Florida swimming team—would have been ashamed to have written.

They were the sort of things that Yardley had produced before he and my brother were attached to each other by the editors of the *Miami Times.*

Yardley ignored his critics and encouraged his imitators, praising them extravagantly for the most ordinary and, in most cases, out-of-place prose. Even when this prose was thrown back at them by old-school editors who told them to fill the holes with facts, not flowers.

My brother was affected neither by the piece in *Time* magazine nor by its appearance on the city room bulletin board, even the part in which he was referred to by Yardley Acheman as "a more traditional, nuts and bolts, kind of reporter"—in contrast to Yardley himself, who, in his own words, was "the one who saw the shapes and meanings of stories in nontraditional ways."

❑

WE WERE TOGETHER all the time, Ward and I. We ate together, we came to work together, we left together. I wondered sometimes which of us was protecting the other, but when I entered my building at night after I'd dropped him off, and the fat man with the frog's eyes came out of his room to watch me walk down the hall, I was always reminded of what happened in Daytona Beach, and felt secure somehow knowing I'd left Ward safely at his own door.

Sometimes the fat man smiled as I passed and sometimes he made clucking sounds out of the side of his mouth. It seemed clear to me that he was violating the rule of the house, bothering me in this way, and some nights, when I'd had trouble of one kind or another at work, I found myself enraged over this violation, an almost unmanageable anger.

I felt oddly whole, to be that angry.

I had wondered, of course, who the man was, and then one morning on the way to my car another resident of the house fell in next to me, wanting a ride to north Palm Beach County, where he said he could get some day work picking fruit, and told me that Froggy Bill, as he was called, had once been a cop. That he lived on a pension now.

"You got to be a real bad cop before they throw you out," he said. "You got to do things that bring you to public attention."

I told the man it was none of my business, and gave him a dollar for the bus, and left him there on the curb while I drove to work.

❏

I DID NOT MENTION Froggy Bill to Ward; in fact, I never spoke to him about the place where I lived. I suppose he assumed it was like his own place—an apartment with a bedroom and a kitchen and a bathroom.

My bathroom, however, was at the end of the hall. I went there early in the morning, before the sun rose, to keep myself removed from Froggy Bill's daily routine.

❏

ONE NIGHT I HEARD a man scream. I was in the hallway and the scream came from Froggy Bill's apartment, and lasted only a second or two and then died, as if the screamer had run out of air.

I stood still, listening, ready to run for the door if Froggy Bill emerged with a body, but there were no other screams. The whole rooming house was quiet. I began to wonder if it was Bill himself who had screamed, but I do not know the answer to that, even now.

❏

WARD DECIDED TO RETURN to Moat County, over the objections of the Sunday editor—the man with the beard who had come to Moat County to push the story ahead when Ward was in the hospital—and Yardley Acheman, who was anxious to leave the Van Wetter matter behind him.

Yardley said it was time to move on to something else, while he and Ward were still "hot," that timing was everything. He did not say what the next story might be, and I don't believe it was anything he had considered. My brother found the stories.

Ward said he would be back in a few days.

They were in the office, Ward, Yardley, and the Sunday editor. I was standing outside, holding a tray of mail to sort. I began to move past the door when I heard Yardley Acheman again. "Maybe I ought to go to Daytona," he said, "see what I can find there."

And he was not talking about matters of sod and condominium builders.

"Whatever you think," Ward said.

❑

THAT NIGHT, after work, we threw a few days' worth of clothes into the back of the Ford and headed north to Moat County. He used vacation days to make the trip.

It was hot even at night, and we drove with the windows open, the bugs as hard as pebbles as they hit my arm.

"I don't think we ought to stay in Lately," I said.

He shrugged. "We can stay at home."

"I don't think we ought to stay there either," I said. "They may be butt-naked in the kitchen."

He considered that and withdrew from the conversation. It did not matter to him how we would be received, it did not matter to him where we would stay. It did not matter to him if we slept in the car.

"I wonder if the girl married him," he said later, speaking of Charlotte. We'd stopped at an all-night gas station and bought a six-pack of beer, and the beer seemed to relax him.

"She said she was going to send us invitations," I said.

"It might be different, what she thinks now of the way this all came out," he said.

I pictured her in the wetlands, waiting with her spoon for the men to finish what they wanted of the ice cream. I did not think she would stay married to Hillary Van Wetter very long. I thought this might cure her of killers forever.

❑

WE CAME IN BY BOAT, and found the place more easily than we had before. Everything in my life was easier without Yardley Acheman around. The old man—Tyree—was in the yard, working on an alligator with a thin, black-handled knife, mak-

234

ing the cuts effortlessly, pulling the skin back from the flesh underneath.

He straightened when he heard the engine, turned and stared at us as I slowed the boat and headed it into the bank. He gave no indication that he remembered us, although I did not believe that he had so many guests he couldn't keep us straight.

I killed the engine a few feet from land and jumped into the river to pull the boat up. The old man turned back to the alligator, putting his knife into the animal's throat and cutting him all the way to the back legs.

He put his hand in then, up near the throat, and pulled it down, the viscera falling out along the line he had cut, just below his hand. When he'd finished, it did not seem possible that there was enough room inside the alligator for everything that had come out.

"Mr. Van Wetter?" my brother said.

The old man put the knife point-down in his back pocket and his hands on either side of the cut and pulled it apart. The muscles in his forearms boiled up into his skin. There was a cracking sound and I glimpsed the cavity inside.

When the old man turned around again, his hands were slick with the animal's juice.

"Mr. Van Wetter, I am Ward James," my brother said. "I was here before."

He nodded, barely, and something wet dripped off his fingers. "You wrote the story in the paper," he said.

My brother nodded.

"Well," he said, "you said you would."

Ward and I stood still and waited.

The old man waited too.

"There are a few more things . . ." my brother said.

"Hillary ain't in prison anymore," he said. He put his hands on his hips, and the muscles sagged in his arms. "When a thing is over, it's over. Paperboys don't understand that. We been bothered to death over this, even had people coming out here to take pictures at night . . ."

There was a sound from the house, and a small, bullet-headed man I had never seen before came through the door holding a baseball bat at about the balance point, his hand covering the label. He walked slowly across the yard, holding the bat and a singular purpose, and I saw that once we were in range, he would begin his work without a word.

You would get as much mercy from a cat.

The old man watched him come, then glanced at me. "Something's telling you to get back in your boat, ain't it?" he said. I nodded yes.

The man was a few yards away now, and the bat moved in his hand until he held it near the handle.

I took a step backward and looked at Ward, making sure I knew where he was.

My brother held his ground, welcoming this.

The man was almost on us when the old man held up his hand, still glistening with alligator. The man with the bat stopped as suddenly as he had started. He held the bat on his shoulder, where he could swing it, and stared at me with a look of absolute indifference.

The old man reconsidered my brother. "You ain't going to just go away, are you?" he said.

"No sir," Ward said.

"I see how you lost that eye," he said.

My brother looked around, first at the man with the bat, then at the house beyond. "I have some things to ask Hillary," he said.

"Hillary's the wrong man to be bothering right now," the old man said. "He's into a mood since they let him out."

Ward glanced at the man with the bat. "What sort of mood?" he said.

"Changed his disposition," the old man said. "Being in prison does that, I suppose."

It was quiet while the old man contemplated Hillary, and the change in him since he returned from prison. He seemed worried about the change and resigned to it at the same time.

"Took the fun out of everything," he said a little later.

My brother nodded, as if he agreed with that.

"He's got the girl," Ward said, and that made the old man smile.

"She ain't the kind of girl that restores fun," he said, "she's the kind that points up the lack." He turned and looked at the man with the bat. "Put that down now," he said quietly, and the man dropped the barrel of the bat to the ground, then leaned on the handle. He continued to stare at us without a glimmer of interest in who we were.

My brother waited, and I waited with him. The old man stretched his neck and stomped a pinecone flat. Absently, he turned and looked at the alligator. The thing had shrunk in the few minutes since it had been emptied, and begun to curl, almost as if it had been set on fire.

"Truth be known, Mr. James," the old man said, "Hillary never was the one to visit."

"I don't want to stay for dinner," Ward said. "I just want to ask him some questions."

The old man stuck his hands in his trousers. "There ain't a thing in this world you can do for him. The only thing can help him is time."

"It isn't for him," Ward said.

The old man seemed surprised. "Then why would he care to have you visit?"

"He knows me," my brother said. "I came to help him when he was in prison."

"He'll hold that against you," the old man said. "He don't like to be helped."

"Where is he?" Ward said.

The old man frowned, "There is a side to you that provokes a person, you know that?"

My brother stood still.

"I told you already he's in a mood. I ain't giving directions, if that's what you want. . . ."

Ward nodded, leaving the question there between them. The old man waited too, and finally Ward said it again.

"Where is he?"

The old man spit on his hands and wiped them on his overalls. "Right back where he was, I expect," he said, and that was as much as he would say. The man with the bat stood flat-eyed, his legs still spread for leverage if he were asked to swing.

"He moved a brother out of that house with an ax handle," the old man said, "a blood relation. Didn't want nobody around."

The old man looked quickly at the man holding the bat. "He would of used it too," the old man said. The man with the bat nodded.

"I need to talk to him," my brother said again.

"You do what you need to do," the old man said. "Tell him I said hello." He turned away and went back to finish skinning the alligator. A rooster walked between the old man's feet, and he turned, faster than I had imagined an old man could move, and kicked the bird halfway to the house.

The man with the bat watched the rooster hit the ground and roll, and then run into the tree line at the edge of the yard. A small smile touched the corners of his mouth.

❑

WE WERE BACK in the boat, and the air blew over my face and through my hair. I sat at the motor, Ward sat in front, facing me. He had gotten in that way and never turned around. He was staring over my shoulder at the encampments along the shore.

❏

ALONE, EITHER MY BROTHER or I might have slipped in and out of Moat County without visiting our father, but together we were somehow enjoined to stop.

We acknowledged that without talking about it, but put the meeting off, spending the night in a tourists' hotel on the other side of the river, south of Palatka, which had no hot water.

I slept badly on the soft mattress and finally moved to the floor, waking up stiff and not liking the day's prospects. We drove in silence to Lately, and then south to Thorn, planning to shower at home.

A disease had claimed most of the town's trees that spring, leaving the houses to the hard light of the sun. It seemed to have bleached them all. I had been gone only a few months.

There were tricycles in a yard across the street from my father's house, and I remembered that the old woman who lived there had died. A long time ago she had stood at the window early in the morning, her hand on the telephone to call my father if my brother walked across her grass delivering the newspaper. I went with him in those days, wanting to be a paperboy myself.

Our own house, without its trees, seemed smaller than it had. The grass needed mowing and a hose had been left lying in the yard, not rolled up and returned to its spot on the garage wall. A stump five feet across marked the elm that had shaded the porch.

There were no cars in the driveway. I steered the Ford in and stopped. I sat looking at the place a moment while Ward got out, carrying clean clothes, and went to the door.

The door did not open when he pushed it. He stared at it a moment, then went through his keys—he had a ring of perhaps fifteen of them, I don't think he ever threw one away—

and found one and fit it into the lock. I stayed in the car a moment longer, thinking of pulling it around to the alley in back.

And then I reconsidered the grass and the hose and the look of the street without its trees, and I remembered that my father had moved a woman into his house, in full sight of the neighbors, and it did not seem so important now that a rusted station wagon was sitting in his driveway.

I went inside. The walls in the living room had been painted a soft beige. There were plants in the corners that had never been there before, and a new sofa, which did not look as if it were designed to sit on. All the furniture, as I looked around, was new, with the exception of my father's chair. The stains from his hair oil were missing, though; it had been reupholstered.

An air conditioner had been stuck into a large side window, and the place had a department store odor. I stood in the living room, trying to remember what color the walls had been before they were painted. Ward went upstairs, and a minute later I heard a door close and then running water.

I walked into the kitchen, and things were more familiar. I found a beer in the refrigerator and sat down at the kitchen table to wait for Ward to finish. There was another shower in the basement, but if you turned it on while the one upstairs was running, the water up there turned cold.

I lay the lip of the beer cap against the table's edge and hit it once with the flat part of my hand. The cap rolled across the floor, and the foam came up out of the bottle and over my hand and pants, and I covered it with my mouth.

At the same moment I tasted the beer, the shower stopped. It didn't seem like he'd been in there long enough to get as wet as I had from the beer.

And then I heard them talking, his voice then hers, and realized slowly that she was still in the house. I walked back into the living room, holding on to the beer, and met her as she came down the stairs.

She was still in her nightshirt, and the flesh around her eyes was swollen from sleep and she had not cleaned the makeup off her eyes the night before. She was barefoot, and her arms looked chubby and dimpled. She crossed them over her chest.

"What do you think you're doing?" she said, looking at the beer.

My brother was moving around upstairs, banging things as he hurried.

"This isn't a public bath," she said.

I sat down on the new couch. "We were here first," I said. The woman was not going to chase me out of the house where I had grown up. I was thinking I would sit in that spot for a month.

"I told your brother, and I will tell you," she said, "don't ever walk into this house again without knocking."

I looked up the staircase. "You got the paperboy up there, or what?"

"That's it," she said. "Get out."

I lifted the beer to my lips and sipped at it again, watching her. I sat back farther into the couch.

"I don't want to make this more unpleasant than it already is," she said.

It seemed suddenly as if my father were in the room too, as if she and I were both weighing our behavior to look good in his eyes, and I was sorry I'd made the remark about the paperboy, knowing that he would not like that.

"We just came over to take showers," I said. "The motel didn't have hot water."

I could see that settle, that we weren't going to stay overnight. Ward came down the stairs then, his hair dripping, carrying his shoes and socks and the clothes he'd worn in.

"Ready?" he said.

"I'm going to take a shower," I said, and I got up and carried my beer and my clean clothes past her and up the stairs. There was a bad moment, climbing the stairs, when I realized I was leaving my brother alone in the living room with her.

"This is going to be unpleasant for us all," she said, but I climbed to the top of the stairs and followed my brother's footprints into the bathroom.

I locked the door, turned on the shower, and sat down on the toilet to finish the beer. My hand was shaking. The part I cannot explain is that I was again entertaining the thought of fucking her. The sink was full of her things—lipstick, makeup, brushes, perfume—and there was a sanitary napkin wrapper in the wastebasket. New towels hung on the racks.

I set the bottle on the floor next to the toilet and stood up. I opened the medicine cabinet and saw that she had taken it over too. Dexedrine.

I wondered if once she had been fat.

I took off my clothes, letting them drop off me onto the floor, and stepped into the shower. There was a brush hanging from the faucet which had never been there before, and I used it to wash my behind. The soap had a peculiar, perfumed smell, and I'd never heard of the shampoo.

I stayed in the shower a long time, thinking I should run all the hot water out of the heater and allow Miss Guthrie to shower cold that morning, but the thought of Ward downstairs with her intruded again, and finally I turned off the water, stepped out of the tub, and dried myself off.

Ellen Guthrie had gone into the kitchen when I got back down, and Ward was outside in the car. I heard her dialing the telephone and a moment later noticed the smell of the dirty clothes in my hand, rancid and sweet at the same time. There is an odor that goes with being scared.

I walked quietly out of the house and dropped the clothes into the garbage can in the driveway. I started the car—the sound of the engine brought one of the neighbors to her window—and drove downtown, toward my father's office, and the smell of the clothes was still on my hands.

MY FATHER WAS SITTING at his desk, running a letter opener he had been given by the Florida Chapter of the National Association for the Advancement of Colored People over the pads of his fingers. I suppose there were no knives available to sharpen there in the office.

He stood up when we came in, not even pretending to be surprised, shaking hands with us in a solemn way, smiling in a way that was both preoccupied and polite. Not pretending that she hadn't already called.

"So," he said, "what brings the *Miami Times* back to Moat County?" And there was a certain reproach in that, directed as much at me as my brother.

"A few things to check," Ward said.

My father nodded, in the same, familiar way he'd nodded for years when my mother spoke to him while he was reading his newspapers after dinner. He wasn't listening.

I sat down in one of the chairs, Ward stood near the desk. He would not sit down without being invited. "We thought maybe we'd take you to lunch," Ward said. I looked at the clock on the wall, a little after eleven. My father settled back into his chair and put his hands behind his head.

"That would be wonderful, boys," he said, "but I'm on the hook with some advertisers." Moments passed. "You know," he said finally, "I got a call a little while ago from Ellen." And he looked at each of us, taking his time, as if he were trying to decide which of us to keep.

"We didn't mean to barge in," Ward said, "we thought she'd be at work."

"She works late and comes in late," he said. "She puts in more hours than any editor here."

"I only meant we wouldn't have gone inside if we'd thought she was there," he said.

I said, "We needed to shower before we went up to Lately, and the hotel didn't have hot water."

But he was not interested in the hotel or what we were going to do in Lately.

"It's always your home too," he said, "you know that, but it might not be a bad idea for now, while Ellen's getting used to me, if you knocked before you went in."

He checked to see if he'd insulted us.

"She might be running around the kitchen in her underwear," he said.

We all sat a moment or two, contemplating that, and then the phone rang and he picked it up. "W. W. James," he said.

It was Ellen; it was in his face before he said a word. I stood up and headed toward the door. "We can wait outside," I said.

He said, "Just a minute," into the mouthpiece and then covered it with his hand and smiled at us as we went out the door. "Thanks for stopping by," he said. And then he hurried around his desk, still holding the phone, and shook hands with each of us again.

I closed the door when we were out of the office, and looked back once. He was sitting in his chair again, the phone cradled under his chin, smiling as he nodded at something she was saying on the other end.

The next time I went to my father's house, the door locks had been changed.

❏

WE DROVE BACK TO Lately in the afternoon, passing the spot where Sheriff Call was found dead, and, a few miles farther north, the little store operated by the Van Wetters.

I glanced into the parking lot and thought of the child's beating, and it seemed like a long time since that had happened. I was angry at my father, that he had asked us to knock at our own house, but Ward was unaffected. He wasn't tied to the place the way I was.

"He wants us to knock," I said.

He said, "Maybe we'll forget about the courthouse, and go straight to the sheriff's."

I followed a long curve in the road and then passed an old truck carrying a load of gravel, pushing the accelerator all the way to the floor as I came up on him from behind, and then, back on my own side of the road, reaching down to the floorboard with my hand to get it unstuck. The car swerved, hit the soft shoulder of the road, and then corrected; eighty miles an hour, and my brother sat as unbothered as if I had leaned forward to take out the cigarette lighter.

❏

THE MAN BEHIND THE DESK at the Moat County Sheriff's Department did not look up until Ward had finished speaking. When he did, I saw his eyes were red, as if he had been drinking. "What is it you want?" he said.

My brother went through it again, saying the same words, and the man behind the desk nodded all the way through, reminding us he had heard it before. And when Ward had finished, the man said, "But what I asked you, what is it you want?"

"I want to know how to get to Hillary Van Wetter's place," Ward said.

The man behind the desk was suddenly angry. "I asked you what for," he said.

Ward held his ground, and when I began to explain that there were a few questions we wanted to ask, he stopped me, interrupting almost before I'd begun.

"That is a private matter," he said.

The deputy smiled at us. "You're the ones wrote that story in the paper, aren't you?" he said. "And now you finding out it wasn't the way you put it down?"

My brother did not answer; he didn't move. He only waited. "You know he cut a man's thumb off?" the deputy said. He was looking at me now, and I nodded. "Over a traffic ticket?"

The deputy looked at his own thumb, and then at Ward. "Is there somebody who can tell us how to get out there?" Ward said.

"You might as well cut off a man's hand," the deputy said. Ward kept himself still, the deputy thought it over.

"I'll tell you exactly where he is," he said finally. "You can go out there and see for yourself what you saved."

My brother took a pen from his pocket to write down the instructions, but the deputy was agitated now, and took a pencil from his drawer and began to draw a map.

The man's fingers were thick and blunted, as if the tips had been caught in a car door, but he drew with a delicate motion, careful of the shapes of intersections, the size of his roads, the shoreline of the river. He stopped from time to time to judge the proportions of the drawing, and then leaned back into it, filling in certain areas with shading, or erasing part of the shoreline, remembering a place where the land hooked into the water. He labeled roads and intersections in perfect block letters.

My brother stayed still, waiting for him to finish. The man enjoyed sketching, and Ward didn't interrupt to say there was no need for block lettering and shading. A pest strip hung from the ceiling near the window, covered with flies.

I wondered what the man might have done with his talent if he hadn't caught on with the sheriff's department. If it might have made him into someone else.

In those days, it didn't seem possible that someday I might wonder what I would have become if things had gone differently for me. I thought all the choices would always be in front of me.

He pulled away from his work and looked at it another moment, enjoying it, and then handed it to my brother.

***

"Anybody was to ask," he said, "you didn't get it here."

My brother folded the paper carefully, acknowledging the work that went into it, and put it into his pocket. "I appreciate this," he said.

"You think so?" the deputy said.

And then he got up and walked through an open door into the back. He was a heavy man, and the creases in his pants where he'd been sitting stayed pressed against his flesh as he went.

❑

WE FOLLOWED THE MAP.

It took us north of Lately and then east, along a dirt road through dense stands of pine, the soil itself gradually getting darker as we came closer to the river. We were perhaps twenty minutes in the pines, driving slowly, as I did not want to be in this place with a broken axle.

The road emptied into a clearing, and we saw the river. Glimpses of the sun reflecting off it, through the trees on the other side. I stopped the car. The road itself seemed for a moment to have disappeared, but then I noticed old car tracks beneath the weeds.

No one had driven through in a long time.

We sat in the car, at the edge of the clearing. My brother looked at the map, laid it on his lap and studied it, looking up from time to time to check a landmark. He put his finger on a spot near a shaded area and the river.

"We're here," he said.

I looked at it and saw the deputy had the road continuing to the river and then another two or three miles north. At the end of his map was a small house with a pitched roof, surrounded by a fence, and the words *Van Wetter* had been printed underneath.

"This isn't a road anymore," I said. Ward studied the map.

"We could get this thing high centered and have to walk out again," I said.

"If there was a road once, it's still there," he said, and I sheared the car into first gear and started through. A doe appeared in the weeds ahead of us, picked up her head and watched us pass, leaving a path of tall grass bent to the ground behind.

I kept the car moving straight, and then we dropped into a deep rut, slamming the underside against the ground. The engine quit, and in the quiet I could hear the insects.

"Are we out of gas?" he said.

I turned the key and the engine turned with it. I found myself wondering if Hillary Van Wetter had heard the car. If he already knew who it was.

The engine caught and the old Ford climbed out of the hole and headed back across the clearing.

Ahead, there were trees, and I drove into them until there was no place else to go.

"It doesn't go any farther," I said, and Ward looked at the map again, then opened his door and stepped out. I turned off the engine and got out too. The heat rose off the old car's hood in waves, and there was a whining sound in the air somewhere close.

Ward was looking from the map to the trees. They were thick here; no road had been cut through.

"He must have had it wrong," I said.

I stepped around the front of the car, feeling the engine's heat, and walked a few feet into the trees. The whine was closer in there, and its pitch changed. It was cool in the shade, and I walked farther in, trying to find the source of the noise. It seemed to come from one place, and then another. I sat down against one of the pines to pull my socks up out of my shoes. The dirt was cool beneath my pants. Ward came through the trees slowly, still holding the map.

"According to this . . ."

"He must have made a mistake," I said.

He put the map into his pocket and walked past me into the trees, tripping once and then stopping to put his heel back into his shoe. He always bought the same brown wing tips; he wore them everywhere. I had seen him shoot baskets in those shoes.

He bent at the waist and leaned with one hand against a tree to prop himself up while he adjusted the slipped shoe. There was a popping noise, about like a light bulb breaking, and then he was on the ground.

I got up; he sat up. A faint burning smell hung in the air around him, and he tried to get back to his feet and fell. Something newborn. He did not seem to know where he was. I put my hands under his arms and pulled him to his feet.

"You all right?" I said.

He did not answer, but concentrated on keeping himself upright. It was always important to him to stay on his feet. I noticed the white insulator in the tree then, and the dark, narrow wire that was strung across it. The humming sound had stopped.

"It's an electric fence," I said, and he nodded as if he understood, but I was still holding more of his weight than he was himself. I had touched an electric fence too, when I was eleven or twelve, out dove hunting with my father. I'd thought I'd shot myself.

"They must be trying to keep out the bears," I said.

Gradually, I moved out from under him, allowing him to stand on his own. "Jesus," he said.

"It was an electric fence," I said again.

"It was like being sucked into a hole," he said. And he ran his hands over his face, as if he were feeling it for the first time.

"Sit down for a little while," I said.

He shook his head and looked at his hand. It felt stung,

he said, and he closed it once and then opened it, testing. He turned and looked at the fence he'd touched, and at the same time stepped away from it.

"Let's get out of here," I said. "Let's forget the whole thing."

He looked into the trees. "It must be farther back," he said.

"There's nothing back there."

"Somebody put up a fence."

A moment later he ducked beneath the wire, giving it wide clearance, and started off into the trees. I stayed on the other side a little while, not satisfied that the matter had been settled, but then, with no one there to settle it with, I went under the wire too and followed him in.

❑

THE HOUSE SAT IN a clearing of stumps—some cut lower than others, but averaging perhaps half a foot. A natural creek ran along the edge of this clearing, and a plank bridge had been constructed over it, substantial enough to hold an automobile or a truck. There were tire tracks on both sides, although I didn't see how a car would get there, over the stumps, or where it would go afterwards.

Ward stood at the bridge, studying the house. The humming noise had resumed in the trees behind us; I had the distinct feeling that we were trapped. There was a sudden absence of birds.

The house itself was smaller than the one farther south where Hillary's uncle lived, but like that one sat off the ground on blocks. It had not been prefabricated—it looked, in fact, as if it had been built at two different times, with two different kinds of shingles on the roof. There was a smaller building behind it where the generator was running.

We stood still, watching the house, and the realization settled on me that Charlotte was inside.

Ward started across the bridge and I fell in next to him, thinking of Charlotte. I wondered if her looks had changed, living in this place. If she spent as much time on her face and clothes now there was no one but Hillary Van Wetter to see them. I knew she had to work at her looks; in some way that made her more attractive.

We had come halfway across the yard when the door opened. Hillary stood above us, naked. Except for a small beard of pale blond pubic hair, his body appeared hairless. He looked thicker than he had in prison; his legs were as big around as my head, and curiously out of proportion. Too short for his size.

Ward took a step or two closer and then stopped. Hillary didn't move. They stared at each other, and then slowly Hillary shook his head.

"What is it now?" he said finally.

"I want to talk," Ward said.

"More talk."

My brother nodded. "About the night you and your uncle stole the sod," he said.

Hillary stood still. He had been more animated in prison, chained to a chair. "What about it?" he said.

"Was it true?"

"You said it was true," he said. "It was in the newspaper that it was true. . . ."

It was quiet again, except for the sound of the generator. "Yardley Acheman said he met the man who bought it," Ward said.

Slowly, Hillary Van Wetter began to smile. "It was in the paper," he said again. "How could it be a lie?"

He looked quickly at me, and then behind me, back into the trees. "Where's the other one?" he said.

"He's done with it," Ward said.

Hillary smiled again. "He got what he wanted, and now he's moved on. . . ."

My brother nodded, and Hillary turned sober. "Tell him

something for me, would you?" he said. "Tell him I done the same thing." And then he turned and went back into the house.

I stood still, the sun pressing against my back. When Hillary reappeared, he was wearing shoes and a pair of pants; the belt hung loose in the waist. He stepped through the doorway and closed the door behind him as if there were a cat inside that he did not want slipping out between his feet.

"You tell him I done the same thing," he said again, happy with the way that sounded.

"I don't know what that means," Ward said.

Hillary Van Wetter smiled. "Ain't that the truth?" he said. Then Hillary put his hands in his pockets and looked at Ward as if something about my brother confused him. "Is there something else?" he said.

"The night you stole the sod . . ." Ward said, "how did you know where to go to sell it?" They looked at each other over the question, and I brushed at a mosquito in my hair and it was hot from the sun.

"You don't just steal the sod off a golf course and then drive around looking for somebody who wants to buy it," Ward said.

Hillary Van Wetter shrugged, comfortable with the story the way it was.

"So either you knew the man before, or there wasn't any man," he said.

Hillary sat down on the step leading to his front door; he leaned forward and dropped a line of spit between his feet.

"You think you come into the prison with all your friends and saved me," he said. He stuck a finger in his ear and screwed it in and then out, and then studied the tip. I noticed again that there were no birds in the trees; I thought perhaps the noise of the generator kept them away. That or something in the spectacle of the stumps.

"Let me tell you something," Hillary said. "Ain't no such

thing." He wiped the earwax off his finger and onto his pants, leaving a stain. He saw me watching him and said, "I secrete abnormal amounts of cerumen."

I nodded without knowing what he was talking about. "Earwax," he said, and then he smiled, almost as if he liked me. "Paperboys don't know everything after all. . . ."

My brother did not seem to be listening.

Hillary said, "The prison doctor told me that; about my abnormal secretion." He paused a moment, thinking of the prison doctor, and then spoke again to me. "Now, there was a man that also needed excitement in his life, just like you two, and he got himself cut for his trouble. . . ."

He spit again, the color of coffee.

"He was there when some colored boys broke in for morphine." He smiled.

My brother sat down on a stump two feet across. He didn't say anything; he had asked his question and now he was waiting for an answer. Hillary turned to him, and the smile that had come with the memory of the colored boys cutting the doctor was gone. "Let me tell you something else you don't know," he said.

"Tell me about the man who bought the sod," Ward said.

"I'll tell you something better," he said. He leaned forward; his elbows rested on his knees and his hands dangled in the air in front of him. He was wearing a ring that he hadn't worn in prison, the kind you get for graduating from high school. "You didn't save nobody. Once a man sees his own death in front of him, you can't bring things back to what they was."

He nodded back in the direction of the house. "How many of you was poking the lady while I was in prison?" he said. "I didn't see nothing about that in the paper, that while the *Miami Times* undertook its investigation into the railroaded prisoner that they was having his fiancée on the side."

Ward shook his head, and seemed about to deny it, and then stopped. "I don't involve myself in other people's copulations," he said quietly. Hillary did not understand the word.

"Pokings," I said, thinking that now we were all even for *cerumen*.

"I mind my own business," Ward said.

"If you was minding your own business, you wouldn't be here sitting on my stump," Hillary said.

I was looking back at the little house again, wondering if Charlotte would come outside. He caught me at it; he seemed to read my thoughts.

"You lovesick?" he said.

"I was just wondering how she is," I said.

"Indisposed," he said.

"She wrote a letter . . ."

"I know about her letters," he said. A moment passed. "I know everything about that girl."

It was quiet again, and I stared at the house, feeling offended that she hadn't at least come out. "Don't come back here," Hillary said, more to my brother than to me.

Ward did not seem the least inclined even to leave.

"Don't come back," Hillary stood up then, slowly, and walked back inside.

Ward reluctantly got to his feet and made his way back through the stumps toward the dark trees beyond, tripping as he went on roots that lay above the ground. Each time he tripped, he caught himself and continued on as if he'd already forgotten that the roots were there.

Lost, as always, in a higher purpose.

❑

WE WENT BACK TO the hotel along the river and I showered in cold water. It was hot outside and I had six beers in a cooler of ice, along with some chicken sandwiches that I'd bought at the same place where I'd gotten the beer.

I came out of the bathroom and opened two of the beers and handed one to Ward, and then I lay down on the bed, still wet from the shower. There was a breeze from the window, a suggestion of coolness.

Ward stood looking out over the river. The sun was setting and the trees in the motel yard framed the boats and the long shadows they threw across the water, but I don't think he saw any of that. I am not sure he knew he was holding a beer. I tasted mine, and it was cold and bitter and good. I began to feel optimistic, as I often did when the first cold beer was still in my hand. Later on, after too many beers, I knew I would slip the other way.

"Was he right about the girl and Yardley?" he said. I could hear it embarrassed him to ask the question.

"About Yardley sleeping with her?"

He nodded, without looking back.

"Yeah, he was right," I said. I looked at him a moment and realized that he was the only one who hadn't wanted Charlotte for himself. That was how he'd missed it.

"There's no way to be sure," he said. He left the window, picked up half the sandwich off the bed, and sat on a table in the corner next to the telephone. "He's always been honest."

I had another drink of beer. "Shit," I said.

"I don't mean his personal life," he said. "I mean he's always been an honest reporter."

"Those are two different things?" I said. "A guy can be Yardley Acheman off the job and somebody honest when he's sitting at the typewriter . . ."

"The best reporters aren't always the best people," he said. "The best ones keep who they are out of it."

"What I think is, if you're Yardley Acheman it doesn't matter what kind of reporter you are, you're still Yardley Acheman."

Ward picked up his beer and drank it, throwing his head back, some of it leaking at the scar and dripping off his chin.

A little time passed.

"That afternoon in the office when you wrestled him to the floor," he said, feeling the alcohol. "What was that about?"

I finished another beer. It seemed to me then—it has always seemed to me—that there are people whom you recognize intuitively as your enemies. And most of the time, as in the case of Yardley Acheman, they recognize you. And even if nothing is ever said or done, the animus is there from the first moment you walk into the same room.

"I suppose we're natural enemies," I said.

❏

I CALLED MY FATHER's office in the morning, before we left for Miami. I had to use the phone outside the lobby of the hotel; there were none in the rooms. It was a warm morning; the birds were making noise from the trees and the river was full of bass fishermen sitting in still boats.

I hung up when he answered.

❏

BY THE TIME WE returned to South Florida, Yardley Acheman was an author.

A publisher in New York had offered him thirty thousand dollars to expand the Moat County articles into a book, an amount almost equal to two years of his salary. I do not know if the offer had initially included my brother, but by the time we heard of it, it was Yardley Acheman's alone.

He told Ward about the book without mentioning the amount of the advance, although I knew from one of the copyboys that he had been bragging about the money for days, going from one desk to another in the newsroom, speaking to people he had not spoken to in months.

What he said to Ward was that for some time he had been

struggling with the feeling that newspapers were too limiting for the things he wanted to write.

"Maybe it's just something I've got to get out of my system," he said, meaning the book. "Something to accomplish, you know, by myself. To find out if I can do it." He paused a moment and then said, "Not that it's the end of our partnership. We're too good together to quit...."

Ward nodded, and listened politely while Yardley, relieved now that Ward had been notified that he was out of the deal, elaborated on his plans for the book, never mentioning the thirty thousand dollars.

When I left the office, Yardley was still discussing his sense of being unfulfilled as a writer. "You know what I'm talking about," he said. "The canvas is too small . . ."

❑

YARDLEY WAS NOT AROUND the office as much for the next few months. He spent much of his time in New York with the magazine writer, whom he in fact married.

At the urging of the editors, Ward undertook an investigation of several of the Dade County commissioners, collecting and filing thousands of pages of documents on landfills and sewer projects and housing developments. He traced corporations through foreign banks, and found their owners back in Miami.

But in spite of growing evidence of an abuse of public trust, Ward had no real interest in the players. He would walk into his office at seven or eight in the morning and reappear an hour later, stretching or going for coffee, and an hour after that I would sometimes pass his office and see him standing at the window, staring out at the city.

❑

YARDLEY ACHEMAN CALLED from his apartment in Miami or from his wife's apartment in New York several times a day, asking for information about Hillary or Thurmond Call that he had lost or forgotten—everything that hadn't appeared in the newspaper article itself.

My brother took the calls cordially, welcoming the chance to talk again about Moat County, often answering in more detail than Yardley Acheman wanted.

Once a week Yardley made an appearance at the office—a gesture of sorts, as he was still drawing his salary—spending a few minutes with Ward, and then an hour or so with his editors, reporting on the progress of the story of the Dade County Commissioners. Nurturing the fading view that he and Ward were equal partners in the work.

He wore expensive suits now, the influence perhaps of New York, but the big city had not been all good to him, as he'd also begun to change colors. His skin had taken on an unnatural cast, as if he were standing in fluorescent light.

On Saturday, Yardley always flew back to New York to be with his wife and friends, and sometimes on his visits to the *Times* he would complain about the complications of living both places at once. Of going, as he put it, from the fastest place in the world to the slowest—to the place where New Yorkers came to retire when they were too slow to keep up.

He spoke of Miami now as he had once spoken of Lately.

I didn't know anything about the literary fraternity in New York, of course, but it didn't seem to me that it could be such an exclusive club if they let him in the first day. It seemed to me that New York must be full of people like Yardley Acheman.

The calls from Yardley to my brother became more constant. Afterwards, sometimes, my brother would slide the patch off his eye and sit at his desk for a long time, his head resting in his hands, still possessed by the documents from Hillary Van Wetter's arrest and trial.

258

He would forget to eat; he would forget to go home. Sometimes he would forget to replace the eye patch. The spectacle of the squeezed, empty socket brought other spectacles to mind, and I would look quickly away when I saw it, unable to reconcile myself to the memory of the beating.

❑

WORKING ALONE, WARD FINISHED the story on the Dade County commissioners, writing it himself. Yardley occupied himself flying back and forth to New York. He turned in fifty pages of the book and was told to rewrite them, and refused to write at all for several weeks.

The newspaper article, which, at Yardley's insistence, bore his name along with my brother's, resulted in the indictment of four of the commissioners, ruining their lives, and in a spirit of celebration the editors gave Ward two weeks off.

Yardley also took two weeks, and returned to New York to resume work on the book. I heard later that he went back to his publishers, asking for and receiving more money on the advance.

❑

MY BROTHER WENT BACK to Moat County. He wanted to go home, he said, for a few days rest.

What he meant by *home*, I didn't know. He didn't intend to move in with my father and his girlfriend. He had seen how welcome he was with her in the house.

I called my father on the day Ward left. I hadn't spoken to him in the months since he told us to knock before we came into the house. He sounded weary when he picked up the phone, and I wondered if Ellen Guthrie had been keeping him up late.

"Jack," he said, "good to hear your voice." And then his

own voice began to improve. He asked if I was swimming, how much I weighed, what sort of things they had me doing at the newspaper. He seemed afraid of running out of things to say; afraid that the conversation would end.

I found myself forgiving him.

"What I do best," I said, "is when somebody says, 'Jack, get me the glue,' I get the glue."

I prided myself then on being the only copyboy in the newsroom who did not have ambitions to become a reporter.

He said that he'd read Ward's story about the Dade County commissioners and he'd been meaning to call to tell him it was a fine piece of journalism. "The most important, best journalism there is," he said, "comfort the afflicted and afflict the comfortable, and it's all local . . ."

He stopped a moment, out of things to say.

"He isn't there, is he?"

"They gave him a couple of weeks off," I said.

"Well," he said, "when you see him tell him to call."

"He's on his way up there," I said.

And there was a small, empty place in the conversation. "Thorn?" he said.

"I guess."

"To visit?" A worried man now. "He isn't doing another story, is he?"

"I don't know what he's doing."

"I thought he was through with us," he said, making a small joke. The connection was quiet while my father weighed my brother's impending visit and its inherent domestic implications.

"Should I tell Ellen to expect him?" he said.

"I don't think so," I said.

I heard relief in his voice.

"Well, we'd love to have him," he said. "At least he could come by for a meal . . ."

I thought of the meals at home, of the steam coming off

boiled food. I was homesick. "How is Anita getting along with your roommate?" I said.

He stalled on that.

"Actually, we had to let her go."

I didn't say anything then. She'd been in my father's house as long as the cracks in the ceiling.

"You know how it is," he said, "two women in one kitchen . . ."

"I didn't know Ellen was in the kitchen."

"It's a figure of speech," he said.

"Anita was there a long time," I said. It seemed to me that he should have said something to us before he got rid of her.

"I took care of her financially," he said. "Don't worry about that." When I didn't speak again, he said, "She worked for us, Jack, she wasn't a member of the family."

"She was part of things," I said.

And it was quiet again.

"Things change," he said finally. "You know that."

❑

FOUR DAYS BEFORE WARD was due back in Miami, the Sunday editor came to me in the newsroom, trying to find him. He was excited and desperate at the same time.

"We need to contact your brother," he said.

I said he was in Moat County. I was sorting mail for the reporters at the time, a job I liked for its solitary nature.

"Where?" he said.

I hadn't heard from him since he left.

"We've got to get him back here," he said.

"He'll be back on Friday."

The Sunday editor shook his head, fretting. "Friday doesn't do us any good," he said.

"I don't know where he's staying," I said.

"Would your father know?"

"I doubt it."

He stuck his hands into his pockets and shook his head. "Jesus, what kind of a family have you got, you go home and don't see each other?"

I turned back to the mailboxes and continued sorting the mail. "Can you find him?" he said.

"I can make some calls. . . ."

"We've got to have him in the office tomorrow," he said.

"For what?"

"I can't tell you for what, just get him."

I handed the Sunday editor the letters in my hand, and he looked at them a moment, realized what they were, and dropped them in the wastebasket. I walked back into Ward's office and shut the door. I called half a dozen motels in Lately, and he was not registered at any of them. I called my father's office, and he was at lunch with Miss Guthrie.

The Sunday editor walked past the office from time to time, looking inside for some signal that I'd found him. I kept shaking my head.

Later, when I reached my father, he said that he'd thought that Ward had changed his mind and stayed in Miami. "If he came up, I assumed he'd have called," he said, sounding hurt.

"Maybe he went somewhere else," I said. His license had been reinstated and he'd bought a car of his own. I tried to think of places he might go.

"What's going on?"

"I don't know, they just want him back in the office," I said. "It's important, but they won't tell me why. . . ."

He paused a moment. "Did they say when?"

"Tomorrow," I said. "They want him back no later than the morning."

He thought a moment, and then, quietly, "Jesus . . ."

"What?"

He said, "He's won the Pulitzer."

The Sunday editor walked past the window again, looking in, and I shook my head no.

❑

YARDLEY ACHEMAN FLEW IN from New York late that night, and appeared in the newsroom in the morning in one of his new suits. Seeing him there, three days before he was due, I knew my father was right.

The Sunday editor set me back to work calling Moat County motels, but some of the urgency was out of it now. It was plain that he was disappointed I wasn't better at calling motels.

❑

THE NAMES OF THE WINNERS came in over the Associated Press wire about eleven, and the celebration began there in the office with an official announcement by the paper's publisher, an ancient, pink-faced man who emerged from his office upstairs to congratulate not only Yardley and my brother, but the entire staff.

The paper was good at winning Pulitzer Prizes, and the speech had been used before.

Bottles of champagne appeared as soon as the publisher returned to his own floor, and a party began there in the city room, some reporters drinking, some of them taking stories over the phone, some doing both. Yardley Acheman kissed all the best-looking women, at least the ones who would let him.

A telegram came in from Lately, my father saying this was the proudest moment of his life.

Later in the day the party moved to a bar across the street, and then to a hotel near the bar.

The hotel had a swimming pool on the roof, and reporters who had never spoken to me before sat down smelling of Scotch and confessed their admiration for my brother even if he was an odd duck, and saying what a shame it was that he couldn't have been there for the party.

Among the thirty or so celebrants gathered at the pool that night was a young police reporter named Helen Drew. Miss Drew was overweight and, like my brother, worked at her job compulsively, even on her own time. She came into Ward's office occasionally for advice on professional matters, as she wanted to be an investigative reporter herself, and was clearly star-struck in his presence. She could not keep herself from finishing his sentences for him, or nodding obsessively in agreement before he even began to speak. Yardley Acheman would have nothing to do with her.

On this evening, however, Yardley was feeling his humanity. She came to him and absently he dropped his arm over her shoulder, and she leaned into him, smiling, like old pals.

Helen Drew's skin was pale and doughy, and she did not see well even with her glasses. Her form was not so much fat as thick—not just her waist and shoulders and legs, but her wrists and fingers too. Her hands looked like an enormous baby's.

She wore loose-fitting dresses to work that draped her body all the way to the shoes, and late at night she took those shoes off—they waited together near a canvas chair, looking squashed, with her glasses laid inside one of them—and dangled a foot in the pool as she drank. And while she was balanced this way, with one foot over the edge, Yardley, who was behind her then with a thinner woman, suddenly dropped his head and butted her back side, knocking her in.

She panicked, blind in the water and unable to swim, but then found the ladder and calmed herself, and then stayed in the pool for a long time, mascara running down her cheeks, laughing and chatting from there with the reporters standing at the edge, putting off that moment as long as she could when she would emerge with the wet material of her dress sticking to the rolls of flesh it was intended to hide.

Yardley kept saying he was sorry, again and again. But he could not apologize without remembering the spectacle as she'd gone in, and he would lose himself and begin to laugh. And she laughed with him.

Helen Drew finally came out of the pool, streaming water like a long-sunken treasure, and wrapped herself in a towel. She drank and laughed for another half hour and left. She was not at work the next day, or the next.

She resigned from the paper later in the week without cleaning out her desk, taking a job at the *Miami Sun,* a small paper which rented offices in the Times Building, where she was promised the chance to become an investigative reporter.

❑

MY BROTHER RETURNED FROM his vacation bone thin and sunburned, with insect bites covering his face and arms and his belt cinched back to the last notch. His pants gathered in bunches at the waist.

He didn't look as if he'd eaten since he left.

I did not ask him where he'd stayed or what he'd done, and he didn't offer to tell me.

We went to dinner, but he only picked at the food. He seemed detached, completely uninterested in the prize he had won, and was only briefly engaged by the news that Ellen Guthrie had talked World War into firing Anita Chester.

"She wants it all to herself, doesn't she?" he said, sounding like an outsider, someone standing to the side, watching a family fall apart.

❑

YARDLEY ACHEMAN MADE a quick trip to New York, using the Pulitzer to leverage a few more thousand dollars from his publisher, and then flew back to Miami to request a leave of absence to finish his book. He lobbied to stay on the payroll during his leave, on the grounds that the paper was still using his picture in full-page advertisements and that the praise for the book would inevitably reflect back on the *Times.* He added that continuation of his salary would also guarantee his return after the manuscript was finished.

The editors gave him the leave of absence, but not his salary. He'd made his demands in the city room before he made them to the editors, and they were afraid of setting a precedent.

He left for New York again that same week, saying he could not promise to come back.

❑

THE SUNDAY EDITOR APPROACHED my brother a few days later, on a mission from the editors above him, to discuss pairing him with another reporter. In spite of several indicted county commissioners, the idea that my brother could work alone hadn't seemed to occur to them.

"We have to face the facts," the Sunday editor said. "Acheman may not be coming back."

My brother said no.

❑

YARDLEY ACHEMAN REDEDICATED HIMSELF to the book, and I watched my brother cast about for a new story, throwing himself into the process as completely as he would into a story itself, but he could not find one with people who interested him. The editors had stories, of course, but they were always too much like the ones he had already done.

The calls came in again, collect, four and five times a day, occasionally that many in an hour. My brother accepted them all, putting aside his own work to answer Yardley's questions, not needing now to go back into the transcripts and notes from the case, even for the smallest details.

There was a certain urgency to these calls, and Yardley's voice, when I picked up the phone, had lost its confidence. It occurred to me that perhaps writing a book was not as entertaining an activity as signing the contract to write it.

I remember another call a few months later, a different kind of call, when my brother simply held the phone, against his ear and listened for a long time. Slowly, he began to nod. "I could let you have a few hundred," he said.

I could hear the voice coming through the phone, and my brother was nodding again. He picked up a pencil and wrote down an address. "I'll put it in the mail tonight," he said, and then he hung up.

He looked at me and said, "Elaine's must be expensive."

He smiled for a moment, enjoying what he'd said, and then went back to the work in front of him, curious, I think, at the meanness of the remark.

❑

THE MONEY DID NOT LAST in New York, and Yardley Acheman returned to the *Times* angry and broke, bringing the unfinished book with him. His wife stayed where she was.

On his first day back, a call came in from Helen Drew. Yardley did not remember who she was until she recalled for him that she had been the one who fell into the pool. That was the way she put it, that she fell.

"Right, right," he said, "how are you?"

I was in the office at the time and he looked up at me and winked.

She asked if he had a few minutes to talk.

"The truth is, with the book and all, I'm not doing interviews right now . . ."

"We were just looking over the Pulitzer story," she said, "and a couple of questions came up."

"We?" he said. "Who is *we?*"

"My editors and I . . ."

"And you just happen to be looking over my Pulitzer story?"

"There were a few things we were wondering about."

Yardley looked at me again, but there was no wink in it now. "I don't have time for this shit," he said. "I don't know what kind of penny-ante, chickenshit journalism you practice over there, but I don't have time for it."

And then he slammed the phone into the receiver and stalked out of the office. A moment later, my brother's phone began to ring.

❑

MY BROTHER SPOKE several times to Helen Drew in the next few months, over the objections of Yardley Acheman. It became clear that she was going back over the entire story, piece by piece. Why, no one knew. She would call over the smallest point, unwilling or unable to go on until everything behind her was clear and accounted for. She never seemed to get things right the first time, but in the end she was thorough. And in the end, that is all a reporter needs.

Yardley Acheman began to believe that she was writing a book of her own. He was infuriated that Ward would talk to her, and went to the editors to complain. Yardley had threatened them too often, however, and did not have the influence he had once had. They said there was nothing they could do.

❑

HELEN DREW SHOWED UP in the city room on a Thursday afternoon in sandals and one of her loose-fitting dresses. She wore a button protesting the war in Vietnam, and her hair was streaked blond in a way that was the fashion that year.

It would be hard to imagine a more harmless-looking human being. Ward was on the telephone when she came in. She offered me her hand and I took it, feeling the weight. She was sweating and breathing heavily, having walked the steps from the first floor, and fanned herself with a copy of the paper that someone at the reception desk had given her. She picked at her dress, pulling it away from her skin.

She looked around the room. "It's bigger than I remember," she said.

❑

SHE WAS WITH Ward most of the afternoon, and left apologizing for taking so much of his time. The office was still warm with the heat from her body when I went in, and smelled of her soap.

"What does she want now?" I said.

He shook his head. "I'm not sure," he said. "She keeps coming back to the timing of it, the story being written while I was in the hospital . . ."

"What did you tell her?"

"I told her that Mr. Van Wetter was facing the electric chair, and the paper didn't think it could hold the story. . . ." He shrugged, as if the arguments were self-evident.

"She ought to talk to Yardley Acheman," I said, making a joke.

"He thinks she's stealing his book," he said. "Something about a swimming pool. He thinks she hates him for pushing her into a swimming pool."

❑

ALTHOUGH AGAIN DRAWING a paycheck, Yardley Acheman had, for all practical purposes, never come back to work. There was no way to quietly fire him, however, and the *Times* had too much invested in him to do such a thing in public.

He worked on his book in spurts, and complained out loud that he could not concentrate, knowing that there were people out to ruin him.

❑

AND MY BROTHER WENT back to what had worked before.

He disappeared into a new project, night and day, collecting the contradictory facts and details of things that had happened, sometimes years before, filing them away against the day when he would look at them again and decide a certain chain of events, a version of history that would be printed. Believing this time it would emerge on the pages of the newspaper exactly as it had happened in life.

Strangely, he refused to discuss what his new project was, and his editors began to worry that they had lost them both, with Yardley Acheman complaining that they had no understanding of the pressures of writing a book, and Ward not talking to them at all.

Neither of them could be fired, of course, and Yardley reminded them of that from time to time, asking out loud in the newsroom how the paper could afford to keep him around.

And while I wasn't there for the conversations with his publisher in New York—he tended to keep that aspect of his life more private than the rest—one morning I did see a draft of a letter he wrote the man, which he'd left beside the copying machine in the office (he was making copies of all his correspondence then, against the day students would be studying his work in English classes), explaining it was impossible to continue to work at the paper and, at the same time, finish the book. "They don't seem to be able to turn on the lights around here without me," he said.

———

270

He believed his wife was having an affair. He called her daily and reported his progress on the book and begged her to come to Miami to visit. She, however, was working on something of her own and could not get away. He would hang up enraged.

He worried out loud about his marriage, and added that to the distractions keeping him from finishing his book. He estimated his marital problems had set him back six months, a figure he offered to anyone who would listen, even to me.

On the day he did that, however, he turned abruptly away, not waiting for an answer, as if he had just realized I was not in a position to forgive his obligations.

❑

HELEN DREW RETURNED to the *Times*'s newsroom, still smelling of the same soap. She seemed happy to see me, as if we were old friends. And perhaps I was as close to an old friend as she had.

She wondered out loud how Yardley was doing with his book, if he might have time to talk to her now. There was something wide-eyed and sweet in her tone which did not quite hide the edge beneath.

❑

I LEARNED OF MY father's engagement to Ellen Guthrie through a wedding invitation mailed to me at the paper. I used the newspaper's address for the little personal correspondence I received because mail which came to me at the rooming house was left on a small table near the front door and inspected by the other tenants as they came and left during the day. Often, one of them opened it.

The invitation was professionally printed and included a small map of Thorn, showing the location of the Methodist church and the country club where the reception would be held, as well as the name of a store in Jacksonville where Ellen Guthrie had established an account of the things she needed in the way of gifts.

I took the invitation straight to my brother, who by now had generated enough piles of documents and records for the new project to cover his desk.

Yardley Acheman was also in the room, on the telephone with his agent in New York.

"Listen," he said, "I need six months to finish this thing, and I have to get back to the city to do it. . . ."

I dropped the invitation in the middle of Ward's documents. "Did you get one of these?" I said.

He looked at it without touching it, cocking his head to read the words, then seemed to follow them off the page, across the desk to some banking records sitting beneath a staple gun at the far corner.

Yardley was asking for another eight thousand dollars.

"It gets better and better," I said.

Ward turned toward a corner of the room where his own mail lay in a mound on a shelf, unopened since he had begun the new project. Some of it had fallen off onto the floor.

Yardley was telling the editor now that the story was timeless.

Ward touched the invitation I'd dropped on his desk, turning it with one finger until he could read it again without moving his head sideways. "He's going to marry her," I said.

He nodded, still looking at the invitation, still touching it with the tip of his finger.

"She's after the whole paper," I said.

He smiled again, and then shook his head no, as if he found the idea implausible.

"If you want it faster, then get me out of this fucking hole and back in New York where I can write," Yardley said. "Six thousand dollars, I'll live on a thousand a month . . ."

Yardley squirmed quietly in his chair while the man on the other end of the line spoke. He looked up at us, then back at the paper in front of him. He had written the number 6,000 and circled it several times, now he crossed it out.

"Well, they seem to get along with each other," Ward said.

Yardley closed his eyes, listening to the man in New York. My brother seemed unaware of the conversation; he seemed only vaguely aware of me.

Yardley suddenly slammed the phone onto the receiver and sat for a moment, breathing hard. He looked at the phone, then across the room at Ward. "Your friend Helen Drew?" he said. "She's been checking on me in New York."

❏

TWO LETTERS ARRIVED at the paper from my father's attorney later that week, one to me, one to Ward, formally notifying us of a change in the structure of the company. My father had named Ellen Guthrie as president, but had held on to the formal editorship of the newspaper, as well as his title of chief executive officer.

She had also been named to the board of directors. There was no explanation of the change, no personal note or call later from my father.

He had simply changed the locks again.

Ward left the office after he opened the letter, brushing past Helen Drew, who was waiting at the receptionist's desk to see Yardley Acheman. He walked to the bar at the corner and drank beer all that afternoon. I found him there after I'd finished work, still wearing his tie snug against the top button of his shirt. He was sitting in a booth against the wall, his head resting against the plastic cushion, a watery look to his eyes. There was no other sign that he was drunk.

I got a beer from the bartender and sat down and offered

a toast. "To the new Mrs. James," I said, and he touched the lip of his bottle against mine, and we both drank.

"Was the girl from the *Sun* still there when you left?" It was a beer or two later.

"Still waiting for Yardley," I said.

He thought a moment and said, "I wish she'd go away."

"I think there's something wrong with her," I said.

"I wish they'd all go away."

"Who?"

He smiled, and drank his beer. "All of them," he said, and then he brought his bottle across the table and touched mine again. And then he laughed.

❏

I WAS HALF DRUNK and on the way back to the paper when I saw them, coming out of the parking lot. First Helen Drew, in a Ford, and then Yardley Acheman, in his Buick. Half a minute apart. She turned the corner and slowed, watching for him in her rearview mirror, and then, after he had turned the corner too, they disappeared together into Miami.

❏

WHEN I SAW Helen Drew again, it was ten o'clock in the morning at the rooming house. It was my day off and I'd just come back from a swim. I suppose she'd been watching for me outside. I was still in a bathing suit when she knocked on the door. She was embarrassed, and stumbled over herself apologizing for the intrusion.

"I tried to call the paper," she said, "but the woman wouldn't take a message."

The receptionist at the paper refused to take messages for the secretaries or the editorial assistants, feeling they were not professional members of the staff, and not entitled to professional courtesies.

I looked around my room, and clothes were strewn most of the places anyone could sit. The sheets were twisted on the bed; I couldn't remember when I'd changed them. She glanced back toward the front door, uncomfortable to be standing in the hall.

I opened the door wider and stepped aside to let her in. Once she was past, I looked up the hallway, and saw Froggy Bill at his regular station, excited by what was going on.

She sat down on a corner of the bed. A single pants leg stuck out from beneath her, as if whoever had been inside had been crushed. I picked up a T-shirt and put it on, and that seemed to make her more comfortable. There was water in my ear from the swim, and I tilted that way and hit my head with the flat of my palm. She winced.

"Sorry," she said, "I'm not used to doing this."

I picked up a pair of pants and a shirt and tossed them into the open closet, then cleared the socks off the chair against the wall and sat down. The bathing suit was damp and sandy. An ancient, cracked mirror hung on the opposite wall, and from where I was sitting I could see her, front and back.

She did not seem to know where to start.

"I don't know how I get into these things," she said finally.

I waited, thinking of the man outside in the hallway, and what he imagined I was doing with this fat girl in my room.

"It's about your brother," she said.

"What about him?"

"About Daytona Beach." She sat perfectly still and waited. I waited too. She looked unhappy and resigned. "Someone who knows," she said, "indicated to me that he didn't get hurt on the beach."

It was quiet a moment.

"What difference does it make?"

She sat very still. "It just gets messier and messier," she said.

"What does?"

"The whole thing," she said. "You start out with something

you want to do, and the next thing you know you're doing things you don't want to do at all. . . ."

"Then don't do them," I said.

She shook her head. "It's gone too far for that."

I glanced quickly in the mirror, at the rolls of flesh under her blouse. She sat up on the bed, straightening herself.

"You were there in Daytona Beach when it happened . . ."

I waited for her to finish.

"It wasn't at the beach, was it?"

"Who said that?"

"My source."

I didn't answer.

"He or she indicated it happened at the hotel," she said. I didn't move.

"The night manager said it happened there too."

"Bullshit," I said. She was not good at lying.

"The question is, if it happened at the hotel, why did he say it happened at the beach?"

"The question is, why would Yardley Acheman tell you it didn't happen at the beach?"

Now she sat still, as if that were a problem she'd thought of too. She did not try to pretend it wasn't Yardley. "I have to have one thing straight in my head before I can go on to the next thing," she said finally. "The person I spoke to said your brother had some sailors in his room, to have sex with them, and they beat him up and tried to rob him."

She looked at me, waiting.

"It happened on the beach," I said.

She sat still, then slowly shook her head. "Look," she said, "could we just tell each other the truth?"

Then, without waiting for me to answer, she said, "Yardley Acheman told me, off the record, what happened in Daytona, and he said the story was hurried into print to draw attention away."

She sat still.

"That doesn't make sense," I said.

She thought a moment. "In a screwy way it does ... it explains the mix-up over the contractor. ..."

My bathing suit had turned cold, and I wanted to shower and then walk to the little Cuban café two blocks south and read the newspapers and eat breakfast.

"The contractor in the story," she said. "I haven't been able to find him, nobody will divulge his name. Maybe your brother was so embarrassed ..." She paused a moment, thinking. "Maybe he got confused."

"You mean he made the guy up."

"To protect his privacy," she said. "Or maybe he got hurt so bad, he just wanted things to be over."

I sat there thinking of Yardley Acheman.

"This is all off the record," she said.

❏

A MOMENT LATER the color drained out of her face, and she dropped back onto her elbows. I stayed where I was, still calculating the enormity of the lie Yardley had told. "Have you got an orange?" she said.

Her eyes were open and she was sweating. I went to the window and opened it wider, but there wasn't enough air to stir the curtains. She looked at me without moving her face.

"What's wrong?" I said.

"My blood sugar," she said. "I need some fruit."

There was a little grocery store on the same block as the rooming house; the old woman who had it ran numbers on the side. I picked up Helen Drew's legs, holding her ankles, to get her all on the bed. The weight was surprising, and when I had them up she moved a little, realigning herself, at the same time holding down her skirt.

I went out the door, hurrying, past Froggy Bill. "I got some rubbers right here," he said, and stuck his hand inside his pocket. He grinned, and his teeth were terrible.

I ran to the store and bought half a dozen oranges and

some grapes and a quart of orange juice and a box of Fig Newtons.

When I came back into the building Froggy Bill was closer to my room than he'd been when I left, still in the hallway but looking in the door. He moved away as I came in, and restationed himself outside his own door.

She was sitting up again, still pale, but looking better. I put the things I'd bought on the bed next to her and she went over them, opening the orange juice first, drinking perhaps half the container, and then ate all the Fig Newtons and a few of the grapes.

Gradually the color came back to her face, and when she felt well enough she was humiliated. "I've been on this diet," she said. I looked at what was left of the cookies on the bed, the empty carton of orange juice. The six oranges lay where I'd put them, untouched. "The idea is all you eat is popcorn, it's supposed to make you lose twenty pounds the first month, but I keep getting dizzy."

She looked at the bed too, as if she just noticed the evidence of what she'd eaten. "A nurse told me it was blood sugar," she said.

She began cleaning it up, picking up the papers the Fig Newtons had been wrapped in, stuffing them into the orange juice carton.

"This is embarrassing," she said.

She stood up, steadying herself, and then put the carton in the garbage. She looked around the room, as if she were going to clean it all.

"It always comes down to the same thing," she said. "In the end, it doesn't matter what I do, I'm still just the fat kid who gets sick at school." I saw that she was about to cry; I didn't know what to do about it. And then she was crying, and that embarrassed her too.

"Oh, shit," she said, "here I go." And she smiled and cried at the same time. I sat still, waiting for her to stop, trying to find somewhere else in the room to look.

She went to my sink and ran some water, bending into her hands. She came up looking damp. She sat heavily on the bed.

"I never wanted to hurt your brother," she said, and blew her nose. "It was that bastard Acheman, but now it's all gone the wrong way. . . ." And there was something in her hopelessness that I trusted, I suppose because I was hopeless most of the time myself.

"I'll tell you some things," I said, "but not for the newspaper."

She looked at me differently.

"This is off the record," I said.

"Completely off the record," she said. And I heard something tinny in that, but I'd already gone too far to stop, and a few moments later I was telling her what it looked like when I walked into my brother's hotel room. The sailors and the police and the ambulance attendants and Ward, broken to pieces.

"It had nothing to do with the story," I said, "nothing to do with the contractor, except Ward was there trying to find him."

"It was Yardley who said he found the guy?"

"Yardley," I said.

And then I was through talking, and she understood that and got up to leave. "This was all so horrible," she said, looking back at the bed. "You must think I'm crazy."

She opened her purse and came out with a five-dollar bill. "What do I owe you for the groceries?"

We looked at each other over the money, not knowing how to get out of the moment.

"It never happened," I said.

She waited a second or two, then set the money on the chair near the wall. I knew then what I'd done. I stepped into the hallway to see her past Froggy Bill, but he'd left his usual spot, I suppose to report what had gone on to the woman who ran the apartment.

I went to the Cuban place for breakfast, and sat over rice and meat sauce and eggs, trying to remember the exact words I'd said to Helen Drew, saying them again, returning again and again to the cold certainty that I'd turned Ward over to the enemy.

❑

THE STORY APPEARED that same week, on Friday, beginning on the front page of the *Miami Sun*, under the headline THE MAKING OF A PULITZER. The piece ran eighty column inches, perhaps half of it simply a reconstruction of the original story, the other half divided between the search for the missing contractor and the incident in the hotel at Daytona Beach.

Reading the story, I heard some of the words I'd said to her in my room; she'd had a tape recorder in her purse. She'd probably turned it on when I went for the groceries. I heard Yardley's voice in the story too.

She reported that it was unclear which of the two reporters—my brother or Yardley Acheman—claimed to have found the contractor, and that in spite of questions now that the man existed, neither the *Times* nor the reporters would reveal his name, citing a principle of confidentiality.

"Lingering questions," she wrote, "have not only split the partnership, but split the paper, and called its credibility into question. According to a spokesman for the *Times*, however, there are no plans at this time to return the Pulitzer Prize."

❑

A FEW DAYS LATER, the Sunday editor came into my brother's office, where I was sitting alone, opening and sorting Ward's mail.

"Is he here?" he said.

I had a look around.

"When's he coming in?" he said.

"He's working at home for a few days," I said. In fact, he had been sitting in his apartment, going out only to buy beer or vodka, which he drank straight over ice or mixed with whatever he found in the refrigerator. He had taken the boxes from Moat County home, and the papers lay open across the furniture in every room of his place.

I had been astounded at the mess.

"Does anybody still work around here?" the Sunday editor said.

I told him again Ward had taken his work home, and was doing it there. He weighed that, nodding, then, casually, he said, "Do you know if he's had any requests for interviews? About the story in the *Sun*?"

"No, I don't think so."

"He shouldn't talk to anyone," he said.

I had nothing to say to that, and a moment later the Sunday editor asked if I would be seeing Ward after work.

"I don't know," I said.

"Tell him not to talk to anyone," he said. "We've got ourselves a situation here, and it's important to contain it."

"We've got ourselves a situation here," I said, "and it's important."

He stared at me a moment, and I stared back.

"You know," he said, "you're kind of a smart aleck, Jack, for somebody who's only in here because his brother's a big shot."

❏

THERE WAS SOMETHING ABOUT my brother's drinking that caused me to drink too. Somehow if we were both doing it, the reason might be in the air, or the newsroom, or Miami. If we were both drinking, he was not going off someplace alone.

That does not mean, however, that I wanted to visit his

apartment every afternoon after work and sit with him in his dimly lit kitchen, the table covered with his notes from Moat County and melting ice trays, and disappear with him soundlessly into the haze.

I was not a great social drinker, but sometimes over the course of an evening, I would find myself with a word or two I wanted to say.

And so after work, while Ward drank at home, I often visited a crowded, stale-smelling place a few blocks from the paper called Johnny's, where reporters and editors were known to go and discuss the ethics of the business of delivering the news. I did not ordinarily join in these conversations, which were without exception circular in nature, and in which the same people took turns making the same pronouncements to one another, night after night.

On certain nights, however—and it was impossible to say in advance when it would happen—some of the women who worked at the paper grew tired of newspaper talk, and eccentric behavior took over the room.

On Halloween the year before, for instance, shortly after I'd arrived in Miami, I walked in the place and saw a *Times* vice president costumed as a winged devil standing near the jukebox while a woman dressed as Snow White kneeled in front of him, working his penis in and out of her mouth.

As the man began to climax, he wrapped the sequined wings around her head and covered her while he shook.

I had been hoping to see something like that again, or perhaps to revisit the night when a young reporter took off her shirt and bra and threw them into the face of the assistant city editor who was her boss, calling him a dirty bastard. The next day, both the assistant city editor and the reporter were back at their desks as if nothing had happened.

On the afternoon the Sunday editor called me a smart aleck, I went to Johnny's, where Yardley Acheman and half a dozen reporters were already sitting at the booth nearest the door. They turned to watch me come in, falling suddenly quiet, and then stole glances at me over their shoulders as I sat at the bar.

I had several drinks, wondering what Yardley Acheman had been saying about my brother. Johnny poured me doubles. I turned once and caught one of the women at his table staring.

She smiled at me and did not look away. I held her look, feeling the hammer cock, and finally turned away myself, flushed.

Later in the evening, the table changed. People went home or to other bars or to other tables, and the woman who had been staring sat down next to me at the bar.

She looked over her shoulder, where Yardley was sitting alone now, folded into the corner. "What a conceited asshole," she said.

"The author," I said.

She lit a cigarette and allowed her hand to rest on my leg in a casual way. "Do you think they'll let them keep it?"

"Keep what?"

"The Pulitzer."

"I didn't know they could take it away," I said.

She shrugged and lifted her hand off my leg to sip at her drink. "The paper might make them give it back," she said.

"I don't think the paper is going to do that."

"It's happened before," she said.

It was quiet a moment, and then I said, "Do you get tired of talking about newspapers all the time?"

"What everyone keeps wondering," she said, "is how your brother's taking all this."

"He was fine when I saw him," I said.

"He hasn't been in the office since the story in the *Sun*."

"He's working at home," I said.

A moment later she put her hand on my arm and leaned so close that I thought she was about to kiss me. "Have you heard what Yardley's saying?" she said.

"About what?"

"About your brother."

I turned in my seat to stare at him, but he had closed his eyes and dropped his head into the back of the booth, his mouth slightly open. In the dark of the bar, he seemed to be smiling.

I suddenly wanted to leave, and took a dollar out of my pocket and set it on the bar, covering it with the glass. As I stood up, I felt her hand again against my leg.

"Where are you going?" she said.

"For a swim," I said.

She looked at me a long time, an appraisal, and then she said, "Tell you what, why don't you come swimming with me?"

❏

I WENT TO SEE Ward in the morning, straight from the woman's lap, to confess what had happened when Helen Drew came to see me at my apartment. He answered the door in his pajamas.

The place was hot and smelled of alcohol which had been filtered through a human body, and I opened some of the windows to air it out. The files from Moat County were all over the floor, some of them were wet. You could not cross the room without stepping on them.

I moved a pile and took a seat on the sofa. "The girl from the *Sun*? Helen Drew?"

"The heavy girl," he said. I nodded, and he took a moment remembering her. "She seemed nice," he said finally. He smiled at me, as if there were something at work I didn't understand.

"The thing is," I said, "she came to see me one morning at my place . . ."

I paused, he waited.

"Yardley told her you were the one who said he found the contractor."

"I know," he said, still smiling. "It's what he told the Associated Press too. He gave it to them off the record, they said it to me off the record. It's all leverage."

"What do they want?"

"Another story," he said. "That's all, just another story. Somebody writes it, somebody prints it, somebody reads it." He shrugged. "It's all anonymous."

"It's not anonymous," I said. "It's you."

"You want a beer?" he said. He frowned at his watch, and then went into the kitchen and returned carrying a beer and a jelly glass half full of warm vodka.

And I drank the beer and he drank the vodka, and then I had another, and another, and after a while it didn't seem so out of place, my brother drinking in the morning, as long as I was there drinking with him.

I thought of the woman I'd spent the night with, and wondered if she would want me back. She was hungover when I left, and hadn't said much one way or the other.

I drank another beer and asked my brother if he'd ever been swimming at night. He thought about the question, then picked up the vodka bottle—he'd brought it into the living room with one of my beers—and poured some into the glass.

"In Lake Okeechobee," he said. "You were four years old, and we went camping one weekend, and Mother and I went swimming at night while you and Father started a charcoal fire." He sat still, remembering it. "It was like bathwater," he said. "And you could taste the lighter fluid in the steaks."

I could remember the fire, faintly remember the fire.

"The lake's dead," I said. "I meant the ocean."

He thought it over. "No," he said, "not in the ocean . . . What's it like?"

"Completely alone," I said. "You've never been alone like that, swimming at night."

"Is it quiet?" he said.

"Yeah," I said, "it's quiet."

We sat still a minute, and then I remembered why I had come. "The girl from the *Sun* . . ." I said.

He smiled at me and swallowed some vodka. "Tell me about swimming, Jack," he said. "Tell me something about swimming."

❏

THE PUBLISHER OF THE *Miami Times* called a meeting for Friday afternoon. Ward, Yardley Acheman, the Sunday editor, the managing editor, the executive editor, and me. Everyone who'd had anything to do with the story from Moat County.

I had never been included in such a meeting before—in fact, I had never been included in any meetings—and I took my invitation as a signal that the paper was in some stage of trying to sort fact from fiction, and prepared myself with dates and times of Yardley Acheman's transgressions against decency and journalism.

The publisher's office was larger than the editor's, and overlooked Biscayne Bay, where he kept his yacht. We sat in leather chairs and sipped coffee which his secretary brought on a silver tray.

The publisher himself sat on the edge of his desk in a casual sort of way, somehow offering the impression that he was very much like the rest of us in the room. Yardley Acheman was wearing a new suit and my brother smelled vaguely of alcohol.

It was the first day Ward had been back in the newsroom, and the editors had asked him to drop by their offices after the meeting. He did not make any promises.

"The reason I asked you here today," the publisher said, "is to get a clearer picture in my mind of exactly what has transpired since the awarding of the Pulitzer Prize to Yardley and Ward."

He looked at them as he spoke, pausing longer on Yardley than my brother. "If we've got a problem," he said, "I want to know it."

The Sunday editor cleared his throat, drawing the publisher's attention. Before he could speak, however, Yardley Acheman interrupted him. "There's no problem, R.E.," he said. It is a curiosity of newsrooms that, top to bottom, everyone is called by first names. Yardley was leaning back into his chair, more relaxed than anyone except the publisher himself. "All we've got here is a few loose ends, that's all."

The publisher turned to the executive editor, to see if he agreed with that. The man looked at his knuckles carefully, then at the tips of his fingers. He had more to lose, and less places to go if he lost.

"It's the kind of thing that comes up once in a while when you win too many Pulitzers," Yardley said, as if he had been through it before. "Somebody gets a hard-on for you and uncovers the little inconsistencies that always show up in a story of this magnitude."

The publisher thought about that a moment, then nodded and looked again at the executive editor. "This ever happened to us before, Bill?" he said.

"There's always grumblings," the editor said in a flat way, "but this is the first time I remember it went public."

"If you can call the *Miami Sun* public," said the Sunday editor. A polite round of smiles went around the room. The *Sun* had a tiny circulation, and was losing a long, painful struggle to stay alive.

"It's just loose ends," the publisher said.

"The kind of thing you always have," the Sunday editor said. The publisher nodded, but he did not seem inclined to let it drop. His eyes moved around the room, coming finally to rest on me. He clearly did not know who I was, or what I was doing in his meeting. He moved on and stared at Ward.

"You agree with that, Ward?" he said.

"With what?" he said.

"That it's just loose ends," the publisher said. "Nothing particularly out of the ordinary . . ."

"It's out of the ordinary for me," he said.

Across the table Yardley Acheman smiled again, but now it didn't seem to fit his face. "You've got to understand something," he said. "The story wasn't written under ideal conditions. We were at a lot of disadvantages . . ."

The publisher looked at him and waited. "Ward was in the hospital, out of touch, I had to write from his notes . . ." The publisher waited, but Yardley Acheman had run out of things to say.

"What about this contractor?" the publisher said.

Yardley began a slow inspection of the backs of his hands too. "Loose ends," he said finally. "It's all loose ends."

"Somebody did speak to this contractor," the publisher said.

"Absolutely," Yardley said.

"And he said the things he was reported in our newspaper as having said."

"Absolutely, word for word."

"But now he's disappeared."

My brother looked at Yardley with more interest now, anxious to hear the answer to this question.

"Apparently," Yardley Acheman said. "I tried to call him, but the line's been disconnected."

The publisher picked a copy of the *Sun* off his desk and looked at it quickly. "The *Sun* says he doesn't exist."

"He exists, don't worry about that," Yardley said. "The whole problem is I gave my word not to reveal his name to anybody. That was the deal, and we're stuck with it. That's the whole problem."

"Could this man be found again?"

Yardley Acheman shook his head. "I don't know," he said. "And even if we found him, he wouldn't let us use his name. He was scared . . . probably in some kind of trouble with the licensing board . . ."

He paused, and the room paused with him. And then the publisher nodded, as if it all made sense. "The paper stands by its story, Bill?" he said finally.

"The paper stands behind it one hundred percent," the executive editor said, as if he were reciting lines from a familiar play. "If we made an error, we will happily correct it. That has always been our policy, and still is."

"And as far as we know, there is nothing to correct . . ."

"The paper stands behind its story," the executive editor said again, and the publisher nodded, and seemed relieved.

And then the feeling seemed to spread through the room, and everyone was relieved.

"Thank you, gentlemen," the publisher said, and we stood to leave. Before anyone got to the door, the publisher spoke again to the executive editor. "You know, Bill," he said, "it might not be a bad idea if we didn't entertain further questions on the matter from other news organizations."

The executive editor nodded, but didn't speak. He was not comfortable with the idea—the heart of the business, after all, lies in the asking and answering of questions—but he ran a large newspaper, and he had done uncomfortable things before.

"It's already taken care of," the Sunday editor said.

The publisher thought it over and smiled. He said, "What if we just leave the old dog lie in the sun a while and see if she don't go to sleep."

❑

THE OLD DOG DID NOT go to sleep. The missing contractor became the subject of articles in cities where no reader ever heard of Hillary Van Wetter or Moat County.

Prizes are a consuming interest of newspaper people, particularly Pulitzer Prizes. They are as consuming as the World Series or natural disasters or national elections. Generally, this interest is held in check and only imposed on the reading public when a newspaper itself wins prizes. The possibility of a tainted Pulitzer, however, stirs great juices in the newsroom.

The phone in my brother's office rang a dozen times a day, reporters wanting to discuss the missing contractor. I took most of these calls, as Yardley and my brother had again stopped coming to work. I told the reporters I did not know when they would be back, and referred questions to the publisher.

Some of the reporters asked for my impressions of the situation at the *Times*, how it was affecting morale. It was all off the record, they said. They had no idea of who I was, or what I did.

The most determined caller was a reporter from *Newsweek*, a magazine whose interest in the story was heightened by *Time's* piece of the year before pronouncing Yardley Acheman a fine example of America's new journalists.

The reporter wanted Yardley's phone number, and I had spoken to him now half a dozen times.

"Listen," he said, "let me tell you exactly what I'm thinking. I'm thinking this whole thing is bullshit."

"What thing?"

"The whole thing," he said. "All I have to do is talk to Yardley Acheman five minutes, ask him a couple of questions, and I'm out of your life." I closed my eyes and pictured the man on the other end of the telephone, and he was handsome and confident; he looked a lot like Yardley Acheman.

"You want to ask him about the contractor," I said.

"Just to make sure I've got the explanation right," he said. "That the one in the hospital got hit over the head and couldn't remember where the contractor was."

"Where did you hear that?" I said.

"It's in the newspapers," the man said. "I just need to check."

When I didn't answer, he said, "What, that's not the way it happened?"

"No," I said.

"So you tell me . . ."

"The one in the hospital," I said, "wasn't the one who forgot where the contractor was. He never saw the contractor."

Now the quiet came from the other end. "That doesn't make sense," the man said finally. "The other guy gets amnesia because his partner gets hit over the head?"

"Let me get you his number," I said.

"Don't worry," he said, "nobody knows where I got it."

I read Yardley Acheman's number into the telephone and hung up.

❑

I WENT TO SEE Ward after work; he was still drinking, shuffling to the kitchen and back over the notes from Moat County. They were still spread out over every room of the apartment, and as he walked absently into the kitchen, he would pick up a page or two and begin reading, forgetting for the moment what he had gone to the kitchen for. He knew the transcripts and the notes so well by now that he could pick up any piece of paper and recognize immediately where it fit into the thousands of other pieces of paper that lay scattered over the floor. He would study it a moment, then carefully put it back on the floor where he had found it, and move on to the refrigerator.

In a different way, he was bewildered by the papers he picked up; as well as he knew them, the meaning had been lost.

"A man called today from *Newsweek*," he said when we were back in the living room. "He wanted to know about my amnesia."

I sipped at my beer, and it tasted bitter and stale at the same time, and a shudder ran through me right to my toes. I set the beer on the table and watched my brother drink vodka.

"What did you tell him?" I said.

"I told him I was working on it."

He smiled at me in a reckless way I only saw when he'd been drinking, and then poured another half inch of liquor into the glass. I tried the beer again, not wanting him to drink alone.

"What are you working on?" I said.

He was still smiling. "Amnesia," he said. "I think that's the answer."

"Good. The editors want to know when you might be finished," I said.

The smile came off his face, and he said, "That's the beauty of it, Jack. You don't know when you're finished because you can't remember."

"Is that what you told the guy from *Newsweek*?"

He shook his head. "I didn't think of it in time," he said. "I wish I'd thought of it . . ." He looked at me differently, then. "What do you think old World War's making of all this?" he said.

I shook my head. "I haven't heard a thing."

"You think it's still the proudest moment of his life?"

I sipped at the beer. "So what did you tell him? The guy from *Newsweek* . . ."

Ward shook his head. "I told him, 'No comment.'" He began to smile again then. "You know," he said, "it's true. At the bottom of everything that's happened, it's 'no comment.' I'm twenty-nine years old, and up till now, I've got no comment." He began to laugh, and barely got the last words out: "I can't think of anything appropriate to say."

I waited for him to stop, and then I said we ought to get something to eat.

Ward fixed himself another drink and took it with him into the bathroom. The sound of the shower began a moment later and I settled into a chair. There were papers under my feet and I picked some of them up. Two pages of preliminary hearing motions, and then a page from Charlotte Bless's first letter to my brother, asking for his help to save her fiancé. The handwriting was round, like a schoolgirl's. I counted the word *innocent* eleven times on the one page.

I set the papers back on the floor, thinking of Charlotte and Hillary. She was afraid of him now, or she would have come out of the house. She was not a person who was used to being afraid, and wouldn't know how to carry it.

The shower had been on a long time. I finished the beer and went into the kitchen for another. There was nothing in the refrigerator except the beer and a piece of uncovered orange cheese, dried and cracked. There were no dishes in the sink, no silverware, no sign that the place had been used at all except to receive and hold papers from Moat County.

I took the beer and went back into the living room. The shower was still running. I found myself listening to it more carefully, and noticed a certain monotony in the rhythm, as if it were beating evenly against the floor of the tub, with nothing interrupting it.

I called his name, and then got up and walked to the bathroom door and tried again. There was no answer. The door was slightly cracked, the steam collecting around the opening as if to seal it. I pushed the door open, and put my head inside.

My brother was sitting on the closed toilet, still holding his drink, staring into the shower. His clothes were on the floor, near more of the papers from Moat County, and he turned as I walked into the bathroom and nodded, as if I had just come into his office.

I looked into the shower too, we studied it a long time, this shower, and then I turned to Ward. A large, black bruise ran the length of his thigh, and there were other bruises on the trunk of his body. His ribs were distinct under his skin, defined all the way to their ends.

It seemed to me that he could not have weighed a hundred and thirty pounds. He looked at me and smiled, and then drank the last little bit of vodka left in the glass. I looked again at the shower.

"The idea is you run the water while you're in there with it," I said. And he stood up, naked and dignified, and handed me his glass and then stepped in.

❏

WE WENT TO A RESTAURANT I did not know, a place he saw as we drove past in my car. It was the kind of place with tablecloths and a wine list, but I was not thinking of how much it would cost. He ordered a bottle of thirty-dollar wine and a salad. He had drunk half a bottle of vodka that day, but it still didn't show.

He sat up straight and spoke all his words accurately, in a soft voice. "You on a diet?" I said.

He looked at me, not understanding the question.

"You're only eating a salad?"

He thought for a moment, remembering, then nodded. That was what he was having, a salad.

"You're losing weight," I said.

He looked down at himself, then either lost the thought or decided it didn't matter. "Have you heard from World War?" he said.

I told him he'd already asked that.

"I meant about the wedding," he said.

"Not a word," I said. "Just the invitation."

The waiter brought the bottle of wine Ward had ordered and removed the cork and set it on the table. He poured a little into my glass to test. Ward watched me taste the wine as if something depended on my opinion of it, and then held his glass while the waiter filled it too.

"Do you think he'll go through with it?" I said.

"World War?" he said, "of course." And he was right. It was my father's nature to see things through. It is the nature of the business. Something moves, and draws the eye, and that is as much as it takes. A day later it is incorporated into the great, messy history of this place and time.

Cautious human beings do not presume to write history on a day's notice. They are aware of the damage mistakes can cause. My father believed that mistakes could always be corrected in the next edition.

Ward drank what was left in his wineglass. He took it directly into his throat, as if it were water, as if it had no taste at all. "Do you think I should go?" he said finally.

"Why not?"

It hadn't occurred to me until that moment that we would not be in Thorn together to witness an error of this magnitude.

He looked at his wineglass and said, "He's probably embarrassed at what's happened . . ." He thought it over. "She doesn't like us around, I'd hate to ruin the day."

"We're his family," I said, and I poured myself another glass of wine. The second taste was better than the first, which perhaps is what separates thirty-dollar wine from the kind you buy at the grocery store. "We were there before Ellen Guthrie, and we'll be there after she's gone."

He nodded—an acknowledgment that I'd spoken, not that he agreed with what I'd said. A beautiful young woman walked across the room, passing by our table, the cloth of her skirt brushed against my shoulder. There were so many things I wanted, and that was the only one that had a name. "You ought to eat something," I said.

He picked at a piece of lettuce with his fork, and put it into his mouth. It did not taste as good to him as the wine. "You're too thin," I said. I leaned across the table and spoke more quietly. "You look like you took a bad spill, too."

He didn't understand.

"The bruise on your leg, the marks on your chest and arms . . ."

He thought a moment and said, "I don't know how that happened."

"You must have fallen," I said.

"I must have."

Ward stared at his wineglass. "Are you going swimming tonight?" he said.

I looked out the window toward the street and saw a ladies' hat tumble past on the sidewalk. It was cool that night, and cloudy, and the wind had been picking up all day. A long ways out, a storm was collecting in the Atlantic.

"There's too much wind," I said. "It has to be still or you're fighting it the whole time."

"You're in the water. How can you feel it if you're in the water?"

"You can feel it," I said, "but if it's calm, you don't have to fight. On a calm night, you're just part of the ocean."

❏

WE DROVE NORTH TO Moat County that weekend, leaving at ten in the morning, both of us hung over and grim. The car smelled of spilled wine, and the rain beat against the windshield one moment, and then settled into a mist the next. Once, coming into Fort Lauderdale, we saw the sun. Afterwards, the windows fogged, and I had to wipe them clean with my hand to see.

Ward sat still in the seat next to me and made no move to clear the glass in front of him, as if he had no interest in seeing what was outside. He had not wanted to leave his apartment. Helen Drew's story about the Pulitzer Prize was dying then the way stories always die—it happens when there is nothing to sustain them—but it did not seem to be dying to my brother.

It grew, in fact, each day he didn't hear from World War. "I wish this weren't hanging over my head right now," he said.

"It isn't as bad as you think. People in Moat County don't care about Miami newspapers or Pulitzer Prizes . . ."

It was no comfort. We listened for a while to the sound of the tires and the rain, and then I turned on the radio and heard in a news report that the hurricane had turned east and was headed into the Keys, its winds right at a hundred miles an hour.

"We ought to stop and get something to drink," he said a little later.

I pulled into a convenience store and bought a cold six-pack of beer, and we drank that as we drove up U.S. 1, and after a while the beer began to make us feel better, and after we had drunk the six beers we pulled the car to the side of the road and stepped outside into a driving rain and urinated against the tires. We stood on opposite sides of the car, look-ing at each other over the hood. Ward's hair was plastered across his pale forehead, and he had to shout to be heard over the wind.

"It's too bad," he said, "that they can't take a picture of this for the wedding album."

The rain seemed to clean us.

❏

"Maybe this won't be so bad," I said. We were back on the road.

Ward shrugged, as if it didn't matter. "We ought to get more beer," he said. There were only a few cars on the high-way, and the ones we saw had their lights on against the rain, somehow making the storm seem all the worse.

We looked for a store, but the ones we passed were all closed. It turned darker, and there was a certain feeling to the afternoon that we were the only two souls in the state not safe at home.

THE WEDDING OF MY FATHER and Ellen Guthrie went off on schedule the next day, in spite of Hurricane Sylvia, which in the end had veered west into the Gulf of Mexico and hit the state just below Bradenton Beach, and then turned north to blow itself out.

The ceremony was held in the Methodist church in Thorn, with the rain beating so hard against the roof and the stained-glass windows I could barely hear the words. There were perhaps a hundred guests sitting in the pews behind me, most of them friends of my father's. It was my impression that Ellen Guthrie had no friends in Moat County.

The woman who had once been my father's managing editor was there, a long skirt covering her legs to mid-calf, and she sat resolute and loyal, banking, I suppose, on the day when this marriage would end. My father had rediscovered slender legs, however, and would never go back.

He wore a pale suit with a white tie, and Ellen Guthrie wore a white dress. I don't know much about wedding dresses, except to say this was not the sort of thing that dragged on the floor behind her.

Ward and I sat in the front row, soaked to the skin, and the lightning and thunder rattled the windows and the rain blew so hard that it did not seem impossible that it would blow the old building down. The organist was nervous, and her padded shoulders hunched at the sound of the wind.

A man my father's age gave Ellen Guthrie in marriage, and there was something in his expression that said he was making the best of a bad situation.

My father's best man was a former editor of the *Atlanta Constitution*.

All members of the wedding party were wet except Ellen Guthrie herself, who had somehow managed to come through

Hurricane Sylvia and arrive at the altar dry. She was, of course, a woman of great determination.

After the ceremony we ran to the limousines my father had hired for the occasion, and rode to the country club where the reception was held. Ward and I shared a car with the man who had given Ellen Guthrie away, and he was precisely as cheerful as the weather.

He introduced himself as her father, and stared out the window in a forlorn way at Thorn. The wind rocked the car and rain seeped in through the windows. "I suppose she knows what she's doing," he said, "but it's always hard on a father, letting your little girl go."

"Imagine how we feel," I said, but it was not a good time for small jokes.

❑

THERE WAS A BOWL OF champagne with flowers floating in it at the club, and I found a spot next to it where I intended to stay for the entire reception, to drink all the champagne and perhaps eat the flowers. Ward was in another part of the room, cornered by my father's newspaper friends, who were talking solemnly of their own trials as young reporters.

My father was freshly shaved and smelled of cologne, and his attention moved from his bride to his friends to the band to the weather, unable to settle anywhere for more than a second or two. He drank as much of the champagne as I did, although he took his from the waiters who walked the room with glasses of it on silver trays. He hugged a lot of people; he kissed Ellen Guthrie with cake still in his mouth.

And the storm blew its way through.

"This is the happiest day of my life," he said, offering one of many toasts.

Another toast:

"My wife, my friends, my dear, old friends, my sons . . ." He looked for his sons and found Ward and hugged him. He turned around then, saying, "Where's Jack?" and came face-to-face with his bride before I could move toward him, and hugged her instead.

Her smile was looking a little practiced by now, but the storm had not diminished, and dinner was stalled in the kitchen. I took a plate of hors d'oeuvres from one of the waiters and ate everything on it.

The lawyer Weldon Pine passed by, smiling. I did not recognize him at first, as he had clearly been sick and was perhaps half the size he had been when we'd visited his office. I returned the smile, and crumbs fell out of my mouth. He walked with a cane now, and nodded at me, although it was impossible to say if he remembered me or not.

Hungry and drunk, and carrying a champagne glass in each hand, I wandered back into the kitchen to find more food. I went through the swinging doors backwards and was hit by the heat of the place—it was at least ninety degrees in there, where the outside room had been almost cool—and then stood for a minute watching half a dozen people at work at different stations, preparing dinner.

A wild boar was lying on an oven rack while two cooks basted it.

The cooks were both black women, dressed in white coats and white chef's hats, and it took a moment, because of the costumes, to see that one of them was Anita Chester. She looked up from the pig and saw me standing in the kitchen, holding my drinks. Her eyes stayed on me one moment, and then moved, without any sign of recognition, back to her work.

I broke into the kind of smile I only find when I am drinking, and moved through the other kitchen workers to her side. She looked at me again quickly, and a moment later I could smell her, familiar and clean, like shirts you get back from the laundry. I stood by her side while she worked on a boar, collecting his juices in a ladle and pouring them back over his skin, the liquid catching the overhead lights as it rinsed over his face, and glistening there, as if the animal had just come awake.

"You missing your party," she said.

"I brought you a glass of champagne," I said, and handed her one of the glasses.

"Thank you," she said, and set it on the table near the stove, and then looked quickly toward the other end of the kitchen where a white man with clouds of black hair on his arms and neck was overseeing the preparations.

He glared at her and at me, holding a long-handled spoon that he was using to taste the soup, imagining that I was some kind of trouble. I smiled at him, and he turned back to his soup, checking a moment later to see if I was still in his kitchen.

"How have you been?" I said.

She finished basting the boar, put down her ladle, and pushed the pig back into the oven. When she closed the door I saw sweat beading in her hairline. She wiped her hands on her apron and went to check on some pies in another oven. I followed her over, happy to be around her again.

"You work here now?" I said.

She bent into her pies, testing the ones in the farthest corner of the oven. "I do unless you get me fired," she said.

I looked again at the white man with the hairy arms and then smiled at her, to tell her he was harmless. She closed the oven door and stood up, wiping her hands on a towel.

"Ward's outside," I said.

She nodded, indicating that this was not entirely a surprise, and then looked me squarely in the face. "You got to get out of the kitchen," she said.

"Come say hello to Ward," I said. "He and I still talk about you down in Miami."

"It isn't a comfortable situation," she said.

301

"I'll go talk to your boss," I said, "tell him you're a friend of the family . . ."

"Don't do that," she said. And when I smiled at her again she said, "I'm no friend of your family, Jack. All I did was cook and maid. I did that and now I do this, and when they don't need me anymore, I'll do something else."

"You're part of the family," I said, and finished the drink in my hand. Without it, I felt suddenly out of place. "It wasn't my father," I said. "He wasn't the one who fired you. . . ."

She walked past me again, back toward the oven which held the wild boar. I noticed more people watching now; I felt the embarrassment I'd caused her, but perhaps because of that I couldn't leave it alone. And then the big man with hairy arms stopped what he was doing on the other side of the room and walked over to where we were standing.

She saw him without looking; her eyes dropped a little, not to meet any of ours. He put his hands on his hips and cocked his head a little, waiting.

"I'm sorry, sir," she said to me, sounding strangely formal, "you'll have to excuse me to do my work."

The man nodded, as if he were not quite satisfied with that, even though it was the right answer.

"You belong out there in the other room," I said.

"No, sir, I don't," she said, and she walked away. I understood she was afraid, and didn't follow her any farther. I looked at the man and said, "She's an old friend of the family," and he nodded as if we both knew that wasn't true. As if in another place—a bar, say, or a restaurant where he was not working—he would take me outside and teach me to stay out of his kitchen.

And I nodded back, thinking of my famous headlock.

❑

I WALKED BACK INTO the main room looking for my brother to tell him that Anita Chester was working in the kitchen. I found him sitting near the front door where a photographer was taking pictures of my father and Ellen Guthrie with various arrangements of family and friends.

Before I made it over, the electricity quit, and at four o'clock in the afternoon, the room—one whole side of which was a wall of windows overlooking the golf course—was dropped into a darkness like night.

When my eyes adjusted to the dark, I sat down next to my brother. There were several glasses of champagne still on a tray, sitting in front of him on the table. The storm blew sheets of rain into the windows.

"Guess who's in the kitchen," I said, taking one of the glasses.

He stared at the ceiling, as if he were trying to understand what had happened to the lights.

"Just like that," Ward said. I saw him smile.

"Just like what?" I said.

I drank that glass, and then another, but the taste had turned sweet.

"Just like that," he said again. He coughed, and at the end of it there was a suggestion of a laugh.

"Anita's in the kitchen," I said.

Somewhere in the room a woman's voice rose and fell, and gradually the hum of conversation returned, not as loud as it had been before, but still filling the room.

My brother coughed again, and then laughed out loud. People turned, and he caught himself momentarily, and then he was laughing again. It was a strange kind of laughing; it built on itself, taking him over, and in a minute or two he was holding his head in his hands, howling like he was crazy.

"Just like that," he said.

I went out into the rain and wind and was sick on the lawn.

❑

HURRICANE SYLVIA PASSED THROUGH Moat County headed east and north, following the course of the St. Johns River, blowing through Jacksonville and then back out to sea.

It dropped eleven inches of rain on Moat County in less than nine hours, raising the river to flood levels and submerging some of the small islands that dot the wetlands along its western shore.

When the water receded, the shape of some of these islands had changed. Parts of them broke off and were lost to the river, exposing the root systems of their trees, and some of them simply disappeared, along with the small hunting or fishing cabins on them.

It was a bass fisherman in a flat-bottom boat, working the holes along the west side of the river, who found the bodies. They were bloated and floating, hidden from the river itself by some trees which had fallen in the storm. The current had brought them into a sort of pocket in the wetlands, where they rose and fell with the debris from the storm, bumping each other as dragonflies hung in the air over their heads.

The fisherman finished working his holes, then returned to the boat landing and called the sheriff's department, and the bodies were recovered.

One was a woman, the other three were men. According to the county coroner, all but the woman had been dead a year or more, one of the men having succumbed to cancer of the liver. The woman had died from knife wounds of an unmentionable nature.

The bodies were found within the boundaries of Moat County, a mile or more from the house occupied by Tyree Van Wetter, and were presumed to have come from a small plot of flat, high ground nearby where the Van Wetters had buried their dead for all the generations they had occupied this part of Florida.

The piece of the cemetery which had washed away was nearest the edge, and represented the most recent deaths. It was the observation of the sheriff's deputy who investigated that the Van Wetters were running out of burial space. He estimated the plot of ground—less than half an acre—held another hundred and forty graves, but could not count them accurately as most were unmarked, or marked only with bricks.

A few headstones had also been placed in the ground, but they had been stolen from Allen's Mortuary in Palatka, and carried no inscriptions.

Charlotte Bless was identified through her fingerprints, recorded at the post office in New Orleans when she began work there as a letter sorter.

❑

A WEEK LATER, Hillary Van Wetter was arrested for the murder after an unidentified member of the Van Wetter family gave his whereabouts to members of the state police, who had been called in by the sheriff, and swarmed through the small encampments along the river in numbers the Van Wetters had never before seen, threatening to exhume the entire graveyard.

And in that way the Van Wetters gave Hillary back to the state, and in compensation were left alone to live as they had.

❑

WARD WAS IN HIS APARTMENT when I went to see him, packing the notes from Moat County into cardboard boxes, stacking them against the wall.

The front door had not been closed and I stood in the doorway watching him until he saw me.

"He killed her," I said.

"I know."

I came in and sat down on the floor. Her death was more

remote to him than it was to me, but it had settled somewhere, another piece of evidence that fit into something
larger.

I thought of her breasts, floating in the water.

My brother went back to his packing.

"Where are we going?" I said.

He looked at the boxes against the wall as if he were trying
to decide. "I can't do it anymore," he said. "It doesn't work."
And I understood that I was part of what he couldn't do. He
didn't want to take care of anyone now, or be taken care of.
I did not try to talk him out of it.

I helped him carry the boxes out to his car. He set them
carefully in the trunk and the backseat, arranging them by
number. They were still there, in precisely the same order, four
months later when I flew to California to claim his things.

❑

AT THE POLICE DEPARTMENT, a friendly sergeant turned over my
brother's shoes and the wallet and keys that had been found
inside them, and asked if Ward often went swimming in the
Pacific Ocean at night.

"We've got more undertow than you do in Florida," he said.

And that was as much as I ever knew about how my brother
died.

❑

AFTER HIS SON DROWNED in California, my father did a reassess-
ment of sorts, and saved what he could, offering me a position at the *Tribune,* working as his assistant against the day I
would take over his paper.

I turned down that offer and stayed in Miami, becoming a
rewrite man on the night desk. And there were times then—
usually a calamity—when the phone was ringing every five

minutes and I was turning two dozen frantic calls into a single story, when I would lose myself in it for an hour or two, and find a certain peace in the confusion and excitement.

That is as close as I have come to understanding what my brother meant when he spoke of the work making it bearable.

❑

YEARS LATER, my father's kidneys failed, and I went back to Moat County and took over his newspaper, replacing his wife on the board of directors. She stays home now, ordering new furniture; a machine cleans his blood.

My father is old—he turned old understanding his son was not coming back from the West Coast—but he holds on to what he can, his stories. He tells them after dinner, mostly to himself, and to the nurses at the medical center while he is hooked up to the kidney machine; Ralph McGill rides again. The stories span three decades but stop in 1969; my brother's name is never mentioned.

It is not old age, but a lifetime habit; he believes that refusing to look at it will keep him whole.

My father still comes to the office in the afternoons to attend the daily news meetings, sitting quietly at the head of the table while his editors argue the placement of the articles which will appear in tomorrow's paper.

He listens a minute or two, then wanders, his gaze moving out the window overlooking his newsroom. He takes a knife from his pocket, and moves the blade in a circular motion over the arm of his chair, as if he were sharpening it.

Sometimes he calls me Ward.

There are no intact men.

February 8, 1994
Whidbey Island

PETE DEXTER lives on an island in the Puget Sound with his wife and daughter.

ABOUT THE TYPE

This book was set in Baskerville, a type-face designed by John Baskerville, an amateur printer and typefounder, and cut for him by John Handy in 1750. The type became popular again when the Lanston Monotype Corporation of London revived the classic Roman face in 1923. The Mergenthaler Linotype Company in England and the United States cut a version of Baskerville in 1931, making it one of the most widely used typefaces today.